Ring

Stephen Baxter was born in 1957. Raised in Liverpool, he has a mathematics degree from the University of Cambridge and a Ph.D from Southampton. He sold his first short stories to *Interzone* in 1986 and was a prizewinner in the Writers of the Future contest. His first novel, *Raft*, was published in 1991, to great acclaim. *Ring* is his fifth novel. He is married and lives in Buckinghamshire.

'In *Ring* Baxter conveys the most up-to-date theories of quantum mechanics and cosmology without losing sight of the ultimate goal, that of telling a story . . . some of the best hard SF I've read this year and probably some of the best I've *ever* read'   *Vector*

'Stephen Baxter is carving himself a reputation for extremely adroit, Big Idea hard science fiction . . . Baxter maintains complete control over a plot that other writers might have allowed to drown in its own Byzantine complexities. And he doesn't let the gosh wow speculative elements swamp the human values'   *The Dark Side*

'*Ring* ought to immediately thrust Baxter into the front rank of hard SF writers'   *Locus*

D1351820

The Time Ships

'*The Time Ships* is the most outstanding work of imaginative fiction since Stapledon's *Last and First Men*, and it is the best possible contribution to *The Time Machine*'s centennial year. I'm almost tempted to say (I know this is blasphemy) that the sequel is better than the original. After all, it should be, with a hundred years of science and discovery for added inspiration . . . This book is the best evidence for reincarnation I've ever encountered. Welcome back, H.G. . . .'

ARTHUR C. CLARKE

'*The Time Ships* is a ripping yarn. Recommended'   *SFX*

'A set of ingenious variations of Wells's original idea, *The Time Ships* is a spectacular and exhilarating ride . . . his aim is to redeem [The Time Machine's] SF content and reaffirm its cosmic sweep, and he does this with considerable panache and style'   *Locus*

'One of Baxter's skills is his ability to strike a balance between scientific plausibility and sheer entertainment values'   *The Dark Side*

'Baxter has excelled himself, and this complex, well-woven tale contains both the despair and the compassion that are proper to his craft'   *Matrix*

Flux

'Arthur C. Clarke, Poul Anderson ... Isaac Asimov and Robert Heinlein succeeded in doing it, but very few others. Now Stephen Baxter joins their exclusive ranks – writing science fiction in which the science is right, the author knowledgeable, and the extrapolations a sheer pleasure to read, admire, enjoy. The reaction is that which C.S. Lewis referred to when he described science fiction as the only genuine consciousness-expanding drug . . . Wonderful stuff! It is a rare thing to find such a good read'

HARRY HARRISON, *New Scientist*

Anti-Ice

'There is a breed of romance that nudges the what-is to the what-if. Stephen Baxter's *Anti-Ice* is one of the most compelling of these. A touch of improper amour and impeccable period detail makes all this alarmingly addictive'

The Times

Timelike Infinity

'*Timelike Infinity* is good science by someone who knows what he is talking about' *Sunday Telegraph*

Raft

'*Raft* is fast paced, strong on suspense, efficiently written, and has moral weight, but it is in the creation of a genuinely strange and believable new universe that Baxter excels . . . rigorous, vigorous SF at its enjoyable best'

LISA TUTTLE, *Time Out*

'Almost perfect . . . *Raft* is very, very hard SF and it's great fun' *Interzone*

ALSO BY STEPHEN BAXTER

Raft
Timelike Infinity
Anti-Ice
Flux
The Time Ships

Voyager

STEPHEN BAXTER

Ring

HarperCollins*Publishers*

Voyager
An Imprint of HarperCollins*Publishers*
77–85 Fulham Palace Road,
Hammersmith, London W6 8JB

This paperback edition 1996

5 7 9 8 6 4

First published in Great Britain by
HarperCollins*Publishers* 1994

Copyright © Stephen Baxter 1994

The Author asserts the moral right to
be identified as the author of this work

ISBN 0 00 648221 X

Set in Palatino

Printed and bound in Great Britain by
Caledonian International Book Manufacturing Ltd, Glasgow

For my nephew
Thomas Baxter

PART I

EVENT: SYSTEM

1

Even at the moment she was born she knew something was wrong.

A face loomed over her: wide, smooth, smiling. The cheeks were damp, the glistening eyes huge. 'Lieserl. Oh, Lieserl . . .'

Lieserl. My name, then.

She explored the face before her, studying the lines around the eyes, the humorous upturn of the mouth, the strong nose. It was an intelligent, lived-in face. *This is a good human being*, she thought. *Good stock . . .*

'*Good stock*'?

This was impossible. *She* was impossible. She felt terrified of her own explosive consciousness. She shouldn't even be able to focus her eyes yet . . .

She tried to touch her mother's face. Her own hand was still moist with amniotic fluid – *but it was growing visibly*, the bones extending and broadening, filling out the loose skin as if it were a glove.

She opened her mouth. It was dry, her gums already sore with budding teeth.

Strong arms reached beneath her; bony adult fingers dug into the aching flesh of her back. She could sense other adults surrounding her, the bed in which she'd been born, the outlines of a room.

Her mother held her high before a window. Lieserl's head lolled, the expanding muscles still too weak to support the burgeoning weight of her skull. Spittle laced across her chin.

An immense light flooded her eyes.

She cried out.

Her mother enfolded her in her arms. 'The Sun, Lieserl. *The Sun . . .*'

*   *   *

9

The first few days were the worst.

Her parents – impossibly tall, looming figures – took her through brightly lit rooms, a garden always flooded with sunlight. She learned to sit up. The muscles in her back fanned out, pulsing as they grew. To distract her from the unending pain, clowns tumbled over the grass before her, chortling through huge red lips, before popping out of existence in clouds of pixels.

She grew explosively, feeding all the time, a million impressions crowding into her soft sensorium.

There seemed to be no limit to the number of rooms in this place, this *House*. Slowly she began to understand that some of the rooms were Virtual chambers – blank screens against which any number of images could be projected. But even so, the House must comprise hundreds of rooms. And she – with her parents – wasn't alone here. There were other people. But at first they kept away, out of sight, apparent only by their actions: the meals they prepared, the toys they left her.

On the third day her parents took her on a trip by flitter. It was the first time she'd been away from the House, its grounds. As the flitter rose she stared through the bulbous windows, pressing her nose to heated glass.

The House was a jumble of white, cube-shaped buildings, linked by corridors and surrounded by garden – grass, trees. Further out there were bridges and roads looping through the air above the ground, more houses like a child's bricks sprinkled across glowing hillsides.

The flitter soared higher.

The journey was an arc over a toylike landscape. A breast of blue ocean curved away from the land, all around her. This was the island of Skiros, Phillida – her mother – told her, and the sea was called the Aegean. The House was the largest construct on the island. She could see huge, brown-painted spheres dotting the heart of the island: carbon-sequestration domes, Phillida said, balls of dry ice four hundred yards tall.

The flitter snuggled at last against a grassy sward close to the shore of the ocean. Lieserl's mother lifted her out and placed her – on her stretching, unsteady legs – on the rough, sandy grass.

Hand in hand, the little family walked down a short slope to the beach.

10

The Sun burned from an unbearably blue sky. Her vision seemed telescopic. She looked at distant groups of children and adults playing – far away, halfway to the horizon – and it was as if she was among them herself. Her feet, still uncertain, pressed into gritty, moist sand.

She found mussels clinging to a ruined pier. She prised them away with a toy spade, and gazed, fascinated, at their slime-dripping feet. She could taste the brine salt on the air; it seemed to permeate her very skin.

She sat on the sand with her parents, feeling her light costume stretch over her still-spreading limbs. They played a simple game, of counters moving over a floating Virtual board, with pictures of ladders and hissing snakes. There was laughter, mock complaints by her father, elaborate pantomimes of cheating.

Her senses were electric. It was a wonderful day, full of light and joy, extraordinarily vivid sensations. Her parents loved her – she could see that in the way they moved with each other, came to her, played with her.

They must know she was different; but they didn't seem to care.

She didn't want to be different – to be *wrong*. She closed her mind against her fears, and concentrated on the snakes, the ladders, the sparkling counters.

Every morning she woke up in a bed that felt too small.

Lieserl liked the garden. She liked to watch the flowers straining their tiny, pretty faces towards the Sun, as the great light climbed patiently across the sky. The sunlight made the flowers grow, her father told her. Maybe she was like a flower, she thought, growing too quickly in all this sunlight.

The House was full of toys: colourful blocks, and puzzles, and dolls. She picked them up and turned them over in her stretching, growing hands. She rapidly became bored with each toy, but one little gadget held her attention. It was a tiny village immersed in a globe of water. There were tiny people in there, frozen in mid-step as they walked, or ran, through their world. When her awkward hands shook the globe, plastic snowflakes would swirl through the air, settling over the encased streets

11

and rooftops. She stared at the entombed villagers, wishing she could become one of them: become frozen in time as they were, free of this pressure of *growing*.

On the fifth day she was taken to a wide, irregularly shaped, sunlight-drenched classroom. This room was full of children – *other children*! The children sat on the floor and played with paints and dolls, or talked earnestly to brilliantly coloured Virtual figures – smiling birds, tiny clowns.

The children turned to watch as she came in with her mother, their faces round and bright, like dapples of sunlight through leaves. She'd never been so close to other children before. Were these children *different* too?

One small girl scowled at her, and Lieserl quailed against her mother's legs. But Phillida's familiar warm hands pressed into her back. 'Go ahead. It's all right.'

As she stared at the unknown girl's scowling face, Lieserl's questions, her too-adult, too-sophisticated doubts, seemed to evaporate. Suddenly, all that mattered to her – all that mattered in the world – was that she should be accepted by these children: that they wouldn't know she was *different*.

An adult approached her: a man, young, thin, his features bland with youth. He wore a jumpsuit coloured a ludicrous orange; in the sunlight, the glow of it shone up over his chin. He smiled at her. 'Lieserl, isn't it? My name's Paul. We're glad you're here. Aren't we, people?'

He was answered by a rehearsed, chorused 'Yes'.

'Now come and we'll find something for you to do,' Paul said. He led her across the child-littered floor to a space beside a small boy. The boy – red-haired, with startling blue eyes – was staring at a Virtual puppet which endlessly formed and reformed: the figure two, collapsing into two snowflakes, two swans, two dancing children; the figure three, followed by three bears, three fish swimming in the air, three cakes. The boy mouthed the numbers, following the tinny voice of the Virtual. 'Two. One. Two and one is three.'

Paul introduced her to the boy – Tommy – and she sat down with him. Tommy, she was relieved to find, was so fascinated by his Virtual that he scarcely seemed aware that Lieserl was present – let alone *different*.

Tommy was resting on his stomach, his chin cupped in his

palms. Lieserl, awkwardly, copied his posture.

The number Virtual ran through its cycle. 'Bye bye, Tommy! Goodbye, Lieserl!' It winked out of existence.

Now Tommy turned to her – without appraisal, merely looking, with unconscious acceptance.

Lieserl said, 'Can we see that again?'

He yawned and stuck a finger into one nostril. 'No. Let's see another. There's a great one about the pre-Cambrian explosion –'

'The what?'

He waved a hand dismissively. 'You know, the Burgess Shale and all that. Wait till you see *Hallucigenia* crawling over your neck ...'

The children played, and learned, and napped. Later, the girl who'd scowled at Lieserl – Ginnie – started some trouble. She poked fun at the way Lieserl's bony wrists stuck out of her sleeves (Lieserl's growth rate was slowing, but she was still expanding out of her clothes each day). Then – unexpectedly, astonishingly – Ginnie started to bawl, claiming that Lieserl had walked through her Virtual. When Paul came over Lieserl started to explain, calmly and rationally, that Ginnie must be mistaken; but Paul told her not to cause such distress, and for punishment she was forced to sit away from the other children for ten minutes, without stimulation.

It was all desperately, savagely unfair. It was the longest ten minutes of Lieserl's life. She glowered at Ginnie, filled with resentment.

The next day she found herself looking forward to going to the room with the children again. She set off with her mother through sunlit corridors. They reached the room Lieserl remembered – there was Paul, smiling a little wistfully to her, and Tommy, and the girl Ginnie – but Ginnie seemed different: childlike, unformed ...

At least a head shorter than Lieserl.

Lieserl tried to recapture that delicious enmity of the day before, but it vanished even as she conjured it. Ginnie was just a kid.

She felt as if something had been stolen from her.

13

Her mother squeezed her hand. 'Come on. Let's find a new room for you to play in.'

Every day was unique. Every day Lieserl spent in a new place, with new people.

The world glowed with sunlight. Shining points trailed endlessly across the sky: low-orbit habitats and comet nuclei, tethered for power and fuel. People walked through a sea of information, with access to the Virtual libraries available anywhere in the world, at a subvocalized command. The landscapes were drenched with sentience; it was practically impossible to get lost, or be hurt, or even to become bored.

On the ninth day Lieserl studied herself in a Virtual holomirror. She had the image turn around, so she could see the shape of her skull, the lie of her hair. There was still some childish softness in her face, she thought, but the woman inside her was emerging already, as if her childhood was a receding tide. She would look like Phillida in the strong-nosed set of her face, her large, vulnerable eyes; but she would have the sandy colouring of her father, George.

Lieserl looked about nine years old. But she was just nine *days* old.

She bade the Virtual break up; it shattered into a million tiny, fly-sized images of her face which drifted away in the sunlit air.

Phillida and George were fine parents, she thought. They were physicists; and they both belonged to an organization they called 'Superet'. They spent their time away from her working through technical papers – which scrolled through the air like falling leaves – and exploring elaborate, onion-ring Virtual models of stars. Although they were both clearly busy, they gave themselves to her without hesitation. She moved in a happy world of smiles, sympathy and support.

Her parents loved her unreservedly. But that wasn't always enough.

She started to come up with complicated, detailed questions. Like, what was the mechanism by which she was growing so rapidly? She didn't seem to *eat* more than the other children she encountered; what could be fuelling her absurd growth rate?

How did she *know* so much? She'd been born self-aware, with even the rudiments of language in her head. The Virtuals she

14

interacted with in the classrooms were fun, and she always seemed to learn something new; but she absorbed no more than scraps of knowledge through the Virtuals compared to the feast of insight with which she awoke each morning.

What had taught her, in the womb? What was teaching her now?

The strange little family had worked up some simple, homely rituals together. Lieserl's favourite was the game, each evening, of snakes and ladders. George brought home an old set – a *real* board made of card, and wooden counters. Already Lieserl was too old for the game; but she loved the company of her parents, her father's elaborate jokes, the simple challenge of the game, the feel of the worn, antique counters.

Phillida showed her how to use Virtuals to produce her own game boards. Her first efforts, on her eleventh day, were plain, neat forms, little more than copies of the commercial boards she'd seen. But soon she began to experiment. She drew a huge board of a million squares. It covered a whole room – she could walk through the board, a planar sheet of light at about waist height. She crammed the board with intricate, curling snakes, vast ladders, vibrantly glowing squares – detail piled on detail.

The next morning she walked with eagerness to the room where she'd built her board – and was immediately disappointed. Her efforts seemed pale, static, derivative: obviously the work of a child, despite the assistance of the Virtual software.

She wiped the board clean, leaving a grid of pale squares floating in the air. Then she started to populate it again – but this time with animated half-human snakes, slithering 'ladders' of a hundred forms. She'd learned to access the Virtual libraries, and she plundered the art and history of a hundred centuries to populate her board.

Of course it was no longer possible to play games on the board, but that didn't matter. The board was the thing, a world in itself. She withdrew a little from her parents, spending long hours in deep searches through the libraries. She gave up her daily classes. Her parents didn't seem to mind; they came to speak to her regularly, and showed an interest in her projects, but they respected her privacy.

The board kept her interest the next day. But now she evolved elaborate games, dividing the board into countries and empires with arbitrary bands of glowing light. Armies of ladder-folk joined with legions of snakes in crude recreations of the great events of human history.

She watched the symbols flicker across the Virtual board, shimmering, coalescing; she dictated lengthy chronicles of the histories of her imaginary countries.

By the end of the day, though, she was starting to grow more interested in the history texts she was consulting than in her own elaborations on them. She went to bed, eager for the next morning to come.

She awoke in darkness, doubled in agony.

She called for light. She sat up in bed.

Blood spotted the sheets. She screamed.

Phillida sat with her, cradling her head. Lieserl pressed herself against her mother's warmth, trying to still her trembling.

'I think it's time you asked me your questions.'

Lieserl sniffed. 'What questions?'

'The ones you've carried around with you since the moment you were born.' Phillida smiled. 'I could see it in your eyes, even at that moment. You poor thing . . . to be burdened with so much *awareness*. I'm sorry, Lieserl.'

Lieserl pulled away. Suddenly she felt cold, vulnerable. '*Who am I*, Phillida?'

'You're my daughter.' Phillida placed her hands on Lieserl's shoulders and pushed her face close; Lieserl could feel the warmth of her breath, and the soft room light caught the grey in her mother's blond hair, making it shine. 'Never forget that. You're as human as I am. But –' She hesitated.

'But what?'

'But you're being – *engineered*.

'There are *nanobots* in your body,' Phillida said. 'Do you understand what a nanobot is? A machine at the molecular level which –'

'I know what a nanobot is,' Lieserl snapped. 'I know all about AntiSenescence and nanobots. I'm not a child, Mother.'

'Of course not,' Phillida said seriously. 'But in your case, my darling, the nanobots have been programmed – not to reverse ageing – but to *accelerate* it. Do you understand?'

Nanobots swarmed through Lieserl's body. They plated

16

calcium over her bones, stimulated the generation of new cells, forced her body to sprout like some absurd human sunflower – they even implanted memories, artificial learning, directly into her cortex.

Lieserl felt like scraping at her skin, gouging out this artificial infection. '*Why*? Why did you let this be done to me?'

Phillida pulled her close, but Lieserl stayed stiff, resisting mutely. Phillida buried her face in Lieserl's hair; Lieserl felt the soft weight of her mother's cheek on the crown of her head. 'Not yet,' Phillida said. 'Not yet. A few more days, my love. That's all ...'

Phillida's cheeks grew warmer, as if she were crying, silently, into her daughter's hair.

Lieserl returned to her snakes and ladders board. She found herself looking on her creation with affection, but also nostalgic sadness; she felt distant from this elaborate, slightly obsessive concoction.

Already she'd outgrown it.

She walked into the middle of the sparkling board and bade a Sun, a foot wide, rise out from the centre of her body. Light swamped the board, shattering it.

She wasn't the only adolescent who had constructed fantasy worlds like this. She read about the Brontës, in their lonely parsonage in the north of England, and their elaborate shared world of kings and princes and empires. And she read about the history of the humble game of snakes and ladders. The game had come from India, where it was a morality teaching aid called *Moksha-Patamu*. There were twelve vices and four virtues, and the objective was to get to Nirvana. It was easier to fail than to succeed ... The British in the nineteenth century had adopted the game as an instructional guide for children called *Kismet*; Lieserl stared at images of claustrophobic boards, forbidding snakes. Thirteen snakes and eight ladders showed children that if they were good and obedient their life would be rewarded.

But by a few decades later the game had lost its moral subtexts. Lieserl found images from the early twentieth century of a sad-looking little clown who clambered heroically up ladders and slithered haplessly down snakes.

The game, with its charm and simplicity, had survived through the twenty centuries which had worn away since the death of that forgotten clown. Lieserl stared at him, trying to understand the appeal of his baggy trousers, walking cane and little moustache.

She grew interested in the *numbers* embedded in the various versions of the game. The twelve-to-four ratio of *Moksha-Patamu* clearly made it a harder game to win than *Kismet*'s thirteen-to-eight – but how much harder?

She began to draw new boards in the air. But these boards were abstractions – clean, colourless, little more than sketches. She ran through high-speed simulated games, studying their outcomes. She experimented with ratios of snakes to ladders, with their placement. Phillida sat with her and introduced her to combinatorial mathematics, the theory of games – to different forms of wonder.

On her fifteenth day she tired of her own company and started to attend classes again. She found the perceptions of others a refreshing counterpoint to her own, high-speed learning.

The world seemed to open up around her like a flower; it was a world full of sunlight, of endless avenues of information, of stimulating people.

She read up on nanobots. She learned the secret of Anti-Senescence, the process which had rendered humans effectively immortal.

Body cells were programmed to commit suicide.

Left alone, a cell manufactured enzymes which cut its own DNA into neat pieces, and quietly closed itself down. The suicide of cells was a guard against uncontrolled growth – tumours – and a tool to sculpt the developing body: in the womb, for example, the withering of unwanted cells carved fingers and toes from blunt tissue buds.

Death was the default state of a cell. Chemical signals had to be sent out by the body, to instruct cells to remain alive. It was a dead-man's-switch control mechanism: if cells grew out of control – or if they separated from their parent organ and wandered through the body – the reassuring environment of chemical signals would be lost, and they would be forced to die.

18

The nanotechnological manipulation of this process made AntiSenescence simple.

It also made simple the manufacture of a Lieserl.

Lieserl studied this, scratching absently at her inhabited, engineered arms.

She looked up the word *Superet* in the Virtual libraries. She had access to no reference to it. She wasn't an expert at data mining, but she thought there was a hole here.

Information about Superet was being kept from her.

With a boy called Matthew, from her class, she took a trip away from the House – without her parents, for the first time. They rode a flitter to the shore where she'd played as a child, twelve days earlier. She found the broken pier where she'd discovered mussels. The place seemed less vivid – less magical – and she felt a sad nostalgia for the loss of the freshness of her childish senses. She wondered why no adult ever commented on this dreadful loss of acuity. Perhaps they just forgot, she thought.

But there were other compensations.

Her body was strong, lithe, and the sunlight was like warm oil on her skin. She ran and swam, relishing the sparkle of the ozone-laden air in her lungs. She and Matthew mock-wrestled and chased in the surf, clambering over each other – like children, she thought, but not quite with complete innocence.

As sunset approached they allowed the flitter to return them to the House. They agreed to meet the next day, perhaps take another trip somewhere. Matthew kissed her lightly, on the lips, as they parted.

That night she could barely sleep. She lay in the dark of her room, the scent of salt still strong in her nostrils, the image of Matthew alive in her mind. Her body seemed to pulse with hot blood, with its endless, continuing growth.

The next day – her sixteenth – Lieserl rose quickly. She'd never felt so alive; her skin still glowed from the salt and sunlight of the shore, and there was a hot tension inside her, an ache deep in her belly, a tightness.

When she reached the flitter bay at the front of the House, Matthew was waiting for her. His back was turned, the low sunlight causing the fine hairs at the base of his neck to glow.

He turned to face her.

He reached out to her, uncertainly, then allowed his hands to drop to his sides. He didn't seem to know what to say; his posture changed, subtly, his shoulders slumping slightly; before her eyes he was becoming shy of her.

She was taller than him. Visibly *older*. She became abruptly aware of the still-childlike roundness of his face, the awkwardness of his manner. The thought of *touching* him – the memory of her feverish dreams during the night – seemed absurd, impossibly adolescent.

She felt the muscles in her neck tighten; she felt as if she must scream. Matthew seemed to recede from her, as if she were viewing him through a tunnel.

Once again the labouring nanobots – the vicious, unceasing technological infection of her body – had taken away part of her life.

This time, though, it was too much to bear.

Phillida had never looked so old. Her skin seemed drawn tight across the bones of her face, the lines etched deep. 'I'm sorry,' she said. 'Believe me. When we – George and I – volunteered for Superet's programme, we knew it would be painful. But we never dreamed how much. Neither of us had children before. Perhaps if we had, we'd have been able to anticipate how this would feel.'

'I'm a freak – an absurd experiment,' Lieserl shouted. 'A *construct*. Why did you make me human? Why not some insentient animal? Why not a Virtual?'

'Oh, you had to be human. As human as possible ...'

'I'm human in fragments,' Lieserl said bitterly. 'In shards. Which are taken away from me as soon as they're found. That's not humanity, Phillida. It's *grotesque*.'

'I know. I'm sorry, my love. Come with me.'

'Where?'

'Outside. To the garden. I want to show you something.'

Suspicious, hostile, Lieserl allowed her mother to take her hand; but she made her fingers lie lifeless, cold in Phillida's warm grasp.

It was mid-morning now. The Sun's light flooded the garden; flowers – white and yellow – strained up towards the sky.

Lieserl looked around; the garden was empty. 'What am I supposed to be seeing?'

Phillida, solemnly, pointed upwards.

Lieserl tilted back her head, shading her eyes to block out the Sun. The sky was a searing-blue dome, marked only by a high vapour trail and the lights of orbital habitats.

Gently, Phillida pulled Lieserl's hand down from her face, and, cupping her chin, tipped her face flower-like towards the Sun.

The star's light seemed to fill her head. Dazzled, she dropped her eyes and stared at Phillida through a haze of blurred, streaked retinal images. 'The *Sun*?'

'Lieserl, you were – constructed. You know that. You're being forced through a human lifecycle at hundreds of times the normal pace –'

'A year every day.'

'Approximately, yes. But there is a purpose, Lieserl. A justification. You aren't simply an experiment. You have a mission.' She waved her hand at the sprawling, friendly buildings that comprised the House. 'Most of the people here, particularly the children, don't know anything about you, Lieserl. They have jobs, goals – lives of their own to follow. But they're here *for* you.

'Lieserl, the House is here to *imprint* you with humanity. Your experiences have been designed – George and I were selected, even – to ensure that the first few days of your existence would be as *human* as possible.'

'*The first few days*?' Suddenly the unknowable future was like a black wall, looming towards her; she felt as out of control of her life as if she were a counter on some immense, invisible snakes-and-ladders board. She lifted her face to the warmth of the Sun. '*What am I*?'

'You are ... artificial, Lieserl.

'In a few weeks your human shell will become old. You'll be transferred into a new form ... Your human body will be –'

'Discarded?'

'Lieserl, it's so difficult. That moment will seem like a death to me. But it *won't* be death. It will be a metamorphosis. You'll have new powers – even your awareness will be reconstructed. Lieserl, you'll become the most conscious entity in the Solar System ...'

'I don't want that. I want to be me. I want my freedom, Phillida.'

'No, Lieserl. You're not free, I'm afraid; you never can be. You have a goal.'

'What goal?'

Phillida lifted her face to the Sun once more. 'The Sun gave us life. Without it – without the other stars – we couldn't survive.

'We're a strong species. We believe we can live as long as the stars – for tens of billions of years. And perhaps even beyond that … If we're allowed to. But we've had – *glimpses* – of the future, the far distant future. Disturbing glimpses.

'People are starting to plan, to assure we're granted our destiny. People are working on projects which will take millions of years to come to fruition … People like those working for Superet.

'Lieserl, you're one of those projects.'

'I don't understand.'

Phillida took her hand, squeezed it gently; the simple human contact seemed incongruous, the garden around them transient, a chimera, before this talk of megayears and the future of the species.

'Lieserl, something is wrong with the Sun. *You* have to find out what. The Sun is dying; something – or someone – is *killing* it.' Phillida's eyes were huge before her, staring, probing for understanding. 'Don't be afraid. My dear, you will live forever. If you want to. And you will see wonders which I can only dream of.'

Lieserl stared into her mother's huge, weak eyes. 'But you don't *envy* me. Do you, Phillida?'

'No,' Phillida said quietly.

2

Louise Ye Armonk stood on the weather deck of the SS *Great Britain*. From here she could see the full length of Brunel's fine steam liner: the polished deck, the skylights, the airy masts with their loops of wire rigging, the single, squat funnel amidships.

And beyond the glowing dome which sheltered the old ship, the sky of the Solar System's rim loomed like a huge, empty room.

Louise still felt a little drunk – sourly now – from the orbiting party she'd left a few minutes earlier. She subvocalized a command to send nanobots scouring through her bloodstream; she sobered up fast, with a brief shudder.

Mark Bassett Friar Armonk Wu – Louise's ex-husband – stood close by her. They'd left the *Great Northern*, with its party still in full swing, to come here, to the surface of Port Sol, in a cramped pod. Mark was dressed in a one-piece jumpsuit of some pastel fabric; the lines of his neck were long and elegant as he turned his head to survey the old ship.

Louise was glad they were alone, that none of the *Northern*'s prospective interstellar colonists had decided to follow them down for a last few moments on this outpost of Sol, to reminisce with this fragment of Earth's past – even though reminiscence was part of the reason Louise had had the old ship brought out here in the first place.

Mark touched her arm; his palm, through the thin fabric of her sleeve, felt warm, alive. 'You're not happy, are you? Even at a moment like this. Your greatest triumph.'

She searched his face, seeking out his meaning. He wore his hair shaven, so that his fine, fragile-looking skull showed through his dark skin; his nose was sharp, his lips thin, and his blue eyes – striking in that dark face – were surrounded by a mesh of wrinkles. He'd once told her he'd thought of getting the wrinkles smoothed out – it would be easy enough in the course of AS-renewal – but she'd campaigned against it. Not that she'd have cared too much, but it would have taken most of the character out of that elegant face – most of its patina of *time*, she thought.

'I never could read you,' she said at last. 'Maybe that's why we failed in the end.'

He laughed lightly, a sparkle of intoxication still in his voice. 'Oh, come on. We lasted twenty years. That's not a failure.'

'In a lifetime of *two hundred* years?' She shook her head. 'Look. You ask me about my feelings. Anyone who didn't know you – us – would think you cared. So why do I think that, in some part of your head, you're laughing at me?'

Mark drew his hand away from her arm, and she could almost see the shutters coming down behind his eyes. 'Because you're an ill-tempered, morose, graceless – oh, into Lethe with it.'

'Anyway, you're right,' Louise said at last.

'What?'

'I'm not happy. Although I'm not sure I could tell you why.'

Mark smiled; the sourceless light of the *Britain*'s dome smoothed away the lines around his eyes. 'Well, if we're being honest with each other for once, I *do* kind of enjoy seeing you suffer. Just a bit. But I care as well. Come on, let's walk.'

He took her arm again, and they walked along the ship's starboard side. The soles of their shoes made soft sucking sounds as the shoes' limited processors made the soles adhere to and release the deck surface, unobtrusively reinforcing Port Sol's microgravity. The shoes almost got it right; Louise felt herself stumble only a couple of times.

Around the ship was a dome of semisentient glass, and beyond the dome – beyond the pool of sourceless light which bathed the liner – the landscape of Port Sol stretched to its close-crowding horizon. Port Sol was a hundred-mile ball of friable rock and water-ice, with traces of hydrogen, helium and a few hydrocarbons. It was like a huge comet nucleus. Port Sol's truncated landscape was filled with insubstantial, gossamer forms: sculptures raised from the ancient ice by natural forces reduced to geological slowness by the immense distance of the Sun.

Port Sol was a *Kuiper object*. With uncounted companions, it circled the Sun beyond the orbit of Pluto, shepherded there by resonances of the major planets' gravitational fields.

Louise looked back at the *Great Britain*. Even against the faery background of Port Sol, still Brunel's ship struck her as a thing of lightness, grace and elegance. She remembered going to see the ship in her dry dock on Earth; now, as then, she compressed her eyes, squinting, trying to make out the *form* of the thing – the Platonic ideal within the iron, which poor old Isambard had tried to make real. The ship was three thousand tons of iron and wood, but with her slim, sharp curves and fine detail she was like a craft out of fantasy. Louise thought of the gilded decorations and the coat-of-arms figurehead around the stern, and the simple, affecting symbols of Victorian industry carved into the bow: the coil of rope, the cogwheels, the set-square, the wheatsheaf. It was impossible to imagine such a delicate thing braving the storms of the Atlantic ...

She tilted back her head, and looked for the brightish star in Capricorn that was Sol, all of four billion miles away. Surely even a visionary like old Isambard never imagined that his first great ship would make her final voyage across such an immense sea as this.

Mark and Louise climbed down a steep staircase amidships to the promenade deck; they strolled along the deck past blocks of tiny cabins towards the engine-room bulkhead.

Mark ran a fingertip over the surface of a cabin wall as they passed. He frowned, rubbing his fingertips together. 'The surface feels odd ... not much like wood.'

'It's preserved. Within a thin shell of semisentient plastic, which seals it, nourishes it ... Mark, the damn boat was launched in 1843. Over two thousand years ago. There wouldn't be much left of her without preservation. Anyway, I thought you weren't interested.'

He sniffed. 'Not really. I'm more interested in why you wanted to come down here: now, in the middle of all the celebrations for the completion of the starship.'

'I try to avoid introspection,' she said heavily.

'Oh, sure.' He turned to her, his face picking up the soft glow of the ancient wood. 'Talk to me, Louise. The bit of me that cares about you is outvoting the bit that enjoys seeing you suffer, just for the moment.'

She shrugged. She couldn't help sounding sour. 'You tell me. You always were good at diagnosing the condition of the inside of my head. At great and tedious length. Maybe I'm feeling melancholy after completing my work on the *Northern*. Could that be it, do you think? Maybe I'm going through some equivalent of a post-coital depression.'

He snorted. 'With you, it was post, pre and during, frankly. No, I don't think it's that ... And besides,' he said slowly, 'your work on the *Northern* isn't finished yet. *You're planning to leave with her*. Aren't you? Spend subjective decades hauling her out to Tau Ceti.'

She heard herself growl. 'How did you find out about that? No wonder you drove me crazy, all those years. You're too damn *interested* in me.'

'I'm right, though, aren't I?'

Now they reached the *Britain*'s dining room. It was a fantastic Victorian dream. Twelve columns of white and gold, with ornamental capitals, ran down its spine, and the room was lined by two sets of twelve more columns each. Doorways between the columns led off to passageways and bedrooms, and the door archways were gilded and surmounted by medallion heads. The walls were lemon-yellow, relieved by blue, white and gold; omnipresent, sourceless light shone from the cutlery and glassware on the three long tables.

Mark walked across the carpet and ran his hand over a table's gleaming, polished surface. 'You should do something about this semisentient plastic: have it give the surfaces some semblance of their natural texture. The touch is half the beauty of a thing, Louise. But you always were ... *remote*, weren't you? Happy enough with the surface of things – with their look, their outer form. Never interested in touching, in getting closer.'

She ignored that. 'Brunel had a lot of style, you know. He worked on a tunnel under the Thames, with his father.'

'Where?' Mark had been born in Port Cassini, Titan.

'The Thames. A river, in England ... on Earth. The tunnel was flooded, several times. Once, when it had been pumped out, Brunel threw a dinner party right up against the working face for fifty people. He got the band of the Coldstream Guards to –'

'Hmm. How interesting,' Mark said dryly. 'Maybe you

26

should put some food on these tables. Why not? It could be preserved, by your sentient plastic. You could have segments of dead animals. As devoured by the great Brunel himself.'

'You never did have any taste, Mark.'

'I don't think your mood has anything to do with the completion of the *Northern*.'

'Then what?'

He sighed. 'It's you, of course. It always is. For a long time, while we were together, I thought I understood your motivation. There would always be another huge, beautiful GUTship to build; another immense undertaking to lose yourself in. And since we're all immortal now, thanks to AntiSenescence, I thought that would be enough for you.'

'But I was wrong. It isn't like that. Not really.'

Louise was aware of intense discomfort, somewhere deep within her; she felt she wanted to talk, read a bookslate, bury herself in a Virtual – anything to drown out his words.

'You always were smarter than me, Mark.'

'In some ways, yes.'

'Just say what you've got to say, and get it over.'

'You want immortality, Louise. But not the dreary *literal* immortality of AS – not just a body-scouring every few years – but the kind of immortality attained by your idols.' He waved a hand. 'By Brunel, for instance. By achieving something unique, wonderful. And you fear you'll never be able to, no matter how many starships you build.'

'You're damn patronizing,' she snapped. 'The *Northern* is a great achievement.'

'I know it is. I'm not denying it.' He smiled, triumph in his eyes. 'But I'm right, aren't I?'

She felt deflated. 'You know you are. Damn you.' She rubbed her eyes. '*It's the shadow of the future, Mark . . .*'

A century and a half earlier, the future had invaded the Solar System.

It had been humanity's own fault; everyone recognized that. Under the leadership of an engineer called Michael Poole the Interface project – a wormhole link to a future a millennium and a half ahead – had been completed.

At the time Louise Ye Armonk was well established in her

chosen field of GUTship engineering ... at least, as established as any mere fifty-year-old could be, in a society increasingly dominated by the AS-preserved giants of the recent past. Louise had even worked, briefly, with Michael Poole himself.

Why had Poole's wormhole time link been built? There were endless justifications – *what power could a glimpse of the future afford?* – but the truth was, Louise knew, that it had been built for little more than the sheer *joy* of it.

The Interface project came at the end of centuries of expansion for mankind. The Solar System had been opened up, first by GUTdrive vessels and later by wormhole links, and the first GUTdrive starship fuelling port – Port Sol – was already operational.

It was difficult now to recapture the mood of those times, Louise thought. Confidence – arrogance ... The anthropic theories of cosmological evolution were somewhere near their paradigmatic peak. Some people believed humans were alone in the Universe. Others even believed the Universe had been *designed*, by some offstage agency, with the sole object of delivering and supporting humans. Given time, humans would do anything, go anywhere, achieve whatever they liked.

But Poole's Interface had been a bridge to the *real* future.

The incident that followed the opening of the wormhole had been confused, chaotic, difficult to disentangle. But it *had* been a war – brief, spectacular, like no battle fought in Solar space before or since, but a war nevertheless.

Future Earth – at the other end of Poole's time bridge, a millennium and a half hence – would be under occupation, by an alien species about whom nothing was known save their name: *Qax*.

Rebel humans from the occupation era were pursued back through time, through Poole's Interface, by two immense Qax warships. The rebels, with the help of Michael Poole, had destroyed the warships. Then Poole had driven a captured warship into the Interface wormhole, to seal it against further invasion – and in the process Poole himself was lost in time. The rebels, stranded in their past, had fled the Solar System in a captured GUTdrive ship, evidently intending to use time dilation effects to erode away the years back to their own era.

The System, stunned, slowly recovered.

Various bodies – like the Holy Superet Light Church – still, after a hundred and fifty years, combed through the fragments of data from the Interface incident, trying to answer the unanswerable.

Like: what had *truly* happened to Michael Poole?

It was known that the Qax occupation itself would eventually be lifted, and humanity would resume its expansion – but now more warily, and into a Universe known to be populated by hostile competitors . . .

A Universe containing, above all, the *Xeelee*. And it was said that before Poole's wormhole path to the future finally closed, some information had been obtained on the *far* future – of millions of years hence, far beyond the era of the Qax. Louise could see how some such data could be obtained – by the flux of high-energy particles from the mouth of the collapsing wormhole, for instance.

And the rumours said that the far future – and what it held for mankind – were bleak indeed.

Louise and Mark stood on the forecastle deck and looked up towards the Sun.

The *Great Northern*, Louise's GUTdrive starship, passed serenely over their heads, following its stately, four-hour orbit through the Kuiper object's shallow gravitational well. The *Northern*'s three-mile-long spine, encrusted with sensors, looked as if it had been carved from glass. The GUTdrive was embedded in a block of Port Sol ice, a silvery, irregular mass at one end of the spine. The lifedome – itself a mile across – was a skull of glass, fixed to the spine's other end. Lights shone from the lifedome, green and blue; the dome looked like a bowlful of Earth, here on the rim of the System.

'It's beautiful,' Mark said. 'Like a Virtual. It's hard to believe it's real.' The light from the *Britain*'s dome underlit his face, throwing the fine lines around his mouth into relief. 'And it's a good name, Louise. *Great Northern*. Your starship will head out where every direction is *north* – away from the Sun.'

Staring up at the shimmering *Northern* now, Louise remembered Virtual journeys through ghostly, still-born craft: craft which had evolved around her as the design software responded to her thoughts. How Brunel would have thrived with

29

modern software, which once again enabled the vision of individuals to dominate such huge engineering projects. And some of those lost ships had been far more elegant and daring than the final design – which had been, as ever, a compromise between vision and economics.

...And that was the trouble. The real thing was *always* a disappointment.

'Louise, you shouldn't fear the future,' Mark said.

Instantly Louise was irritated. 'I don't *fear* it,' she said. 'Lethe, don't you even understand that? It's Michael Poole and his damn Interface incident. I don't fear the future. The trouble is, I *know* it.'

'We all do, Louise,' Mark said, his patience starting to sound a little strained. 'And most of us don't let it affect us –'

'Oh, really. Look at yourself, Mark. What about your *hair*, for instance? – or rather, your lack of it.'

Mark ran a self-conscious hand up and over his scalp.

She went on, 'Everyone knows that this modern passion for baldness comes from those weird human rebels from the future, the Friends of Wigner. So you can't tell me you're not influenced by knowing what's to come. Your very hairstyle is a statement of –'

'All right,' he snapped. 'All right, you've made your point. You never know when to shut up, do you? But, Louise – the difference is we aren't all *obsessed* by the future. Unlike you.'

He walked away from her, his gait stiff with annoyance.

They climbed down into the engine room. Multicoloured light filtered down through an immense skylight. Four inclined cylinders thrust up from the floor of the ship; the pistons stood idle like the limbs of iron giants, and a vast chain girdled the drive machinery.

Louise rubbed her chin and stared at the machinery. 'Obsessed? Mark, the future contains the Xeelee – godlike entities so aloof from us that we may never understand what they are trying to achieve – and with technology, with *engineering*, like magic. They have a *hyperdrive*.' She let her voice soften. 'Do you understand what that means? It means that somewhere in the Universe, *now*, the damn Xeelee are riding around in FTL chariots which make my poor *Northern* look like a horse-drawn cart.

'And we believe they have an intraSystem engine – their so-called *discontinuity drive* – which powers night-dark ships with wings like sycamore leaves, hundreds of miles wide ...

'I'm not denying my GUTdrive module is a beautiful piece of engineering. I'm *proud* of it. But compared to what we understand of Xeelee technology, Mark, it's – it's a damn steam engine. Why, we even use ice as reaction mass. Think of that! What's the point of building something which I know is outdated before I even start?'

Mark laid a hand on her shoulder and squeezed. His touch was warm, firm, and – as he'd no doubt intended – disconcertingly intimate. 'So that's why you're running away.'

'I'd hardly call leaving on a one-way colonizing expedition to Tau Ceti "running away".'

'Of course it is. *Here* is where you can achieve things – here, with the resources of a Solar System. You're an engineer, damn it. What will you build on some planet of Tau Ceti? A *real* steam engine, maybe.'

'But –' She struggled to find words that didn't sound, even to her, like self-justifying whines. 'But maybe that would count for more, in the greater scheme of things, even than a dozen bigger and better *Northerns*. Do you see?'

'Not really.' His voice sounded flat, tired; perhaps he was letting himself sober up.

They stood for a while, in a silence broken only by their breathing. Then he said, 'I'm sorry, Louise. I'm sorry you're letting such moods spoil your night of triumph. But I've had enough; I feel as if I've been listening to that stuff for half my life.'

As usual when his mood turned like this, she was filled with regret. She tried to cover his hand, which still lay on her shoulder. 'Mark –'

He slid his hand away. 'I'm going back to the pod, and up to the ship, and I'm going to get a little more drunk. Do you want to come?'

She thought about it. 'No. Send the pod down again. Some of the cabins here are made up; I can –'

There was a sparkling in the air before him. She stumbled back, disconcerted; Mark moved closer to her to watch.

Pixels – thumbnail cubes of light – tumbled over each other, casting glittering highlights from Brunel's ancient machinery. They coalesced abruptly into the lifesize, semitransparent Virtual image of a human head: round, bald, cheerful. The face split into a grin. 'Louise. Sorry to disturb you.'

'Gillibrand. What in Lethe do *you* want? I thought you'd be unconscious by now.'

Sam Gillibrand, forty going on a hundred and fifty, was Louise's chief assistant. 'I was. But my nanobots were hooked up to the comms panel; they sobered me up fast when the message came in. Damn them.' Gillibrand looked cheerful enough. 'Oh, well; I'll just have it all to do again, and –'

'The comms panel? What was the message, Sam?'

Gillibrand's grin became uncertain. 'City Hall. There's been a change to the flight plan.' Gillibrand's voice was high, heavily accented mid-American, and not really capable of conveying much drama. And yet Louise felt herself shudder when Gillibrand said: 'We're not going to Tau Ceti after all.'

3

The old woman leaned forward in her seat, beside Kevan Scholes.

The surface of the Sun, barely ten thousand miles below the clear-walled cabin of the *Lightrider*, was a floor across the Universe. The photosphere was a landscape, encrusted by granules each large enough to swallow the Earth, and with the chromosphere – the thousand-mile-thick outer atmosphere – a thin haze above it all.

Scholes couldn't help but stare at his companion. Her posture was stiff, and her hands – neatly folded in her lap, over her seatbelt – were gaunt, the skin pocked by liver-spots and hanging loosely from the bones. *Like gloves*, he thought. She wore a simple silver-grey coverall whose only decoration was a small brooch pinned to the breast. The brooch depicted a stylized snake entwined around a golden ladder.

The little ship passed over a photosphere granule; Scholes watched absently as it unfolded beneath them. Hot hydrogen welled up from the Solar interior at a speed of half a mile a second, then spread out across the photosphere surface. This particular fount of gas was perhaps a thousand miles across, and, in its photosphere-hugging orbit, the *Lightrider* was travelling so rapidly that it had passed over the granule in a few minutes. And Scholes saw as he looked back that the granule was already beginning to disintegrate, the hydrogen spill at its heart dwindling. Individual granules persisted less than ten minutes, on average.

'How beautiful this is,' his companion said, gazing down at the Sunscape. 'And how *complex* – how intricate, like some immense machine, perhaps, or even a world.' She turned to him, her mouth – surrounded by its dense web of wrinkles –

folded tight. 'I can imagine whiling away my life, just watching the slow evolutions of that surface.'

Scholes looked across the teeming Sunscape. The photosphere was a mass of ponderous motion, resembling the surface of a slowly boiling liquid. The granules, individual convective cells, were themselves grouped into loose associations: *supergranules*, tens of thousands of miles across, roughly bounded by thin, shifting walls of stable gas. As he watched, one granule exploded, its material bursting suddenly across the Solar surface; neighbouring granules were pushed aside, so that a glowing, unstructured scar was left on the photosphere, a scar which was slowly healed by the eruption of new granules.

Scholes studied his companion. The sunlight underlit her face, deepening the lines and folds of loose flesh there. It made her look almost demonic – or like something out of a distant, unlamented past. She'd fallen silent now, watching him; some response was expected, and he sensed that his customary glib flippancy – which usually passed for conversation in the Solar habitat – wouldn't do.

Not for her.

He summoned up a smile, with some difficulty. 'Yes, it's beautiful. But –' Scholes had spent much of the last five years within a million miles of the Sun's glowing surface, but even so had barely started to become accustomed to the eternal presence of the star. 'It's impossible to forget it's *there* ... Even when I'm in Thoth, with the walls opaqued – when I could really be anywhere in the System, I guess.' He hesitated, suddenly embarrassed; her cold, rheumy eyes were on him, analytical. 'I'm sorry. I don't know how to explain it any better.'

Was there a hint of a smile on that devastated face? 'You needn't be self-conscious.'

Kevan Scholes had volunteered for this assignment – a simple three-hour orbital tour with this mysterious woman who, a few days earlier, had been brought to Thoth, the freefall habitat at the centre of the wormhole project. It should have been little more than a sightseeing jaunt – and a chance to learn more about this ancient woman, and perhaps about the true goals of Superet's wormhole project itself.

And besides, it was a break from his own work. Scholes was supervising the assembly of one vertex of a wormhole Interface from exotic matter components. When the wormhole was complete, one of its pair of tetrahedral Interfaces would be left in close orbit around the Sun. The other, packed with an ambitious AI complex, would be dropped into the Sun itself.

The work was well paid, though demanding; but it was dull, routine, lacking fulfilment. So a break was welcome ... But he had not expected to be so disconcerted by this extraordinary woman.

He tried again. 'You see, we're all scientists or engineers here,' he said. 'A sense of wonder isn't a prerequisite for a job on this project – it's probably a handicap, actually. But that's a *star* out there, after all: nearly a million miles across – *five light-seconds* – and with the mass of three hundred thousand Earths. Even when I can't see it, I know it's there; it's like a psychic pressure, perhaps.'

She nodded and turned her face to the Sun once more. 'Which is why we find speculation about its destruction so extraordinarily distressing. And, of course, to some extent we are actually *within* the body of the Sun itself. Isn't that true?'

'I guess so. There's no simple definition of where the Sun ends; there's just a fall-off of density, steep at first, then becoming less dramatic once you're outside the photosphere ... Let me show you.'

He touched his data slate, and the semisentient hull suppressed the photosphere's glow. In its new false colours the Sunscape became suffused with deep crimsons and purples; the granules seethed like the clustering mouths of undersea volcanoes.

'My word,' she murmured. 'It's like a landscape from a medieval hell.'

'Look up,' Scholes said.

She did so, and gasped.

The chromosphere was a soft, featureless mist around the ship. And the corona – the Sun's outer atmosphere, extending many Solar diameters beyond the photosphere – was a cathedral of gas above them, easily visible now that the photosphere light was suppressed. There were ribbons, streamers of high density in that gas; it was like an immense, slow explosion all around them, expanding as if to fill space.

'There's so much *structure*,' she said. She stared upwards, her

35

watery eyes wide and unblinking. Scholes felt disquieted by her intensity. He restored the transparency of the hull, so that the corona was overwhelmed once more.

A sunspot – deep black at its heart, giving an impression of a wound in the Sun's hide, of immense depth – unfolded beneath them, ponderously.

'We seem to be travelling so *slowly*,' she said.

He smiled. 'We're in free orbit around the Sun. We're actually travelling at three hundred miles a *second*.'

He saw her eyes widen.

He said gently, 'I know. It takes a little while to get used to the *scale* of the Sun. It's not a planet. If the Earth were at the centre of the Sun, the whole of the Moon's orbit would be contained within the Sun's bulk ...'

They were directly over the spot now; its central umbra was like a wound in the Sun's glowing flesh, deep black, with the penumbra a wide, grey bruise around it. This was the largest of a small, interconnected family of spots, Scholes saw now; they looked like splashes of paint against the photosphere, and their penumbrae were linked by causeways of greyness. The spot complex passed beneath them, a landscape wrought in shades of grey.

'It's like a tunnel,' Lieserl said. 'I imagine I can see into it, right down into the heart of the Sun.'

'That's an illusion, I'm afraid. The spot is dark only by contrast with the surrounding regions. If a major spot complex could be cut out of the Sun and left hanging in space, it would be as bright as the full Moon, seen from Earth.'

'But still, the illusion of depth is startling.'

Now the spot complex was passing beneath them, rapidly becoming foreshortened.

Scholes said uncertainly, 'Of course you understand that what you see of the Sun, here, is a false-colour rendering by the hull of the *Lightrider*. The *'Rider'*s hull is actually almost perfectly reflective. Excess heat is dumped into space with high-energy lasers fixed to the hull: the *'Rider'* refrigerates itself, effectively. In fact, if you could see the ship from outside it would actually be glowing more brightly than the photosphere itself ...' Scholes was uncomfortably aware that he was jabbering.

'I think I follow.' She waved her claw-like hand, delicately, at

36

the glowing surface. 'But the features are real, of course. Like the spot complex.'

'Yes. Yes, of course.' *Lethe*, he thought suddenly. *Am I patronizing her?*

His brief had been to show this strange old woman the sights – to give her the VIP tour. But he knew nothing about her – it was quite possible she knew far more about the subjects he was describing than he did.

The Holy Superet Light Church was notoriously secretive: about the goals of this Solar wormhole project, and the role the old woman would play in it ... although everyone knew, from the way she had been handled since arriving in near-Solar space – as if she was as fragile and precious as an eggshell – that this woman was somehow the key to the whole thing.

But how much did she *know?*

He watched her birdlike face carefully. The way her grey hair had been swept back into a small, hard bun made her strong-nosed face even more gaunt and threatening than it might otherwise have been.

She asked, 'And is this refrigeration process how the wormhole probe is going to work – to become able to penetrate the Sun itself?'

He hesitated. 'Something like it, yes. The key to refrigerating a volume is to suck heat out of the volume faster than it's allowed in. We'll be taking Solar heat away from the AI complex out through the wormhole, and dumping it outside the Sun itself; actually we're planning to use that energy as a secondary power source for Thoth ...'

She shifted in her chair, stiff and cautious, as if afraid of breaking something. 'Dr Scholes, tell me. Will we be leaving freefall?'

The question was surprising. He looked at her. 'During this flight, in the *Lightrider*?'

She returned his look calmly, waiting.

'We're actually in free orbit around the Sun; this close to the surface the period is about three hours ... We'll make a complete orbit. Then we'll climb back out to Thoth ... But we'll proceed the whole way at low acceleration; you should barely feel a thing. Why do you ask?' He hesitated. 'Are you uncomfortable?'

'No. But I would be if we started to ramp up the gees. I'm a little more fragile than I used to be, you see.' Her tone was baffling – self-deprecating, wistful, perhaps with a hint of resentment.

He nodded and turned away, unsure how to respond.

'Oh, dear.' Unexpectedly, she was smiling, revealing small, yellow-gold teeth. 'I'm sorry, Dr Scholes. I suspect I'm intimidating you.'

'A little, yes.' He grinned.

'You really don't know what to make of me, do you?'

He spread his hands. 'The trouble is, frankly, I'm not sure how much you know.' He hesitated. 'I don't want to feel I'm patronizing you, by –'

'Don't feel that.' Unexpectedly she let her hand rest on his; her fingers felt like dried twigs, but her palm was surprisingly warm, leathery. 'You're fulfilling the request I made, for this trip, very well. Assume I know nothing; you can treat me as an empty-headed tourist.' Her smile turned into a grin, almost mischievous; suddenly she seemed much less *alien*, in Scholes' eyes. 'As ignorant as a visiting politician, or Superet high-up, even. Tell me about sunspots, for instance.'

He laughed. 'All right ... To understand that, you need to know how the Sun is put together.'

The Sun was a thing of layers, like a Chinese box.

At the Sun's heart was an immense fusion reactor, extending across two hundred thousand miles. This core region – contained within just a quarter of the Sun's diameter – provided nearly all the Sun's luminosity, the energy which caused the Sun to shine.

Beyond the fusing core, the Sun consisted of a thinning plasma. Photons – packets of radiation emitted from the core – worked their way through this radiative layer, on average travelling no more than an inch before bouncing off a nucleus or electron. It could take an individual photon millions of years to work its way through the crowd to the surface of the Sun.

Moving outwards from the core, the density, temperature and pressure of the plasma fell steadily, until at last – four-fifths of the way to the surface – electrons could cling to nuclei to form atoms – and, unlike the bare nuclei of the plasma, the atoms were able to *absorb* the energy of the photons.

It was as if the photons, after struggling out from the fusing centre, had hit a brick wall. All of their energy was dumped into the atoms. The gas above the wall responded – like a pan of water heated from below – by *convecting*, with hot material rising and dragging down cooler material from above.

The wormhole probe, with its fragile cargo, would be able to penetrate as far as the bottom of this convective zone, twenty per cent of the way towards the centre of the Sun.

She nodded. 'And the photosphere which we see, with its granules and supergranules, is essentially the top layer of the convective zone. It's like the surface of your pan of boiling water.'

'Yes. And it's the properties of the material in the convective zone that cause sunspots.'

The convective zone matter was highly charged. The Sun's magnetic field was intense, and its flux tubes, each a hundred yards across, became locked into the charged material.

The Sun's rotation spread the frozen-in flux lines, stretching them around the Sun's interior like bands of elastic. The tubes became tangled into ropes, disturbed by bubbles of rising gas and twisted by convection. Kinks in the tangled ropes became buoyant enough to float up to the surface and spread out, causing spots and spot groups.

She smiled as he spoke. 'You know, I feel as if I'm returning to my childhood. I studied Solar physics intensely,' she said. 'And a lot else, besides. I remember doing it. But ...' She sighed. 'I seem to retain less and less.

'The Sun is my life's work, you see, Dr Scholes. I've known that since I was born. I once knew much about the Sun. And in the future,' she went on ambiguously, 'I shall once again know a great deal. More, perhaps, than anyone who has yet lived.'

He decided to be honest with her. 'That doesn't make a lot of sense.'

'No. No, I don't suppose it does,' she said sharply. 'But that doesn't matter, Dr Scholes. Your brief is to do just what you've been doing: to show me the sights, to let me *feel* the Sun from a human perspective.'

A human perspective?

Now she turned and looked directly into his eyes; her gaze, watery as it was, was open and disconcerting, searing. 'But your curiosity about my role isn't what's throwing you off balance. Is it?'

'I –'

'It's my *age*.' She grinned again, deliberately – it seemed to him – showing her grotesque, yellowed teeth. 'I've seen you studying me, from the corner of your eye ... Don't worry, Kevan Scholes, I don't take offence. My age is the subject you've been politely skirting since I climbed aboard this flying refrigerator of yours.'

He felt resentful. 'You're mocking me.'

She snorted. 'Of course I am. But it's the truth, isn't it?'

He tried not to let his anger build. 'What reaction do you expect?'

'Ah ... honesty at last. I expect nothing less than your rather morbid fascination, of course.' She raised her hands and studied them, as if they were artefacts separate from her body; she turned them around, flexing her fingers. 'How awful it is that this *ageing* was once the lot of all of humanity, this slow disintegration into decay, physical and mental. Especially the physical, actually ... My body seems to crowd out my awareness; sometimes I've time for nothing else but to cater to its pressing, undignified needs ...' She frowned. 'But perhaps AS treatment has robbed our species of rather more than it has given us. After all, even the most vain, or most attention-seeking, refuse to be AS-frozen at more than, say, physical-sixty. So meaningful interaction is restricted to a physical range of a mere six decades. How sad.'

He took a breath. 'But you must be – physical-eighty?'

Her mouth twitched. 'That's not a bad guess, for someone who's never met an *old* person before ... unless you've ever encountered an unfortunate individual for whom AS treatment has failed to take. These are humans in their natural state, if you think about it, but our society treats them as ill – to be feared, shunned.'

Gently, he asked, 'Is that what's happened to you?'

'Failed AS treatments?' Her papery cheeks trembled briefly, and again he perceived resentment, a deep anger, just under her abrasive, disconcerting surface. 'No. Not exactly.'

He touched her arm. 'Look there ... ahead of us.'

There was a structure before them, looming out of the

40

flat-infinite horizon, rising from the photosphere itself. It was like a viaduct – a series of arches, loops of crimson-glowing gas which strode across the Solar surface.

Once again he heard her gasp.

He checked his data slate. 'Prominences. The whole structure is a hundred thousand miles long, twenty thousand high …' He glanced up and checked their heading. 'We're only ten thousand miles above the surface ourselves. We're going to pass *through* one of those arches.'

She clapped her hands in delight, and suddenly she seemed astonishingly, unnervingly young – a child trapped in a decaying husk of a body, he thought.

Soon the arch through which they would pass was huge before them, and the mouths of the others began to close up, foreshortened. In this landscape of giants, Scholes found he had trouble visualizing the scale of the structures; their approach seemed to take forever, yet still they grew, thrusting out of the Sun like the dreams of some insane engineer. Now he could make out detail – there were places were the arch was not complete, and he could see knots of higher density in the coronal gas which flowed, glowing, down the magnetically shaped flanks towards pools of light at the feet of the arch. But despite all this the illusion of artifice persisted, making the structure still more intimidating.

At last the arch swept over them, immense, aloof, grand.

'Five thousand miles thick,' he said slowly. 'Just think; you could hang the Earth up there, at the apex of that arch, like a Christmas tree ornament.'

She snorted, and pressed the back of her hand to her mouth.

He looked at her curiously. She was – he realized slowly – *giggling*.

They passed through the arch; the vast sculpture of gas receded slowly behind them.

Scholes checked his data slate. 'We've almost completed our orbit. Three million miles of a Solar great circle traversed in three hours …'

'So our journey's nearly done.' She folded her hands neatly in her lap once more, and turned her face to the clear wall; corona light played around her profile, making her look remote, surprisingly young.

41

He felt suddenly moved by her – by this lonely, bitter woman, isolated by her age and fragility from the rest of mankind ... and, he suspected obscurely, isolated by some much more dramatic secret.

He tried to reassure her. 'Another hour and you'll be safely inside the habitat. You'll be a lot more comfortable there. And –'

She turned to him. She wasn't smiling, but her face seemed to have softened a little, as if she understood what he was trying to do. Again she reached out and touched the back of his hand, and the sudden human contact was electric. 'Thank you for your patience, Dr Scholes. I've not given you an easy time, have I?'

He frowned, troubled. 'I don't think I've been patient at all, actually.'

'Oh, but you have.'

His curiosity burned within him, like the Sun's fusion core, illuminating everything he saw. 'You're at the heart of all this, aren't you? The Superet project, I mean. I don't understand what your role is ... But that's the truth, isn't it?'

She said nothing, but let her hand remain on his.

He frowned. She seemed so *fragile*. 'And how do you feel about it?'

'How do I *feel*?' She closed her eyes. 'Do you know, I'm not sure if anyone has asked me that before. How do I feel?' She sighed, raggedly. 'I'm scared, Dr Scholes. *That's* how I feel.'

He let his fingers close around hers.

There was a subtle push in the base of his spine, and the sound of the *Lightrider*'s drive was a deep, low vibration, a seismic rumble he felt deep within the fabric of his body.

Slowly, the little ship climbed away from the Sun's boiling surface.

4

The flitter tumbled from the shimmering throat of the wormhole transit route from Port Sol to Earthport. Louise Ye Armonk peered out of the cramped cabin, looking for Earth. Mark sat beside her, a bookslate on his lap.

Earthport was a swarm of wormhole Interfaces clustered at L4 – one of the five gravitationally stable Lagrange points in the Earth-Moon system, leading the Moon in its orbit around Earth by sixty degrees. From here, Earth was a swollen blue disc; wormhole gates of all sizes drifted across the face of the old planet like electric-blue, tetrahedral snowflakes.

The flitter – unmanned save for its two passengers – surged unhesitatingly through the tangle of Interfaces, the mesh of traffic which passed endlessly through the great cross-System gateways. In contrast to the desolation of the outer rim, Louise received a powerful, immediate impression of bustle, prosperity, activity, here at the heart of the System.

At the flitter's standard one-gee acceleration the final leg from L4 to Earth itself would take only six hours; and already the old planet, pregnant and green, seemed to Louise to be approaching rapidly, as if surfacing through the complex web of wormhole Interfaces. Huge fusion stations – constructed from ice moons towed into Earth orbit from the asteroid belt and beyond – sparkled as they crawled above green-blue oceans. The planet itself was laced with lights, on land and sea. In the thin rim of atmosphere near the North Pole Louise could just make out the dull purple glow of an immense radiator beam, a diffuse refrigerating laser dumping a fraction of Earth's waste heat into the endless sink of space.

Louise felt an absurd, sentimental lump rise to her throat as she studied the slowly turning planet. At moments like this she felt impelled to make private vows about spending more time here: *here*, at the vital core of the System, rather than on its desolate edge.

. . . But, she reminded herself harshly, the rim was where the *Northern* was being built.

Louise had work to do. She was trying to equip a starship, damn it. She didn't have the time or energy to hop back to Earth to play guessing games with some unseen authority.

Growling subvocally, Louise rested her head against her couch and tried to sleep. Mark, patient and placid, called a new page of his bookslate.

The little ship landed in North America, barely thirteen hours after leaving Port Sol – all of four billion miles away. The flitter brought them to a small landing pad near the heart of Central Park, New York City. Louise saw two people – a man and a woman – approaching the pad across the crisp grass.

The flitter's autopilot told them to make their way to a small, anonymous-grey building close to the pad.

Louise and Mark emerged into the sunshine of a New York spring. Louise could see the shoulders of tall, ancient sky-scrapers at the rim of the park, interlaced by darting flitters. Not far away, shielded by trees at the heart of the park, she made out one of the city's carbon-sequestration domes. The dome was a sphere of dry ice four hundred yards tall: sequestration was an old Superet scheme, with each dome containing fifty million tons of carbon dioxide boldly frozen out of the atmosphere and lagged by a two-yard layer of rock wool.

Mark raised his face to the Sun and breathed deeply. 'Mmm. Cherry blossom and freshly cut grass. I love that smell.'

Louise snorted. 'Really? I didn't know cherry trees grew wild, on Titan.'

'We have domes,' he said defensively. 'Anyway, every human is allowed to be sentimental about a spring day in New York. Look at those clouds, Louise. Aren't they beautiful?'

She looked up. The sky was laced by high, fluffy, dark clouds. And beyond the clouds she saw crawling points of light: the habitats and factories of near-Earth space. It was a fine view – but quite artificial, she knew. Even the clouds were fakes: they were doped with detergent, to limit the growth of the water droplets which comprised them. Smaller droplets reflected more sunlight than larger ones, making the semi-permanent clouds an effective shield against excessive Solar heating.

So much for sentiment. Everything was manufactured.

Louise dropped her head. As always on returning to Earth, she felt disoriented by the openness of the sky above her – it seemed to counter every intuition to have to believe that a thin layer of blue air could protect her adequately from the rigours of space.

'Come on,' she said to Mark. 'Let's get this over with.'

Following the instructions of the autopilot they approached the nearby building. The structure was brick-shaped, perhaps ten feet tall; there was a low doorway in the centre of its nearest face.

As they got closer, the two people Louise had noticed from the air walked slowly towards them from the rear of the building.

The two parties stared at each other curiously.

The man stepped forward, his hands behind his back. He was thin and tall, physical-fifty, with a bald, pallid scalp fringed by white hair. He stared frankly at Louise. 'I know your face,' he said.

Louise let her eyebrows lift. 'Really? And you are –'

'My name is Uvarov. Garry Benson Deng Uvarov.' He held out his hand; his voice had the flat, colourless intonation of the old Lunar colonies, Louise thought. 'My field is eugenics. And my companion –' He indicated the woman, who came forward. 'This is Serena Milpitas.'

The woman grinned. She was plump but strong-looking, about physical-forty, with short-cropped hair. 'That's Serena *Harvey Gallium Harvey* Milpitas,' she said. 'And I'm an engineer.'

Uvarov gazed at Louise, his eyes a startling blue. 'It's very pleasant to meet you, Louise Ye Armonk. I've followed the construction of your starship with interest. But I am a busy man. I'll be very pleased to learn why you've summoned us here.'

'Me too,' Milpitas growled. She had the lazy, nasal pitch of a Martian.

Louise felt confused. 'Why *I* summoned you . . . ?'

Mark stepped forward and introduced himself. 'I think you've got it wrong, Dr Uvarov. We don't know any more than

45

you do, it seems. *We* were summoned *too*.'

Louise stared at Uvarov, feeling an immediate dislike for the man gather in her heart. 'Yeah. And I bet we had further to come than you, too.'

Mark looked sour. 'First blood to you, Louise. Well done. Come on; the only way we're all going to get away from here is to go through with this, it seems.'

Striding confidently, he led the way towards the low building.

Studying each other suspiciously, the rest followed.

Louise passed through the squat, open doorway – and was plunged immediately into the darkness of space.

She heard Mark gasp; he stopped a pace behind her, his step faltering. She turned to him. He'd raised his head to a darkened dome above them; a sliver of salmon-pink (Jovian?) cloud slid across the lip of the dome, casting a light across his face, a light which softened the shadows of his apparent age. She reached out and found his hand; it was thin, cold. 'Don't let it get to you,' she whispered. 'It's just a stunt. A Virtual trick, designed to put us off balance.'

He pulled his hand away from hers; his fingernails scratched her palm lightly. 'I know that. Lethe, you'll never learn to stop patronizing me, will you?'

She thought of apologizing, then decided to skip it.

Uvarov walked forward briskly – hoping, it seemed, to catch the Virtual projectors of this illusion off guard. But the chamber moved past him fluidly, convincingly, shadows and hidden aspects unfolding with seamless grace.

The four of them were in a dome, a half-sphere a hundred yards across. At the geometric centre of the dome were tipped-back control couches. A series of basic data entry and retrieval desks clustered around the couches. The rest of the floor area was divided by shoulder-high partitions into lab areas, a galley, a gym, a sleeping area and shower. The shower was enclosed by a spherical balloon of some clear material – obviously designed for zero-gee operation, Louise thought.

The sleeping zone contained a single sleep pouch. There was a noticeable absence of decoration – of any real sign of *personality*, Louise thought. There was no concession to comfort –

no sign of entertainment areas, for example. Even the gym was functional, bare, little more than an open coffin surrounded by pneumatic weight-simulators. The only colour in the chamber came from the screens of the data desks, and from the slice of Jovian cloud visible through the dome.

Serena Milpitas strolled towards Louise, her footsteps clicking loudly on the hard floor. She ran a fingertip along the surface of a data desk. 'It's a high-quality Virtual projection, with semisentient surface backup,' she said. 'Feel it.'

'I don't need to,' Louise groused. 'I'm sure it is. That's not the bloody point. This is obviously meant to be the lifedome of a GUTship – a small, limited, primitive design compared to my *Northern*, but a GUTship nevertheless. And –'

Light, electric-blue, flooded the dome. The explosion of brilliance was overwhelming, drenching; Louise couldn't help but cower. Her own shadow – sharp, black, utterly artificial – seemed to peer up at her, mocking her.

She lifted her head. Beyond the transparent dome above her, an artefact – a tetrahedron glowing sky-blue – sailed past the limb of the Jovian planet. It was a framework of glowing rods: at first sight the framework looked open, but Louise could make out glimmers of elusive, brown-gold membranes of light stretched across the open faces. Those membranes held tantalizing images of starfields, of suns that had never shone over Jupiter.

'A wormhole Interface,' Milpitas breathed.

'Obviously,' Uvarov said. 'So we're in a Virtual GUTship, sailing towards an Interface in orbit around Jupiter.' He turned to Louise, letting his exasperation show. 'Haven't you got it yet?' He waved a hand. 'The meaning of this ludicrous stunt?'

Louise smiled. 'We're in the *Hermit Crab*, aren't we? On Michael Poole's ship.'

'Yes. Just before it flew into Poole's Interface – just before Poole got himself killed.'

'Not quite.'

The new voice came from the control couches at the heart of the lifedome. Now one of the couches spun around, slowly, and a man climbed out gracelessly. He walked towards them, emerging into the glaring blue overhead light of the Interface. He said, 'Actually we don't know if Poole was killed or not. He was certainly *lost*. He may still be alive – although it's difficult to say what meaning words like "still" have when spacetime flaws spanning centuries are traversed.'

The man smiled. He was thin, tired-looking, with physical age around sixty, Louise supposed; he wore a drab one-piece coverall.

The face – the clothes – were startling in their familiarity to Louise; a hundred memories crowded, unwelcome, for her attention.

'I know you,' she said slowly. 'I *remember* you; I worked with you. But you were lost in time . . .'

'My name,' the man said, 'is Michael Poole.'

Lieserl wanted to die.

It was her ninetieth day of life, and she was ninety physical-years old. She was impossibly frail – unable to walk, or feed herself, or even clean herself. The faceless men and women tending her had almost left the download too late, she thought with derision; they'd already had one scare when an infection had somehow got through to her and settled into her lungs, nearly killing her.

She was *old* – physically the oldest human in the System, probably. She felt as if she was underwater: her senses had turned to mush, so that she could barely feel, or taste, or see anything, as if she was encased in some deadening, viscous fluid. And her mind was failing.

She could *feel* it, towards the end. It was like a ghastly reverse run of her accelerated childhood; she woke every day to a new diminution of her self. She came to dread sleep, yet could not avoid it.

And every day, the bed seemed too large for her.

But she retained her pride; she couldn't stand the indignity of it. She hated those who had put her into this position.

Her mother's last visit to the habitat, a few days before the download, was bizarre. Lieserl, through her ruined, rheumy old eyes, was barely able to recognize Phillida – this young, weeping woman, only a few months older than when she had held up her baby girl to the Sun.

She could not forgive her mother for the artifice of her exist-ence – for the way understanding of her nature, even data on

48

Superet, had been *kept* from her until *others* thought she was ready.

Lieserl cursed Phillida, sent her away.

At last Lieserl was taken, in her bed, to the downloading chamber at the heart of Thoth. The chamber's lid, disturbingly coffin-like, closed over her head. She closed her eyes; she felt her own, abandoned, frail body around her.

And then –

It was a sensory explosion. It was like sleeping, then waking – no, she thought; it was more – far more than that.

The focus of her awareness remained in the same functional hospital room at the centre of the Solar habitat. She was standing, surveying the chamber – no, she realized slowly, she wasn't standing: *she had no real sensation of her body* . . .

She felt disembodied, discorporeal. She felt an instant of panic.

But that moment of fear faded rapidly, as she looked out through her new eyes.

The drab, functional chamber seemed as vivid to her as the golden day she had spent as a small child, with her parents on that remote beach, when her senses had been so acute they were almost transparent. In an instant she had become young again, with every sense alive and sharp.

And, slowly, Lieserl became aware of new senses – senses beyond the human. She could see the sparkle of X-ray photons from the Solar photosphere as they leaked through the habitat's shielding, the dull infra-red glow of the bellies and heads of the people working around the shell of her own abandoned body – and the fading sheen of that cold husk itself.

She probed inwards. She retained her memories from her old body, from prior to the downloading, she realized; but those memories were qualitatively different from the records she was accumulating now. Limited, partial, subjective, imperfectly recorded: like fading paintings, she thought.

She had died, and she was reborn. She felt pity, for the person who once called herself Lieserl.

The clarity of her new senses was remarkable. It was like being a child again. She immersed herself, joyously, in the objective reality of the Universe around her.

*　　*　　*

He – *it* – was a Virtual, of course. The realization brought Louise crushing disappointment.

Uvarov snorted. 'This is an absurdity. A pantomime. You're wasting my time here.'

The Virtual of Poole looked disconcerted; his smile faded. 'How so?'

'I've read of Michael Poole. And I know he hated Virtuals, of all kinds.'

Virtual-Poole laughed. 'All right. So this simulacrum is offensive; you think Poole would have objected. Well, perhaps. But at least it's got your attention.'

Milpitas touched Uvarov's arm. 'Why are you so damn hostile, Doctor? No one's doing you any harm.'

Uvarov snatched his arm away.

'She's right.' Virtual-Poole waved a hand to the couches at the heart of the lifedome. 'Why don't you sit down? Do you want a drink, or –'

'I don't want to sit down,' Louise said icily. 'And I don't want a drink. What am I, a kid to be impressed by fireworks?' Even as she spoke, though, she was aware that the wormhole, sliding across space above them, had frozen in its track at the moment Virtual-Poole had climbed out of his couch; exotic-energy light flooded down over the little human tableau, as if suspending them in timelessness. She felt confused, disoriented. *This isn't Michael Poole*. But all Virtuals were conscious, to some degree. *This Virtual remembers being Poole*. She wanted to lash out at it – to hurt it. 'Damn it, it would have been cheaper to take us to Jupiter itself rather than to set up this charade, here on Earth.'

'Perhaps,' Virtual-Poole said drily. 'But this diorama isn't just for show. I have something to demonstrate to you. This setup seemed the best way to achieve that. As, if you've the patience, you'll see.'

Louise felt her jaw muscles tighten. 'Patience? I'm trying to launch a starship. I need to be at Port Sol, working on the *Northern* – not stuck here in this box in New York, talking to a damn puppet.'

Poole winced, looking genuinely hurt. Louise despised herself.

Uvarov said, 'I, too, have projects which demand my time.'

The sky-blue light cast convincing shadows over Poole's

cheekbones and jaw. 'This simulation is serving severai purposes. And one of those purposes is *discretion*. Look – I'm only partially self-aware. But I am autonomous, within this environment. There is no channel in or out of here; no record will exist of this conversation, unless one of you chooses to make one.'

Milpitas snorted. 'Why should we believe you? We still don't know who you represent.'

A trace of anger showed in the hardening of Virtual-Poole's mouth. 'Now *you're* being absurd. Why should I lie? Louise Ye Armonk, I have a proposal for you. A challenge – for you all, actually. You may refuse the challenge. You certainly can't be forced to accept it. And so, we meet in secrecy; if you refuse, no one will ever know.'

'Bullshit,' Uvarov growled; pink Jovian light gleamed from his bald pate. 'Let's skip the riddles and get on with it. Who's behind you, Poole?'

Briefly, Virtual-Poole looked pained – almost as if he was too tired for such confrontations. Louise remembered that although Michael Poole had accepted AS treatment, he'd persistently refused consciousness adjustment treatment. A deep dread of memory editing kept people like Poole away from the reloading tables, even when the efficiency of their awareness – clogged by decades of memory – started to downgrade.

Virtual-Poole seemed to rouse himself. 'Tell me what you know.'

Mark spoke up. 'Very little. We got a call to come in here from the Port Sol authorities.' He smiled. 'We got the impression we didn't have a lot of choice but to comply. But it wasn't clear who was behind the summons, or why we were wanted.'

Milpitas and Uvarov confirmed that they, too, had received similar calls.

'But,' Louise said drily, 'it was obviously someone a bit more senior than the Port Sol harbour master.'

Virtual-Poole rubbed his nose; shadows moved convincingly across his hand. 'Yes,' he said. 'And no. You've no doubt heard of us. We don't report to Port Sol – or to any single nation. We're a private corporation, but we're not working for profit. We get some backing from the UN, but also from most of the individual nation-states in the System as well. And a variety of corporations, who –'

Louise studied Virtual-Poole suspiciously. *'Who are you?'*

Poole's face stiffened, and Louise wondered how much restriction had been placed on the Virtual's free will. *Lethe, I hate sentience technology*, she thought. *Poole doesn't deserve this.*

Poole said, 'I'm a representative of a group called Superet. The Holy Superet Light Church . . .'

'Superet.' Mark smiled. He looked relieved. 'Is that all? Superet is innocuous enough. Isn't it?'

'Maybe.' Virtual-Poole smiled. 'Not everyone agrees. Superet is well known for the Earth-terraforming initiatives of the past. But not all Superet's projects are simple balls of dry ice, you see. Some are rather more – ambitious. And not everyone thinks that projects with such timescales should be permitted to progress.'

Louise shoved her face forward, seeking understanding in the Virtual's bland, simulated expression. 'What timescales? How long-term?'

'Infinite,' Virtual-Poole said quietly. 'Superet's backers are people who wish to invest in the survival of the species itself, Louise.'

There was a long silence.

'Good grief.' Milpitas shook her head. 'I don't know about you, but I need to sit down. And how about that drink, Poole?'

5

Lieserl was suspended inside the body of the Sun.

She spread her arms wide and lifted up her face. She was deep within the Sun's convective zone, the broad mantle of turbulent material beneath the glowing photosphere. Convective cells larger than the Earth, tangled with ropes of magnetic flux, filled the world around her with a complex, dynamic, three-dimensional tapestry. She could hear the roar of the great gas founts, smell the stale photons diffusing out towards space from the remote core.

She felt as if she were alone in some huge cavern. Looking up she could see how the photosphere formed a glowing roof over her world perhaps fifty thousand miles above her, and the inner radiative zone was a shining, impenetrable sea another fifty thousand miles beneath her. The radiative zone was a ball of plasma which occupied eighty per cent of the Sun's diameter – with the fusing core itself buried deep within – and the convective zone was a comparatively thin layer above the plasma, with the photosphere a crust at the boundary of space. She could see huge waves crossing the surface of the radiative-zone 'sea': the waves were g-modes – gravity waves, like ocean waves on Earth – with crests thousands of miles across, and periods of days.

Lieserl? Can you hear me? Are you all right?

She thrust her arms down by her sides and swooped up into the convective-zone 'air'; she looped the loop backwards, letting the floor and roof of this cavern-world wheel around her. She opened up her new senses, so that she could feel the turbulence of the gas, with its almost terrestrial density, as a breeze against her skin, and the warm glow of hard photons diffusing out from the core was no more than a gentle warmth against her face.

53

Lieserl?

She suppressed a sigh.

'Yes. Yes, Kevan. I'm perfectly all right.'

Damn it, Lieserl, you're going to have to respond properly. Things are difficult enough without –

'I know. I'm sorry. How are *you* feeling, anyway?'

Me? I'm fine. But that's hardly the point, is it? Now come on, Lieserl, the team here are getting on my back; let's run through the tests.

'You mean I'm not down here to enjoy myself?'

The tests, Lieserl.

'Yeah. Okay, electromagnetic first.' She adjusted her sensorium. 'I'm plunged into darkness,' she said drily. 'There's very little free radiation at any frequency – perhaps an X-ray glow from the photosphere; it looks a little like a late evening sky. And –'

Come on, Lieserl. We know the systems are functioning. I need to know what you see, what you feel.

'What I feel?'

She spread her arms and sailed backwards through the buffeting air. She *opened* her eyes again.

The huge semistable convection cells around her reached from the photosphere to the base of the convective zone; they buffeted against each other like living things, huge whales in this insubstantial sea of gas. And the honeycomb of activity was driven by the endless flux of energetic photons out of the radiative sea of plasma beneath her.

'I feel wonderful,' she said. 'I see fountains. A cave-full of them.'

Good. Keep talking, Lieserl. You know what we're trying to achieve here; your senses – your Virtual senses – are composites, constructs from a wide variety of inputs. I can see the individual elements are functioning; what I need to know is how well the Virtual sensorium is integrating –

'Fine.' She rolled over onto her belly, so that she was gliding face-down, surveying the plasma sea below her.

Lieserl, what now?

She adjusted her eyes once more. The flux tubes came into prominence, solidifying out of the air; beyond them the convective pattern was a sketchy framework, overlaid. 'I see the magnetic flux,' she reported. 'I can see what I want to see. It's all working the way it's supposed to, I think; I can pick out whatever feature of the world I choose, here.'

'*World*'?

'Yes, Kevan.' She glanced up at the photosphere, the symbolic barrier separating her forever from the Universe of humanity. 'This is my world, now.'

Maybe. Just don't lose yourself down there, Lieserl.

'I won't.'

It sounded as if there was some sympathy in his voice – knowing Kevan, there probably was; they had grown almost close in the few days she'd had left after her tour with him around the Sun.

But it was hard to tell. The communication channel linking them was a path through the wormhole, from the Interface fixed among the habitats outside the Sun to the portal which had been dropped into the Sun, and which now sustained her. The comms link was ingenious, and seemed reliable, but it wasn't too good at relaying complex intonations.

Tell me about the flux tubes.

The tubes were each a hundred yards broad, channels of magnetic energy cutting through the air; they were thousands of miles long, and they filled the air around her, all the way down to the plasma sea.

Lieserl dipped into a tube, into its interior; she felt the tingle of enhanced magnetic strength. She lowered her head and allowed herself to soar along the length of the tube, so that its walls rushed past her, curving gracefully. 'It's terrific,' she said. 'I'm in an immense tunnel; it's like a fairground ride. I could follow this path all the way round the Sun.'

Maybe. I don't know if we need the poetry, Lieserl. What about other tubes? Can you still see them?

'Yes.' She turned her head, and induced currents in her Virtual body made her face sparkle with radiation. 'I can see hundreds, thousands of the tubes, all curving through the air –'

The 'air'?

'The convective zone gases. The other tubes are parallel with mine, more or less.' She sought for a way to convey the sensation. 'I feel as if I'm sliding around the scalp of some immense giant, Kevan, following the lines of hairs.'

Scholes laughed. *Well, that's not a bad image. The flux tubes can tangle, or break, but they can't intersect. Just like hair.*

'You know, this is almost relaxing . . .'

Good. Again she detected that hint of sympathy – or was it pity? – in Kevan's voice. *I'm glad you're feeling – ah – happy in yourself, Lieserl.*

She let the crisp magnetic flux play over her cheeks, sharp, bright, vivid. 'My new self. Well, it's an improvement on the old; you have to admit.'

Now the flux tube curved away, consistently, to the right; she was forced to deflect to avoid crashing through the tube's insubstantial walls.

In following the tube she became aware that she was tracing out a spiral path. She let herself relax into the motion, and watched the cave-world beyond the tube wheel around her. The flux tubes neighbouring her own had become twisted into spirals, too, she realized; she was following one strand in a rope of twisted-together flux tubes.

Lieserl, what's happening? We can see your trajectory's altering, fast.

'I'm fine, Kevan. I've got myself into a rope, that's all . . .'

Lieserl, you should get out of there.

She let the tube's path sweep her around. 'Why? This is fun.'

Maybe. But the rope is heading for the photosphere. It isn't a good idea for you to break the surface; we're concerned about the stability of the wormhole –

Lieserl sighed and let herself slow. 'Oh, damn it, Kevan, you're just no fun. I would have enjoyed bursting out through the middle of a sunspot. What a great way to go.'

Lieserl –

She slid out of the flux tube, relishing the sharp scent of the magnetic field as she cut across it. 'All right, Kevan. I'm at your service. What next?'

We're not done with the tests yet, Lieserl. I'm sorry.

'What do you want me to do?'

One more . . .

'Just tell me.'

Run a full self-check, Lieserl. Just for a few minutes . . . Drop the Virtual constructs.

She hesitated. 'Why? I thought you said you could tell the

systems were functioning to specification, and –'

They are. That's not the point ... We're still testing how well integrated they are –

'Integrated into my sensorium. Why don't you just say what you're after, Kevan? You want to test how *conscious* this machine called Lieserl is. Right?'

Lieserl, you don't need to make this difficult for me. Scholes sounded defensive. *This is a standard suite of tests for any AI which –*

'All right, damn it.'

She closed her eyes, and with a sudden, impulsive, stab of will, she let her Virtual image of herself – the illusion of a human body around her – crumble.

It was like – what? Like waking from a dream, a soft, comfortable dream of childhood, waking to find herself entombed in a machine, a crude construct of bolts and cords and gears.

But even *that* was an illusion, she thought, a metaphor for herself behind which she was hiding.

She considered herself.

The wormhole Interface was suspended in the body of the Sun. The thin, searing-hot gas of the convective zone poured into its triangular faces, so that the Interface was embedded in a sculpture of inflowing gas, a flower carved dynamically from the Sun's flesh. That material was being pumped through the wormhole to the second Interface in orbit around the Sun; there, convection zone gases emerged, blazing, making the drifting tetrahedron into a second, miniature Sun around which orbited the fragile human habitat called Thoth.

Thus the Interface refrigerated itself, enabling it to survive with its precious, fragile cargo of data stores ... The stores which sustained the awareness of herself. And the flux of matter through the Interface's planes was controlled, to enable her to move the Interface through the body of the Sun.

She inspected herself, at many levels, simultaneously.

At the *physical* level she studied crisp matrices of data, shifting, coalescing, the patterns of bits which, together, comprised her memories. Then, overlaid on that – visually, if she willed it, like a ghostly superstructure – was her *logical* level, the data storage and access paths which represented the components of her consciousness.

Good ... Good, Lieserl. You're sending us good data.

She traced paths and linkages through the interleaved and interdependent structures of her own personality. 'It's functioning well. To specification. Even beyond. I –'

We know that. But, Lieserl, how are you feeling? That's what we can't tell.

'You keep asking me that, damn it. I feel –'

Enhanced.

No longer trapped in a single point, in a box of bone a few inches behind eyes made of jelly.

She was supremely *conscious*.

What was her consciousness? It was the ability to be aware of what was happening in her mind, and in the world around her, and in the past.

Even in her old, battered, rapidly ageing body, she had been conscious, of course. She could remember a little of what had happened to her, or in her mind, a few moments earlier.

But now, with her trace-function memory, she could *relive* her experiences, bit by data bit if she wanted to. Her senses went far beyond the human. And as for inner perception – why, she could see herself laid open now in a kind of dynamic blueprint.

By any test, she was more conscious than any other human had ever been – because she had more of the *mechanism* of consciousness. She was the most conscious human who had ever lived.

... If, she thought uneasily, *I am still human.*

Lieserl?

'Yes, Kevan. I can hear you.'

And?

'I'm a lot more conscious.' She laughed. 'But possibly not much smarter.'

She heard him laugh in reply. It was a ghostly Virtual sound, she thought, transmitted through a defect in spacetime, and – perhaps – across a boundary between species.

Come on, Lieserl. We have work to do.

She let her awareness implode, once more, into a Virtual-human form.

Her perception was immediately simplified. To be seeing

through apparently human eyes was comforting ... in a way. And yet, she thought, *restrictive.*

No wonder Superet had been so concerned to imprint her with sympathy for mankind ... before it had robbed her completely of her humanity.

Perhaps it wouldn't be much longer before she felt ready to abandon even this thin vestige of humanity.

And then what?

Bathed in Jovian light, Louise, Uvarov, Milpitas and Mark sat in the soft, reclined couches. The Virtual of Michael Poole held a snifter of old brandy; the glass was filled with convincing blue-gold Interface light sparkles, and Virtual-Poole sipped it with every sign of enjoyment – as if it were the first, and last, such glass he would ever enjoy.

As, probably, it was, for this particular autonomous sentient copy, Louise thought.

'To the survival of the species.' Louise raised her own glass and sipped at whisky, a fine peaty Scotch. 'But what's it got to do with me? I don't even have any kids.'

'Superet has a long history,' Virtual-Poole said stiffly. 'You may not be aware of it, but Superet is already a thousand years old. It took its name from an ancient, obscure religious sect in North America that worshipped the first nuclear weapons ...'

The Superet creed, in some ways, Louise thought, embodied the essence of the pre-Poole optimism of humanity. Superet believed that nothing was beyond the capabilities of mankind.

Poole gazed into his drink. 'Superet believes that if something is physically possible, then it's just a question of engineering.' The Virtual's expression was complex – almost tormented, Louise thought. The Virtual went on, 'But it takes *planning* – perhaps on immense timescales.'

Louise felt a vague anger build in her. *Uvarov was right. This isn't Michael Poole. Poole would not have defended the grandiose claims of Superet like this. This is a travesty of programming in conflict with sentience.*

'In the past,' the Virtual went on, 'Superet sponsored many of the eco-engineering projects which have restored much of the biosphere of Earth – the carbon-sequestration domes, and so on.'

Louise knew that was true. The great macroengineering projects of the last millennium, supplemented by the nano-engineering of the atmosphere and lithosphere and the transfer offplanet of most power-generating and industrial concerns, had stabilized and preserved Earth's fragile ecosystem. There was more woodland covering the temperate regions, now, than at any time since the last glaciation, locking in much of the excess carbon dioxide which had plagued previous centuries. And the great decline in species suffered after the industrialization of a couple of thousand years ago had long since been reversed, thanks to the use of genetic archives and careful reconstruction – from disparate descendants – of lost genotypes.

Earth had been the first planet to be terraformed.

The Virtual said, 'But Superet's goals were modified, following the Friends of Wigner incident ...'

'If Superet is such a saintly organization,' Uvarov growled, 'then why is it such a thing of shadows? Why the secrets?'

Poole said, 'Superet is a thousand years old, Doctor. No human organization of such longevity has ever been fully open. Think of the great established religions, societies like the Templars, the Masons. Groupings like Superet have a way of accreting tradition, and isolation, around themselves with time.'

'And,' Uvarov said sharply, 'no doubt the long career of Superet has a few dark phases ...'

Poole didn't reply.

Louise said, 'You said the goals of Superet were changed by the Friends incident.'

'Yes. Let me use this Virtual box of tricks to explain.'

The tetrahedron came to life again. It rotated above them, a gaudy trinket miles across.

'The *Cauchy* Interface,' the Virtual said. 'At the time, the largest wormhole mouth constructed – in fact, the largest exercise in exotic-matter engineering.'

The Virtual's face was gaunt in the shifting Interface light – wistful, Louise thought.

Michael Poole had been rightly celebrated for his achievements, she thought. He had been the Brunel of his day, and more. His wormhole projects had opened up the System much as the great railroads had opened up Great Britain two thousand years earlier.

A wormhole was a flaw in spacetime – a throat, connecting two events in spacetime that would otherwise be separated by light-years, or millennia. Wormholes existed naturally on all scales, most of them around the size of the Planck length – ten to minus forty three inches, the level at which space itself became granular.

Working in the orbit of Jupiter, Michael Poole and his team had taken natural wormholes and expanded them; Poole had made wormholes big enough to permit spaceships to pass through.

Wormholes were inherently unstable. Poole had threaded his wormholes with frameworks of *exotic matter* – matter with negative energy density, with pressure greater than rest mass energy. The exotic matter set up repulsive gravity fields able to hold open the wormholes' throats and mouths.

Louise remembered the excitement of those times. Poole Interfaces were towed out of Jovian orbit and set up all over the System. The wormholes enabled the inner System to be traversed in sublight GUTships in a matter of hours rather than months. The Jovian system became a hub for interplanetary commerce. Port Sol – a converted Kuiper object on the rim of the System – was established as the base for the first great interstellar voyages.

Michael Poole had opened up the Solar System in an explosion of accessibility, more dramatic than anything since the days of the great sea-going voyages of exploration on old Earth.

'It was a wonderful time. But you had greater ambitions in mind,' she said. 'Didn't you, Michael?'

The Virtual stared upwards at the display above, expression frozen, evidently unable to speak.

Mark said gently, 'You mean the *Cauchy*, Louise?'

'Yes. Michael Poole used wormhole technology to travel – not just across space – but across *time*.' She pointed up to the tetrahedron in the dome. 'This is just one Interface from Poole's greatest wormhole project: termini three miles across, and the throat itself no less than a mile wide. The wormhole's second Interface was attached to a GUTship – the *Cauchy*.'

The GUTship was launched on a subrelativistic flight beyond

the fringe of the Solar System – a circular tour, designed to return at last to Jupiter. The *Cauchy* carried one of Poole's wormhole Interfaces with it. The other was left in orbit around Jupiter.

The flight lasted fifteen centuries – but thanks to time dilation effects, only two subjective centuries had passed for the *Cauchy*'s crew.

The two Interfaces remained linked by the wormhole flaw. Because of the link, when it returned to the Solar System more than a millennium into the future of the System it had left, the *Cauchy*'s Interface was still connected to its twin in orbit around Jupiter – where only two centuries had passed since the departure of the *Cauchy*, as they had for the *Cauchy*'s crew.

'By passing through the wormhole,' Louise said, 'it was possible to travel back and forth through time. Thus, Poole had used wormhole technology to establish a bridge across fifteen hundred years, *to the future.*'

Mark pulled at his lips. 'We all know what became of this great time bridge. But – I've never understood – *why* did Poole build it?'

The Virtual spoke, his voice tired, dry – so familiar that Louise felt her heart move. Michael Poole said, 'It was an experiment. I was more interested in proving the technology – the concepts – than in the final application. But –'

'Yes, Michael?' Louise prompted.

'I had a vision – a dream perhaps – of establishing great wormhole highways across time, as well as across space. If the technology is possible, why not? What power might be afforded to the human species with the opening up of such information channels?'

'But the future didn't welcome this great dream,' Uvarov said drily.

'No, it didn't,' Virtual-Poole said.

The floor of the *Hermit Crab*'s lifedome turned transparent; space-darkness washed across it in a sudden flood that made Milpitas gasp audibly.

Louise stood and looked down. There was space-emptiness beyond her feet; her eyes told her she was suspended above an immense drop, and she had to summon all her will not to stumble, weakly, back to her chair . . .

And then, belatedly, she registered what she was seeing: beneath the lifedome, and extending for hundreds of yards in every direction, was a *floor* of some broken, irregular, bloody material – a floor of (what looked like, but couldn't possibly be) *flesh*.

Louise turned slowly around, trying to make out the geometry of what she was seeing.

The flesh-surface, bathed in sickly Jovian light, curved away from her in all directions; the 'floor' was actually the outer surface of a sphere – as if the *Crab* were embedded in an impossible moon of flesh, perhaps a mile wide. If the *Crab*'s drive section still existed, it was buried somewhere deep inside this immense carcass. The clean metal lines of the GUTship's spine – which connected lifedome to drive unit – were enveloped in a gaping wound in this floor of flesh.

Apart from this huge wound in the fleshy floor caused by the *Crab* (a wound which pooled with what looked unnervingly like blood) there were a number of pockmarks in which metal glistened – weapons emplacements? – and others ... *eyes*, huge, dimmed analogues of her own eyeballs.

There was a sense of suffering here, she thought: of pain, on an immense scale – the agony of a wounded god.

She peered more closely at the nearest pockmark, trying to make out the nature of the device embedded there. But the image was little more than a sketch – a suggestion of form, rendered in shining chrome.

Virtual-Poole, with Mark, Uvarov and Milpitas, stood beside her. The Virtual studied the flesh landscape sombrely. 'The wormhole route to the future became a channel for invasion – by the *Qax*, an extraSolar species which had occupied the System by the time the bridge was established. You're seeing here a reconstruction of one of the two Qax warships which came back through the wormhole. These are *Spline* – living creatures, perhaps even sentient – a technology unlike anything we've developed.'

Uvarov pointed to the sketchy surface of the Spline. 'Your reconstruction isn't so impressive.'

Virtual-Poole seemed more composed now, Louise thought – more *Virtual*, less *Poole*. She felt grateful for that. He said, 'We know little about the Spline, save their name and gross form. I – Poole – with the help of the rebel humans from the occupation future, destroyed the invading Spline ships.' He peered down at the *Crab*'s spine, the huge, disrupted epidermis. 'You can see how I – how *he* – rammed one of the warships, spearing it with the *Crab*'s GUTdrive. The warship was disabled – but not destroyed; in fact it was possible to take over some of the warship's higher functions.

'I'm going to show you a reconstruction of the last few minutes of Michael Poole's known existence.'

The sky-blue light around them started to shift, to slide over the equipment desks. Louise looked up. The Interface above the ship was moving gracefully across the sky; one triangular face, three miles wide, opened up –

– and, like some immense mouth, descended towards them.

Serena Milpitas said, 'Lethe. We're going through it, aren't we? We're going into the future.'

Louise looked at Poole. The Virtual gazed upwards, his eyes hardening with memory. 'I drove the Spline into the wormhole. The wormhole had to be destroyed – the bridge to the future closed ...' That was my only goal.'

The triangular frame passed around the bulk of the Spline warship now; the lifedome shuddered – delicately, but convincingly. Blue-white flashes erupted all around the perimeter of the lifedome – damage inflicted on the flesh of the Spline, Louise guessed, by grazing collisions with the exotic-matter framework.

Suddenly they were inside the tetrahedral Interface – and the wormhole itself opened up before them. It was a tunnel, above the lifedome, delineated by sheets of autumn-gold light – and leading (impossibly) *beyond* the Interface framework, and arcing to infinity.

Louise wished she could touch Poole. This copy was closer to Michael Poole than any cloned twin; he shared Poole's memories, his consciousness even. How must it be to relive one's death like this?

Poole said, 'The flashes in the wormhole throat represent the decay of heavy particles, produced in turn by the relaxing of shear energy in the curved-spacetime walls of the wormhole, which –'

Uvarov growled, 'Skip the fairground ride; just tell us what happened. How did Poole destroy the wormhole?'

The Virtual turned his face towards Louise, his strong, aged features outlined by shuddering wormhole light. 'The Spline ships had a hyperdrive, of unknown nature. I opened up my captive hyperdrive *here* –'

The Virtual raised his hands.

The floor bucked beneath them. The wormhole was flooded with sheets of blue-white light which raced towards them and down past the lifedome, giving Louise the sudden impression of huge, uncontrolled speed.

Poole shouted, 'However the hyperdrive works, it must be based on manipulating the multidimensionality of space. And if so – and if it were operated inside a wormhole, where spacetime is already distorted . . .'

Now the sheets of light gathered into threads, sinuous snakes of luminosity which curved around the GUTship, sundering the spacetime walls.

Mark said, 'So the hyperdrive made the wormhole collapse?'

'Perhaps. Or –' Virtual-Poole lifted his simulated head to the storm of wormhole light.

The threads of light seemed to sink into the fabric of the wormhole itself. Defects – cracks and sheets – opened up in the wormhole walls, revealing a plethora of wormhole tunnels, a hydra-like explosion of ballooning wormholes.

The *Hermit Crab*, uncontrolled, plunged down one wormhole after another into the future.

The *Crab*, at last, came to Virtual rest.

The last wormhole mouth closed behind it, the stresses of its distorted spacetime fabric finally yielding in a gush of heavy particles.

The sky beyond the lifedome was dark – almost empty, save for a random scattering of dimmed, reddened stars. There was no sign of life: no large-scale structure, no purposeful motion.

The sudden flood of darkness was startling. Louise, looking up, shivered; she had a feeling of intense age. 'Michael – you surely expected to die, in the destruction of the wormhole.'

'Yes . . . but as you can see – *perhaps* – the wormhole didn't simply collapse.' He looked confused. 'I'm a simulacrum,

Louise; I don't share these memories with Poole ... But there is evidence. Some of the particles which emerged from the collapsing Interface, in our own time, were of much too high energies to have been generated in the collapse of a single wormhole.

'We think the impact actually *created* – or at any rate widened – more, branching wormholes, which carried the *Crab* further into the future. Perhaps much further.

'We have simulations which show how this could happen, given the right form of hyperdrive physics – particularly if there were other cross-time wormholes already extant in the Solar System of the occupation era – perhaps set up by the Qax. In fact, the assumption that the branching *did* occur is allowing us to rule out classes of hyperdrive theory ...'

The Virtual stood, and paced slowly across the transparent floor. 'I was determined to close off the time bridge – to remove the threat of invasions from the future. But – I have to tell you – Superet thinks this was a mistake.' The Virtual twisted his hands together. 'After all, we had already beaten off one Spline incursion. After Poole's departure the study of the Qax incident became the prime focus of Superet. But because the wormhole is closed, Superet is reduced to *inferring* the truth about the future of our species from fragments, from indirect shards of evidence ...'

Louise said, 'You don't believe it was a mistake, Michael.'

Poole looked haunted; again, Louise realized with an inner ache, his personality was conflicting with the programming imposed on it by Superet.

Mark peered up at the dying stars. 'So. Did Poole survive?'

Louise said, 'I'd like to think he did. Even just for a short while, so that he could understand what he saw.'

Milpitas lay back in her couch and stared up at the scattering of dim, reddened stars. 'I'm no cosmologist ... but those stars look so *old*. How far in time did he come?'

The Virtual did not reply.

Uvarov said, 'Why have you shown us all this? What do you want?'

Virtual-Poole raised his thin arms to the desolate sky. 'Look around you, Uvarov. Perhaps this is the end of time; it is certainly the end of the stars, of baryonic life. Perhaps there are other life forms out there, not perceived by us – creatures of dark matter, the non-baryonic stuff which makes up nine-tenths of the Universe. But – *where is man*? In fact there's no evidence of life at all here, human or otherwise.

'Superet has pieced together some fragments of the history of the future, from the rubble the *Crab* left behind. We know about the Xeelee, for example. We even know – we think – the name of the Xeelee's greatest project: the *Ring*. But – *what happens to us*? What happens to the human species? What destroys us, even as it extinguishes the stars?

'And – Superet asks – is there anything we can do to avert this, the final catastrophe?'

Louise looked up at the dying stars. 'Ah. I think I understand why I'm here. Superet wants me to follow the *Hermit Crab*. To take the *Great Northern* – not to Tau Ceti – but on a circular trip, like Poole's *Cauchy*, to establish a time bridge. Superet wants to set up a way – a stable way – of reaching *this* era: the end of time.

'I get it. We've long since taken responsibility for the management of our planets – for the survival of their ecologies. Why, now, should we not take responsibility for our own long term survival as a species?' She felt like laughing. 'Superet really does think big, doesn't it?'

Milpitas sat on the edge of her couch. 'But what does *survival* mean, on such timescales? Surely even with AS treatments, survival of individuals – of *us* – into the indefinite future is impossible. What, then? Survival of the genotype? Or of the culture of our species – the memes, the cultural elements, perhaps, preserved in some form –'

Uvarov looked fascinated now, Louise thought; all his impatience and irritability gone, he stared up at the Virtual rendition of the future hungrily. 'Either, or both, perhaps. Speaking as a flesh-and-blood human, I share a natural human bias to the survival of the actual genotype in some form. The preservation of mere information appears a sterile option to me.

'But, whatever survival means, *it doesn't matter*. Look beyond the dome. In this time to which Michael Poole travelled, *nothing* of us has survived, *in any form*. And *that's* the catastrophe Superet is determined – clearly – we must work to avert.'

Louise pulled her lip. 'If this is such a compelling case, why is Superet a small, covert operation? Why shouldn't Superet's goals motivate the primary activity of the race?'

Poole sighed. 'Because the case *isn't* so compelling. Obviously. Louise, as a species we aren't used to thinking on such timescales. Not yet. There is talk of hubris: of comparisons with the Friends of Wigner, who came back through time – evidently – to manipulate history, to avert the Qax occupation.' He looked at Louise wearily. 'There isn't even agreement about what you're seeing here. I've shown you just one scenario, reconstructed from the Interface incident evidence. Maybe, it's argued, we're addressing problems that don't really exist.'

Louise folded her arms. 'And what if that's true?'

Uvarov said, 'But if there's even the smallest chance that this interpretation is correct – then isn't it worth some investment, against the possibility?'

Mark frowned. 'So we use the *Northern* to fly to the future. The flight to Tau Ceti is only supposed to take a century.'

Poole nodded. 'With modern technology, the flight of the *Northern* into the future should last no more than a thousand subjective years –'

Mark laughed. 'Poole, that's impossible. No ship could last that long, physically. No closed ecology could survive. A closed society would tear itself apart ... We don't even know if AS treatment can keep humans alive over such periods.'

Louise stared up at the simulated stars. *A thousand years?* Mark was right; it was inhumanly long – but she had the feeling *it wasn't long enough* ...

Uvarov nodded. 'But that is clearly why you have been chosen: Louise, the best engineer of the day, *and* with will enough to sustain immense projects. You, Mark Wu, a good social engineer –'

'There are better ones,' Mark said.

'Not married to Louise.'

'Formerly married.'

Poole turned to Milpitas. 'The proposal is that you, Serena, will make the *Great Northern* herself viable for its unprecedented thousand-year flight. And you, Dr Uvarov, have a deep understanding of the strengths and limitations of the engineering of the *human* form; you will help Mark Wu keep the people – the species – alive.'

Louise saw Uvarov's eyes gleam.

'I've no intention of going on this flight,' Mark said. 'And besides, the *Northern* already has a ship's engineer. And a damn doctor, come to that.'

Poole smiled. 'Not for this mission.'

'Hold it,' Louise said. 'There's something missing.' She thought over what she had to say: relativistic math, done in the head, was chancy. But still ... 'Poole, a thousand-year trip can't be long enough.' She looked up at the decaying stars. 'I'm no cosmologist. But I see no Main Sequence stars up there at all. I'd guess we're looking at a sky from far into the future – tens of billions of years, at least.'

Poole shook his head. His Virtual face was difficult to see in the faded starlight. 'No, Louise. You're wrong. A thousand-subjective-year trip is quite sufficient.'

'How can it be?'

'Because the sky you're seeing isn't from tens of billions of years hence. It's from *five million years* ahead. That's all – five megayears, *nothing* in cosmological time ...'

'But how –'

'More than time will ruin the stars, Louise. If this reconstruction is anything like accurate, there's an agency at large – which must be acting *even now* – systematically destroying the stars ...

'And, as a consequence, us.'

Uvarov turned his face, expressionless, up to the darkling sky.

Virtual-Poole said, 'We have reason to believe that even our own Sun is subject to this mysterious assault.' He stood before Louise. 'Look, Louise, you know I don't advocate cosmic engineering – I was the one who opposed the Friends of Wigner, who did my damnedest to close my own bridge to the future. *But this is different.* Even I can sympathize with what Superet is attempting here. *Now* can you see why they want you to follow the *Crab*?'

The light show began to fade from the dome; evidently the display was over.

Poole still stood before Louise, but his definition was fading, his outlines growing blocky in clouds of pixels. She reached out a hand to him, but his face had already grown smooth, empty; long before the final pixels of his image dispersed, she realized, all trace of consciousness had fled.

*　　*　　*

69

Lieserl soared through her convective cavern, letting her sensory range expand and contract, almost at random.

She thought about the Sun.

For all its grandeur, the Sun, as a machine, was simple. When she looked down and *opened* her eyes she could see evidence of the fusing core, a glow of neutrino light beneath the radiative plasma ocean. If that core were ever extinguished, then the flood of energetic photons out of the core and into the radiative and convective layers would be staunched. The Sun was in hydrostatic equilibrium – the radiation pressure from the photons balanced the Sun's tendency to collapse inwards, under gravity. And if the radiation pressure were removed the outer layers would implode, falling freely, within a few hours.

The Sun hadn't always been as stable as this ... and it wouldn't always remain so.

The Sun had formed from a contracting cloud of gas – a *protostar*. At first the soft-edged, amorphous body had shone by the conversion of its gravitational energy alone.

When the central temperature had reached ten million degrees, hydrogen fusion had begun in the core.

The shrinkage had been halted, and stability reached rapidly. The fusion was restricted to an inner core, surrounded by the plasma sea and the convective 'atmosphere'. The Sun, stable, burning tranquilly, had become a *Main Sequence* star; by the time Lieserl entered the convective zone, the Sun had burned for five billion years.

But the Sun would not remain on the Main Sequence forever.

The mass converted to energy was millions of tons per second. The Sun's bulk was so huge that this was a tiny fraction; in all its five-billion-year history so far the Sun had burned only five per cent of its hydrogen fuel ...

But, relentlessly, the fuel in the core would be exhausted. Gradually an ash of helium would accumulate in the core, and the central temperature would drop. The delicate balance between gravity and radiation pressure would be lost, and the core would implode under the weight of the surrounding, cooler layers.

Paradoxically, the implosion would cause the core temperature to *rise* once more – so much so that new fusion processes would become possible – and the star's overall energy output would rise.

The outer layers would expand enormously, driven out by the new-burning core. The Sun would engulf Mercury, and perhaps more of the inner planets, before reaching a new gravity-pressure equilibrium – as a *red giant*. This hundred-million-year phase would be spectacular, with the Sun's luminosity increasing by a factor of a thousand.

But this profligate expansion was not sustainable. Complex elements would be burned with increasing desperation in the expanding, clinker-ridden core, until at last all the available fuel was exhausted.

As the core's temperature suddenly fell, equilibrium would be lost with sudden abandon. The Sun would implode once more, seeking a new stability. Finally, as a *white dwarf*, the Sun would consist of little more than its own dead core, its density a million times higher than before, with further contraction opposed by the pressure of high-speed electrons in its interior.

Slowly, the remnant would cool, at last becoming a *black dwarf*, surrounded – as if by betrayed children – by the charred husks of its planets.

... At least, Lieserl thought, that was the theory.

If the laws of physics were allowed to unravel, following their own logic unimpeded, the Sun's red giant stage was still billions of years away ... not mere *millions* of years, as Superet's evidence suggested was the case.

Lieserl's brief was to find out what was damaging the Sun.

Lieserl. Try to pick up the p-modes; we want to see if that sensory mechanism works ...

'Absolutely. Helioseismology, here I come,' she said flippantly.

She *opened* her eyes once more.

A new pattern was built up by her processors, a fresh overlay on top of the images of convective cells and tangled flux tubes: gradually, she made out a structure of ghostly-blue walls and spinning planes that propagated through the convective cavern. These were *p-modes*: sound waves, pressure pulses fleeing through the Solar gas from explosive events like the destruction of granules on the surface. The waves were trapped in the convective layer, reflected from the vacuum beyond the photosphere and bent away from the core by the increasing sound speed in the interior. The waves cancelled and reinforced each other until only standing waves survived, modes of vibration which matched the geometry of the convective cavern.

The modes filled the space around her with ghostly, spinning patterns; their character varied as she surveyed the depth of the cavern, with length scales increasing as she looked into the interior. Looking up with her enhanced vision Lieserl could see how patches – thousands of miles wide – of the Sun's surface *oscillated* as the waves struck, with displacements of fifty miles and speeds of half a mile a second.

The Sun *rang*, like a bell.

Good . . . good. This is terrific data, Lieserl.

'I'm glad to oblige,' she said drily.

All right. Now let's try putting it together. Use the neutrino flux, such as it is, and the helioseismology data, and everything else you've got . . . Let's find out how much we can see.

Lieserl felt a thrill of excitement – subtle, but real – as she began to comply. Now she was moving to the core of her mission, even of her life: to look into the heart of the Sun, as no human had done before.

As the processors worked to integrate the data she called up from her long-term memory a template: the *Standard Model* of the Sun. The processors overlaid the cavern around her with yet another level of complexity, as they populated it with icons, graphics, grid lines and alphanumeric labels, showing her the basic properties of the Standard Model. The Model – refined and revised over millennia – represented humanity's best understanding of how the Sun worked. She looked in towards the core and saw how, according to the Model, the pressure and temperature rose smoothly towards the core; the temperature graph showed as a complex three-dimensional sphere in pink and red, reaching an intensely scarlet fifteen million degrees at the very heart.

Slowly, her processors plotted the reality – as she perceived it now – against the theory; graphs and schematics blossomed over each other like clusters of multicoloured flowers.

After a few minutes, her vision stabilized. She stared around at the complex imagery filling the cavern, zooming in on particular aspects, highlighting differences.

Oh, no, Scholes said. *No. Something's wrong.*

'What?'

The discrepancies, Lieserl. Particularly towards the core. This simply can't be right.

She felt amused. 'You've gone to all the trouble of constructing me, of sending me in here like this, and now that I'm here you're going to disbelieve what I tell you?'

But look at the divergences from the Model, Lieserl. Under a command from Scholes, the actual and predicted temperature gradients were picked out in glowing, radiant pinks. *Look at this.*

'Hmm ...'

According to the Standard Model, the temperature should have fallen quite rapidly away from the fusion region – down by a full twenty per cent from the central value after a tenth of the Sun's radius. But in fact, the temperature drop was much more shallow ... falling only a few per cent, Lieserl saw, over more than a *quarter* of the radius.

'That's not so surprising. Is it?' In riposte she superimposed a graphic of her own, a variant of the Standard Model. 'Look at this. Here's a model with a dark matter component – photinos, orbiting the core.' The dark matter – fast-moving, almost intangible particles kept clustered around the heart of the Sun by its gravity field – transferred energy out of the core and to the surrounding layers. 'See? The photinos just leak kinetic energy – heat energy – out of the core. The central temperature is suppressed, and the core is made isothermal – uniform temperature – out to about ten per cent of the radius.'

Scholes sounded testy, impatient. *Yes,* he said, *but what we're looking at here is an isothermal region covering three times that radius – twenty-five times the volume predicted even by the widest of the Standard Model's variants. It's impossible, Lieserl. Something must be going wrong with –*

'With what? With the eyes you've built for me? Or with your own expectations?'

Irritated, she cancelled all the schematics. The spheres and contour lines imploded in sparkles of pixels, exposing the native panorama of the convective cavern, a complex, ghostly overlay of flux tubes, p-modes and convection cells.

Frustrated, with some analogue of nervous energy building in her, she sent her Virtual self soaring around the cavern. She chased the rotating p-wave modes, sliced through flux tubes. 'Kevan. What if the effect we're seeing is *real*? Maybe this divergence in the core is what you've sent me in here to find.'

Maybe ... Lieserl, what will you do next?

'It's early days, but I think I'll soon have learned all I can out here.'

Out here?

'In the cavern – the convective zone. All the evidence we have is indirect, Kevan. The real action is deeper in, at the core.'

But you can't go any deeper, Lieserl. Your design ... the wormhole will implode if you try to penetrate the radiative zone ...

'Maybe. Well, it's up to you to sort that out, Kevan.'

She swooped up to the glowing roof of the cavern, and plunged down, at hundreds of miles a second, towards the plasma sea, past the slow-pulsing flanks of giant p-modes.

6

Like an insect circling an elephant the pod skimmed around the hull of the *Great Northern*.

Mark Wu, Louise Armonk, Garry Uvarov and Serena Milpitas sat and watched as their tiny pod skirted the starship. Their silence, Mark thought, was suitably deep and awe-struck, even for four who had been as close to the final stages of the project as these. And maybe that was Louise's intention today, he thought, the subtext under what was ostensibly a simple inspection tour of the ship by her top management team.

Well, if so, she was certainly succeeding.

The lifedome of the *Northern* was a squat, transparent cylinder a mile wide. It was extraordinary to think that the whole of Michael Poole's GUTship – drive section and all – would have fitted inside that sparkling box; Mark tried to imagine the *Hermit Crab* suspended in that great cylinder like some immense model under glass.

Mark could see clearly the multiple decks of the dome, and throughout the dome there was movement and light, and the deep, refreshing green of growing things. He was aware that the adaptation of much of the dome, and the rest of the ship, was still unfinished; most of what he saw was little more than a Virtual projection. But still he was impressed by the scale and vigour of it all. This lifedome would be a self-contained city – no, more than that: a world in itself, a biosphere suspended between the stars.

Home to five thousand people for a thousand years.

Now they wheeled to the underside of the lifedome. The pod approached the immense, tangled structure of the *Northern*'s main spine, and flew parallel to the spine for some three hundred yards towards the base of the dome.

The spine was a three-mile highway of metal littered with

supply modules and antennae and other sensors, turned up to the distant stars like mouths. Behind them the spine led to the mysterious darkness of the drive section, where the lights of workers – human and robotic – crawled like flies. And, attached to the spine by bands of gold just before the drive section, was the huge Interface, the wormhole terminus which they would tow to the future. The tetrahedral frame looked like a gaudy, glittering toy of shining blue ribbon.

Uvarov spread his long, intelligent fingers and rested his hands against the gleaming hull of the pod. 'Lethe,' he said. The pod's lights struck highlights from his bony profile as he peered out at the spine. 'It might not be real, but it's beautiful.'

Louise laughed; beside the thin, gaunt eugenicist she looked short, compact, Mark thought. 'Real enough,' she said. 'The spine's framework is a hundred per cent realized. It's just the superstructure that remains nebulous.' She thought for a moment, then called, 'Configure 3-B.'

The flower-like antennae clustered along the spine melted away, dissolving into showers of pixel cubes which tumbled like snowflakes. For a few surreal seconds Virtual configurations of equipment modules blossomed over the spine; through the snowstorm of modules Mark could see the basic – and elegant – structure of triangular vertebrae at the core of the spine.

At last the storm of images stilled; the spine settled into a new scattering of lenses and antennae. To Mark's untutored eye this looked much the same as the original – perhaps rather sparser – but he became aware that Serena Milpitas was nodding, almost wistfully.

'This is the original configuration,' she said. 'It's what was planned when the ship was being designed for its one-way hop to Tau Ceti, just a century away.'

Mark studied Milpitas curiously. The project's new chief engineer affected physical-forty, but Mark knew she was at least twice as old as that. He also knew there had been quite a bit of friction between Milpitas and Louise; so he was surprised to find, now, Milpitas praising Louise's design. 'You sound a little – nostalgic. Do you really think this is a better design?'

'Oh, yes.' Milpitas' broad face split in a smile; she seemed surprised by the question. 'Don't you? Can't you see it?'

Uvarov grunted. 'Not particularly.'

'Inelegance was forced on us. Look – for a thousand-year flight the problems of reliability are enormous.' Her accent was broad, confident Martian. 'This ship has around a thousand million distinguishable components. And all of them have to work perfectly, all of the time. Right? Now, we estimate that the chance of a significant failure of any one of those components – of a failure serious enough to knock out a ship's system, say – is a tenth of one per cent per year. Pretty good odds, you might think. But as the years go by the chances of a failure mount up, and they work cumulatively.' She fixed Mark with a direct stare. 'What would you guess the chances of such a failure would be after a hundred years?'

Uvarov growled, 'Oh, please, spare us games.'

Mark shrugged. 'A few per cent?'

'Not bad. Ten per cent. Not wonderful, but liveable with.'

Uvarov clicked his tongue. 'I hate your Mons Olympus grammar, engineer.'

Milpitas ignored him. 'But after a *thousand* years, you're looking at a failure probability of over *sixty* per cent. You reach fifty-fifty after just seven centuries –'

'What she's trying to tell you,' Uvarov said heavily, his flat Lunar tones conveying his boredom, 'is the obvious fact that they've had to perform extensive redesign to enable the ship to survive a thousand-year flight.'

'How? Louise doesn't tell me a damn thing.'

Uvarov grinned. 'Ex-wives never do. I should know. I –'

Milpitas cut in, 'With current technology, we couldn't get the reliability rates high enough for the mechanical, electrical or semisentient components.' She waved a hand at the half-Virtual panorama beyond the hull. 'Amazing, isn't it? We think we've come so far. We thought that with nanobotic technology – continual repair and replacement at the sub-visible level – reliability problems were a thing of the past. I mean, look at that spine out there. There's sentience in it *everywhere*, right down to the nuts and bolts.'

'There are *no* nuts and bolts, Serena,' Louise said drily.

Milpitas ignored her. 'And yet it doesn't take much of a challenge to move us beyond the envelope of our capabilities. Strictly speaking, a thousand-year flight is still beyond our means.'

'That sounds ominous,' Mark said uneasily.

'So,' Louise said, 'we had to look to the past – simple methods used to improve reliability on projects like the first off-Earth flights.' She called out, 'Central configuration,' and the blizzard of virtual components swirled once more around the spine, settling at last into the pattern Mark remembered from before Louise's change.

Milpitas pointed. 'And this is what we're going to the stars with. Look at it. Even at this gross macroscopic level you can *see* there are many more components.' And, indeed, Mark realized now that there were more antennae, more sensor snouts, more maintenance pods; the spine structure looked busier, far more cluttered.

'Triple redundancy,' Milpitas said with a grimace. 'Words – and a technique – from the twenty-fifth century. Or further back, even, for all I know; probably from the time of those disgusting old fission reactors. Carrying three of everything – or more, for the key components – to reduce the chance of a catastrophe to the invisibly small.'

'Gripping,' Uvarov said. 'But shall we move on, some time today? We do have the whole of the ship to inspect, as I recall.'

The base of the lifedome expanded in Mark's vision until it covered the sky, becoming an immense, complex, semitransparent roof; guide lights and the outlines of ports – large and small – encrusted the surface with colour, and everywhere there was movement, a constant flow of cargo, pods and spacesuited figures through the multiple locks. Again Mark had the impression that this was not so much a ship as a city: immense, busy, occupied with the endless business of maintaining its own fabric.

Suspended beneath the lifedome, cradled in cables, was the dark, wildly incongruous form of the *Great Britain*. It looked like an immense lifeboat, suspended there, Mark thought; he grinned, relishing this evidence of Louise's sentimentality.

The pod, working autonomously, made a flawless entry into one of the huge airlocks. After a couple of minutes the lock had completed its cycle.

The four of them emerged, drifting, into the air at the base of the *Northern*'s lifedome. It seemed to Mark that the base itself – constructed with the universal semisentient transparent plastic

78

– was a wall dividing the Universe into two halves. Before him was the elaborate, sparkling-clean interior of the lifedome; behind him was the tough, angular spine of the GUTship, and the static darkness of transPlutonian space.

Louise led them to a row of zero-gee scooters; the scooters nuzzled against the transparent base, neat and efficient. Mark took a scooter. It was a simple platform, its pneumatic jets controlled by twists of its raised handles.

They formed into pairs – Louise and Uvarov in the lead, with Mark and Milpitas following. With near-silent sighs of scooter air the four moved off in formation, up towards the heart of the lifedome.

The lower fifth of a mile of the lifedome was known as the loading bay: a single, echoing hall, brilliantly lit and free of partitions. The roof of the loading bay – the underside of the first habitable section, called the maintenance bulkhead – was a mist-shrouded tangle of infrastructure, far above. Today, the loading bay was filled with bulky machinery and crates of supplies; huge masses, towed by people on scooters or by 'bots, crossed the air in all directions, emerging from a dozen locks.

Serena Milpitas performed a slow, easy spiral as she rose up through the air beside Mark. 'I love these scooter things, don't you?'

Mark smiled. 'Sure. But they're a lazy way to travel in zero gee. And they won't be a lot of use when we're underway.'

'No. A constant one-gee drive for a thousand years. What a drag.'

Mark studied the engineer as she went through her rolls; her expression was calm, almost vacuous, with every sign that she was lost in the simple physical pleasure of the scooter-ride. Mark said, 'How did you feel about having to dig up those old techniques – the reliability procedures?'

'How did I *feel*?' Milpitas stabilized her scooter and studied Mark, a half-smile on her face. 'You sound like a Keplerian ... They're dippier than anyone else back home on Mars. Ah, but I guess that's your job, isn't it? The social engineer.'

Mark smiled. 'Maybe. But I'm off-duty now.'

'Sure you are.' Milpitas thought for a moment. 'I guess our work isn't so dissimilar, Mark. Your job – as I understand it – is to come up with ways for us to live with each other over a thousand years. Mine is to ensure that the ship itself – the external fabric of the mission – can sustain itself. When it came to redesigning *Northern*, I didn't like messing up Louise's nice, clean designs, frankly. But if you're going to succeed at something like this you have to take no chances. You have to *plan*.' Her eyes lost their focus, as if she were looking at something far away. 'It had to be done. And it was worth it. Anything's worth it, for the project, of course.' Her expression cleared, and she looked at Mark, appearing confused. 'Is that answering your question?'

'I think so.'

Mark hung back a little, and let Milpitas move ahead, up towards the complex maintenance bulkhead. He fell into line with Louise.

'You don't look so happy,' Louise said.

Mark shrugged. 'Just a little spooked by Serena, I guess.'

Louise snorted. 'Aren't we all.'

Many of the original crew of the *Northern* – who had, after all, seen themselves as potential colonists of the Tau Ceti system, not as time travellers with quasi-mystical goals about saving the species – had decided not to stay with the ship after its new flight plan was announced by Louise. Louise had lost, for instance, the genial Sam Gillibrand, her original first assistant. On the other hand, Serena Milpitas – and Uvarov, for that matter – had seemed eager to join the project after its rescoping by Superet.

Both Milpitas and Uvarov seemed natural Superet supporters, to Mark; they'd absorbed with a chilling alacrity the induction programmes Superet had offered them all.

Milpitas and Uvarov had become *converts*, Mark thought uneasily.

'You know, I always liked Sam Gillibrand,' he said wistfully. 'Sam wants to go to Tau Ceti and build houses under the light of a new sun; the dark possibilities of five megayears hence couldn't be of less interest to him. Serena is different, though. Under all that bluff Martian chatter and confident engineering, there's something darker – more driven. Obsessive, even.'

'Maybe,' Louise said. 'But, just as human engineering isn't yet up to thousand-year flights, so the average human head isn't capable of thinking on thousand-year timescales.' She sighed and ran her fingers through her close-cropped hair. 'Serena Milpitas can win through for the mission, Mark. Both Milpitas and Uvarov seem able to think in millennia – megayears, even. And as a consequence, or as a cause, they are dark, multilevelled, complex people.' She looked at Mark sadly. 'The Superet stuff is spooky, I agree. But I think it comes with the territory, Mark.'

Maybe in the complexities of the future the home-builders like Sam would be obsolete, their simple skills and motivation displaced in a dangerous Universe, Mark thought. Perhaps Superet and its converts represented the human of the future – the next wave of evolution, what the species would have to become to survive on cosmic timescales.

Maybe. But – judging by Milpitas and Uvarov – there wouldn't be too many laughs.

Anyway, he thought gloomily, he was going to have *ten centuries* with these people to find out about them ... And it was going to be Lethe's own challenge for him to construct a viable society around them.

'It still surprises me that *you* agreed to sign up for this,' he said. 'I mean, they took away your mission.'

Louise shrugged. 'We've been over this enough times. Let's face it, they would have taken *Northern* away from me anyway. I want to see the ship perform. And –'

'Yes?'

She grinned. 'Besides, after I got over my irritation at the way Superet runs its affairs, I realized no one's ever tried a thousand-year flight before. *Or* tried to establish a time bridge across five million years. I can get one over on Michael Poole, wherever he is –'

'Yes, but look what happened to him.'

Mark could see what was going on inside Louise's head. With the Superet mission – with this immense *stunt* – she was going to be able to bypass the intimidating shadow of the future, simply by leaping over it. And she was obviously entranced by the idea of taking her technology to its limits. But he wondered if she really – *really* – had any idea of the scale of the problems they would face.

He opened his mouth to speak.

Louise, with unusual tenderness, laid a finger over his lips, closing them. 'Come on, Mark. We've a thousand years to think of all the problems. Time enough. Today, the ship is bright and new; today, it's enough for me to believe the mission is going to be *fun*.'

With a sudden access of vigour she twisted the handle of her scooter and hurried after the others.

Lieserl. Take it easy. You're doing fine.

She looked up, tipping back her head. Already she was dropping out of the complex, exhilarating world of the convection region, with its immense turbulent cells, tangled flux tubes and booming p-waves. She stared upwards, allowing herself the luxury of nostalgia. The convective-zone cavern had come to seem almost homely, she realized.

Homely ... at least compared to the regions she was going to enter now.

We're still getting good telemetry, Lieserl.

'Good. I'm relieved.'

Lieserl, how are you feeling?

She laughed. With a mixture of exasperation and affection, she said, 'I'll feel better when you lose your "good telemetry", Kevan, and I don't have to listen to your dumb-ass questions any more.'

You'll miss me when I'm gone.

'Actually,' Lieserl said, 'that's probably true. But I'm damned if I'm going to tell you so.'

Scholes laughed, his synthesized voice surprisingly unrealistic. *You haven't answered my question.*

Her arms still outstretched, she looked down at her bare feet. 'Actually, I feel a little like Christ. Dali's Christ, perhaps, suspended in the air over an uncaring landscape.'

Yeah, Scholes said casually. *My thought exactly.*

Now she plunged through the last ghost-forms of convective cells. It was exactly like falling out of a cloud bank. The milky-white surface of the plasma sea was exposed beneath her; huge g-mode waves crawled across its surface, like thoughts traversing some huge mind.

Her rate of fall suddenly increased. It felt as if the bottom had dropped out of her stomach.

'Lethe,' she whispered.

Lieserl?

She found her chest tightening – and that was absurd, of course, because she *had* no chest. She struggled to speak. 'I'm okay, Kevan. It's just a little vertigo.'

Vertigo?

'Virtual vertigo. I feel like I'm falling. This illusion's too damn good.'

Well, you are falling, Lieserl. Your speed's increased, now you're out of the convective stuff.

'I'm *scared*, Kevan.'

Take it easy. The telemetry is –

'Screw the telemetry. Just talk to me.'

He hesitated. *You're a hundred thousand miles beneath the photosphere. You're close to the boundary of the radiative zone; the centre of the Sun is another seven hundred thousand miles below you.*

'Don't look down,' she breathed.

Right. Don't look down. Listen, you can be proud; that's deeper than any probe we've dropped before.

Despite her fear, she couldn't let that go. 'So I'm a probe, now?'

Sorry. We're looking at the new material squirting through the other end of your refrigerator-wormhole now. I can barely see the Interface for the science platforms clustered around it. It's a great sight, Lieserl; we've universities from all over the System queuing up for observation time. The density of the gas around you is only about one per cent of water's. But it's at a temperature of half a million degrees.

'Strong stuff.'

Angel tears, Lieserl . . .

The plasma sea was rushing up towards her, bland, devouring. Suddenly she was convinced that she, and her flimsy wormhole, were going to disappear into that well of fire with barely a spark. 'Oh, Lethe!' She tucked her knees up to her chest and wrapped her arms around her lower legs, so that she was falling curled up in a foetal ball.

Lieserl, you're not committed to this. If you want to pull out of there –

'No.' She closed her eyes and rested her forehead against her

83

knees. 'No, it's all right. I'm sorry. I'm just not as tough as I think I am, sometimes.'

The wormhole is holding together. We think, after the redesign we've done, that you can penetrate at least the first few thousand miles of the radiative zone, without compromising the integrity of the wormhole. Maybe deeper; the temperature and pressure gradients are pretty small. But you know we didn't advise this dive –

'I know it.' She opened her eyes and faced the looming sea once more. The fear was still huge, like a vice around her thinking. 'Kevan, I'd never assemble the courage to go through this a second time. It's now or never. I'll even try to enjoy the ride.'

Stay with it, Lieserl.

'Yeah,' she growled. 'And you stay with me –'

Suddenly her fall was halted. It felt as if she had run into a wall of glass; her limbs spread-eagled against an invisible barrier and the breath was knocked out of her illusory lungs. Helpless, she was even thrown back up into the 'air' a short distance; then her fall resumed, even more precipitately than before.

She screamed: *'Kevan!'*

We saw it, Lieserl. I'm still here; it's okay. Everything's nominal.

Nominal, she thought sourly. *How comforting.* 'What in Lethe was *that?*'

You're at the bottom of the convective layer. You should have been expecting something like that.

'Yes?' she snarled. 'Well, maybe you should have damn well told me – yike!'

Again, that sudden, jarring arrest, followed by a disconcerting hurl into the air, as if she were an autumn leaf in the breeze.

Like snakes and bloody ladders, she thought.

You're passing through the boundary layer between the radiative and convective zones, is all, Scholes said with studied calm. *Below you is plasma; above you atomic gas – matter cool enough for electrons to stick to nuclei.*

The photons emerging from the fusing core just bounce off the plasma, but they dump all their energy into the atomic gas. It's the process that powers the convective zone, Lieserl. A process that drives convective founts bigger than worlds. So you shouldn't be surprised if you encounter a little turbulence. In fact, out here we're all interested by the fact that the boundary layer seems to be so thin ...

We're still tracking you, Lieserl; you shouldn't be afraid. You're through the turbulence now, aren't you? You should be falling freely again.

'Yes. Yes, I am. So I'm in the sea, now?'

The sea?

'The plasma sea. The radiative zone.'

Yes.

'But –'

Suddenly, almost without warning, the familiar skyscape of convection cells and flux tubes was misting from her sight, whiting out. There was whiteness above, before, below her; it was like being suspended inside some huge, chilling eggshell.

But what? What is it, Lieserl? What's wrong?

For the first time she felt real panic creep around her mind.

'I can't *see*, Kevan.'

Mark, rising through brightly lit air, looked down. He was nearing the top of the loading bay now. The base was a floor of glass far below him, with the spine and drive section ghostly forms beyond; people and 'bots criss-crossed the bay, hauling their cargo.

Mark tried to analyse his own impressions as they rose. For a moment he fought an irrational surge of vertigo: a feeling – despite the evidence of his eyes that he was in zero-gee – that if he tumbled from this scooter he would plummet to that floor of glass, far below. He concentrated on the environment close to him, the thick layer of warm, bright air all round him. But that made the glimpses of the spine and drive – the brutal limbs of the ship – seem unreal, as if the emptiness of space beyond the fragile walls of the dome was an illusion.

Mark felt uneasy. The ship was so huge, so complex – so *convincing*. After a few decades, it would be terribly easy to believe that this ship was a world, to forget that there was anything real, or significant, beyond its walls.

Now they were approaching the roof of the bay: the maintenance bulkhead. Mark drew level with Garry Uvarov, and they stared up at the mile-wide layer of engineering above them. The bulkhead was a tangle of pipes, ducts and cables, an inverted industrial landscape. There were even tree-roots, Mark saw.

People and 'bots swarmed everywhere, working rapidly and apparently efficiently; even as Mark watched the bulkhead's complex surface seemed to evolve, the ducts and tubes creeping across the surface like living things. It was a little like watching life spread through some forest of metal and plastic.

'Extraordinary how primitive it all is,' Mark said to Uvarov. 'Cables and ducts – it's like some sculpture from a museum of industrial archaeology.'

Uvarov waved a cultured hand towards the pipes above him. 'We're carrying human beings – barely-evolved, untidy sacks of water and wind – to the stars. We are cavemen inside a starship. That's why the undersurface of this bulkhead seems so crude to you, Mark; it's simply a reflection of the crudity of our own human design. We sail the stars. We even have nanobots to rebuild us when we grow old. But we remain primitives; and when we travel, we need immense boxes with pipes and ducts to carry our breath, piss and shit.' He grinned. 'Mark, my passion – my career – is the improvement of the basic human stock. Do you imagine the *Xeelee* carry all this garbage around with them?'

They passed through access ports in the maintenance bulkhead and ascended into the habitable sections.

There were fifteen habitable Decks in the mile-deep lifedome, each around a hundred yards apart. Some of the main levels were subdivided, so that the interior of the lifedome was a complex warren of chambers of all sizes. Elevator shafts and walkways pierced the Decks. The shafts were already in use as zero-gee access channels; they'd be left uncompleted, without machinery, until closer to departure.

Now the little party entered one shaft and began to rise, slowly, past the cut-through Decks.

Many of the chambers were still unfinished, and a succession of Virtual designs were being tried out in some of them; Mark peered out at a storm of parks, libraries, domestic dwellings, theatres, workshops, blizzarding through the chambers.

Uvarov said, 'How charming. How Earthlike. More concessions to the primitive in us, of course.'

Mark frowned. 'Primitive or not, Uvarov, we have to take *some* account of human needs when designing an environment like this. As you should know. The chambers have been laid out on a human scale; it's important people shouldn't feel dwarfed to insignificance by the scale of the artefacts around them – or, on the other hand, cramped and confined by ship walls. Why, some of the chambers are so large it would be possible for an inhabitant to forget he or she was inside a ship at all.'

Uvarov grunted. 'Really. But isn't that more evidence that we as a species aren't really yet up to a flight like this? It would be so easy to be immersed in the sensory impressions of the here-and-now, which are so much more *real* than the fragility of the ship, the emptiness outside the thin walls. It would be tempting to accept this ship as a world in itself, an invulnerable background against which we can play out our own tiny, complex human dramas, much as our distant forefathers did on the plains of Africa, billions of miles away.

'Think of the pipes and ducts under that maintenance bulkhead. Perhaps our ancestors, in simpler times, imagined that some such infrastructure lay underneath the flat Earth. The Universe was a box, with the Earth as its floor. The sky was a cow whose feet rested on the four corners of the Earth – or perhaps a woman, supporting herself on elbows and knees – or a vaulted metal lid. Around the walls of the box-world flowed a river on which the sun and moon gods sailed each day, entering and vanishing through stage doors. The fixed stars were lamps, suspended from the vault. And, presumably, underneath it all lay some labyrinth of tunnels and ducts through which the waters and the gods could travel to begin their daily journeys afresh. The heavens could change, but they were predictable; to the human consciousness – still half-asleep – this was a safe, contained, cosy, womb-like Universe. Mark Wu, is our *Northern*, today, so unlike the Earth as envisaged by – let us say – a Babylonian, or an Egyptian?'

Mark rubbed his chin. Uvarov's patronizing style irritated him, but his remarks plugged in closely to his own vague sense of disquiet. 'Maybe not,' he replied sharply. 'But then you and I, and the others, have a responsibility to ensure that the inhabitants of the ship don't slip back into some pre-rational state. That they don't *forget*.'

'Ah, but will that be so easy, over *a thousand years*?'

Mark peered out at the half-built libraries and parks uneasily.

Uvarov said, 'I've heard about some of the programmes you

and your social engineering teams are devising. Research initiatives and so forth – make-works, obviously.'

'Not at all.' Mark found himself bridling again. 'I'm not going to deny we need to find something for people to *do*. As you keep saying, we're primitives; we aren't capable of sitting around in comfort for a thousand years as the journey unravels.

'Some of the work is obvious, like the maintenance and enhancement of the ship. But there will be programmes of research. Remember, we'll be cut off from the rest of the human Universe for most of the journey. Some of your own projects come into this category, Uvarov – like your AS enhancement programme.' He thought about that, then said provocatively, 'Perhaps you could come up with some way of replicating Milpitas' triple-redundancy ideas within our own bodies.'

Uvarov laughed, unperturbed. 'Perhaps. But I would hope to work in a rather more *imaginative* way than that, Mark Wu. After all AS treatment represents an enormous advance in our evolutionary history – one of our most significant steps away from the tyranny of the gene, which has ruthlessly cut us down since the dawn of our history. But must we rely on injections of nanobots to achieve this end? How much better it would be if we could change the fundamental basis of our existence as a species . . .'

Mark found Uvarov chilling. His cold, analytical view of humanity, coupled with the extraordinarily long-term perspective of his thinking, was deeply disturbing. The Superet conversion seemed only to have reinforced these trends in Uvarov's personality.

And, Lethe, Uvarov was supposed to be a *doctor*.

'We should not be restrained by the primitive in us, Mark Wu,' Uvarov was saying. 'We should think of the *possible*. And then determine what must be done to attain that . . . Whatever the cost.

'Your proposals for the social structure in this ship are another example of limited thinking, I fear.'

Mark frowned, his anger building. 'You disapprove of my proposals?'

Uvarov's voice, under its thick layer of Lunar accent, was mocking. 'You have a draft constitution for a unified democratic structure –'

'With deep splits of power, and local accountability. Yes. You have a problem with that? Uvarov, I've based my proposals on the most successful examples of closed societies we have – the early colonies on Mars, for example. We must learn from the past ...'

Louise was the nominal leader of the expedition. But she wasn't going to be a *captain*; no hierarchical command structure could last a thousand years. And there was no guarantee that AS treatments could sustain any individual over such a period. AS itself wasn't that well established; the oldest living human was only around four centuries old. And who knew what cumulative effect consciousness editing would have, over centuries?

...So it could be that none of the crew alive at the launch – even Louise and Mark themselves – would survive to see the end of the trip.

But even if the last person who remembered Sol expired, Louise and her coterie had to find ways to ensure that the mission's purpose was not lost with them.

Mark's job was to design a *society* to populate the ship's closed environment – a society stable enough to persist over ten centuries ... *and* to maintain the ship's core mission.

Uvarov looked sceptical. 'But a simple democracy?'

Mark was surprised at the depth of his resentment at being patronized like this by Uvarov. 'We have to start somewhere – with a framework the ship's inhabitants are going to be able to use, to build on. The constitution will be malleable. It will even be possible, legally, to abandon the constitution altogether –'

'You're missing my point,' Uvarov said silkily. 'Mark, democracy as a method of human interaction is already millennia old. And we know how easy it is to subvert any democratic process. There are endless examples of people using a democratic system as a games-theory framework of rules to achieve their own ends.

'Use your imagination. Is there truly nothing better? Have we learned *nothing* about ourselves in all that time?'

'Democracies don't go to war with each other, Uvarov,' Mark said coldly. 'Democracies – however imperfectly – reflect the will of the many, not the few. Or the *one*.

'As you've told me, Uvarov, we remain primitives. Maybe

we're still too primitive to trust ourselves *not* to operate without a democratic framework.'

Uvarov bowed his elegant, silvered head – but without conviction or agreement, as if merely conceding a debating point.

The four scooters rose smoothly past the half-finished Decks.

7

She was suspended in a bath of charged particles. It was isotropic, opaque, featureless . . .

She had entered a new realm of matter.

Lieserl. Lieserl! I know you can hear me; I'm monitoring the feedback loops. Just listen to me. Your senses are overloaded; they are going to take time to adapt to this environment. That's why you're whited out. You're not designed for this, damn it. But your processors will soon be able to interpret the neutrino flux, the temperature and density gradients, even some of the g-mode patterns, and construct a sensorium for you. You'll be able to see again, Lieserl; just wait for the processors to cut in . . .

The voice continued, buzzing in her ear like some insect. It seemed irrelevant, remote. In this mush of plasma, she couldn't even see her own body. She was suspended in isotropy and homogeneity – the same everywhere, and in every direction. It was as if this plasma sea, this radiative zone, were some immense sensory-deprivation bath arranged for her benefit.

But she wasn't afraid. Her fear was gone now, washed away in the pearl-like light. The silence . . .

Damn it, Lieserl, I'm not going to lose you now! Listen to my voice. You've gone in there to find dark matter, not to lose your soul.

Lieserl, lost in whiteness, allowed the still, small voice to whisper into her head.

She dreamed of photinos.

Dark matter was the best candidate for ageing the Sun.

Dark matter comprised all but one hundredth of the mass of the Universe; the visible matter – *baryonic matter* which made up stars, galaxies, people – was a frosting, a thin scattering across a dark sea.

The effects of dark matter had been obvious long before a

single particle of the stuff had been detected by human physicists. The Milky Way galaxy itself was embedded in a flattened disc of dark matter, a hundred times the mass of its visible components. The stars of the Milky Way didn't orbit its core, as they would in the absence of the dark matter; instead the galaxy turned as if it were a solid disc – the illuminated disc was like an immense toy, embedded in dark glass.

According to the Standard Model there was a knot of cold, dark matter at the heart of the Sun – perhaps at the heart of every star.

And so, Lieserl dreamed, perhaps it was dark matter, passing through fusing hydrogen like a dream of winter, which was causing the Sun to die.

Now, slowly, the isotropy bleached out of the world. There was a hint of colour – a pinkness, a greater warmth, its source lost in the clouds below her. At first she thought this must be some artefact of her own consciousness – an illusion concocted by her starved senses. The shading was smooth, without feature save for its gradual deepening, from the zenith of her sky to its deepest red at the nadir beneath her feet. But it remained in place around her, objectively real, even as she moved her head. It was *out there*, and it was sufficient to restore structure to the world – to give her a definite *up* and *down*.

She found herself sighing. She almost regretted the return of the external world; she could very quickly have grown accustomed to floating in nothingness.

Lieserl. Can you see that? What do you see?

'I see elephants playing basketball.'

Lieserl –

'I'm seeing the temperature gradient, aren't I?'

Yes. It's nice to have you back, girl.

The soft, cosy glow was the light of the fusion hell of the core, filtered through her babyish Virtual senses.

There was light here, she knew – or at least, there were photons: packets of X-ray energy working their way out from the core of the Sun, where they were created in billions of fusion flashes. If Lieserl could have followed the path of a single photon, she would see it move in a random, zigzag way, bouncing off charged particles as if in some subatomic game.

The steps in the random walk – traversed at the speed of light – were, on average, less than an inch long.

The temperature gradient in this part of the Sun was tiny. But it was real, and it was just sufficient to encourage a few of the zigzagging photons to work their way outwards to the surface, rather than inwards. But the paths were long – the average photon needed a thousand billion *billion* steps to reach the outer boundary of the radiative layer. The journey took ten million years – and because the photons moved at the speed of light, the paths themselves were ten million light-years long, wrapped over on themselves like immense lengths of crumpled ribbon.

Now, as other 'senses' cut in, she started to make out more of the environment around her. Pressure and density gradients showed up in shades of blue and green, deepening in intensity towards the centre, closely matching the temperature differentials. It was as if she were suspended inside some huge, three-dimensional diagram of the Sun's equation of state.

As if on cue, the predictions of the Standard Model of theoretical physics cut in, overlaying the pressure, temperature and density gradients like a mesh around her face. The divergences from the Standard Model were highlighted in glowing strands of wire.

There were still divergences from the Model, she saw. There were divergences *everywhere*. And they were even wider than before.

Dark matter and baryonic matter attracted each other gravitationally. Dark matter particles *could* interact with baryonic matter through other forces: but only feebly, and in conditions of the highest density – such as at the heart of stars. In Earthlike conditions, the worlds of baryonic and dark matter slid through and past each other, all but unaware, like colonies of ghosts from different millennia.

This made dark matter hard to study. But after centuries of research, humans had succeeded in trapping a few of the elusive particles.

Dark matter was made up of *sparticles* – ghostly mirror-images of the everyday particles of baryonic matter.

Images in what mirror? Lieserl wondered feebly. As she framed the question the answer assembled itself for her, but –

drifting as she was – it was hard to tell if it came from the voice of Kevan Scholes, or from the forced-learning she'd endured as a child, or from the data stores contained within her wormhole.

Hard to tell, and harder to care.

The particle mirror was *supersymmetry*, the grand theory which had at last shown how the diverse forces of physics – gravitational, electromagnetic, strong and weak nuclear – were all aspects of a single, unified superforce. The superforce emerged at extremes of temperature and pressure, shimmering like a blade of some tempered metal in the hearts of supernovas, or during the first instants of the Big Bang itself. Away from these extremes of time and space, the superforce collapsed into its components, and the supersymmetry was broken.

Supersymmetry predicted that every baryonic particle should have a supersymmetric twin: a sparticle. The electron was paired with a *selectron*, the photon with the *photino* – and so on.

The particular unified-theory variant called *Spin (10)* had, with time, become the standard. Lieserl rolled that around her tongue, a few times. *Spin (10)*. A suitably absurd name for the secret of the Universe.

The divergence, of theory from observation, was *immense* – and increased towards the centre of the Sun.

'Kevan, it's *way* too hot out here.'

We see it, Lieserl, he said wryly. *For now we're just logging the data. Just as well you didn't pack your winter coat.*

She looked within herself, at some of her subsidiary senses. 'And I'm already picking up some stray photino flux.'

Already? This far out from the centre? Scholes sounded disturbed. *Are you sure?*

As a star like the Sun swept along its path about the centre of the galaxy – through a huge, intangible sea of dark matter – photinos fell into its pinprick gravity well, and clustered around its heart.

The photinos actually *orbited* the centre of the Sun, swarming through its core around the geometric centre like tiny, circling carrion-eaters, subatomic planets with orbital 'years' lasting mere minutes. The photinos passed through fusing hydrogen as if it were a light mist . . .

Almost.

The chances of a photino interacting with particles of the plasma were remote – but not zero. Once every orbit, a photino would scatter off a baryonic particle, perhaps a proton. The photino took some energy away from the proton. The gain in energy boosted the orbital speed of the photino, making it circle a little further out from the heart of the Sun.

Working this way, passing through the fusing hydrogen with its coagulated mass of trapped photons, the photinos were extremely efficient at transporting heat out from the centre of the Sun.

According to the Standard Model, the temperature at the centre should have been suppressed by a tenth, and the fusion heat energy smoothed out into the surrounding, cooler regions, making the central regions nearly *isothermal* – at a uniform temperature. The core would be a little cooler than it should otherwise have been, and the surrounding material a little warmer.

. . . Just a little. According to the Standard Model.

Now, Lieserl studied the temperature contours around her and realized how far the reality diverged from the ancient, venerated theoretical image. The isothermal region stretched *well* beyond the fusion core – far, far beyond the predictions of the Standard Model with its modest little knot of circling photinos.

'Kevan, there is *much* more heat being sucked out of the core than the Standard Model predicted. You do realize that there's no way the Model can be made to fit these observations.'

No. There was a silence, and Lieserl imagined Scholes sighing into his microphone. *I guess this means goodbye to an old friend.*

She allowed the contour forms of the Standard Model to lapse from her sensorium, leaving exposed the gradient curves of the physical properties of the medium around her. Without the spurious detail provided by the overlay of Standard-Model contours, the gradient curves seemed too smooth, deceptively featureless; she felt a remnant of her earlier deprived-sensorium tranquillity return to her. There was no sense of motion, and no real sense of scale; it was like being inside overlaid clouds glowing pink and blue from some hidden neon source.

'Kevan. Am I still falling?'

You've reached your nominal depth now.

'Nominal. I hate that word.'

Sorry. You're still falling, but a lot more slowly; we want to be sure we can handle the energy gradients.

But she'd barely breached the surface of the plasma sea; eighty per cent of the Sun's radius – a full two light-seconds – still lay beneath her.

And you're picking up some lateral drift, also. There are currents of some kind in there, Lieserl.

It was as if her Virtual senses were dark-adapting; now she could see more structure in the waxy temperature-map around her: pockets of higher temperature, slow, drifting currents. 'Right. I think I see it. Convection cells?'

Maybe. Or some new phenomenon. Lieserl, you're picking up data they've never seen before, out here. This stuff is only minutes old; it's a little early to form hypotheses yet, even for the bright guys in Thoth.

I wish you could see the Interface – out here, at the other end of your heat sink. Deep Solar plasma is just spewing out of it, pumping from every face; it's as if a small nova has gone off, right at the heart of the System. Lieserl, you may not believe this, but you're actually illuminating the photosphere. Why, I'll bet if we looked hard enough we'd find you were casting shadows from prominences.

She smiled.

I can hear you smiling, Lieserl. I'm smart like that. You enjoy being the hero, don't you?

'Maybe just a little.' She let her smile broaden. *I'm casting shadows onto the Sun. Not a bad monument.*

The uppermost level of the *Northern*'s habitable section was a square mile of rain forest.

The four air-scooters rose through a cylindrical Lock. Mark found himself rising up, like some ancient god, into the midst of jungle.

The air was thick, stifling, laden with rich scents and the cries and hoots of birds and animals. He was surrounded by the branchless boles of trees, pillars of hardwood – some extravagantly buttressed – that reached up to a thick canopy of leaves; the boles disappeared into the gloom, rank on rank of them, as if he were inside some nature-born temple of Islam. The floor of the forest, starved of light by the canopy, was surprisingly bare and looked firm underfoot: it was a carpet of leaves, pierced by

Lock entrances which offered incongruous glimpses of the cool, huge spaces beneath this sub-world. Fungi proliferated across the floor, spreading filaments through the leaf litter and erecting fruiting bodies in the shape of umbrellas and globes, platforms and spikes hung about by lace skirts.

On a whim, Mark rose through a hundred feet alongside the rotting carcass of a dead tree. The bark was thick with ferns and mosses which had formed a rich compost in the bark's crevices. Huge, gaudy orchids and bromeliads had colonized the bark, drawing their sustenance from leaf mould and collecting moisture from the air with their dangling roots.

He drew alongside a wild banana. Its broad, drooping leaf was marked by a line of holes on either side of the midrib. Mark lifted the leaf, and found suspended from the underside a series of white, fur-coated balls perhaps two inches across: nomadic bats, sheltering from the rainfall of this artificial forest.

There was a motion behind him; he turned.

Uvarov had followed him, and was now watching appraisingly. 'Each day,' Uvarov intoned, his face long in the gloom, 'an artificial sun will ride its chariot across the glass sky of this jungle-world. And machines will pipe rainfall into artificial clouds. We're living in a high-technology realization of our most ancient visions of the Universe. What does the fact that we've built this ship in such a way tell us about ourselves, I wonder?'

Mark didn't answer. He pushed himself away from the tree, and they descended to join the others, just above the forest floor.

Louise slapped the bole of a tree. She grinned. 'One of the few real objects in the whole damn ship,' she said. She looked around. 'This is Deck Zero. I wanted our tour today to end here. I'm proud of this forest. It's practical – it's going to be the lungs of the ship, a key part of our ecology – and it has higher purposes too; with this aboard we'll never be able to forget who we are, and where we came from.'

She looked from one to the other, in the green gloom. 'We've all come into this project from different directions. I'm interested in the technical challenge. And some of you, with Superet sympathies, have rather more ambitious goals to achieve. But we four, above all others, have the responsibility of making this project work. The forest is a symbol for us all. If these trees survive our ten centuries, then surely our human cargo will too.'

Serena Milpitas tilted back her head; Mark followed her example, and found himself peering up at the remote stars through a gap in the canopy. Suddenly he had a shift of perspective – a discontinuity of the imagination which abruptly revealed to him the true nature of this toy jungle, with empty, lightless space above it and a complex warren of humans below.

Garry Uvarov said, 'But if the Superet projections are correct, who knows what stars will be shining down on these trees in a thousand years?'

Mark reached out and touched a tree bole; he found something comforting about its warm, moist solidity. He heard a shrieking chorus, high above him; in the branches above his head he saw a troupe of birds of paradise – at least a dozen of them – dancing together, their ecstatic golden plumage shimmering against the transPlutonian darkness beyond the skydome.

A thousand years . . .

Dark matter could age a star.

The photino knot at the heart of the Sun lowered the temperature, and thereby suppressed the rate of fusion reaction. Naively, Lieserl supposed, one might think that this would *extend* the life of the Sun, not diminish it, by slowing the rate at which hydrogen was exhausted.

But it didn't work out like that. Taking heat energy out from the core made the Sun more *unstable*. The delicate balance between gravitational collapse and radiative explosion was upset. The Sun would reach *turnoff* earlier – that is, it would leave the Main Sequence, the family of stable stars, sooner than otherwise.

According to the Standard Model, photinos should reduce the life of the Sun only by a billion years.

Only?

A billion years was a long time – the Universe itself was only around twenty billion years out of its Big Bang egg – but the Sun would still be left with many billions of years of stable, Main Sequence existence . . .

According to the Standard Model. But she already knew the Model was wrong, didn't she?

Lieserl.

'Hmm?'

We have the answer. We think.

'Tell me.'

The Standard Model predicts the photino cloud should be contained within the fusing core, within ten per cent of the total Solar diameter. Right? But, according to the best fits we've made to your data —

'Go on, Kevan.'

There are actually significant photino densities out to thirty per cent of the diameter. Three times as much as the Model; nearly a third of the —

'Lethe.' She looked down. The heart of the Sun still glowed peacefully in interleaved shades of pink and blue. 'That must mean the fusion core is swamped with photinos.'

Even through the crude wormhole telemetry link she could hear the distress in his voice. *The temperature at the centre is way, way down, Lieserl. In fact —*

'In fact,' she said quietly, 'it's possible the fusion processes have already been extinguished altogether. Isn't it, Kevan? Perhaps the core of the Sun has already gone out, like a smothered flame.'

Yes. Lieserl, the most disturbing thing for me is that no one here can come up with a mechanism for such a photino cloud to form naturally . . .

'What's the lifecycle prediction? How long has the Sun left to live?'

No hesitation this time. *Zero.*

At first the blunt word made no sense. 'What?'

Zero, on the scales we're talking about — timescales measured in billions of years. In practice, we're looking at perhaps one to ten million years left. Lieserl, that's nothing in cosmic terms.

'I know. But it ties in with the predictions out of Superet, doesn't it? The data they collected through Michael Poole's wormhole daisy-chain.'

Yes.

'Kevan, you shouldn't feel too distressed. Five million years is fifty times the length of human history so far —'

Maybe. Kevan's voice took on a harder edge, as if he per-

sonally resented the ageing of the Sun. But I have kids. I hope to have descendants still alive in five million years. Damn it, I hope to be sentient still myself. Why not? It's only five megayears; we're out of the Dark Ages now, Lieserl.

She peered deep into the heart of the Sun, subvocally trying to press more of her functions into play. She had senses to pick up the ghostly shades of neutrino and photino fluxes, and if she just – *tried* – hard enough, she ought to be able to make out the dark matter cloud itself.

'I'll have to go deeper,' she murmured.

What?

'I said I'm going deeper. I want to find out what's down there. In the core.'

Lieserl –

'Come on, Kevan. Spare me any warnings about caution. You can't tell me that Superet has invested so much in me so far, only to have me turn back just inside the damn photosphere.'

You've already achieved an astonishing amount.

'And I can achieve a lot more. I'm going in, Kevan. Just as I've been designed to. I want to see just what has put out our Sun.' *Or,* she thought uneasily, *who.*

Scholes hesitated. *The truth is, you're only an experiment, Lieserl. Damn it, we didn't even know what conditions you would encounter in there.*

'So I'll take my time. You can redesign me en route. I've all the time in the world.

'I'll follow the bouncing photons. Maybe it will take me a million years to drift into the centre. But I'm going to get there.'

Lieserl, Superet wants you to go on. But – you must listen to this – it is prepared to risk you not returning. Your trip could be one way, Lieserl. Do you understand? Lieserl?

She shut out the whispering, remote voice, and stared into the oceanic depths of the Sun.

PART II

TRAJECTORY: TIMELIKE

8

His legs locked around a branch of the kapok tree, Arrow Maker raised his bow towards the skydome. The taut bowstring dug into the tough flesh of his three middle fingers, and the bow itself had a feeling of heaviness, of power. The arrow balanced in his grasp, light, perfect.

Maker's bare, hairless skin was slick from the exertion of climbing. He was close to the top of the canopy here, and the clicks, rustles, trills and coughs of the approaching evening sounded from everywhere within the great layer of life around him. Somewhere a group of howler monkeys were calling out their territorial claims, their eerie, almost choral wails rising and falling.

He released the bow string.

The arrow hissed into the air, and the guide line it towed unravelled past Arrow Maker's face with the faintest of breezes.

He heard a clatter in the branches, a few yards away from him, as the arrow returned. But the line didn't fall back; Maker had succeeded in hooking it over an upper branch of the kapok.

He slung his bow across his shoulder, retrieved his quiver, and clambered across the branches, his bare feet easily finding purchase on moss-laden bark. He found the arrow in a mound of moss at the junction of a banyan's trunk with a branch. Working quickly and efficiently, Arrow Maker unravelled a rope from his waist and attached it to the line; the rope – spun by his daughter from liana fibre – was as thick as his finger, and, working by touch, Maker found the rope heavy and difficult to knot.

When the rope was firmly attached Arrow Maker began to haul at the guide line. The rope slithered up through layers of leaves. Soon Maker had pulled the rope over the branch above. He tugged at the rope; there was some give, as the unseen kapok branch flexed, but the hold was more than strong enough to support his weight.

He detached the guide line and wrapped it around his waist. He clipped two metal hand-grips onto the rope. There was a webbing stirrup attached to each grip, and Arrow Maker placed his feet in these. Standing with his weight in one stirrup he moved the other a few feet upwards. Then he raised himself and moved the other grip, up past the first. Thus Arrow Maker climbed smoothly up through the remaining layers of canopy. The grips slid upwards easily, but ratchets prevented them from slipping down. One of the grips felt a little loose – it was worn, he suspected – but it was secure enough.

As he climbed up through layers of greenery towards the sky, Maker relaxed into the familiar rhythm of the simple exercise, enjoying the glowing feeling in his joints as his muscles worked. The heavy belt around his waist, with its pockets of webbing for his tools and food, bumped softly against his skin; he barely noticed the bow and quiver slung over his shoulder.

The grips, and ropes and stirrups, had belonged to Arrow Maker for at least twenty years. They were among his most treasured possessions: his life depended on them, and they were almost irreplaceable. The people of the forest could make rope, and bows, and face paint, but they simply didn't have the raw materials to manufacture grips and stirrups – or, come to that, knives, spectacles and many other essential day-to-day objects. Even old Uvarov – rolling around the forest floor in his chair – admitted as much.

To get his set of climbing gear, the younger Arrow Maker had traded with the Undermen.

He'd spent many days collecting forest produce: fruit, the flesh of birds, bowls of copaifera sap. He piled his goods in one of the great Locks set in the floor of the forest. He'd communicated his needs to the Undermen by an elaborate series of scratches made with the point of his knife in the scarred surface of the Lock.

When he'd returned to the Lock the next day, there lay the climbing gear he'd wanted, gleaming new and neatly laid out. Of the forest goods there was no sign.

The forest folk relied on Underman artefacts to stay alive. But similarly, Arrow Maker had often thought, perhaps the

Undermen needed forest food to survive. Perhaps it was dark down there, beneath the forest, cut off from the light; perhaps the Men couldn't grow their own food. Arrow Maker shivered; he had a sudden vision of a race of nocturnal, huge-eyed creatures skulking like loris through the lifeless, ever-darkened levels below his feet.

He reached the top of his rope. The anchoring branch was only a couple of hand's-breadths thick, but it was solid enough. A tree-swift's nest – a ball of bark and feathers, glued by spittle – clung to the side of the branch, sheltering its single egg.

He selected a fatter branch and sat on it, wrapping his legs around its junction with the trunk. He placed his bow and quiver carefully beside him, lodging them safely. He drew some dried meat from his belt and chewed at the tough, salty stuff as he gazed around.

Now he'd climbed close to the crown of the kapok tree. The great tree's last few branches were silhouetted against the darkling skydome above him, their clusters of brownish leaves rustling.

The mass of the canopy was perhaps thirty yards below the skydome, but this single giant kapok raised its bulk above the rest, its uppermost branches almost grazing the sky. The darkness of the evening rendered this upper world almost as dark as the forest floor, far below him. But Maker knew his way around the kapok; after all he'd been climbing it for most of his eighty years.

He was at the top of the world. In the distance a bird flapped across the sky, its colours a gaudy splash against the fading light. Beyond the skydome, the stars were coming out. The kapok's branches were a dense, tangled mass beneath him, obscuring its immense trunk. Seeds – fragments of fluffy down – floated everywhere, peppering the leaves with the last of the daylight. Ten yards below the tree's crown, the canopy was a rippling carpet, a dense layer of greenery – turning oily black as night approached – which stretched to the horizon, lapping against the walls of the skydome itself.

Garry Uvarov had sent Arrow Maker up here to inspect the sky. So Maker tipped up his face.

It was tempting to reach up and see if he could touch the sky. He couldn't, of course – the skydome was still at least twenty feet above him – but it would be easy enough to shoot up an arrow, to watch it clatter against the invisible roof.

The sky was unchanged. The stars were a thin, irregular sprinkling, hardly disturbing the sky's deep emptiness. Most of the stars were dull red points of light, like drops of blood, that were often difficult to see.

Uvarov had never shown interest in the stars before; now, suddenly, he'd ordered Arrow Maker to climb the trees, telling him to expect a sky blazing with stars, white, yellow and blue. Well, he'd been quite wrong.

Maker felt that old Uvarov was important: precious, like a talisman. But, as the years wore by, his words and imperatives seemed increasingly irrational.

Maker looked for the sky patterns he'd grown to know since his boyhood. There were the three stars, of a uniform brightness, in a neat row; there the familiar circle of stars dominated by a bright, scarlet gleam.

Nothing had changed in the sky above him, in the stars beyond the dome. Arrow Maker didn't even know what Uvarov was expecting him to find.

He clambered down into the bulk of the kapok treetop, so that there was a comforting layer of greenery between himself and the bare sky. Then he tied himself to the trunk with a loop of rope, laid his head against a pillowing arm and waited for sleep.

The klaxon's oscillating wail echoed off the houses, the empty streets, the walls of the sky.

Morrow woke immediately.

For a moment he lay in bed, staring into the sourceless illumination which bathed the ceiling above him.

Waking, at least, was easy. Some mornings the klaxon failed to sound – it was as imperfect and liable to failure as every other bit of equipment in the world – but on those mornings Morrow found his eyes opening on time, just as usual. He pictured his brain as a worn, ancient thing, with grooves of habit ground into its surface. He woke at the same time, every day.

Just as he had for the last five centuries.

Stiffly he swung his legs from his pallet and stood up. He started to think through the shift ahead. Today he was due for

106

an interview with Planner Milpitas – *yet another interview*, he thought – and he felt his heart sink.

He walked to the window and swung his arms back and forth to generate a little circulation in his upper body. From his home here on Deck Two Morrow could make out, through the open, multilayered flooring, some details of Deck Three below; he looked down over houses, factories, offices and – looming above all the other buildings – the imposing shoulders of the Planner Temples, scattered across the split levels like blocky clouds. Beyond the buildings and streets stood the walls of the world: sheets of metal, ribbed for strength. And over it all lay the multilevelled sky, a lid of girders and panels, enclosing and oppressive.

He worked through his morning rituals – washing, shaving his face and scalp, taking some dull, high-fibre food. He dressed in his cleanest standard-issue dungarees. Then he set off for his appointment with Planner Milpitas.

The community occupied two Decks, Two and Three. The inhabited Decks were laid out following a circular geometry, in a pattern of sectors and segments divided from each other by roads tracing out chords and radii. Deck Four, the level beneath Three, was accessible but uninhabited; Superet had long ago decreed that it be used as a source of raw materials. And there was also one level above, called Deck One, which was also uninhabited – but served other purposes.

Morrow had no idea what lay above Deck One, or below Deck Four. The Planners didn't encourage curiosity.

There were few people about as he crossed the Deck. He walked, of course; the world was only a mile across, so walking or cycling almost always sufficed. Morrow lived in Segment 2, an undesirable slice of the Deck close to the outer hull. The Temple was in Sector 3 – almost diametrically opposite, but close to the heart of the Deck. Morrow was able to cut down the radial walkways, past Sector 5, and walk almost directly to the Temple.

Much of Sector 5 was still known as Poole Park – a name which had been attached to it since the ship's launch, Morrow had heard. There was nothing very park-like about it now, though. Morrow, in no hurry to be early for Milpitas, walked slowly past rows of poor, shack-like dwellings and shops. The shops bore the names of their owners and their wares, but also crude, vivid paintings of the goods to be obtained inside. Here and there, between the walls of the shops, weeds and wild flowers struggled to survive. He passed a couple of maintenance 'bots: low-slung trolleys fitted with brushes and scoops, toiling their way down the worn streets.

The rows of small dwellings, the boxy shops and meeting-places, the libraries and factories, looked as they always did: not drab, exactly – each night everything was cleansed by the rain machines – but *uniform*.

Some old spark stirred in Morrow's tired mind. *Uniform. Yes, that was the word. Dreadfully uniform.* Now he was approaching the Planners' Temple. The tetrahedral pyramid was fully fifty yards high, built of gleaming metal and with its edges highlighted in blue. Morrow felt dwarfed as he approached it, and his steps slowed, involuntarily; in a world in which few buildings were taller than two storeys, the Temples were visible everywhere, huge, faceless – and *intimidating*.

As, no doubt, they were meant to be.

Planner Milpitas turned the bit of metal over and over in his long fingers, eyeing Morrow. His desk was bare, the walls without adornment. 'You ask too many questions, Morrow.' The Planner's bare scalp was stretched paper-thin over his skull and betrayed a faint tracery of scars.

Morrow tried to smile; already, as he entered the interview, he felt immensely tired. 'I always have.'

The Planner didn't smile. 'Yes. You always have. But my problem is that your questions sometimes disturb others.'

Morrow tried to keep himself from trembling. At the surface of his mind there was fear, and a sense of powerlessness – but beneath that there was an anger he knew he must struggle to control. Milpitas could, if he wished, make life very unpleasant for Morrow.

Milpitas held up the artefact. 'Tell me what this is.'

'It's a figure-of-eight ring.'

'Did you make it?'

Morrow shrugged. 'I don't know. Perhaps. It's a standard design in the shops on Deck Four.'

'All right.' Milpitas placed the ring on his desk, with a soft clink. 'Tell me what else you make. Give me a list.'

Morrow closed his eyes and thought. 'Parts for some of the machines – the food dispensers, for instance. Not the innards, of course – we leave that to the nanobots – but the major external components. Material for buildings – joists, pipes, cables. Spectacles, cutlery: simple things that the nanobot maintenance crews can't repair.'

Milpitas nodded. 'And?'

'And things like your figure-of-eight ring.' Morrow struggled, probably failing, to keep a note of frustration out of his voice. 'And ratchets, and stirrups. Scrapers –'

'All right. Now, Morrow, the value of a joist, or a pair of spectacles, is obvious. But what do you think of this question: what is the *value* of your figure-of-eight rings, ratchets and stirrups?'

Morrow hesitated. This was exactly the kind of question which had landed him in trouble in the first place. 'I don't know,' he blurted at last. 'Planner, it drives me crazy not to know. I look at these things and try to work out what they *might* be used for, but –'

The Planner raised his hands. 'You're not answering me, Morrow.'

Morrow was confused. He'd long since learned that when dealing with people like Milpitas, words turned into weapons, fine blades whose movements he could barely follow. 'But you asked me what the ratchets were for.'

'No. I asked you what you thought of the *question*, not for an answer to the question itself. That's very different.'

Morrow tried to work that out. 'I'm sorry. I don't understand.'

'No.' The Planner rested his long, surgery-scarred fingers on the desk before him. Milpitas seemed to be one of those unfortunate individuals suffering a partial AS failure, necessitating this kind of gross rework of his body. 'No, I really believe you don't. And that's precisely the problem, isn't it, Morrow?'

He stood and walked to the window of his office. From here Morrow could see the outer frame of the Temple; its face was a tilted plane of golden light. Milpitas' wide, bony face was framed by the iron sky, the sourceless daylight.

'The question has *no* value,' Milpitas said at length. 'And so an answer to it would have no value – it would be meaningless, because the question in itself has no reference to anything meaningful.' He turned to Morrow and smiled searchingly. 'I know you're not happy with that answer. Go ahead; don't be afraid. Tell me what you think.'

Morrow sighed. *I think you're crazy.* 'I think you're playing with words.' He picked up the ring. 'Of *course* this thing has a purpose. It exists, physically. We expend effort in making it –'

'Everything we do has a purpose, Morrow, and one purpose only.' Milpitas looked solemn. 'Do you know what that is?'

Morrow felt vaguely irritated. 'The survival of the species. I'm not a child, Planner.'

'Exactly. Good. That's why we're here; that's why Superet built this ship-world of ours; that's why my grandmother – dead now, of course – and the others initiated this voyage. That's the purpose that informs everything we do.'

Morrow's irritation turned into a vague rebelliousness. *Everything? Even the elimination of the children?*

He wondered how many interviews, like this, he had suffered over the years.

Vaguely he remembered a time when things hadn't been like this. Right at the start of his life, half a millennium ago, the great Virtual devices, hidden somewhere in the fabric of the world, had covered the drab hull walls with scenes of lost, beautiful panoramas: he remembered Virtual suns and moons crossing a Virtual sky, children running in the streets.

There had been a feeling of space – of *infinity*. The Virtuals had had the power to make this box-world seem immense, without constraints.

But Superet had closed down the Virtuals, one by one, exposing the skull-like reality of the world which lay beneath the illusion. No one now seemed to know where the Virtual machines were, or how to get access to them, even if they still worked.

At the same time Superet had first discouraged, then abolished, childbirth. Morrow had been one of the last children to be born, in fact.

Virtual dioramas – and the voices of children – were no longer necessary, Superet said.

There were no young, and the people grew *old*. There

110

was neither day nor night, but only the endless, steel-grey, sourceless light which – diffused from the metal hull – gave the impression of a continual dawn. Leisure activities – theatres, study groups, play groups – had fallen into disuse. The world was structured only by the endless drudgery of work.

Work, and study of the words of the founders of Superet, of course.

Milpitas turned his wide, rather coarse face to Morrow. 'Superet's one imperative is to ensure the survival of the species – physically, through our genes, and culturally, through the memes we carry – into the indefinite future.' He pointed to the iron sky. 'Everything we do is driven by that logic, Morrow. For all we know, we are the only humans alive, anywhere. And so we must optimize the use of our resources.

'At present we're succeeding. Our population is well-adjusted; we have no need of new generations – not until our resource situation changes.'

But, Morrow thought wildly, *but the population isn't stable*. Every year people died – through accident, or obscure AS-failure. So, every year, the population actually *fell*.

Over the centuries he had witnessed the steady drop in population, the slow retreat from the lower Decks. When Morrow had been born, he was sure that the lifedome had been inhabited all the way down to Deck Eight – and it was said there were another seven or eight Decks below that. Now, only Decks Two and Three were occupied.

Could there be a point, he wondered, below which the race couldn't regenerate itself, even if the temporary sterility was reversed?

What would Superet do then?

Milpitas sat down once more. When he spoke again, the Planner seemed to be trying to be kind. 'Morrow, you must not torment yourself – and those around you – with questions that can't be answered. You know, in principle, *why* our world is as it is. Isn't that sufficient? Is it really necessary for you to understand every detail?'

But if I don't understand, Morrow thought sourly, *then you can control me. Arbitrarily. And* that's *what I find hard to accept*.

Milpitas steepled his fingers. 'Here's another dimension you need to think about.' His voice was harsher now. 'Tell me, what

111

are your views on the internal contradictions of the meme versus gene duality?'

Morrow, glowering, refused to answer.

Milpitas smiled, exquisitely patronizing. 'You don't understand the question, do you? Can you read?'

'Yes, I can read,' Morrow said testily. 'I had to teach myself, but, yes, I can read.'

Milpitas frowned. 'But you don't *need* to be able to read. Most people don't need to. It's a luxury, Morrow; an indulgence.

'We must all accept our limitations, Morrow; *you have to accept* that there are people who know better than you do.'

Morrow steeled himself. *Here it comes.* No punishment was going to be terribly onerous, but he found any disruption from his daily routine increasingly difficult, even painful.

'Four weeks on Deck One,' Milpitas said briskly, making a note. 'I'll co-ordinate this with your supervisor in the shops. I'm sorry to do this, Morrow, but you must see my position; we can't have you disrupting those around you with your – your ill-disciplined thinking.'

Deck One. The Locks. One of the most difficult – if not frightening – places to work on all the Decks. This was a tough punishment, for what he still couldn't accept as a crime . . .

But, nevertheless, he found himself suppressing a grin at the irony of this. For the Locks – and the strange, illicit trade that went on through them – were an explicit embodiment of the contradictions within his society.

The first tendrils of morning light snaked up over the skydome like living things. The dim stars fled.

Arrow Maker unwrapped himself from his branch and stretched the stiffness out of his limbs. The breeze up here was fresh and dry. He urinated against the bole of the tree; the hot liquid darkened the wood and coursed down towards the canopy. He chewed on some of the meat from his belt, and lapped up dew moisture from the kapok's leaves. The water wasn't much, but he'd find more later, in the bowls of orchids and bromeliads.

He retrieved his bow and quiver, made his way to the rope he'd left dangling, and prepared for the first stage of his descent. He passed the rope through a metal figure-of-eight ring, clipped the ring to his belt, and stood up in his webbing stirrups. He slid easily downwards, controlling the run of the rope through the ring with his hand. The figure-of-eight ring, scuffed and worn with use, rang softly as he descended.

The canopy, fifty yards above the forest floor, was a twenty-yard-deep layer of vegetation. Arrow Maker was soon screened from the breeze of the topmost level, and the air grew moist, humid, comfortable.

He found a liana and cut it open; water spurted into his mouth. On his last visit to the canopy, Arrow Maker had spotted a fig-tree which had looked close to fruiting; he decided to take a detour there before returning to Uvarov. He wrapped his rope around his waist, tucked his climbing gear into his belt, and clambered across the canopy, working his way from branch to branch.

Moss and algae coated the bark of the trees and hung from twigs in sheets, making the wood dangerously slippery. Lianas, fig roots and the dangling roots of orchids, bromeliads and ferns festooned the branches like rope. Leaves shone in the gloom, like little green arrow-heads. Some of the flowers, designed to catch the attention of hummingbirds and sunbirds, gleamed red in the gloom; others, pale, fetid, waited patiently for bats to eat their fruit and so propagate their seeds.

Beyond the clutter of life, Maker could see the branchless trunks of the canopy trees. The trunks rose like columns of smoke through the greenery, smooth and massive.

The fig-tree was an incongruous tangle sprouting from the trunk of a canopy tree, a parasite feeding off its host tree. As he approached the fig he knew he'd been right about the fruiting. A parrot hung upside down from a branch, its feathers brilliant crimson, munching at a fig it held in one claw. The rich smell of ripe figs wafted from the leaves, and the branches were alive with animals and birds.

There was even a family of silver-leaf monkeys. Maker got quite close to one female, with a baby clinging to her back. For a few moments Maker watched her working at the fruit; she seemed to sniff each fig individually, as if trying to determine from the perfume if it was ready to consume. At last she found a fig to her liking and crammed it whole into her mouth, while her baby mewled at her neck.

The female suddenly became aware of Arrow Maker. Her small, perfect head swivelled towards him, her eyes round, and for an instant she froze, her gaze locked with Maker's. Then she turned and bounded away through rustling leaves, lost to his sight in a moment.

He worked his way towards the fig, shouting and clapping his hands to scare the scavengers away. He even roused a cluster of fruit bats, unusually feeding during the day; they scattered at his approach, their huge, loose, leathery wings rustling.

At length he reached the bough of the canopy tree, which was wrapped around with fig roots. This was actually a strangler fig, he realized; the crown of the fig was so dense that it was blocking out the light from its host and would eventually take its place in the canopy.

'Arrow Maker.'

His name was whispered, suddenly, close behind him. He turned, startled, and almost lost his grip on the algae-coated branch below him; his bow rattled against his bare back, clumsily.

It was Spinner-of-Rope. Her face was round in the gloom as she grinned at him. Spinner, his older daughter, was fifteen years old, and her short, slim body was as lithe as a monkey's. She bore a full sack at her back. A bright smear of scarlet dye crossed her face, picking out her eyes and nose like a mask; her hair was shaven back from her scalp and dangled in a fringe over her ears down to her shoulders, rich black. Her metal spectacles shone in the green light.

'Got you,' she said.

He tried to recover his dignity. 'That was irresponsible.'

She snorted and rubbed at her stub of a nose. 'Oh, sure. I saw you creeping up on that poor silver-leaf. With her baby, too.' Squatting in the branches, she moved towards him menacingly. 'Maybe I should climb on your back and see how you like it –'

'Don't bother.' He settled against the bough of the tree, pulled a fig from a branch and bit into it. 'What's in the sack?'

'Figs, and honeycombs, and a few tubers I dug up earlier from the floor ... I breakfasted on beetle grubs from inside a fallen trunk down there.' She looked remote for a moment as she remembered her meal. 'Delicious ... What are you doing here anyway? I thought you were down with old Uvarov.'

'I am. In principle. It's my turn ...'

The tribe's fifty people lived out most of their lives in the canopy. So Garry Uvarov had instituted a rota, designating folk who had to spend time with him on the floor below. Uvarov raged if the rota was broken, insisting that even the rota itself was older than any human alive, save himself.

'Uvarov sent me up top – to the giant kapok – to see if the stars had changed.'

Spinner grunted; she took a fig herself and ate it whole, like a monkey. She wiped her lips on a leaf. 'Why?'

'I don't know ...'

'Then he's an old fool. And so are you.'

Arrow Maker sighed. 'You shouldn't say things like that, Spinner. Uvarov is an old man – an ancient man. He remembers when the ship was launched, and –'

'I know, I know.' She picked seeds from her teeth with her little finger. 'But he's also a *crazy* old man, and getting crazier.'

Arrow Maker decided not to argue. 'But whether that's true or not, we still have to care for him. We can't let him die. Would you want that?' He searched her face, seeking signs of understanding. 'And if you – and your friends – don't take your turns in the rota –'

'Which we don't.'

'– then it means that people like me have to carry more than our fair share.'

Spinner-of-Rope grinned in triumph, her face paint vivid. 'So you admit you *resent* having to tend for that old relic down there.'

'Yes. *No.*' With a few words she'd made him intensely uncomfortable, as she seemed to manage so often, and so easily. 'Oh, I don't know, Spinner. But we can't let him die.'

She bit into another fig, and said casually, 'Why not?'

'Because he's a human being who deserves dignity, if nothing else,' he snapped. 'And –'

'And what?'

And, he thought, *I'm afraid that if Uvarov is allowed to die, the world will come to an end.*

The world was so obviously *artificial.*

The forest was contained in a box. It was possible to shoot an arrow against the sky. There were holes in the floor, and whole levels – the domain of the Undermen – underneath the world. Hidden machines brought light to the skydome each day, caused the rain to fall over the waiting leaves, and pumped the air around the canopy tops. Perhaps there were more subtle machines too, he speculated sometimes, which sustained the little closed world in other ways.

The world must seem huge to Spinner. But it had become small and fragile in Arrow Maker's eyes, and as he grew older he became increasingly aware of how dependent all the humans of the forest were on mechanisms that were ancient and inaccessible.

If the mechanisms failed, they would all die; to Arrow Maker it was as simple, and as unforgettable, as that.

Garry Uvarov was an old fool in a wheelchair, with no obvious influence on the mechanisms which kept them all alive. And yet, it seemed undoubtedly true that he was indeed as old as he claimed – that he was a thousand years old, as old as the ship itself – *that he remembered Earth.*

Uvarov was a link with the days of the ship's construction. Arrow Maker felt, with a deep, superstitious dread, that if Uvarov were to die – if that tangible link to the past were ever broken – then perhaps the ship itself would die, around them.

And then, how could they possibly survive?

He looked at his daughter, troubled, wondering if he would ever be able to explain this to her.

9

Lieserl roused – slowly, fitfully – from her long sleep.

She stirred, irritated; she peered around, blinking her Virtual eyes, trying to understand what had disturbed her. Motion of some kind?

Motion, in this million-degree soup?

Virtual arms folded against her chest, legs tucked beneath her, she floated slowly through the compressed plasma of the radiative zone. Around her, all but unnoticed, high-energy photons performed their complex, million-year dance as they worked their way out of the core towards the surface.

After all this time, she had drifted to within no more than a third of a Solar radius of the centre of the Sun itself.

She ran brief diagnostic checks over her remaining data stores. She found more damage, of course; more cumulative depredation by the unceasing hand of entropy. She wondered vaguely how much of her original processing and memory capacity she was left with by now. Ten per cent? Less, perhaps?

How would she *feel*, if she roused herself to full awareness now? She'd never used her full capacity anyway – there was immense redundancy built into the systems – but she would surely be aware of some loss: gaps in her memory, perhaps, or a degradation of her sense of her Virtual body – a numbness, imperfectly realized skin.

Lieserl, she told herself, *you're getting old, all over again. The first human in history to grow old for the second time.*

Another first, for the freak lady.

She smiled and snuggled her face closer to her knees. Once, her depth of self-awareness and her ability to access huge memory stores had made her the most conscious human – or quasi-human, anyway – in history. So she'd been told.

117

Well, that couldn't be true any more.

Always assuming there were still humans left to compare herself against, of course.

Plasma still poured through the faces of the Interface which cradled her ancient, battered data stores; somewhere beyond the Sun, the energy dumped through the refrigerating wormhole must still blaze like a miniature star, perhaps casting its shadows across the photosphere. She knew the wormhole refrigerating link must be operating still, and that the various enhancements the engineers had made to it, as she'd gone far beyond her design envelope in her quest deeper into the Sun, must still be working. After a fashion, anyway.

She knew all that, because if the link wasn't working, she would be dead.

It was even conceivable that there were still people at the other end of the wormhole, getting useful data out of the link. In fact, she vaguely hoped so, in spite of everything. That had been the point of this expedition in the first place, after all. Just because they no longer chose to speak to her didn't mean they weren't *there*.

Anyway, it scarcely mattered; she'd no intention of waking out of the drowsy half-sleep within which she had whiled away the years – and centuries, and millennia . . .

But there was that hint of motion again. Something elusive, transient –

It was no more than a shadow, streaking across the rim of her sensorium, barely visible even to her enhanced senses. She tried to turn, to track the elusive ghost; but she was stiff, clumsy, her 'limbs' rusty from centuries of abandonment.

The fizzing shadow arced across her vision again, surging along a straight line and out of her sight.

Working with unaccustomed haste, she initiated self-repair routines throughout her system. She analysed what she'd seen, decomposing the compound image presented to her visually into its underlying component forms.

She felt dimly excited. If she'd been human still, she knew, her heart would be beating faster, and a surge of adrenaline would make her skin tighten, her breathing speed up, her senses become more vivid. For the first time in historic ages she felt impatience with the cocoon of shut-down Virtual senses which swaddled her; it was as if the machinery stopped her from *feeling* ...

She considered the results of her analysis. The image scarcely existed; no wonder it had looked like a ghost to her. It was no more than a faint shadow against the flood of neutrinos from the Solar core, a vague coherence among scintillas of interaction with the slow-moving protons of the plasma ...

The shadow she'd seen had been a structure of dark matter. A thing of photinos, orbiting the heart of the Sun.

She felt jubilant. *At last* – and just at the depth, a third of a Solar radius out from the centre, that she and Kevan had deduced it would be all those years ago, she'd found what she'd come here for – the prize for which her humanity had been engineered away. At last she'd penetrated to the edge of the Sun's dark matter shadow core, to the near-invisible canker which was smothering its fusion fire.

She waited for the photino object to return.

Arrow Maker slid towards the ground.

He passed through another layer of leaves: this was the forest's understorey, made up of darkness-adapted palms and a few saplings, young trees growing from seeds dropped by the canopy trees. The light at this level – even now, at midday – was dim, drenched in the green of the canopy. The air was hot, stagnant, moist.

Arrow Maker reached the ground, close to the base of a huge tree. Under one of his bare soles, a beetle wriggled, working its way through decaying leaf matter. Arrow Maker reached down, absently, picked up the beetle and popped it into his mouth.

He hauled his rope down from the tree and set off across the forest floor.

Beneath the thin soil he could feel the tree's thick mat of rootlets. The trees were supported by immense buttresses: triangular fins, five yards wide at their base, which sprouted from the clustering trunks. A thin line of termites – a ribbon hundreds of yards long – marched steadily across the floor close to his feet, on their way to the tree trunk cleft that housed their nest.

He passed splashes of colour amid the corruption of the forest floor – mostly dead flowers, fallen from the canopy – but there was also one huge rafflesia: a single flower a yard across, leafless, its maroon petals thick, leathery and coated with warts. A revolting stench of putrescence came from its interior, and flies, mesmerized by the scent, swarmed around the vast cup.

Arrow Maker, preoccupied, walked around the grotesque bloom.

'... Where in Lethe have you been?'

Uvarov's chair came rolling towards Maker, out of the shadows of his shelter.

Maker, startled, stumbled backwards. 'I stopped to gather figs. They were ripe. I met my daughter – Spinner-of-Rope – and –'

Garry Uvarov was ignoring him. Uvarov rolled his chair back into the shelter, its wheels heavy on the soft forest floor. 'Tell me about the stars you saw,' he hissed. 'The *stars* ... '

Uvarov's shelter was little more than a roof of ropes and palm leaves, a web suspended between a cluster of tree trunks. Beneath this roof the jungle floor had been cleared and floored over with crudely cut planks of wood, over which Uvarov could prowl, the wheels of his chair humming as they bore him to and fro, to and fro. There were resin torches fixed to the walls, unlit. Uvarov kept his few possessions here, most of them incomprehensible to Arrow Maker: boxes fronted by discs of glass, bookslates worn yellow and faded with use, cupboards, chairs and a bed into which Uvarov could no longer climb.

None of this had ever worked in Arrow Maker's lifetime.

Garry Uvarov was swaddled in a leather blanket, which hid his useless limbs. His head – huge, skull-like, fringed by sky-white hair and with eyes hollowed out by corruption – lolled on a neck grown too weak to support it. If Uvarov could stand, he'd be taller than Arrow Maker by three feet. But, sprawled in his chair as he was, Uvarov looked like some grotesque doll, a crude thing constructed of rags and the skull of some animal, perhaps a monkey.

Maker studied Uvarov uneasily. The old man had never exactly been rational, but today there seemed to be an additional edge to his voice – perhaps a knife-edge of real madness, at last.

And if that was true, how was he – Arrow Maker – going to deal with it?

'Do you want anything? I'll get you some –'

Uvarov lifted his head. 'Just tell me, damn you ...' His leaf-like cheeks shook and spittle flecked his chin, signifying rage. But his voice – reconstructed by some machine generations ago – was a bland, inhuman whisper.

'I climbed the kapok – the tallest tree ...' Arrow Maker, stumbling, tried to describe what he'd seen.

Uvarov listened, his head cocked back, his mouth lolling.

'*The starbow*,' he said at last. 'Did you see the starbow?'

Arrow Maker shook his head. 'I've never seen a starbow. Tell me what it looks like.'

Rage seemed to have enveloped Uvarov now; his chair rolled back and forth, back and forth, clattering over loose floorboards. 'I knew it! No starbow ... The ship's slowing. We've arrived. I knew it ...

'They've tried to exclude me. Those survivalist bastard Planners, and maybe even that wizened bitch Armonk. If she's still alive.' He wheeled about, trying to point himself at Arrow Maker. 'Don't you see it? If there's no starbow *the ship must have arrived*. The journey is over ... After a thousand years, we've returned to Sol.'

'But you're not making sense,' Arrow Maker protested weakly. 'There's never been a starbow. I don't know what –'

'The bastards ... The bastards.' Uvarov continued his endless rolling. 'We've returned, to fulfil our mission – *Superet*'s mission, not Louise Ye bloody Armonk's! – and they want to shut me out. You, too, my children ... My immortal children.

'Listen to me.' Uvarov wheeled about to face Maker again. 'You must hear me; it's very important. You're the future, Arrow Maker ... You, poor, ignorant as you are: *you* and your people are the future of the species.'

He wheeled to the lip of his flooring, now, and lifted his head to Arrow Maker. Maker could see pools of congealed blood at the pits of those empty eye sockets, and he recoiled from the heavy, fetid stink of the decaying body under its blanket. 'You'll not be betrayed by your damn AS nanobots the way I was. When the 'bots withered my limbs and chopped up my damn eyes, five centuries ago, I saw I'd been right all along ...

'But now we've come home. The mission is over. That's what the stars are telling you, if you only had eyes to see.

'I want you to gather the people. Get weapons – bows, blowpipes – anything you can find.'

'Why?'

'Because you're going to go back into the Decks. For the first time in centuries. You have to reach the Interface. *The wormhole Interface*, Maker.'

The Decks ...

Arrow Maker tried to envisage going *through* the Locks in the forest floor, entering the unknown darkness of the endless levels beneath his feet. Panic rose, sharp and painful in his throat.

Maker stumbled away from the little hut, and back into the familiar scents of the jungle. He raised his face to the canopy above, and the glowing sky beyond.

Could Uvarov be right? Was the thousand-year journey over – at last?

Suddenly Arrow Maker's world seemed tiny, fragile, a mote adrift among impossible dangers. He longed to return to the canopy, to lose himself in the thick, moist air, in the scent of growing things.

'Milpitas was right,' Constancy-of-Purpose said. 'Your trouble is you think too much, Morrow.' Her big voice boomed out, echoing from the bare metal walls of Deck One; Constancy-of-Purpose seemed oblivious of the huge emptiness around them – the desolate dwellings, the endless, shadowed places of this uninhabited place.

Constancy-of-Purpose opened up a Lock. The Lock was a simple cylinder which rose from the floor and merged seamlessly with the ceiling, a hundred yards above their heads. Constancy-of-Purpose had opened a door in the Lock's side, but there was also (Morrow had noticed) a hatch inside the cylinder twenty feet above them, blocking off the cylinder's upper section.

All the Locks were alike. But Morrow had never seen an upper hatch opened, and knew no one who had.

Today, this Lock contained a pile of pineapples, plump and ripe, and a few flagons of copafeira sap. Morrow held open a bag, and Constancy-of-Purpose started methodically to shovel the fruit out of the Lock and into the bag, her huge biceps working. 'You have to accept things as they are,' she went on. 'Our way of life here hasn't changed for centuries – you have to admit that. So the Planners must be doing *something* right. Why not give them the benefit of the doubt?'

Constancy-of-Purpose was a big, burly woman who habitually wore sleeveless tunics, leaving the huge muscles of her arms exposed. Her face, too, was strong, broad and patient, habitually placid beneath her shaven scalp. The lower half of her body, by contrast, was wasted, spindly, giving her a strangely unbalanced look.

Morrow said to Constancy-of-Purpose, 'You always talk to me as if I were still a child.' As, in Constancy-of-Purpose's eyes, he probably always would be. Constancy-of-Purpose was twenty years older than Morrow, and she had always assumed the role of older mentor – even now, after five centuries of life, when a mere couple of decades could go by barely noticed. The fact that they'd once been married, for a few decades, had made no long-term difference to their relationship at all. 'Look, Constancy-of-Purpose, so much of our little world just doesn't make sense. And it drives me crazy to think about it.'

Constancy-of-Purpose straightened up and rested her fists on her hips; her face gleamed with sweat. 'No, it doesn't.'

'What?'

'It *doesn't* drive you crazy. Nobody as old as you – or me – is capable of being driven crazy by anything. We don't have the energy to be mad any more, Morrow.'

Morrow sighed. 'All right. But it *ought* to drive me crazy. And you. There's so much that is simply – *unsaid*.' He hoisted the half-full sack of fruit. 'Look at the work we're doing now, even. This simply isn't *logical*.'

'Logical enough. Copafeira sap is a useful fuel. And we need the fruit to supplement the supply machines, which haven't worked properly since –'

'Yes,' Morrow said, exasperated, 'but where does the fruit *come* from? Who brings it here, to these Locks? And –'

'And what?'

'And what do they want with the ratchets, and knives, and figure-of-eight rings we bring *them*?'

Morrow picked up the sap flagons, and Constancy-of-Purpose slung the fruit bag over her shoulder. They began the hundred-yard walk to the next Lock. Constancy-of-Purpose moved with an uneven, almost waddling motion, her stick-like legs seeming almost too weak to support the massive bulk of her upper body. Some obscure nanobot failure had left her legs shrivelled, spindly and – Morrow suspected, though Constancy-of-Purpose never complained – arthritic.

'I don't know,' said Constancy-of-Purpose simply. 'And I don't think about it.' She looked sideways at Morrow.

'But it doesn't make *sense*.' Morrow looked up, nervously, at the bulkhead above him. 'This fruit must come from *somewhere*. There must be *people* up there, Constancy-of-Purpose – people we've never seen, whose existence has never been acknowledged by the Planners, or –'

'People whose existence doesn't matter a damn, then.'

'But it *does*. We *trade* with them.' He stopped and held out his sack of fruit. 'Look at this. We've carried on this trade with them – thereby implicitly acknowledging their existence – for decades now.'

Constancy-of-Purpose kept walking, painfully. 'Centuries, actually.'

When he was a young man, Morrow had been angry just about the whole time, he recalled. Now – even now – he felt a ghostly surge of that old anger. He felt obscurely proud of himself: a feeling of anger was as rare an event as achieving an erection, these days. 'But that means our society is, at its core, slightly insane.'

Constancy-of-Purpose shook her massive head and studied Morrow, a tolerant look on her face. 'Keep up that talk, and you'll spend the rest of your life up here. Or somewhere worse.'

'Just think about it,' Morrow said. 'A whole society, labouring under a mass delusion ... No wonder they shut down the Virtuals. No wonder they banned *kids*.'

'But we're all kept fed. Aren't we? So it can't be that crazy.' She smiled, her broad face assuming a look of wisdom. 'Humans are a very flawed species, Morrow. We simply don't seem to be able to act rationally, for very long. This sort of thing – a trade with the nonexistent unknowns upstairs – seems a minor aberration to me.'

Morrow studied her curiously. 'You believe that? And I think of *me* as sceptical.'

Constancy-of-Purpose had reached the next Lock; she dropped her sack and leant against the curving metal wall, her hands resting on her knees. 'You know, we have this conversation every few years, my friend.'

Morrow frowned. 'Really? Do we?'

'Of course.' Constancy-of-Purpose smiled. 'At our age, even *doubting* becomes a habit. And we never come to any conclusion, and the world goes on. Just as it always has.' She straightened up, cautiously flexing her thin legs. 'Come on. Let's get on with our work.'

With a twist of her huge upper arms Constancy-of-Purpose hauled open the door of the Lock.

Then – instead of stepping forward to gather the foodstuffs – she frowned, and looked at Morrow uncertainly. '...I don't understand.'

'What is it?'

'Look.'

The Lock was *empty*.

Morrow stared at Constancy-of-Purpose, and then into the empty chamber. He couldn't take in what he was seeing. These trades had *never* gone wrong before.

'The knives have gone,' he said.

'We left them here yesterday.'

'But there's no meat.'

'But the scratches clearly said the knives were what they wanted ...'

This dialogue went on for perhaps five minutes. Part of Morrow was able to step outside – to look at himself and Constancy-of-Purpose with a certain detachment, even with pity. Here were two old people, too hopelessly habit-bound to respond to the unexpected.

Constancy-of-Purpose is right. I've become like a machine, he thought with anger and sadness. *Worse than a machine.*

Constancy-of-Purpose said, 'I'll go in and check the markings. Maybe we made some mistake.'

'We never made a mistake before. How could we?'

'I'll go check anyway.'

Constancy-of-Purpose stepped forward into the Lock and peered up, squinting, at the trade markings.

... And the hatch at the top of the Lock, twenty feet above

Constancy-of-Purpose's head, *started to open.*

Inside the plasma sea, time held little meaning for Lieserl.

As she sank into the Sun she'd abandoned all her Virtual senses, save for sight and a residual body awareness; drifting through the billowing, cloudy plasma was like a childhood vision of sleep, or an endless, oceanic meditation. She'd slowed the clocks which governed her awareness, and allowed herself to slip into long periods of true 'sleep' – of unawareness, when she drifted with only her autonomic systems patiently functioning.

And she had allowed, without regret, the crucial link of synchronization between her sensorium and the Universe outside to be severed. While she had drifted around the core of the Sun, sinking almost imperceptibly deeper into its heart, dozens of centuries had worn away on the worlds of mankind . . .

Here came the photino structure again.

This time she was ready. She strained at the structure as it passed her, every sense open.

Still, she could barely make it out; it was like a crude charcoal sketch against the glowing plasma background.

Wistfully she watched the photino cloud soar out of sight once more, passing through the plasma as if it were no more substantial than mist, on its minutes-long orbit around the Sun.

But –

But, had it *diverged* from its orbit as it passed her? Was it possible that the photino object had actually reacted to her presence?

Now she became aware of more motion, below and ahead of her. The moving forms were shadowy, infuriatingly elusive against the gleaming, almost featureless background. Frustrated, she strained at her senses, demanding that her aged processors extract every last bit of information content from the data they were receiving.

Slowly the images enhanced, gaining in definition and sharpness.

There were hundreds – no: thousands, *millions* – of the photino traces. Maybe they were standing-wave patterns, she wondered, traces of coherence on the dark matter cloud.

Slowly she built up an image in her head, a composite model of the patterns: a roughly lenticular form, with length of

126

perhaps fifty yards – and, she realized slowly, some hints of an internal structure.

Internal structure?

Well, so much for the standing-wave theory. These things seemed to be discrete *objects*, not merely patterns of coherence in a continuum.

She watched the objects as they traced their orbits around the centre of the Sun. The soaring lens-shapes reminded her of graphics of the contents of a blood stream; she wondered if the structures were indeed like antibodies, or thrombocytes – blood platelets, swarming in search of a wound. They swarmed over and past each other, miraculously never colliding –

No, she realized slowly. There was nothing *miraculous* about it. The objects were *steering* away from each other, as they soared through their orbits.

This was a flock. The dark matter structures were *alive*.

Alive and purposeful.

Slowly she drifted into the flock of photino birds (as she'd tentatively labelled them). They swooped around her, avoiding her gracefully.

They were clearly reacting to her presence. They were obviously *aware* – if not intelligent, she thought.

She wondered what to do next. She wished she had Kevan Scholes to talk to about this.

Sweet, patient Kevan had come to the Sun as a junior research associate; his tour of duty had been meant to be only a few years. But he'd stayed on much longer in near-Solar orbit to serve as her patient capcom, far beyond the call of duty or friendship. In the end her long-distance relationship with Scholes had lasted decades.

Well, she'd been grateful for his loyalty. He'd helped her immeasurably through those first difficult years inside the Sun.

Fitfully, she tried to remember the last time he spoke to her.

In the end he'd simply been removed. Why? To serve some organizational, political, cultural change? She'd never been told.

She had come to learn, with time, that human organizations – even if staffed by AS-preserved semi-immortals – had a half-life

127

of only a few decades. Those that survived longer persisted only as shells, usually transmuted far from the aims of their founders. She thought of the slow corruption of the Holy Superet Light Church, apparent even in her own brief time outside the Sun, into a core organization of fanatics huddled around some eternal flame of ancient belief.

A succession of capcoms had taken their places at the microphones at the other end of her wormhole link. She'd been shown their faces, by images dumped through the telemetry channels. So she knew what they looked like, that parade of ever more odd-looking men and women with their evanescent fashions and styles and their increasing remoteness of expression. Language evolution and other cultural changes were downloaded into her data stores, so the drift of the human worlds away from the time she'd grown up in (however briefly) didn't cause her communication problems. But none of it *engaged* her. After Kevan Scholes she found little interest in, or empathy with, the succession of firefly people who communicated with her.

Sometimes she had wondered how she must seem to *them* – a cranky, antique quasi-human trapped inside a piece of rickety old technology.

Then, at last, they had stopped talking to her altogether.

Oddly, though, she still felt – in spite of everything – *loyal* to humanity. They'd manufactured her quite cynically for their own purposes and finally abandoned her here, in the heart of this alien world; and yet she couldn't cut herself off from people, in her mind. After all, whether they would speak to her or not, her wormhole refrigeration link could easily have been closed down – her consciousness terminated – as trivially as turning out a light. But that hadn't happened.

So, she thought resentfully, they hadn't bothered to kill her off. For this did she owe them loyalty? She tried to be cynical. Should she have to bow and scrape, just for the favour of her continuing life?

But, despite her determination to be tough-minded, she found she retained a residual urge to *communicate* – to broadcast her news beyond the Sun, to tell all she had found out about the photino birds – just in case anyone was listening.

It wasn't logical. And yet, she did care; it was a nagging sense of responsibility – even of duty – that she simply couldn't flush out of her consciousness.

After a time, in fact, she had begun to grow suspicious of this very persistence. After all, she had represented quite an investment, for the Superet of her time. Her brief had been to find out what was happening to the Sun, and she could only fulfil her brief, clearly, if she reported back to *somebody*. So maybe the need to communicate, even with non-receptive listeners, had been deeply embedded into the programming of the systems which underlay her awareness. Perhaps it was even hard-wired into the physical systems.

After all this time, they're still manipulating me, she thought sourly.

But even if that were true, there wasn't much she could do about it; the result was, though, that she was left with an irritating itch – and no way to scratch it.

Morrow simply stared. He didn't feel fear, or curiosity. The upper hatch had never opened before. And – even though his eyes told him otherwise – it couldn't be happening now.

Beyond the hatch was a tunnel, rising upwards – the tunnel was the inside of the cylindrical Lock, he realized. The light from above the hatch was dim, greenish. The air from the cylinder felt hot, humid, laden with secret, fruit-like scents.

He tried to find some appropriate response, to formulate some plan; but this new event skittered across the habit-worn surface of his mind like mercury across glass, unable to penetrate. He could only watch the events unfold, one after the other, as if he had been reduced to the state of a child, unable to connect incidents in any causal sequence.

Constancy-of-Purpose, too, seemed to be having trouble accepting any of this. She stood in the Lock with her head tipped back, gazing up, mouth slack . . .

Then there was a hissing noise, a soft, moist impact.

Constancy-of-Purpose clutched her arm.

She looked at Morrow with blank incomprehension – and then it was as if her wizened legs had failed her at last, for they crumpled, slowly, bearing her down to the floor of the Lock. For a few seconds she sat, her legs folded awkwardly under her. She looked surprised, confused. Then the great torso toppled sideways, sending the legs sprawling.

At last Morrow was able to move. He rushed into the Lock and, with effort, hauled Constancy-of-Purpose upright. Constancy-of-Purpose's eyes were open but only the whites were showing; spittle drooled from her mouth. Her skin felt moist, cold. Morrow searched frantically for a pulse at Constancy-of-Purpose's wrist, then amid the massive tendons of her neck.

A rope curled down from the hatch above, fraying, brown. Someone – *something* – descended, hand-over-hand, dropping lightly to the floor.

Morrow tried to study the invader, but it was as if he couldn't even *see* him – or her. This was simply too strange, too shocking; his eyes seemed to slide away from the invader, as if refusing to accept its reality.

Cradling Constancy-of-Purpose in his arms, he forced himself to take this one step at a time. First of all: *human*, certainly. He stared at four limbs, startlingly bright eyes behind spectacles, white teeth. Very short, no more than four feet tall. A child, then? Perhaps – but with the form, the breasts and hips, of a woman. And clothed in some suit of brown, with colourful flashes; dungarees, perhaps, which –

No. He forced himself to *see*. Save for a belt at the waist, bulging with pockets, this person was *naked*. Her skin was a rich brown. Her head was shaven at the scalp, but sported a fringe of thick, black, oiled hair. A mask of red paint sliced across her nose and eyes. She was carrying a long, fine-bored tube of wood. Her face was round – not pretty, but ...

But *young*. She couldn't be more than fifteen or sixteen years old.

But it wasn't possible to AS-preserve at that age. So this was a *child* – a genuine child; the first he'd seen in five centuries.

She raised the tube warily, as if preparing to strike him, or fend him off.

'My name is Spinner-of-Rope,' she said. 'I won't hurt you.'

The old Underman was *grotesque*. Nearly as bad as Uvarov: bald, skinny, faded skin, dressed in some kind of stuffy, drab garment – and as tall as Uvarov would be, if he was laid out lengthways.

The Underman's unconscious friend, the woman, was worse, with that huge upper body and spindly legs. The pair of them looked so *old*, so unnatural.

She felt revolted. There was an air of corruption about these people: of decay, of mould. She wanted to destroy them, get away, back to the clean air of the forest –

'What's happening?' Maker's voice came booming down the Lock shaft. 'Spinner? Are you all right?'

She forced herself to put aside her emotions, to *think*. This tall old man was disgusting. But he was clearly no threat.

'Yes,' she called up the shaft. 'I'm fine, Arrow Maker. Come down.'

She waited in silence for the few minutes it took her father – grunting, clumsy – to work his way down the rope from the forest floor. At last he dropped the last few feet to the Deck; he landed at a crouch, with his knife in one hand.

He was startled to find the two Underpeople there, but he seemed to take in the situation quickly. 'Is she dead? Are you all right?'

'No, and yes.' She held up her blowpipe, apologetically. 'I used this. Now, I don't think I needed to. I –'

'It doesn't matter.'

The old Underman's eyes were pale blue and watery; he seemed to be having trouble focusing on them. He pointed at the blowpipe. 'You killed Constancy-of-Purpose ... with that?' His accent was strange, lilting, but quite comprehensible.

Spinner hesitated. 'No ...' She held out the pipe to him, but the Underman didn't take it; he simply sat cradling his friend. 'The pipe is bamboo. You give the darts an airtight seal inside the pipe with seed fibres. You get the poison from frogs, roasted on a spit, and —'

'We're sorry about your friend,' Arrow Maker said. 'She will recover. And it was – unnecessary.'

The Underman looked defiant. 'Yes,' he said. 'Yes, it damn well was.' He looked from one to the other. 'What do you want?'

Spinner and her father looked at each other, uncertainly. At length Arrow Maker said, 'We've an old man. Uvarov. He says he remembers Earth. And he says that the journey's over – that the starship has arrived at its destination. And now we must travel to the Interface.' Maker looked at the Underman, hesitant, baffled. 'Will you help us? Will you lead us to the Interface?' Then his expression hardened. 'Or must we fight our way past you, as Uvarov predicts?'

The Underman stared at Maker. Somehow, Spinner thought, he seemed to be emerging from his paralysis and confusion. '*Uvarov – Interface –* I've no idea what you're talking about . . .'

Then, unexpectedly, he said wonderingly, 'But I've heard of Earth.'

The three of them stood in the cold light of the Lock, studying each other with fearful curiosity.

She descended deeper into the Sun, through the core-smothering flock of photino birds. The birds soared past and around her, tiny planets of dark matter racing through their tight Solar orbits.

The birds continually nudged towards or away from each other, like a horde of satellites manoeuvring for docking. Many of the transient clusters which they formed – and swept by her, too fast to study properly – seemed immensely complex, and she stored away a succession of images. There had to be a *reason* for all this activity, she thought.

Some of the motion, on the fringe of the spherical flock, was simpler in pattern and easier to interpret.

Individual photino birds sailed in from beyond the flock, sweeping through the outer layers of the Sun on hyperbolic paths, and settled into the swarm of their orbiting cousins. Occasionally a bird would break away from the rest, and go soaring off on open trajectories to –

To where? Back to some diffuse ocean of dark matter beyond the Sun? Or to some other star?

And if so, why?

Patiently she watched the birds coming and going from their flock, letting the patterns build up in her head.

10

The hatch at the top of the Lock was jammed open, revealing a circle of luxuriant greenery. It was a window to another world. The howls of a troupe of some unimaginable animals echoed down into the metal caverns of Deck One.

Morrow stood at the base of the Lock shaft, trying to suppress the urge to *run*, to bury himself again in the routine rhythms of his everyday life.

Squatting around the rim of the upper hatch, peering down at Morrow, were four or five of the forest folk. They were all naked, their bare, smooth skins adorned with splashes of fruit-dye colour, and they seemed impossibly young. Between them they were supporting a cradle of rope, and suspended in the cradle – descending slowly, shakily as the forest folk paid out lengths of rope – was Garry Uvarov.

The head of the extraordinary ancient protruded from a mass of thick blankets. Through the blankets Morrow could make out the chunky, mechanical box-shape of the mobile chair which sustained Uvarov, so that Uvarov looked nearly inhuman – as if he had been merged with his chair, a bizarre, wizened cyborg.

The girl with the spectacles – *Spinner-of-Rope* – came to stand beside Morrow, at the bottom of the shaft. She wore a loose necklace of orchid-petals, and little else. Her head was at a level with Morrow's elbow, and – now that he was growing used to her – her fierce crimson face paint looked almost comical. She touched his arm; her hand was delicate, small, impossibly light. 'Don't be afraid,' she said.

He was startled. 'I'm not afraid. What is there to be afraid of? Why do you think I'm afraid? If I was afraid, would I be here helping you?'

'It's the way you look. The way you're standing.' She shrugged her bare shoulders. 'Everything. Uvarov looks like – I don't know; some huge larva – but he's just a human. A very old human.'

'Actually I was thinking he looks like a kind of god. A half-human, half-mechanical god. With you people as his attendants.'

She wrinkled her small nose and pushed her spectacles further up her face, smudging the paint on her cheeks; glaring up at him, she looked irritated. 'Really. Well, we aren't superstitious savages. As you Undermen think we are. Don't you?'

'No, I –'

'We know Uvarov is no god. He's just a man – although a very ancient, strange and special man; a man who seems to remember what this ship was actually *for*.

'Morrow, I live in a tree and make things out of wood, and vine. You live –' she waved a hand vaguely '– in some boxy house somewhere, and make things out of metal and glass. But that's the only difference between us. My people aren't primitives, and we aren't ignorant. We *know* that we're all living inside a huge starship. Maybe we understand that better than you do, since we can actually see the sky.'

But that's not the point. You and I are different, he thought, exasperated. *More different than you can understand*.

Spinner-of-Rope was a fifteen-year-old girl – lively, inquisitive, fearless, disrespectful. It had been five centuries since Morrow had been fifteen. Even then, he would have found Spinner a handful. Morrow suspected, wistfully, that Spinner was more alien to him than Garry Uvarov.

One of the forest folk walked up to them. Through a sparse mask of face paint the man smiled up at Morrow. 'Is she giving you a hard time?'

Spinner snorted resentfully.

Morrow stared down at the newcomer, trying to place him. *Damn it, all these little men look the same* – He remembered; this was Arrow Maker, Spinner's father. He made an effort to smile back. 'No, no. Actually I think she was trying to comfort me. She was explaining I shouldn't be frightened of old Uvarov.'

Uvarov's chair bumped down on the surface of Deck One. Tree people clustered around Uvarov, loosening the ropes around the chair; the ropes were pulled back up through the hatch above them, snaking up like living things. Uvarov's sightless eye sockets opened, and he growled instructions to his attendants.

Arrow Maker was watching Morrow's face. 'And *do* you fear Uvarov?'

Morrow became aware that he was pulling at his fingers, his motions tense, stabbing; he tried to be still. 'No. Believe me, in my world, there are many AS-failure cases just as – ah, startling – as Uvarov. Though perhaps no one quite so *old*.'

Spinner-of-Rope approached them. 'Uvarov's ready. So unless you want to stand here talking all day, I think we should get on ... '

The little party formed up on Deck One. Morrow led the way, at a slow walking pace. Uvarov in his chair followed him, the chair's hidden motor whirring noisily. Arrow Maker and Spinner flanked the chair, guiding the sightless Uvarov with gentle, wordless touches on his shoulder.

As the forest folk walked across the Deck, their feet padded softly on the worn metal; they left behind a trail of marks, imprints of forest dirt and sweat. Arrow Maker wore a bow and quiver, slung over his shoulder, and Spinner's blowpipe dangled at her waist, obscure and deadly. Their bare, painted flesh made splashes of extraordinary colour against the drab grey-brown shades of the Decks. Their eyes, peering through bright masks of paint, were wide with alert suspicion and wariness, an effect hardly softened by Spinner's eye-glasses.

Morrow had managed to arrange an interview with Planner Milpitas. He had decided to restrict this venture into the interior of the Decks – this first mixture of cultures in centuries of the ship's two worlds – to just these three. He didn't want to expose the society of the Decks to any more cultural stress than he had to.

They moved away from the open Lock, with its last glimpse of the forest, and entered the metal-walled environment typical of the Decks. Spinner's gait, at first confident, became more hesitant; she seemed to lose some of her brashness, and turned pale under her face paint.

Morrow felt a certain relish. 'What's the matter with you? Nervous?'

She looked at him defiantly, swallowing hard. 'Shouldn't I be? Aren't you?'

Arrow Maker began, 'Spinner –'

'But it's not that.' She wrinkled up her round face, making her glasses slip on her nose. 'It's the *stench*. It's everywhere. Oppressive, stale ... Can't you smell it?'

Morrow raised his face, vaguely alarmed. Even old Uvarov, blind, trapped in his chair, turned his face, dragging air through his ruin of a nose.

Morrow said, 'I don't understand ...'

'Spinner.' Arrow Maker's voice was patient. 'I don't think there's anything wrong. That's just – *people*. People, and metal, and machinery. It's a different world down here; we'll have to learn to accept it.'

Spinner looked briefly horrified. 'Well, it's disgusting. They should do something about it.'

Morrow felt exasperated and amused. 'Do something? Like what?'

'Like plant a few trees.' Defiantly, she lifted the orchid garland around her neck and pressed it against her face, ostentatiously breathing in the petals' scent.

Arrow Maker walked beside Morrow. 'She does not mean to give offence,' he said seriously.

Morrow sighed. 'Don't worry about that. But ... I'm an old man, Arrow Maker. Older than you can understand, perhaps.' He glanced sideways at the little man from the forest. Arrow Maker looked competent, practical – and his four-feet-tall body, his bare feet and his painted face were utterly out of place in the sterile surroundings of Deck One. 'I'm a bit more restless than most people down here. And I've had enough trouble over that. But, even so, I'm *old*. I can't help but fear *change* – unpredictability – more than anything else. You people represent an enormous irruption into the Decks – almost an invasion. My life will never be the same. And that's uncomfortable.'

Arrow Maker slowed. 'Will you help us?' he asked levelly. 'You said –'

'Yes, I'll help you. I won't lose my nerve, Arrow Maker; I'll keep my word. I've been aware for a long time that the way things are run, down here, isn't *logical*. Maybe, by helping you – by helping Uvarov – I'll be able to make sense of a little more of it. Or maybe not.' *At least*, he thought, *now I understand what all those ratchets and loops of metal I've been making for so many decades are actually for.* He grinned and ran a hand over his shaven head. 'But I don't quite know what's going to come out of this. You're so – *different*.'

Arrow Maker smiled. 'Then being fearful – cautious, at least – is the only rational response.'

'Unless you're fifteen years old.'

'I heard that.' Spinner rejoined them; she punched Morrow, lightly, in the ribs; her small, hard fist sank into layers of body-fat, and he tried not to react to the sudden, small pain.

They descended a ramp, and passed down from Deck One and onto Deck Two, the first of the inhabited levels.

Morrow tried to see his world through the fresh eyes of the forest people. The drab, stained surfaces of the bulkheads above and below, the distant, slightly mist-shrouded, hull walls, all provided a frame around the world – regular, ordered, enclosed. Immense banners of green copper-stain disfigured one hull wall. Stair-ramps threaded between the Decks like hundred-yard-long traceries of spider-webs, and the elevator shafts were vertical pillars which pierced the levels, apparently supporting the metal sky. The rigid circular-geometry layout of Deck Two was easy to discern. Buildings – homes, factories, the Planners' Temples – clustered obediently in the Deck's neat sectors and segments.

Morrow felt embarrassed, obscurely depressed. His world was unimaginative, constricting – like the interior of some huge machine, he thought. And a battered, failing, ageing machine at that.

They set off down a chord-way which ran directly to Milpitas' Temple.

A woman came near them. Morrow knew her – she was called Perpetuation; she ran a shop in a poor part of Sector 4. She walked steadily along the way towards them, eyes downcast. She looked tired, Morrow thought; it must be her shift end.

Then she looked up, and saw the forest folk. Perpetuation slowed to a halt in the middle of the chord-way, her mouth hanging slack. Morrow saw beads of sweat break out over her scalp.

In his peripheral vision, Morrow saw Spinner-of-Rope reach for her blowpipe.

137

He raised a hand and tried to smile. 'Perpetuation. Don't be alarmed. We're on our way to the Temple, to ...'

He let his voice trail off. He could *see* Perpetuation wasn't hearing him. In fact, she seemed to be having difficulty in believing the evidence of her own eyes; she kept looking *past* Morrow's party, along the chord-way towards her home.

It was as if the forest party didn't exist – *couldn't* exist – for her.

She looked absurd. But she reminded Morrow, disturbingly, of his own first reaction to Spinner-of-Rope.

Perpetuation scurried off the path, ran *around* them, and continued on her way without looking back. Spinner seemed to relax. She slung her blowpipe over her shoulder once more.

'For the love of Life,' Morrow snapped at the girl, suddenly impatient, 'you were in no danger from that poor woman. She was terrified. Couldn't you see that?'

Spinner returned his stare, wide-eyed.

Uvarov turned up his blind face; Arrow Maker explained briefly what had happened. Uvarov barked laughter. 'You are wrong, Morrow. Of *course* Spinner was in danger here. We all are.'

Arrow Maker, plodding beside Morrow, frowned. 'I don't understand. This place is strange, but I've seen no danger.'

Morrow said, 'I agree. You're under no threat here ...'

Uvarov laughed. 'You think not? Maker, try to remember this lesson. It might keep you alive a little longer. The most precious thing to a human being is a *mind-set*: more precious than one's own life, even. Human history has taught us that lesson time and again, with its endless parade of wars – human sacrifices *en masse* – thousands of deaths over the most trivial of differences of religious interpretation.

'We do not fit into the mind-set of the people within these Decks. That poor woman walked *around* us, convincing herself we are not real! By our presence here – by our very existence, in fact – we are disturbing the *mind-set* of the people here ... in particular, of those ancients who control this society.

'They may not even realize it themselves, but they will seek to destroy us. The lives of three or four strangers is a cheap price to pay for the preservation of a mind-set, believe me.'

'No,' Morrow said. 'I can't accept that. I don't always agree with the Planners. But they aren't killers.'

'You think not?' Uvarov laughed again. 'The survivalists – your "Planners" – are psychotic. Of course. As I am. And you. We are a fundamentally flawed species. Most of humanity, for most of its history, has been driven by a series of mass psychotic delusions. The labels changed, but the nature of the delusions barely varied . . .'

Uvarov sighed. 'We built this marvellous ship – we created Superet. We dreamed of saving the species itself. We launched, towards the stars and the future . . .

'But, unfortunately, we had to take the contents of our heads with us.'

Morrow recalled Perpetuation's expression, as she had systematically shut out the existence of the forest folk. Maybe, he thought grimly, this was going to be even harder than he'd anticipated.

Lieserl remembered the first time she'd lost contact with the outside human worlds altogether. It had hurt her more than she'd expected.

She'd tested her systems; the telemetry link was still functioning, but input from the far end had simply ceased – quite abruptly, without warning.

Confused, baffled, resentful, she had withdrawn into herself for a while. If the humans who had engineered her, and dumped her into this alien place, had now decided to abandon her – well, so would she them . . .

Then, when she calmed down a little, she tried to figure out *why* the link had been broken.

From the clues provided by Michael Poole's quixotic wormhole flight into the future, Superet had put together a sketchy chronology of man's future history. Lieserl mapped her internal clocks against the Superet chronology.

When she first lost contact, already millennia had passed since her downloading into the Sun.

Earth was occupied, she'd found.

Humans had diffused out beyond the Solar System in their bulky, ponderous slower-than-light GUTships. It had been a time of optimism, of hope, of expansion into an unlimited future.

Then the first extra-Solar intelligence had been encountered, somewhere among the stars: the *Squeem*, a race of group-mind entities with a wide network of trading colonies.

Impossibly rapidly, the Squeem had overwhelmed human military capabilities and occupied Earth. The systematic exploitation of Solar resources – for the benefit of an alien power – was begun.

Sometimes, Lieserl speculated about why the dire warnings of Superet – based on Poole's data – had failed to avert the very catastrophes, like the Squeem occupation, that Superet had predicted. Maybe there was an inevitability to history – maybe it simply wasn't possible to avert the tide of events, no matter how disastrous.

But Lieserl couldn't accept such a fatalistic view.

Probably the simple truth was that – by the time enough centuries had passed for the predictions of Superet to come true – those predictions simply weren't accepted any more. The people who had actually encountered the Squeem must have been pioneers – traders, builders of new worlds. To them, Earth and its environs had been a remote legend. If they'd ever even heard of Superet, it would have been dismissed as a remote fringe group clinging fanatically to shards of dire prediction from the past, with no greater significance than astrologers or soothsayers.

But, Lieserl realized, Superet's predictions had actually been *right*.

After the Squeem interregnum, contact with her had suddenly been restored.

She remembered how words and images had suddenly come pouring once more through the revived telemetry links. At first she had been terrified by this sudden irruption into her cetacean drifting through the Sun's heart.

Her new capcom – ragged, undernourished, but endlessly enthusiastic – told her that the yoke of the Squeem had been cast off. Humans were free again, able to exploit themselves and their own resources as they saw fit. Not only that, Lieserl learned, the Squeem occupation had left humans with a legacy of high technology – a *hyperdrive*, a faster-than-light means of travelling between the stars.

Hyperdrive technology hadn't originated with the Squeem, it

was learned rapidly. They had acquired it from some other species, by fair means or foul; just as humanity had now 'inherited' it.

The true progenitors, of much of the technology in the Galaxy, were known ... at least from afar.

Xeelee.

The lost human colonies on the nearby stars were contacted and revitalized, and a new, explosive wave of expansion began, powered by the hyperdrive. Humans spread like an infection across the Galaxy, vigorous, optimistic once more.

Lieserl, drifting through her fantasy of Sun-clouds, watched all this from afar, bemused. Contact with her was maintained only fitfully; Lieserl with her wormhole technology was a relic – a bizarre artefact from the past, drifting slowly to some forgotten goal inside the Sun.

In the first few years after the overthrow of the Squeem, humans had prospered – flourished, expanded. But Lieserl grew increasingly depressed as she fast-forwarded through human history. The Universe beyond the Solar System seemed to be a place full of petty, uncreative races endlessly competing for Xeelee scraps. But maybe, she thought sourly, that made it a good arena for mankind.

Then – devastatingly – a war was fought, and lost, with another alien power: the *Qax*.

Earth was occupied again.

There were more birds joining the flock than leaving it, she realized slowly.

The birds joining the cloud came in from random directions. But there was a pattern to the paths of the departing birds: there was a steady flow of the outgoing birds in one direction, in the Sun's equatorial plane, to some unknown destination.

The point was, more birds were arriving than departing. The cloud at the heart of the Sun was *being grown*. The birds were expanding the cloud *deliberately*.

She felt as if she were being dragged along a deductive chain, reluctantly, to a place she didn't want to go. She found, absurdly, that she *liked* the birds; she didn't want to think ill of them.

But she had to consider the possibility.

141

Was it really true? What if the birds *knew* what they were doing, to the Sun? Oh, the precise form of their intelligence – their awareness – didn't matter. They might even be some form of group consciousness, like the Squeem. The key question was their *intent*.

Could the wildest speculations of Superet be, after all, correct? Did the birds represent some form of malevolent intelligence which intended to extinguish the Sun?

Were they smothering the Sun's fusion fire by design?

And if so, why?

Brooding, she sank deeper into the flock, watching, correlating.

They reached the Superet Planners' Temple in Sector 3.

The little party slowed. Arrow Maker and Spinner seemed to have coped well with the sights and sounds of their journey so far, but the glowing, tetrahedral mass of the Temple, looming above them, seemed to have awed them at last. Morrow found it hard to control his own nervousness. After all it was only a few shifts since his own last, painful, personal interview with Milpitas; and now, standing here, he wondered at his own temerity at coming back like this.

Garry Uvarov stirred in his cocoon of stained blanket, his sightless face questing. When he spoke his cheeks, paper-thin, rustled. 'What's going on? Why have we stopped?'

'We've arrived,' Morrow said. 'This is the Planners' Temple. And –'

Uvarov snorted, cavernously. '*Temple*. Of course they'd call it that. Arrow Maker,' he snapped. 'Tell me what you see.'

Arrow Maker, hesitantly, described the tetrahedral pyramid, its glowing-blue edges, the sheets of glimmering brown-gold stretched across the faces.

Uvarov's head quivered; he seemed to be trying to nod. 'An Interface mockup. These damned survivalists; always so full of themselves. *Temple*.' He twisted his head; Morrow, fascinated, could see the vertebrae of his neck, individually articulating. 'Well? What are we waiting for?'

Morrow, his anxiety and nervousness tightening in his chest, moved forward towards the Temple.

* * *

'Milpitas? *Milpitas*?' Uvarov's gaunt face showed some interest. 'I knew a Milpitas: Serena Harvey Gallium Harvey Milpitas . . .'

'My grandmother,' Planner Milpitas said. He sat back in his chair and steepled his long fingers, a familiar gesture that Morrow watched, fascinated. 'One of the original crew. She died a long time ago –'

Uvarov's chair rolled, restlessly, back and forth across Milpitas' soft carpet; Arrow Maker, Morrow and Spinner were forced to crowd to the back of Milpitas' small office to avoid Uvarov. 'I know all that, damn it. I didn't ask for her life history. I said I knew *her*. Glib tongue, she had, like all Martians.'

Milpitas, behind his desk, regarded Uvarov. Morrow conceded with a certain respect that the Planner's composure, his *certainty*, hadn't been ruffled at all by the irruption into his ordered world of these painted savages, this gaunt ancient from the days of the launch itself.

The Planner asked, 'Why have you come here?'

'Because you wouldn't come out to meet *me*,' Uvarov growled. 'You arrogant bastard. I should have –'

'But why,' Milpitas pressed with patient distaste, 'did you wish to meet me at all?' Now he let his cold eyes flicker over the silent forest folk. 'Why not stay in your jungle, climbing trees with your friends here?'

Morrow heard Spinner-of-Rope *growl* under her breath.

Uvarov's nostrils flared, the papery skin stretching. 'I won't be spoken to like that by the likes of you. Who's in charge here?'

'I am,' Milpitas said calmly. 'Now answer my question.'

Garry Uvarov raised his face; in the subdued, sourceless light of Milpitas' office his eye sockets looked infinitely deep. 'You people were always the same.'

Milpitas looked amused. 'What people, exactly?'

'You *survivalists*. Your blessed grandmother and the rest of the crew she fell in with, who thought they were the only ones, the sacred guardians of Superet's mission. Always trying to control everybody else, to fit us all into your damn hierarchies.'

'If you've come all this way to debate social structures, then let's do so,' Milpitas said easily. 'There are reasons for devising hierarchical societies – *purposes* for devising bureaucracies. Did you ever think of that, old man?' He waved a languid hand. 'We're confined here – obviously – within a finite environment.

143

We have limited resources. We've no means of obtaining more resources. So we need control. We must *plan*. We need consistency of behaviour: a regulated society designed to maximize efficiency until the greater goal is reached. And a bureaucracy is the best way of –'

'*Power!*' Uvarov's voice was a sudden rant.

His head jerked forward on its stem of neck. 'You've built walls around the world, walls around people. Consistency of behaviour my *arse*. We're talking about *power*, Milpitas. That's all. The power to flatten and control – to impose illiteracy – even to remove the right to reproduce. You're damned inhuman; you people always were. And –'

Milpitas laughed; he seemed completely unperturbed. 'How long have you been isolated up there in the trees, Dr Uvarov? How many centuries? And have you cherished this bitterness all that time?'

'You're obsessed with control. You survivalists . . . With your perverted vision of the Superet goal, your exclusive access to the truth.'

Milpitas' laughter faded, and a cold light came into his eyes. 'I know your history, Dr Uvarov. It's familiar enough. Your rejection of AS treatment, your bizarre experiment to *breed* longevity into your people – your *victims*, I should say . . . And you talk to me of obsession. Of *control*. You dare talk to *me* of these things . . .'

In his brief time with the forest folk, Morrow had learned of Uvarov's eugenic ambitions.

Uvarov had rejected AS treatment – and any artificial means – as the way to immortality. To improve the stock, it was necessary to *change the species*, he argued.

Humans were governed by their genes. They – and every other living thing – were machines, designed by the genes to ensure their own – the genes' – survival. Genes gave their hosts life – and killed them.

Genes which killed their hosts tended to be removed from the gene pool. Thus, a gene which killed young bodies would have no way of being passed on to offspring. But a gene which killed *old* bodies *after* they'd reproduced could survive.

So, perversely, lethal genes in older bodies could propagate.

Uvarov had come to understand that senile decay was simply the outcome of late-acting lethal genes, which could never be selected out of the gene pool by breeding among the young.

After two centuries of flight, Garry Uvarov had determined to improve the stock of humanity the starship was carrying to the future. AS treatment used nanobotic techniques to eliminate ageing effects directly, at the biochemical level, but did not challenge the genes directly.

Even before AS treatment had started to fail him, Uvarov had declared war on the lethal genes which were killing him.

He and his followers had occupied the forest Deck, effectively sealing it off. He sent his people into the forest and told them that they would have a simple life: take nourishment from the forest, make simple tools. AS treatment was abandoned, and within a few years the forest floor and canopy were alive with the voices of children.

Then, Uvarov banned any reproduction before the age of forty.

Uvarov had enforced his rule with iron discipline; stalking through the forest, or ascending, grim-faced, into the canopy, Uvarov and a team of close followers had performed several quick, neat abortions.

After some generations of this, he pushed the conception limit up to forty-five. Then fifty.

The population in the forest dipped, but slowly started to recover. And, gradually, the lethal genes were eliminated from the gene pool.

Over time, some contact – a kind of implicit trade – opened up between the inhabitants of the lower levels and the jungle folk. But there was no incursion from below, no will to break open Deck Zero. And so, with iron determination, Uvarov enforced his huge experiment, century after century.

Arrow Maker and Spinner-of-Rope – face-painted, young-old pygmies – were the extraordinary result.

Milpitas listened, apparently bemused, as Uvarov ranted. 'When I started this work the average lifespan, without AS, was about a hundred. Now we have individuals *over two hundred and fifty years old* ...' Spittle looped across his toothless mouth. 'A thousand AS years isn't enough. Ten thousand wouldn't suffice. I'm talking about changing the nature of the *species*, man . . .'

Milpitas laughed at him. 'Was there ever a more obsessive control of any unfortunate population than that? To deny the benefits of AS to so many generations –' The Planner shook his bare, scarred head. 'To waste so much human potential, so many "mute, inglorious Miltons" . . .'

'I'm transforming the species itself,' Uvarov hissed. 'And it's working, damn you. Arrow Maker, here –' he cast about vaguely '– is eighty years old. *Eighty*. Look at him. By successively breeding out the lethal genes, I've –'

'If your programme was so laudable, then why did you feel it necessary to barricade yourself into the forest Deck?'

Morrow, helpless, felt as if he had wandered into an old, worn-out argument. He remembered his last interview with Milpitas, in which Milpitas had – calmly and consistently – denied the reality of the society above Deck One: a society whose independent existence had been obvious long before Arrow Maker and the others came firing darts down through the opened hatches of the Locks. And now – even when *confronted* with Uvarov and these painted primitives – Milpitas seemed unable to break away from his own restricted world-view.

Uvarov was noisy, of alien appearance, visibly half-insane, and locked inside a partial, incomplete – yet utterly inflexible – mind-set. Milpitas, by contrast, was calm, his manner and speech ordered, controlled. And yet, Morrow reflected uneasily, Milpitas was, in his way, just as rigid in his thinking, just as willing to reject the evidence of his senses.

We're a frozen society, Morrow thought gloomily. *Intellectually dead. Maybe Uvarov is right about mind-sets. Perhaps we're all insane, after this long flight. And yet – and yet, if Uvarov is correct about the end of the flight – then perhaps we can't afford to remain this way much longer.*

With a sense of desperation, he turned to Milpitas. 'You must listen to him. The situation's changed, Planner. The ship –'

Milpitas ignored him. He looked weary. 'I'm growing bored with this. I will ask my question once more. And then you will leave. All of you.

'Uvarov, why have you come here?'

146

Uvarov wheeled his chair forward; Morrow heard a dull thud as the chair frame collided softly with Milpitas' desk. 'Survivalist,' he said, *'the journey is over.'*

Milpitas frowned. 'What journey?'

'The flight of the *Great Northern*. Our odyssey through time, and space, to the end of history.' His ruined face twisted. 'I hate to admit it, but our factionalism serves no more purpose. Now, we have to work together – to reach the wormhole Interface, and –'

'Why,' Milpitas asked steadily, 'do you believe the journey is over?'

'Because *I've seen the stars.*'

'Impossible,' Milpitas snapped. 'Your eyes are gone. You're insane, Uvarov.'

'My people –' Uvarov's voice dried to a croak. Spinner-of-Rope stepped forward, took a wooden bowl of water from a rack within the body of the chair, and allowed a little of the fluid to trickle into Uvarov's cavern of a mouth.

'My people are my eyes,' Uvarov said, gasping. 'Arrow Maker climbed the tallest tree and studied the stars. I *know*, Milpitas. And I understand.'

Milpitas' eyes narrowed. 'You understand nothing.' He glanced, briefly and dismissively, at Arrow Maker, who returned his look with cool calculation. 'I've no idea what this – person – saw, when he climbed his tree. But I know you're wrong, Uvarov. We've nothing to discuss.'

'But the stars – don't you see, Milpitas? *There was no starbow.* The relativistic phase of the flight must be over . . .'

Milpitas smiled thinly. 'Even now, through the fog that has swamped your intellect, you'll probably concede that one great strength of the bureaucracies you despise so much is record-keeping.

'Uvarov, we keep good records. And we *know* that you're wrong. After all this time there's some uncertainty, but we know that the thousand-year flight has at least half a century to run.'

Something stirred in Morrow's heart at that. Somehow, he suspected, he'd never quite believed Uvarov's pronouncement – but the authority of a Planner was something else. *Just fifty years . . .*

147

'You're a damn fool,' Uvarov railed; his chair jerked back and forth, displaying his agitation.

Milpitas said coolly, 'No doubt. But we'll cope with journey's end when it comes. Now I want you out of my office, old man. I have more than enough work to do without –'

Morrow couldn't help but come forward. 'Planner. Is that all you have to say? The first contact between the Decks for hundreds of years –'

'And the last, if I've anything to do with it.' Milpitas raised his face to Morrow; his remodelled flesh was like a sculpture, Morrow thought abstractedly, a thing of cold, hard planes and edges. 'Get them out of here, Morrow. Take them back to their jungle world.'

'Was I wrong to bring them here?'

'Get them out.' Tension showed in Milpitas' voice, and the prominence of the muscles in his neck. *'Get them out.'*

She wondered how she must appear to these photino creatures.

They would find it as difficult to perceive baryonic matter as she, a baryonic creature, found it to see them. Perhaps the birds saw a pale tetrahedron, the faint dark-matter shadow of the exotic matter Interface framework which formed the basis of her being. Perhaps they caught some dim sense of the wormhole itself, the throat of space and time through which she pumped away the heat which would otherwise destroy her.

The old theories had predicted dark-matter particles colliding with the swarming protons of the Solar core, absorbing a little of their energy and so transporting heat out from the fusing heart. This was how, it was thought, dark matter cooled the Sun.

She saw now that these notions had been right in essence, but too crude. The *birds* absorbed Solar heat energy. They fed on interactions with protons in the plasma. Incorporating energy from photino-proton interactions within their structures, the birds grew, and spiralled out from the hotter, denser heart of the Sun, taking the heat energy with them.

The ancient theorists had envisaged a particle-based physical process to extract core heat, and so suppress the fusion processes there. The truth was, the birds *fed* on the Sun's heat.

And, by feeding – like unwise parasites – they would eventually kill their host.

Unwise – unless, of course, that had been the intention all along.

Lieserl had learned about the Qax.

The Qax had originated as clusters of turbulent cells in the seas of a young planet. Because there were so few of them the Qax weren't naturally warlike – individual life was far too precious to them. They were natural traders; the Qax worked with each other like independent corporations, in perfect competition.

They had occupied Earth simply because it was so easy – because they *could*.

The only law governing the squabbling junior races of the Galaxy was, Lieserl realized, the iron rule of economics. The Qax enslaved mankind simply because it was an economically valid proposition.

They had to learn the techniques of oppression from humans themselves. Fortunately for the Qax, human history wasn't short of object lessons.

The wormhole station maintaining contact with Lieserl was abandoned, once again, during the Qax occupation.

Finally the Qax were overthrown. The details hadn't been clear to Lieserl; it was something to do with a man named Jim Bolder, and an unlikely flight in a stolen Xeelee derelict craft, to the site of the Xeelee's greatest project: the Ring . . .

This was the first time Lieserl had heard of the Ring.

After the overthrow, once more humans returned to the Sun, and restored contact with the ageing, increasingly incongruous artefact that contained Lieserl.

This time, Lieserl was shocked by the humans who greeted her.

The Qax, during the occupation, had withdrawn AntiSenescence technology. Death, illness, had returned to the worlds of mankind. It hadn't taken long for toil and disease to erase most of the old immortals – some of whom had still remembered the days before the Squeem, even – and, within a few generations, humans had forgotten much of their past.

The discontinuity in human culture after the Qax was

immeasurably greater than that arising from the Squeem occupation. The new people who emerged from the Qax era – and who now peered out of sketchy images at Lieserl in her cocoon of Solar plasma – seemed alien to her, with their shaven heads and gaunt, fanatical expressions.

Expansion had begun again, but this time fuelled by a hard-edged determination. Never again would humanity be made to serve some alien power. Lieserl in her whale-dream, watching centuries flicker by in fragments of image and speech, saw humans erupt out of their systems once more. A new period began – a period called the *Assimilation*.

During the Assimilation, humans – aggressively and deliberately – absorbed the resources and technologies of other species.

Human culture evolved rapidly in this period. The link with Lieserl was maintained, but with increasingly long interruptions. The motivation of these remote humans seemed to be a brand of hostile curiosity; she saw only calculation in the faces presented to her. She was seen, she suspected, only as another resource to be exploited for the continuing, endless expansion of mankind.

Soon – astonishingly quickly – humans became the dominant of the junior races. Humanity's growth in power and influence grew exponentially.

At last, only the Xeelee themselves were more potent than mankind . . . And the legend of the Xeelee's achievements – the construction material, the manipulation of space and time, the Ring itself – grew into a deep-rooted mythology.

Then, for the last time, her wormhole telemetry link was shut down.

Drifting through her endless, unchanging ocean of plasma, she felt a distant twinge of regret – a feeling that soon dispersed into the peaceful, numb silence around her.

Humans had become alien to her. She was better off without them.

The birds must have some lifecycle, she thought; a circle of birth and life and death, much like every baryonic creature. Individual photino birds moved past her too rapidly to follow; but still, she studied them carefully, and was rewarded with glimpses – she thought – of *growth*.

Eventually she saw a bird reproduce.

She could see there was something unusual about this bird, even as it approached. The bird was fat, swollen with proton heat-energy. It seemed somehow more solid – more *real*, to Lieserl's baryonic senses – than its neighbours.

The bird shuddered – once, twice – its lenticular rim quivering. She almost felt some empathy with the creature; it seemed in agony.

Abruptly – startling Lieserl – the bird shot away from its orbital path. It hovered for a moment – then it hurtled down into the heat-rich core of the Sun once more. Lieserl's processors told her that the bird seemed a little less massive than before.

And it had left something behind.

Lieserl enhanced her senses as far as they would go. The mother-bird had left behind a *copy* of herself – a ghostly copy, rendered in clumps of higher density in the plasma proton-electron mix. It was a three-dimensional image of the mother, *in baryonic matter*. Within fractions of a second the clumps had started to disperse – but not before more photinos had clustered around the complex pattern of baryonic matter, rapidly plating over its internal structure.

The whole process took less than a second. At the end of it, a new photino bird, sleek and small, moved away from the site of its birth; the last traces of the higher-density baryonic material left behind by the mother bird drifted away.

Lieserl ran the image sequence over and over. As a method of reproduction, it was a long way from any Earth-bound form – even cloning. It was more like making a straight copy – an imprint from a three-dimensional mould, mediated by baryonic matter.

The newborn must be an almost exact copy of its parent – more exact than any clone, even. Presumably it carried a copy of its parent's memories – even, perhaps, of its awareness . . .

And, presumably, a copy too of the generation before that – and before that, and . . .

Lieserl smiled. Each photino child must carry within it the soul of all of its grandmothers, a deep tree of awareness reaching right back to the dawn of the species.

And all mediated by baryonic matter, she thought wonderingly. The birds *depended* on the relative transparency of dark and baryonic matter to take their detailed, three-dimensional copies of themselves.

But this meant, she realized, that the photino birds could only breed in places where they could find high densities of baryonic matter. They could only breed in the hearts of stars.

She replayed the birth images, over and over.

There was something graceful, immensely appealing, about the photino birds, and she found herself warming to them. Spiritually she felt much closer to the birds, now, than to the hard-eyed humans of the Assimilation, beyond the Solar ocean.

She hoped her theory – that the birds were deliberately destroying the Sun – was wrong.

The return journey seemed much longer. Morrow felt angry, disappointed, weary. 'I can't understand how Milpitas reacted.' He shook his head. 'It's as if he didn't even *see* you people ...'

'Oh, I understand.' Uvarov twisted his head. '*I* understand. We are all too *old*, you see. In a way Milpitas was right about me; after all I share some of these flaws myself.' Uvarov's voice, while still distorted by age, was calmer, more rational than at any point during the interview with Milpitas, Morrow thought.

Uvarov went on, 'But at least I can *recognize* my limitations – the tunnel-vision of my age and condition. And, by recognizing it, deal with it.'

Spinner-of-Rope had been leading the way up the hundred-yard ramp to Deck One. Now, as she neared the top, she slowed. Her hand dropped, seemingly automatically, to her blowpipe and the little sack of feathered darts at her waist.

'What is it?' Morrow asked drily. 'More problems with human body odour?'

She turned, her eyes huge behind her spectacles. 'Not that. But *something* ... Something's wrong.'

Arrow Maker raised his face. 'I can smell it, too.'

'Describe,' Uvarov snapped.

'Sharp. Smoky. A little like fire, but more intense ...'

Uvarov grunted. He sounded somehow satisfied. 'Cordite, probably.'

Arrow Maker looked blank. 'What?'

They reached the top of the ramp. Hastily, with both forest people bearing their weapons in their hands, they made for the

Lock down which Uvarov had been carried.

As they approached the Lock, they slowed, almost as if synchronized. The three of them – Arrow Maker, Morrow and Spinner – stood and stared at the Lock.

Uvarov twisted his face to left and right. 'Tell me what's wrong. It's the Lock, isn't it?'

'Yes.' Morrow stepped forward cautiously. 'Yes, it's the Lock.' The cylinder of metal had been burst open, somewhere near its centre; bits of its fabric, twisted, scorched, none larger than his hand, lay scattered across the Deck surface. There was a stink of smoke and fire – presumably Uvarov's cordite.

Arrow Maker stood clutching his bow, open-mouthed, impotent. Spinner ran off towards the next Lock, her bare feet padding against the metal floor.

Uvarov nodded. 'Simple and effective. We should have expected this.'

Morrow bent to pick up a piece of hull metal; but the twisted, scorched fragment was still hot, and he withdrew his fingers hastily.

Spinner came running back. She looked breathless, wide-eyed and very young; she stood close to her father and clutched his arm. 'The next Lock's been blown out as well. I think they all have. The Locks are impassable. *We can't get home.*'

Uvarov whispered, 'We should check. But I am sure she is right.'

Morrow slammed his fist into his palm. '*Why?* I just don't understand. Why this destruction – this *waste*?'

'I *told* you why,' Uvarov said evenly. 'The existence of the upper level was an unacceptable challenge to the mind-set of Milpitas and the rest of your damn Planners. I doubt if they will have done any damage to the forest Deck itself. Sealing it off – sealing it away from themselves, apparently forever – should do the trick just as well.'

'But that's *insane*,' Morrow protested.

Uvarov hissed, 'No one ever said it wasn't. We're *human beings*. What do you expect?'

Arrow Maker paced about the floor. Morrow became aware, nervously, of the muscles in the back of the little man which flexed, angrily; Maker's face paint flared. 'Whether it was

153

intended or not, we're trapped here. We're in real danger. Now, what in Lethe are we going to do?'

Morrow's fear seemed to have been burned out of him by his anger at the foolishness, the wastefulness of the destruction of the Locks. 'I'll help you. I'll not abandon you. I'll take you to my home – I live alone; you can hide there. Later, perhaps we can find some way to open up a Lock again, and –'

Arrow Maker looked grateful; but before he could speak Uvarov wheeled forward.

'*No*. We won't be going back to the forest.'

Arrow Maker said, 'But, Uvarov –'

'Nothing's changed.' Uvarov turned his blind face from side to side. 'Don't you see that? Arrow Maker, you saw the stars yourself. *The ship's journey is over.* And *we* have to go on.'

Spinner clutched at her father's arm. 'Go on? Where?'

'Regardless of the reaction of these damn fool survivalists, we will continue. Down through these Decks, and onwards ... On to the Interface itself.'

Arrow Maker, Spinner and Morrow exchanged stricken glances.

Uvarov tilted back his head, exposing his bony throat. 'We've travelled across five million years, Arrow Maker,' he whispered. '*Five million years* ... Now it's time to go home.'

11

She shivered. Suddenly, she felt oddly cold.

Cold? No. Come on, Lieserl, think.

Sometimes her Virtual-human illusory form was a hindrance; it caused her to anthropomorphize genuine experiences.

Something had *happened* to her just now; somehow her environment had changed. How?

There it came again – that deep, inner stab of illusory cold.

She looked down at herself.

A ghost-form – a photino bird – emerged from her Virtual stomach, and flew away on its orbit around the Sun. Another came through her legs; still more through her arms and chest – and at last, one bird flew through her head, the place where *she* resided. Her cold feeling was a reaction to the slivers of energy the birds took away from her as they passed through.

Before, the photino birds had avoided her; presumably residually aware of her, they'd adjusted their trajectories to sweep around her. Now, though, they seemed to be doing quite the opposite. They seemed to be aiming at her, veering from their paths so that they deliberately passed through her.

She felt like screaming – struggling, beating away these creatures with her fists.

Much good that will do. She forced herself to remain still, to observe, to wait.

Behind her the birds seemed to be gathering into a new formation: a cone with herself at the apex, a cone into which they streamed.

Could they damage me? Kill me, even?

Well, could they? Dark matter could interact with baryonic to a limited extent. If their density, around her, grew high enough – if the rate of interaction between the birds and the particles which comprised her grew high enough – then, she realized, the birds could do *anything*.

And there wasn't a damn thing she could do about it; embedded in this mush of plasma, she could never get away from them in time.

She felt as if a hard, needle rain were sleeting through her. It was uncomfortable – tingling – but not truly painful, she realized slowly.

Maybe they didn't mean to destroy her, she wondered drowsily. Maybe – maybe they were trying to *understand* her . . .

She held out her arms and submitted herself to inspection by the photino birds.

They formed into a rough column – Arrow Maker leading, then Uvarov, followed by Morrow and Spinner-of-Rope, with Spinner occasionally boosting Uvarov's chair.

Morrow stepped over the ramp's shallow lip and began the gentle, hundred-yard descent back into the comparative brightness and warmth of Deck Two.

'Listen to me,' Garry Uvarov rasped. 'We're at the top of the lifedome. We have to get to the bottom of the dome, about a mile below us. Then we'll need to find a pod and traverse half the length of the *Northern*'s spine, towards the drive unit; and that's where we'll find the Interface. Got that?'

Most of this was unimaginable to Morrow. He tried to concentrate on the part he understood. 'What do you mean by the bottom of the lifedome? Deck Four?'

A bark of laughter from Uvarov. 'No; I mean the loading bay. Below Deck Fifteen.'

Morrow felt something cringe within him. *I'm too old for this* . . . 'But, Uvarov, there is *nothing* below Deck Four –'

'Don't be so damn stupid, man.'

'. . . I mean, nothing inhabited. Even Deck Four is just used as a mine.' He tried to imagine descending *below* the gloomy, cavernous Deck in which he'd spent so much of his working life. It might be airless down there. And it would certainly be *dark*. And –

There was a whisper of air past his ear, a clatter as something hit the metal of the ramp behind him.

Arrow Maker froze, reaching for his bow instantly. Spinner

hauled Uvarov's chair to a halt, and the old doctor stared around with his sightless eyes.

'What was that?' Uvarov snapped.

Morrow took a couple of steps back up the ramp and searched the surface. Soon he spied the glint of metal. He bent to pick up the little artefact.

It was a piton, he realized – a simple design he'd turned out hundreds of times himself, in the workshops of Deck Four, for the trade with the forest folk. Perhaps Arrow Maker and Spinner had pitons just like this in their kit even now.

But this piton seemed to have been sharpened; its point gleamed with rough, planed surfaces . . .

There was another whisper of air.

Spinner cried out. She clutched her left arm and bent forward, tumbling slowly to the Deck.

Arrow Maker bent over her. 'Spinner? *Spinner?*'

Spinner held her left arm stiff against her body, and blood was seeping out through the fingers she'd clamped over her flesh.

Arrow Maker prised his daughter's hand away from her arm. Blood trickled down her bare flesh, from a neat, clean-looking puncture; a metal hook protruded from the centre of the puncture. Spinner showed no pain, or fear; her expression was empty, perhaps with a trace of dull surprise showing in the eyes behind her spectacles.

Without hesitation Maker grabbed the hook, spread his fingers around its base across Spinner's flesh, and pulled.

The device slid out neatly. Spinner murmured, her face pale beneath its lurid paint.

Arrow Maker held up the blood-stained artefact. It was another piton. 'Someone's shooting at us,' he said evenly.

'Shooting?' Uvarov turned his blind face towards Morrow. 'What's this, paper-pusher? Is Superet arming you all now?'

Morrow took a few steps down the ramp, further into the light of Deck Two, and peered down.

Four people were climbing the ramp towards him: two women and two men, in drab, startlingly ordinary work uniforms. They looked scared, even bewildered; but their advance was steady and measured. They were pointing devices at his chest. He squinted to see the machines: strips of gleaming metal, bent into curves by lengths of cable.

'I don't believe it,' he whispered. 'Cross-bows. They're carrying *cross-bows*.'

The weapons were obviously of scavenged interior partition material. They must have been constructed in the Deck Four workshops – perhaps mere yards from the spot where Morrow had whiled away decades making climbing rings, ratchets, spectacle frames and bits of cutlery for forest folk he'd never expected to meet.

One of the four assailants, a woman, lifted her bow and began to adjust it, increasing its tension by working a small lever. She drew a piton from her tunic pocket and fitted it into a slot on top of the bow. She raised the bow and sighted along it, at his chest.

Morrow watched, fascinated. He thought he recognized this woman. *Doesn't she work in a hydroponics processor in Segment 2?* And –

A compact mass crashed into his legs. His body was flung to the hard, ridged surface of the ramp, his cheek colliding with the floor with astonishing force.

Another sigh of air over his head; again he heard the clatter of a sharpened piton hitting metal.

Arrow Maker's hand was on his back, pinning him against the ridged ramp surface. 'You'd better damn well wake up, if you want to stay alive,' the forest man hissed. 'Come on. Back up the ramp. Spinner, help Uvarov.'

Spinner-of-Rope, blood still coating her lower arm, clambered up behind Uvarov's chair and began to haul it backwards up the ramp.

Morrow sat up cautiously. His cheek ached, his left side – where he'd landed – was sore, and the ramp felt astonishingly hard beneath his legs. The sparks of pain were like fragments of a sensory explosion. He realized slowly that he hadn't been in a fight – or any kind of violent physical situation – since he'd been a young man.

Arrow Maker's hand grabbed at his collar and hauled him backwards, flat against the ramp. 'Keep *down*, damn it. Watch me. Do what I do.'

Morrow, with an effort, turned on his belly; the ramp ridges dug painfully into the soft flesh over his hip.

Arrow Maker worked rapidly up the ramp. He was small, compact, determined; his bare limbs squirmed across the metal like independent animals. Beyond him, Spinner had already pulled Uvarov out of the line of sight, into the darkness of Deck One.

Morrow tried to copy Arrow Maker's motion, but his clothes snagged on rough edges on the ramp, and the coarse surface rubbed at his palms.

Another piton whispered over his head.

He clambered to a crawling position and – ignoring the agony of kneecaps rolling over ridges in the surface – he scurried up the few yards of the ramp and over its lip.

Arrow Maker tore a strip from Uvarov's blanket and briskly wrapped it around his daughter's wounded arm. Maker said, 'They're coming up the ramp. They'll be here in less than a minute. Which way, Morrow?'

Morrow rolled onto his backside and sat with his legs splayed. He couldn't quite believe what had happened to him, all in the space of less than a minute. 'Weapons,' he said. 'How could they have made them so quickly? And –'

From the gloom of Deck One he heard Uvarov's barked laughter. 'Are you really so naïve?'

Arrow Maker finished his makeshift bandage. 'Morrow. Which way do we go?'

'The elevator shafts,' Uvarov croaked from the darkness. 'They'll be covering all the ramps. The shafts are our only chance. And the shafts cut right through the Decks, all the way to the base of the dome ...'

'But the shafts are disused,' Morrow said, frowning. The shafts had been shut down after the abandonment of the lower Decks, centuries before.

Uvarov grimaced. 'Then we'll have to climb, won't we?'

Morrow could hear the slow, cautious footsteps of their four assailants as they came up the ramp.

The Decks weren't a very big world, and he'd been alive for a long time. He must *know* these people.

And they were coming to *kill* him. If someone else had had the misfortune to be on Deck One when Maker and Spinner first stuck their heads through the hatch, then maybe he, Morrow, would now be in this hunting party, with cross-bows and bolts of scavenged hull-metal ...

A shadow fell across him. He looked up into the eyes of the

woman who worked in the Segment 2 hydroponics. She held a gleaming cross-bow bolt pointed at his face.

There was a whoosh of air.

The woman raised her hand to her face, the palm meeting her cheek with a dull clap. She fell backwards and rolled a few paces down the ramp. The cross-bow dropped from her loosening fingers and clattered to the Deck.

Beyond the fallen woman Morrow caught a brief impression of the other three Deck folk scrambling back down the ramp.

Spinner-of-Rope lowered her blowpipe; beneath her spectacles, her lips were trembling.

'It's all right, Spinner-of-Rope,' Maker said urgently. 'You did the right thing.'

'Morrow,' Uvarov said. 'Show them the way.'

Morrow pushed himself to his feet and stumbled away from the ramp.

The elevator shaft was a cylinder of metal ten yards across; it rose from floor to ceiling, a hundred yards above them.

Spinner-of-Rope, blood soaking through her dark bandage, leaned against the shaft. She looked tired, scared, subdued. *She really is just a kid*, Morrow thought.

But she said defiantly, 'You Undermen aren't used to fighting, are you? Maybe those four weren't expecting us to fight back. So they'll be scared. Cautious. It will slow them down –'

'But not stop them,' Arrow Maker murmured. He was running his hand over the surface of the shaft, probing at small indentations in its surface. 'So we haven't much time ... Morrow, how do we get into – *Oh*.'

In response to Arrow Maker's random jabs, a panel slid backwards and sideways. A round-edged doorway into the shaft was opened up, about as tall as Morrow and towering over the forest folk.

Within the shaft, there was only darkness.

Arrow Maker stuck his head inside the shaft, and peered up and down its length. 'There are rungs on the inner surface. It's like a ladder. Good. It will be easy to climb. And –'

Spinner touched his arm. 'What about Uvarov?'

Arrow Maker turned to the old doctor, his face creasing with concern.

Morrow looked with dismay at the gaping shaft. 'We'll never be able to carry that chair, not down a *ladder* –'

'Then carry *me*.' Uvarov's ruined, crumpled face was deep in shadow as he lifted his head to them. 'Forget the chair, damn it. Carry *me*.'

Morrow heard footsteps, echoing from the bare walls of Deck One. 'There's no time,' he said to Arrow Maker. 'We have to leave him. We can't –'

Maker looked up at him, his face drawn and haughty beneath its gaudy paint. Then he turned away. 'Spinner, give me a hand. Get his blanket off.'

The girl took hold of the top of the black blanket and gently drew it back. Uvarov's body was revealed: wasted, angularly bony, dressed in a silvery coverall through which Morrow could clearly see the bulge of ribs and pelvis. There were lumps under Uvarov's tunic: perhaps colostomy bags or similar medical aids. Although he must have been as tall as Morrow, Uvarov's body looked as if it massed no more than a child's. One hand rested on Uvarov's lap, swaying through a pendular tremble with a period of a second or so, and the other was wrapped around a simple joystick which – Morrow presumed – controlled the chair.

Arrow Maker took Uvarov's wrist and gently pulled his hand away from the joystick; the hand stayed curled, like a claw. Then Maker leaned forward, tucked his head into Uvarov's chest, and straightened up, lifting Uvarov neatly out of his chair and settling him over Maker's shoulder. As Arrow Maker stood there Uvarov's slippered feet dangled against the floor, with his knees almost bent.

Uvarov submitted to all this passively, without comment or complaint; Morrow, watching them, had the feeling that Arrow Maker was accustomed to handling Uvarov like this – perhaps he served the old doctor as some kind of basic nurse.

As he studied the tough little man, almost obscured by his dangling human load, Morrow felt a pang of shame.

Spinner-of-Rope picked up Uvarov's blanket and slung it over her shoulder. 'Let's go,' she said anxiously.

'You lead,' Arrow Maker said.

Spinner took hold of the frame of the open hatch and vaulted neatly into the shaft. She twisted, grabbed onto the rungs beneath the door frame, and clambered down out of sight.

'Now you, Morrow,' Arrow Maker hissed.

Morrow put his hands, now sweating profusely, on the door frame. Damn it, he was five hundred years older than Spinner. And even when he'd been fifteen he'd never been *lithe* . . .

'*Move!*'

He raised one leg and hoisted it over the lip of the door frame. The frame dug into his crotch. He tried to bring his second leg over – and almost lost his grip in the process. He clung to the frame with both hands, feeling as if the entire surface of his skin was drenched in cold sweat.

He tried again, more slowly, and this time managed to get both legs over. For a moment he sat there, feet dangling over a drop whose depth was hidden by darkness.

If the shaft was open all the way to the bottom of the lifedome, there was a mile's drop below him.

He thought, briefly, of climbing back out of the shaft. Could he really face this? He could try surrendering, after all . . . But, oddly, it was the thought of the consequent shame in the face of Arrow Maker and Spinner made that option impossible.

He reached out and down, cautiously, with his right foot. It seemed a long way to the first rung, but at last he caught it with his heel. The rung felt fat and reassuringly solid. He got both feet onto the rung and straightened up. Then, still being minutely careful, he turned around, letting the soles of his feet swivel over the metal rung.

He bent his knees and reached out for the next rung. It was about eighteen inches below the first. Once he'd gone down two or three rungs and he started to settle into a routine, with both hands and feet fixed to the rungs, the going got easier –

Until he suddenly became aware that he was climbing down *into the dark*.

He couldn't see a damn thing, not even the metal shaft surface before his face, or the whiteness of his own hands on the rungs.

He stopped dead and looked up, suddenly desperate even for the dim light of Deck One. Instantly he felt warm, bare feet trampling over the backs of his hands on the rungs, and the clumsy pressure of Arrow Maker's legs on his shoulders and head; something clattered against his back – Uvarov's feet, presumably.

Spinner's voice drifted up from the shaft. 'What's going on?'

'What in Lethe are you doing?' Arrow Maker hissed.

'I'm sorry. It was dark. I –'

'Morrow, your friends are going to reach the shaft any moment –'

Something metallic rattled from the walls of the shaft, the resounding bounces coming further apart as it fell.

Uvarov's voice sounded from the region of Maker's upper legs. 'Correction,' he said drily. 'They *have* reached the shaft . . .'

Desperately, urgently, Morrow began to climb down once more.

Lieserl lay back in the glowing hydrogen-helium mix with arms outstretched and eyes closed, and felt fusion-product photons dance slowly around her. Following their minutes-long orbits around the core of the Sun, the long, lenticular forms of the photino birds flowed past Lieserl. She let the swarming birds cushion her as she sank into the choking heart of the Sun, floating as if in a dream.

And, at last, she came to a region, deep inside the Sun, in which no new photons were produced.

She and Scholes had been right, all those years ago. The core had gone out.

The persistent leeching-out of energy from the Sun's hydrogen-fusing core, by the flocks of photino birds, had at last become untenable. A long time ago – probably before Lieserl's birth – the temperature of the core had dropped so far that the fusion of hydrogen into helium flickered out, died.

Now, its heart already stilled, the Sun was working through its megayear death throes. Despite the slow, continuing migration of the last photons outward from the stilled fusion processes, there was little radiation pressure, here at the heart of the Sun, to balance the core's tendency to collapse under gravity. So the extinguished core fell in on itself further, seeking a new equilibrium, its temperature rising as its mass compressed.

Lieserl knew that in the heart of every star of the Sun's mass, these processes would at last take place – even without the intervention of an agent like the dark matter photino birds. Once the core hydrogen was exhausted, hydrogen fusion processes would die there, and this final subsidence, of a helium-soaked core, would begin.

The difference was, the Sun's core was still replete with unburned hydrogen; fusion processes had died, not because of hydrogen exhaustion, but because of the theft of energy by untiring flocks of photino birds.

And, of course, the Sun should have enjoyed ten billion years of Main Sequence life before reaching this dire state. The photino birds had allowed Sol mere *millions* of years, before forcing this decrepitude.

Around him there was the noise of his own breathing, the soft, ringing sound of his hands and feet on the metal rungs, and – further away, and distorted by echo – the subtle noises of the forest folk as they climbed. There was an all-pervading smell of metal, overlaid by a tang of staleness.

In the darkness Morrow had no way of judging time, and only the growing ache in his muscles to measure the distance he'd travelled. But slowly – to his surprise – his vision began to return, adapting to the gloom. There was actually quite a lot of light in here: there was the open portal at the top, on Deck One, and fine seams in the walls of the shaft shone like arrows of grey silver in the darkness. He could see the dim, foreshortened silhouettes of Arrow Maker and Spinner, above and below him; they climbed with a limber grace, like animals. And in the shaft itself he could see the shadow of cables, dangling, useless.

As he worked his muscles seemed to lose some of their stiffness. He was, he realized with surprise, *enjoying* this . . .

'Stop.' Spinner's voice, softened by echo, came up to him.

He halted, clinging to the rungs, and hissed a warning up to Arrow Maker.

'What is it?'

'We're in trouble,' Spinner said softly.

'No, we're not,' Maker said. 'We're descending more quickly than those thugs with the cross-bows. They didn't follow us down here. So they have to follow the ramps; we're going straight down.'

Spinner sighed. 'Damn it, Maker, I wish you'd listen to me. Look *down*. See?'

Arrow Maker straightened his arms and leaned out over the shaft; Uvarov, passive, dangled against his frame. '*Oh.*'

Morrow twisted his head to see.

There was a rough framework crossing the shaft, some distance below them. He felt a sudden surge of hope; was his climb nearly done? 'Is that the base of the shaft?'

He saw the flash of Spinner's teeth in the gloom as she grinned up at her father. 'No,' she said. 'No, not exactly.'

Maker said, 'How far would you say we've descended, Spinner? Five hundred yards? ... Barely a third of the way to the base of the lifedome, if Uvarov's dimensions are correct.'

Five hundred yards ... They were scarcely past Deck Four, Morrow realized: beyond the scuffed walls of the shaft here were the shops to which he strolled to work every shift. Or *had*, before he'd become a hunted criminal.

The transient enjoyment leached out of him; a trembling ache descended on his legs and upper arms. There was still *twice as far to go* as he'd travelled already ...

'Do you understand their amusement, Morrow?' Uvarov asked acidly, his voice obscured by his limp posture. 'The shaft has been *blocked*.'

'Maker,' Spinner whispered. 'I can see someone moving down there.'

Morrow hooked his arm across a rung and looked down more carefully.

The platform blocking the shaft was quite a crude thing, of beams and plates lashed quickly together, roughly welded. A shadow crawled cautiously across the platform; there was a flare of laser-weld light, a small shower of sparks.

Spinner is right. Someone is *moving down there – building the thing even as we watch. Deliberately blocking off the shaft, to stop us.* How many times had *he* used laser tools like that? Thousands? It could easily have been *him* down there.

... In fact, he realized suddenly, he ought to know who that worker was.

He leaned further out and stared, squinting, trying to make out more of the stocky figure. He saw a sleeveless tunic, brawny arms and torso, surprisingly wasted legs ...

'Constancy-of-Purpose. *Constancy-of-Purpose.*'

At the sound of Morrow's voice, floating out of the gloom above her, Constancy-of-Purpose started. She dropped her laser weld, which died immediately, and scrambled backwards across the platform she'd been building. Morrow saw how she held her wounded arm away from her body, stiffly.

Morrow clambered briskly down the ladder, shouldering Spinner aside. He reached the platform and jumped down onto it. 'Constancy-of-Purpose,' he whispered. 'It's me. Morrow.'

Constancy-of-Purpose got to her feet, warily. She pushed goggles up from her eyes. Morrow saw sweat gleam from her wide shoulders; where the goggles had been, dirt ringed her eyes. 'What in Lethe –'

'It's all right. You don't have to be afraid.'

'Morrow. What's going on?'

'You have to let us through.'

'Us?' Constancy-of-Purpose glanced up into the darkness nervously.

'I have the forest folk with me. You remember.'

'Of course I damn well remember.' Constancy-of-Purpose reflexively rubbed her stiff arm and backed towards the wall of the shaft. 'That little criminal *shot* me.'

'Yes, but – well, she was scared. Listen to me – you must let us through. Past this barrier.'

Constancy-of-Purpose looked at him, bafflement and suspicion evident in her face. 'Why? What are you doing?'

'Don't you know?' Actually, Morrow reflected, Constancy-of-Purpose probably *didn't* know ... The Planners had most likely sent out instructions to block off all the old shafts, without explanation. All to trap *him*, and these forest folk. *I was just lucky to find Constancy-of-Purpose ...*

'I'm not stupid, Morrow,' Constancy-of-Purpose said. 'I don't know what's going on, quite. But the Planners are obviously trying to trap these tree people. And I'm not surprised. They're *killers*. And if you're helping them –'

'Listen. The *Planners* are the killers. Or at least, they're trying to turn the likes of *us* into killers.' Morrow described the crossbows and sharpened pitons, weapons created from horribly mundane objects.

As he talked, Morrow's mind seemed to race, making leaps of

induction. He remembered how Uvarov had taunted him for naïveté. Was it *really* possible that Superet had machined these weapons so quickly, in response to the arrival of the forest folk?

No, he decided. There hadn't been time. Superet must have weapons *stockpiled*.

But Constancy-of-Purpose was shaking her head. 'I don't believe you,' she said.

'Believe it,' Morrow snapped. 'Spinner – the tree girl – got shot in the arm. By a *piton*, for Lethe's sake. Do you want me to show you the wound?'

Constancy-of-Purpose looked up uncertainly. 'I ... no.'

'Constancy-of-Purpose, if you let us past we'll be home free. The Planners surely won't pursue us below Deck Four; this is the last point they can stop us ... But if you keep us here, *you'll kill us*, just as surely as if you wielded the cross-bow yourself ...'

Morrow tried to keep control of his own ragged breathing, not to let Constancy-of-Purpose be aware of his mounting fear.

'... All right.' Suddenly Constancy-of-Purpose, symbolically, moved aside. Hurry. I'll say I didn't see you.'

Morrow reached out his hand, then let it drop. 'Thank you.'

Constancy-of-Purpose frowned. 'Just go, man.' She bent and, with the strength of her uninjured arm, began to prise up a partially welded plate, making a narrow gateway through the blocking platform.

After a moment's hesitation the forest folk scrambled down the ladder and dropped to the platform, lightly. Constancy-of-Purpose glared at Spinner-of-Rope. Spinner returned her stare, thoughtfully stroking the blowpipe at her waist.

'*Go on*,' Morrow told Spinner. 'Through that plate.'

The forest folk hurried across the platform, their bare feet padding, and Spinner began to work her way through the hole.

Now Constancy-of-Purpose stared at Uvarov, still slung over Maker's shoulder.

'Is he dead?'

'Who? The old man? Not quite, but as near as damn it, I suppose ... If I come by this way again, I'll explain.'

'But you *won't* be coming back, will you?' Constancy-of-Purpose's blunt face was serious.

'... No. I don't suppose I will.'

Constancy-of-Purpose backed away, her hands upraised. 'You're crazy. Maybe I should have stopped you after all.'

Arrow Maker, with Uvarov, was already through the platform, and Morrow sat down on the edge of the hole. He looked up. 'Wish me luck.'

But Constancy-of-Purpose had already gone, out of the shaft and back to the mundane world of the Decks: to Morrow's old life.

Morrow eased himself through the platform.

Before long Morrow's shoulders and legs stiffened up again and began to hurt, seriously, and he was forced to take longer and longer breaks. The base of the shaft – illuminated by a ring of open ports – was a remote island of light that climbed towards him with infinite, cruel slowness.

Now they were far below the deepest inhabited level. Beyond the shaft's cold walls, he knew, there was only darkness, stale air, abandoned homes. The cold seemed to pervade the shaft; he felt small, fragile, isolated.

They found ledges on which it was possible to rest – to stretch out, and even doze a little. Arrow Maker laid Uvarov down flat on the hard metal surfaces, and he showed Morrow how to massage his own muscles to stop them seizing up. Spinner produced food – dried fruit and meat – from a pouch at her waist; Morrow tried to eat but his stomach was a knot.

He counted the Decks as they passed them. *Ten ... Eleven ... Twelve ...* The Decks above Four – all the world he had known, really – were an increasingly distant bubble of light and warmth, far above him.

And yet, if this journey was strange and disturbing for him, how much more difficult must it be for the forest folk? At least Morrow was *used* to metal walls. Spinner and her father had grown up with trees – animals, birds – living things. They must wonder if they would ever see their home again.

At last, though, the time came when he could count the last twenty rungs; then the last dozen; and then –

He staggered a few paces away from the ladder and laid himself out against a metal floor, spread-eagled. Here at the base of the shaft, a series of open, illuminated hatchways pierced the walls. 'By Lethe's waters,' he said. 'What a day. I

168

never thought I'd be so happy simply not to be in danger of *falling.*'

Arrow Maker lifted Uvarov from his shoulder and gently rested him, like a doll, against the wall of the elevator shaft. Morrow saw how Uvarov's hand continued its endless, pendular tremble, and his mouth opened and closed with soft, obscene sounds. 'Are we there? Are we down?'

Maker flexed his unburdened shoulder, swinging his arm around. 'Yes,' he said. 'Yes, we're there . . .' He approached one of the hatchways, but slowed nervously as he approached the light.

Morrow got to his feet. He tried to remember how alien all this must be to these people; perhaps it was time for him to take charge. Picking a hatchway at random he walked confidently out of the shaft, and into bright, sourceless light.

The brightness, after the gloom of the shaft, was dazzling and huge. For a moment he stood there, by the entrance to the shaft, his hands shading his watering eyes.

He was in a bright, clean chamber. It must have been a mile wide and a fifth of a mile deep. The underside of the lowest Deck was a ceiling far above him, a tangle of pipes and cables, dark with age. The chamber was quite empty, although there were some dark, anonymous devices – *cargo handlers?* – stored in slings from the walls and upper bulkhead. Morrow felt himself quail; the emptiness of this huge enclosed space seemed to bear down on him. And below him –

He looked down.

The floor was transparent. Below his feet, there were stars.

12

After an unknowable, dreamlike interval, Lieserl became aware of a vague sense of discomfort – not *pain*, exactly, but a non-localized ache that permeated her body.

She sighed. If the discomfort wasn't specific to any part of her Virtual body, there had to be something wrong with the autonomic systems that maintained her awareness – the basic refrigeration systems embedded in the wormhole throat, or maybe the shielded processor banks within which her consciousness resided.

Reluctantly she called up diagnostics from her central systems. *Damn* ...

There *had* been a change, she realized quickly. But the problem wasn't actually with her own systems. The change was in the external environment. There was a much greater flux of photons, from the Solar material, into her wormhole Interface. Her refrigeration units could cope with this greater influx of energy, but they'd had to adjust their working to do it – and that autonomic adjustment was what she had registered as a vague discomfort.

The increased photon flux puzzled her. Why should it be so? She ran some brief, brisk studies of the Solar environment. The remnant photons still diffused out on their million-year random walks towards the photosphere. Could it be that the core-killing action of the birds, their continual leaching away of core energy, was having some effect on the photon flux?

She looked for, and found, a structure to the increased flux. The flux strength was strongest, by far, in the direction of the orbits of the photino birds. That correlation couldn't be a coincidence, surely; somehow the birds *were* influencing the flux rates.

And – she learned – the increased flux was quite localized. It didn't show up more than a few miles from her *own* position.

Understanding came slowly, almost painfully.

The photon flood followed *her* around.

She forced herself to accept the fact that the photino birds were doing this *deliberately*. They were diverting the random walks of photons to flood her with the damn things.

For a while, fear touched her heart. Were the birds trying to kill this unwanted alien in the midst of their flocks – perhaps by seeking to overload her refrigeration system?

If so, there wasn't much she could do about it. She didn't have any help to call on, and no real way to escape. For a long time she limped after the birds in their endless circling of the core, monitoring the photon flux and trying to control her fear, her sense of imprisonment and panic.

But the flux remained steady – increased, but easily tolerated by her onboard systems. And the birds showed no sign of hostile intent to her; they continued to swirl around her in gaudy streams, or else they gathered behind her in their huge, neat, cone-shaped formations. They made no attempt to shield their young from her, or to protect their fragile-looking interior structures.

And, slowly, she began to understand.

This deliberate diversion of the photon flux into her wasn't a threat, or an attempt to destroy her. Perhaps they thought she was injured, or even dying. They must be able to perceive radiant energy disappearing into her wormhole gullet. The birds were *helping* her – trying to supply her with more of what must seem to them to be her prerequisites for life.

The gift was useless, of course – in fact, given the increased strain on her refrigeration systems, worse than useless. *But*, she thought wryly, *it's the thought that counts*.

The birds were trying to *feed* her.

Feeling strangely warmed, she accepted the gift of the photino birds with good grace.

As time wore on, she watched the Sun's death proceed, with increasing pace. She felt an obscure, dark thrill as the huge physical processes unravelled around her.

The core, still plagued by the photino bird flocks, contracted and continued to heat up. At last, a temperature of tens of millions of degrees was reached in the layers of hydrogen *surrounding* the cankered core. A shell of fusing hydrogen ignited, *outside* the core, and began to burn its way out of the heart of the Sun. At first Lieserl wondered if the photino birds would try to quench this new shell of energy, as they had the hydrogen core. But they swept through the fusing shell, ignoring its brilliance. Helium ash was deposited by the shell onto the dead core; the core continued to grow in mass, collapsing still further under its own weight.

The heat energy emitted by the shell, with that of the inert, collapsing core, was greater than that which had been emitted by the *original* fusing core.

The Sun couldn't sustain the increased heat output of its new heart. In an astonishingly short period it was forced to expand – to become *giant*.

Louise Ye Armonk stood on the forecastle deck of the *Great Britain*, peering down at the southern pole of Triton.

The *Britain* sailed through space half a mile above the satellite's thin, gleaming cap of nitrogen ice; steam trailed through space, impossibly, from the ship's single funnel. The ice cap curved beneath the prow of the ship as seamlessly as some huge eggshell. The southern hemisphere of Neptune's largest moon was just entering its forty-year summer, and the ice cap was receding; when Louise tilted back her head she could see thin, high cirrus clouds of nitrogen ice streaming northwards on winds of evaporated pole material.

She walked across the deck, past the ship's bell suspended in its elaborate cradle. The huge, misty bulk of Neptune was reflected in the bell's gleaming surface, and Louise ran her hand over the cool contours of the shaped metal, making it rock gently; the multiple, amorphous images of Neptune slid gracefully across the metal.

From here the Sun was a bright star, a remote point of light; and the blue light of Neptune, eerily Earthlike, bathed the lines of the old ship, making her seem ethereal, not quite substantial – paradoxical, Louise reflected, since the *Britain* was actually the only real artefact in her sensorium at present.

As the *Britain* neared the ragged edge of Triton's ice cap, a geyser blew, almost directly in front of the floating ship. Dark substrate material laced with nitrogen ice plumed into the air, rising ten miles from the plain; as it reached the thin, high altitude wind the plume turned through a right angle and streamed across the face of Triton. Louise walked to the lip of the forecastle deck and followed the line of the plume back down to the surface of the moon, where she could just see the fine crater in the ice at the plume's base. The geyser was caused by the action of the sun's heat on pockets of gas trapped beneath thin crusts of ice. Shards of ice were sprinkled around the site of the eruption, and some splinters still cartwheeled through the thin nitrogen atmosphere, slowly returning to the surface under the languid pull of Triton's gravity.

This was one of her favourite Virtual dioramas, although it was actually one of the least familiar. The capability of her processors to generate these dioramas was huge, but not infinite; she'd deliberately kept the Neptune diorama in reserve, rationing its use over the unchanging centuries, to try to conserve its appeal.

It wasn't hard to analyse why this particular Virtual scene appealed to her so much. The landscape of this remote moon was extraordinary and unfamiliar, and surprisingly full of change, fuelled by the energies of distant Sol; and Neptune's blue mass, with its traceries of nitrogen cirrus, was sufficiently Earthlike to prompt deep, almost buried feelings of nostalgia in her – and yet different enough that the references to Earth were almost subliminal, obscure enough that she was not tempted to descend into morbid longing. And –

Pixels swirled before her suddenly, a thousand self-orbiting blocks of light. Surprised, she almost stumbled; she gripped onto the rail at the edge of the deck for support.

The pixels coalesced with a soundless concussion into the image of Mark Wu. The projection was poor: the Virtual floated a few inches above the deck, and cast no shadow in Neptune's pale light.

'Lethe's waters,' Louise said, 'don't do that. You startled me.'

'I'm sorry,' Mark said. Even his voice was coarse and blocky, Louise noticed. 'It was urgent. I had to interrupt you. I –'

'*And* this projection's lousy. What's the matter with you?' Louise felt her mind slide comfortably into one of its familiar sets – what Mark called her *analytical griping*. She'd be able to

173

while away a good chunk of the empty day interrogating the processor, picking over details of this representation of Mark. 'You're even floating above the deck, damn it. I wouldn't be surprised if you start losing the illusion of solidity next. And –'

'Louise. I said it was *urgent*.'

She found her voice trailing off, her concentration dissolving.

Mark stepped towards her, and his face enhanced visibly, fleshing out and gaining violet-blue tones of Neptunian light. The processors projecting Mark were obviously trying to help her through this interaction. But the rest of his body remained little more than a three-dimensional sketch – a sign that he was diverting most of the available processing power to another priority. 'Louise,' Mark said, his voice soft but insistent. 'Something's happened. Something's changed.'

'Changed?' *Nothing's changed – not significantly – for nearly a thousand years ...*

Mark smiled. 'Your mouth is open.'

She swallowed. 'I'm sorry. I think you're going to have to give me a bit of time with this.'

'I'm going to turn off the diorama.'

She looked up with unreasonable panic at the remote face of Neptune. 'Why?'

'Something's happened, Louise –'

'You said that already.'

'*The lifedome.*' His eyes were fixed on hers.

She felt dreamy, light, almost unconcerned, and she wondered if the nanobots working within her body were feeding her some subtle tranquillizer. 'Tell me.'

'Someone is trying to use one of the ports in the lifedome base.' Mark's eyes were deep, probing. 'Do you understand, Louise? Can you hear what I'm saying?'

'Of course I can,' she snapped.

After five centuries without contact, someone was leaving the lifedome. She tried to grasp the reality of Mark's statement, to envisage it. *Someone was coming.*

'Turn off the projection,' she told Mark wearily. 'I'm ready.'

Neptune collapsed suddenly, like a burst balloon; Triton shrivelled into a billion dwindling pixels, and the light of Sol flickered out. For a moment there was only the *Great Britain*, the undeniable reality of Brunel's old ship hard and incongruent at the centre of this infinity of greyness, of the absence of form; Mark stood before her on the battered deck, his too-real face fixed on hers, reassuring.

Then the Universe returned.

Arrow Maker was falling out of the world.

He sat in the craft – this *pod*, as Uvarov had called it – with his bow and quiver piled neatly on the seat next to him. His bare legs dangled over his chair's smooth lip. There was a simple control console, just within his reach before him.

The pod's walls were transparent, making the cylindrical hull almost invisible. The pod was *nothing*, less sheltering than an insubstantial dream; the four seats, with Maker and his incongruous, futile bow, seemed to be dropping unsupported through the air.

Uvarov had pointed out the pod to him. Maker had barely been able to *see* it – a box of translucent strangeness in a world of strangeness.

Uvarov had told him to get into the pod. Maker, without thought, it seemed, had obeyed.

Through the floor of the pod he could see the port approaching. It was a rectangle set in the base of the lifedome, bleak and unadorned, bordered by a line of pale brilliance. He could still see stars through the lifedome base, but he realized now that it wasn't perfectly transparent. It returned some reflection of the sourceless inner light of the lifedome, making it a genuine floor across the world. Perhaps a layer of dust had collected over the base during the long centuries, spoiling its pristine clarity.

By contrast there was nothing within the expanding frame of the port – *nothing*, not even Uvarov's stars. The frame was rising towards him, preparing to swallow him and this foolish craft like an opening mouth.

The port was a doorway to emptiness.

He felt his bowels loosen. Fear was constantly with him, constantly threatening to erupt from his control . . .

Spinner's voice sounded small, distorted, emanating from the air. 'Maker? Can you hear me? Are you all right?'

He cried out and gripped the edges of his seat. His throat was so tight with tension he couldn't speak. He closed his eyes, shutting out the huge, bizarre unrealities around him, and tried to get some control. He lifted his hands to his waist; he touched the liana rope Spinner had wrapped around him as a good luck talisman, just before his departure.

'Maker? Arrow Maker?'

'. . . Spinner,' he gasped. 'I can hear you. Are you all right?'

She laughed, and just for a moment he could visualize her round, sardonic face, the way she would push her spectacles up her short nose. 'That's hardly the point, is it? The question is, are *you* all right?'

'Yes.' He opened his eyes, cautiously. The invisible engines of this bubble-pod hummed, almost silently, and below him the exit from the lifedome was a floor of grey emptiness, expanding towards him with exquisite slowness. 'Yes, I'm all right. You startled me a bit, that's all.'

'I'm not surprised.' The voice of the tall, dry man from the Decks – Morrow – was rendered even more flat than usual by the distortions of the hidden communications devices. 'Maybe we should have spent more time showing you what to expect.'

'Is there anything you want?'

'Yes, Spinner-of-Rope.' Arrow Maker felt small, fragile, isolated, like a child in a vehicle made for adults. All around him there was a sharp, *empty* smell: of plastic and metal, an absence of life. He longed for the rich humidity of the jungle. 'I wish we could go home,' he told his daughter.

'For Life's sake, stop this babbling.' The voice of Garry Uvarov was like a rattle of bone against glass. 'Arrow Maker,' Uvarov said. 'Where are you?'

Maker hesitated. The lifedome exit was huge beneath him now – he was so close to it, in fact, that its corners and edges were foreshortened; the semi-transparent surface of the lifedome turned into a rim of distant, star-spangled carpet around this immense cavity. He felt himself cringe. He reached out blindly for his bow and clutched it to his chest; it was a small token of normality in this world of strangeness. 'I can't be more than a dozen feet from the exit. And I –'

The lip of the port, brightly lit, slid upwards around the pod, now; Arrow Maker felt as if he were being immersed in some bottomless pool.

* * *

When she understood the birds were trying to feed her, she

tried to pick out individuals among the huge flocks. She told herself she wanted to study the birds: learn more of their life-cycle, mediated as it was by baryonic matter, and perhaps even try to become *empathetic* with the birds, to try to comprehend their individual and racial goals.

But making friends with photino birds – forming contact with individuals in anything like a conventional human sense – simply wasn't a possibility for her, it emerged. They were so nearly alike – after all, she reflected, given their simple reproductive strategy the birds were very nearly clones of each other – that it was all but impossible for her to tell them apart. And, on their brief orbits around the Sun, they flashed past her so quickly. She certainly couldn't identify them closely enough to follow individuals through consecutive orbits past her.

So – though she was surrounded by the birds, and bathed in their strange, luminous generosity – Lieserl remained, still, fundamentally alone.

She felt intense disappointment at this. At first she told herself that this was a symptom of her limited understanding of the birds: Lieserl, as the frustrated scientist.

But this was just a rationalization, she knew.

She forced herself to be honest. What some part of her really wanted, deep down, was for the photino birds to *accept* her – if not as one of their own, then as a tolerable alien in their midst.

When she first diagnosed this about herself, she felt humiliat-ed. For the first time she was glad there was nobody observing her, no latter-day equivalent of Kevan Scholes studying her telemetry and deducing her mental state. Was she really so pathetic, so internally weak, that she needed to cling to crumbs of friendship – even from these dark-matter creatures, whose alienness from her was so fundamental that it made the differences between humans and Qax look like close kinship?

Was she *really* so lonely?

The subsequent embarrassment and fit of self-loathing took a long time to fade.

Individual contact with the birds would be meaningless anyway. Since they were so alike, their behaviour as individ-uals so undifferentiated, racial goals seemed far more import-ant to the birds than individual goals. Personality was

177

subsumed beneath the purpose of the species to a far greater extent than it ever had been with humans – even at the time of the Assimilation, she thought, when opposition to the Xeelee had emerged as a clear racial goal for humanity.

She watched the birds breed, endlessly, the swarms of clumsy young sweeping on uncontrolled elliptical orbits around the Sun's core in pursuit of their parents.

The birds' cloning mode of reproduction seemed to shape the course of their lives.

At first the cloning seemed restrictive – even claustrophobic. Racial goals, downloaded directly from the mother's awareness into the young, overrode any individual ambitions. The young were robots, she decided, programmed from birth to fulfil the objectives of the species.

But then, so had *she* been programmed by her species – and so, to some extent, had every human who had ever lived, she thought. It was all a question of degree.

And anyway, would it really be so terrible, to be a photino bird?

With species-objective programming must come an immense fund of wisdom. The youngest photino bird would come to awareness with an expanded set of racial memories and drivers surely beyond the comprehension of any human.

Phillida had boasted that she – Lieserl – would become, with her close and accurate control of her memories and the functions of her mind, the most *conscious* human who had ever lived. Maybe that was once true. But, even at the height of her powers, Lieserl's degree of awareness was surely a mere candle compared to the immense conscious power available to the humblest of the photino birds.

And perhaps, she thought wistfully, these birds *were* all components of some extended group-mind – perhaps to analyse the consciousness of any individual bird would be as meaningless as to study the awareness of a single component in her own processing banks, or one neurone in the brain of a conventional human.

Perhaps.

But that didn't seem important to Lieserl, compared to the sense of *belonging* the birds must share.

Lieserl, the eternal outsider, watched the birds sweep past

her in their lively, co-ordinated flights. She felt awe – and something else: *envy*.

She pulled away from the shrinking core of the Sun, out through the searing hydrogen-fusing shell, and soared up into the envelope – the bloated, gaseous mantle that the outer forty per cent of giant-Sun's mass had become. The envelope was a universe of thin gas – so thin, she imagined, that if she tried hard enough she could see out through these teeming layers, to the stars beyond (or what was left of them).

The Sun was a red giant. It had become a pocket cosmos in itself, with its own star – the hydrogen-fusion shell around the dead core – blazing at the centre of this clogged, gas-filled space. But the outer layers, the mantle, had become so swollen that they utterly dwarfed the core. In fact, the dimensions of the Sun were like those of an atom, she realized, with the shrunken, blazing core occupying the same proportion of space within its mantle-cloud as did the nucleus of an atom within its cloud of electrons.

The photino birds clustered around the Sun's shrinking heart, sipping relentlessly at its energy store. She was outside the bulk of the flock now – although some outriders still swept past her, on their way into the flock from the Universe outside. With a new feeling of detachment, she started to experience a deepening sense of disquiet at the activities of the birds. From this perspective, the birds seemed like carrion, she thought, or tiny, malevolent parasites.

Restless, disturbed, Lieserl moved through the huge envelope. There was *structure* here, even in this immense volume, she saw. The photosphere of the new red giant – its huge, glowing surface – had actually become less opaque to radiation; its temperature had fallen so far that electrons had recombined with nuclei, increasing the transparency of the surface layers. So – even though its surface temperature had dropped – the Sun was actually radiating more energy, overall, than it had done before its swelling.

To fuel this increased luminosity, immense convection cycles had started – cells which spanned millions of miles, and which would persist for hundreds of days. The convection cycles dug deep into the mantle to haul energy out of the core regions to be pumped out to space – and along with the energy dredging, Lieserl saw, the convection was changing the composition of the Sun, polluting the outer regions with nucleosynthesis products like nitrogen–14, dug out of the core regions.

Coherent maser radiation flashed along the flanks of the convection cells, startling her with its intensity.

As she travelled through the thin gas she felt a faint buffeting, a rocking of the exotic-matter framework of her Interface.

There was turbulence here. The convection process wasn't perfectly efficient, and energy, struggling to escape from the inner regions, was forced to dissipate itself in a complex, space-filling array of turbulent cells. The Sun's magnetic field was affected by this turbulence. She saw how the flux was pushed out of the interior of the cells, to form fine sheets across the cells' surfaces – but the sheets were unstable, and they burst like sheets of soap film, leaving ropes of flux at the intersections of the turbulence cells. Lieserl swam through a million-mile mesh of the magnetic flux ropes.

It was bizarre to think that – if she wished – she could travel out as far as the old orbital radius of Earth, without ever leaving the substance of the Sun.

Lieserl knew – with remote, abstract sadness – that the inner planets, out as far as Earth, must have been consumed in the Sun's cooling, red-tinged mantle. She remembered her brief, golden childhood: the sparkling beaches of the Aegean, the sharp, enticing scent of the sea, the feel of sand between her babyish toes. Perhaps humans, somewhere, were still enjoying such experiences.

But Earth, the only world *she* had known, was gone forever.

13

'Arrow Maker, *tell me what you see*. Can you see the stars?'

Arrow Maker looked down, through the pod hull. 'I don't understand.'

Uvarov's voice, disembodied, became ragged; Arrow Maker imagined the old man thrashing feebly beneath his blanket. 'Can you see Sol? You should be able to, by now. Arrow Maker – *is Earth there*? Is –'

'No.'

'Maker –'

'*No.*'

Arrow Maker shouted the last word, and Uvarov subsided.

The illuminated lip of the port had passed right over the pod now; it was visible to Maker as a frame of light above his head. The outer darkness had enclosed the pod ... No, he was thinking about this in the wrong way. The darkness was the Universe; as if in some obscene, mechanical birth, the pod had been *expelled* from the lifedome into the dark.

The base of the lifedome hung over him like a huge belly of glass and metal, receding slowly, its curvature becoming apparent. And through it – distorted, rendered misty by the base material – he made out the light-filled interior of the dome. He could see bits of detail: elevator shafts from the decks above, control consoles like the one at which he'd left Spinner, Morrow and Uvarov – why, if he had eyes sharp enough, he could probably look up now and see the soles of his daughter's feet.

Suddenly the reality of it hit him. He had travelled *outside the lifedome*. He was beyond its protective hull – perhaps the first human to have ventured outside in half a millennium – and now he was suspended in the emptiness which made up most of the forbidding, lifeless Universe.

'*Arrow Maker*. Talk to us.'

Arrow Maker laughed, his voice shrill in his own ears. 'I'm suspended in a glass bubble, surrounded by emptiness. I can see the lifedome. It's like –'

'Like what?' Morrow's voice, sounding intrigued.

'Like a box of light. Quite – beautiful. But very fragile-looking . . .'

Uvarov cut in, 'Oh, give me strength. *What else, Arrow Maker?*'

Arrow Maker twisted his head, to left and right.

To the right of the pod, an immense pillar of sculpted metal swept through space. It was huge, quite dwarfing the pod, like the trunk of some bizarre artificial tree. It merged seamlessly with the lifedome, and it was encrusted with cups, ribs and flowers of shaped metal.

Maker described this.

'The spine,' Uvarov said impatiently. 'You're travelling parallel to the spine of the GUTship. Yes, yes; just as I told you. Arrow Maker, can you see the Interface? The wormhole –'

Arrow Maker leaned forward and peered down, past the seats and stanchions, through the pod's base. This *spine* descended for a great distance, its encrustation of parasitic forms dwindling with perspective, until the spine narrowed to a mere irregular line. The whole form was no less than three miles long, Uvarov had told him.

Beyond the spine's end was a sheet of light which hid half the sky. The light was eggshell-blue and softly textured; it was like a vast, inverted flower petal, ribbed with lines of stronger, paler hue. As Arrow Maker watched he could see a slow evolution in the patterns of light, with the paler lines waving softly, coalescing and splitting, like hair in a breeze. The light cast blue highlights, rich and varying, from the structures along the spine.

He was looking at the GUTdrive: the light came from the primeval energies, Uvarov had told him, which had hurled the ship and all its cargo through space and time for a thousand years.

Silhouetted against the sheet of creation light, just below the base of the spine, was a dark, irregular mass, too distant for Arrow Maker to resolve: that was the tethered ice asteroid, which still – after all these years – patiently gave up its flesh to serve as reaction mass for the great craft. And –

'Uvarov. *The Interface.* I see it.'

There, halfway down the spine's gleaming length, was a tetrahedral structure: edged in glowing blue, tethered to the spine by what looked like hoops of gold.

'Good.' He heard a tremulous relief in Uvarov's voice. '*Good.* Now, Arrow Maker – look around the sky, and describe the stars you see.'

Arrow Maker stared, beyond the ship. The spine, the Interface, were suspended in darkness.

Uvarov's speech became rushed, almost slurred. 'Why, we might be able to place our position – and the *date* – by the constellations. If I can find the old catalogues; those damn survivalists in the Decks must have retained them. And –'

'Uvarov.' Arrow Maker tried to inject strength into his voice. 'Listen to me. There's something wrong.'

'There can't be. I –'

'There are no constellations. *There are no stars.*' Beyond the ship there was only emptiness; it was as if the great ship, with its flaring drive and teeming lifedome, was the only object in the Universe ...

No, that wasn't quite true. He stared to left and right, scanning the equator of the grey-black sky around him; there seemed to be *something* there – a ribbon of light, too faint to make out colour.

He described this to Uvarov.

'The starbow.' Uvarov's voice sounded much weaker, now. 'But that's impossible. If there's a starbow we must be travelling, still, at relativistic velocities. But we can't be.' The old, dead voice cracked. 'Maker, you've seen the stars yourself.'

'No.' Arrow Maker tried to make his voice gentle. 'Uvarov, all I've ever seen were points of light in a skydome ... Maybe they weren't stars at all.'

If, he thought ruefully, *the stars ever existed at all.*

He stared at the mass of the spine as it slid upwards past him, suddenly relishing its immensity, its detail. He was *glad* there were no stars. If this ship was all that existed, anywhere in the Universe, then it would be enough for him. He could spend a lifetime exploring the worlds contained within its lifedome, and there would always be the forest to return to. And –

Light filled the cabin: a storm of it, multicoloured cubes and spheres which swarmed around him, dazzling him. Then, as suddenly as they had appeared, the cubes hurtled together and coalesced.

There was a man sitting beside Arrow Maker, *inside the pod*, dressed in a grey-silver tunic and trousers. His hands were in his lap, folded calmly, and through his belly and thighs Arrow Maker could see the quiver of arrows he'd left on the chair – *he could actually see the quiver*, through the flesh of the man.

The man smiled. 'My name's Mark – Mark Bassett Friar Armonk Wu. Don't be frightened.'

Arrow Maker screamed.

Lieserl swam with the photino birds through the heart of the bloated Sun. The photino birds appeared to relish Sol's new incarnation. Plasma oscillations caused energy to flood out of the core, in neutrino-antineutrino pairs, and the birds swooped around the core, drinking in this glow of new radiance.

The matter in the inert, collapsing core had become so compressed it was *degenerate*, its density so high that the intermolecular forces that governed its behaviour as a gas had broken down. Now, the gravitational infall was balanced by the pressure of electrons themselves: the mysterious rule of quantum mechanics called the Pauli Exclusion Principle, which ensures that no two electrons can share the same energy level.

But this new state of equilibrium couldn't last for long, Lieserl realized. The shell of fusing hydrogen around the core continued to burn its way outward, raining helium ash down on the core; and so the core continued to grow, to heat up.

Now that the inner planets were gone, she felt utterly isolated.

Why, even the stone-faced bureaucrats of the Assimilation period had been contact of a sort. She'd found it immensely valuable to be able to share impressions with somebody else – somebody outside her own sensorium. In fact she wondered if it were possible for any human being to remain sane, given a long enough period without communication.

But then again, she thought wryly, she *wasn't* a human being ...

Into Lethe with that. She closed her eyes and stretched. She took a slow, careful inventory of her Virtual body-image. She wriggled her fingers, relishing the detailed feel of sliding tendons and stretching skin; she arched her back and felt the muscles at the front of her thighs pull taut; she worked her feet forward and back, as if she were training for some celestial ballet, and focused on the slow, smooth working of her ankles and toes.

She was human, all right, and she was determined to stay that way – even despite the way she'd been treated by humans themselves, in her brief, but still vivid, corporeal life. What had she been but a freak, an experiment that had ultimately been abandoned?

She didn't owe *people* anything, she told herself.

Maybe.

But again that buried urge to *communicate* all this gripped her: she felt she had to tell someone about all this, to warn them.

But those feelings weren't logical, she knew. Since the wormhole telemetry link had been shut down she had no way to communicate anyway. And while she had dreamed, here inside the imperilled heart of the Sun, five million years had worn away in the Solar System outside. For all she knew there might be no humans left alive, anywhere, to hear whatever she might have to say.

... Still, she *itched* to talk.

Again, maser radiation shone out of a convection cell and sparkled over her, bright and coherent.

Intrigued, she followed the path of one of the convection cells as it swept out of the heart of the Sun, bearing its freight of heat energy; she tried to trace the source of the maser light.

The radiation, she found, was coming from a thin trace of silicon monoxide in the mantle gas. Collisions between particles were *pumping* the gas with energy, she saw – leaving the monoxide molecules in an unstable, excited state, rotating rapidly.

A photon of just the right frequency, impacting a pumped molecule, could cause the molecule to tip out of its unstable state. The molecule shed energy and emitted another photon of the same frequency. So the result was *two* photons, where one had been before ... And the two photons stimulated two more atoms, resulting in four photons ... A chain reaction followed, growing geometrically, with a flood of photons from the stimulated silicon monoxide molecules – all at the same micro-wave frequency, and all coherent – with the same phase.

Lieserl knew that to get significant maser effects, pumped molecules had to be arranged in a line of sight, to get a long path of coherence. The convection cells, with their huge, multi-million-mile journeys to the surface and back, provided just such pathways. Maser radiation cascaded up and down the long flanks of the cells, spearing into and out of the helium core.

The maser radiation could even escape from the Sun altogether, she saw. The convection founts grazed the surface, at their most extreme points; maser energy was blasted out, tangential to the surface of the swollen Sun, forming tiny, precise beacons of coherent light.

And the maser beacons were, she realized with a growing excitement, very, very distinctive.

Excited, she swept back and forth through the huge convection cells. It wasn't difficult, she found, to disrupt the form of the coherent silicon monoxide maser beams; she imposed structure on the beams' polarization, phasing and coherent lengths.

She started with simple signals: sequences of prime numbers, straightforward binary arrays of symbols. She could keep that up almost indefinitely; thanks to the time it took for the coher-ent radiation to reach their firing points at the surface, it was sufficient for her to return to the convection cells every few days to re-initiate her sequence of signals. She could trace echoes of her signals, in fact, persisting even in the downfalling sides of the cells.

Then, as her confidence grew, she began to impose meaning-ful information content on her simple signal structure. With binary representations of images in two and three dimensions, and with data provided in every human language she knew, she began to relate the story of what had happened to her, here in the heart of the Sun – and of what the photino birds were doing to mankind's star.

Feverishly she worked at the maser signals, while the final death of the Sun unravelled.

In the stern galley of the *Great Britain*, Louise sat before her data desks. The little pod from the lifedome showed up as a block of pixels sliding past a schematic of the *Northern*.

Over the radio link she heard screams.

'Oh, for Lethe's sake, Mark, don't scare him *completely* out of his mind.'

Mark sounded hurt. 'I'm doing my best.'

Louise felt too tired, too used up, to cope with this sudden flood of events.

She tried, sometimes, to remember how it had been to be young. Or even, not quite so *old*. It might have been different if Mark had survived, of course: his AS system had imploded after four centuries, not long after he and Louise had moved out of the lifedome and into the *Britain*. Maybe if Mark *had* lived, if she'd spent all these years with another person – *not alone* – she wouldn't have ended up feeling so damn *stale*.

She comforted herself with the thought that, whatever was going on today, the *Northern*'s immense journey was nearing its end, now. Another few decades, when she had shepherded the wormhole Interface and motley inhabitants of the lifedome – those who'd survived among those battling, swarming masses – through all these dreadful years, she would be able to let go at last. Maybe *she* would implode then, she thought, like some dried-up husk.

She called up a projection of its trajectory. 'Well, it's not heading for the *Britain*,' she told Virtual-Mark. 'It's moving past us ...'

A new voice came crackling out of her data desk now. 'Arrow Maker. *Arrow Maker*. Listen to me. You must reach the Interface. Don't let them stop you ...'

To Louise, this was a voice from the dead past. It was distorted by age, almost reduced to a caricature, echoing as if centuries were empty rooms.

She localized the source of the transmission – a desk in the base of the lifedome, near the pod hangars – and she threw open a two-way link. 'Uvarov? Garry Uvarov?'

The voice fell silent, abruptly.

She heard Mark, in the pod, saying, 'Now just take it easy. I know this is strange for you, but I'm not going to hurt you.' A pause. 'I couldn't if I tried. I'll tell you a secret: *I'm not real*. See? My hand is passing right through your arm, and –'

More screams, even shriller than before.

187

Oh, Mark . . .

'Come on, Uvarov,' she said. 'I know it's you. I still recognize that damn Moon accent. Speak to me.'

'Oh, Lethe, Louise,' Mark reported, 'he's gone crazy. He's grabbed the stick: he's accelerating – right towards the Interface.'

Mark was right, she saw; the craft's speed had increased, and it was clearly heading to where the wormhole Interface was cradled in its web of superconducting hoops, bound magnetically to the structure of the GUTship.

She punched in quick queries. Less than two minutes remained before the pod reached the Interface.

'Uvarov, listen to me,' she said urgently. 'You must respond. Please.' While she spoke her hands flew over the desks; she ordered her processors to find some way to take control of the pod. She cursed herself, silently, for her carelessness. She'd had centuries, literally, to find ways of immobilizing the lifedome pods. But she'd never imagined this scenario, some crazy savage with a painted face taking a pod into the Interface while they were still relativistic.

Well, she damn well *should* have imagined it.

'Uvarov. You must respond. We're still in flight.' She tried to imagine the old eugenicist's condition, extrapolating wildly from the few words she'd heard him speak. 'Uvarov, can you hear me? You have to stop him – the man in the pod, this *Arrow Maker*. He'll destroy himself . . .' *And*, she thought sourly, *maybe the whole damn ship as well*. 'You know as well as I do that the Interface can't be used during the flight. The kinetic energy difference between our Interface and the one back in the past will make the wormhole unstable. If your Arrow Maker flies that pod in there, he'll wreck the wormhole.'

'You're lying,' Uvarov rasped. 'The journey's over. We've seen the stars.'

'Uvarov, listen to me. *We're still relativistic*.' She turned to peer out of the galley's small windows. The *Britain* was suspended beneath the belly of the lifedome, so that the dome was huge and brilliant above her; the spine pierced space a few hundred yards away. And, all around the spine, the starbow – the ring of starlight aberrated by their motion – gleamed dully, infinitely far away.

With a small corner of her mind, she longed to shut this out, to erect some Virtual illusion to hide in.

'I can see the damn starbow, Uvarov. With my own eyes, right now. We're decelerating, but we're still relativistic. We have decades of this journey ahead of us yet ...' Was it possible Uvarov had *forgotten*?

In the background she could hear Mark's voice patiently pleading with the primitive in the pod; her desks showed her endless representations of the processors' failed attempts to override the pod's autonomous systems, and the astonishingly rapid convergence of the pod with the Interface.

He pushed the crude control as far forward as it would go. The pod hurtled past the spine. He felt mesmerized, bound up in the extraordinary events around him, beyond any remnants of fear.

Once again a frame of light embraced the pod, expanding, enclosing, like a swallowing mouth. This time, the frame was triangular, not rectangular; it was rimmed by blue light, not silver-white. And it contained – not a bleak, charcoal-grey emptiness – but a pool of golden light, elusive, shimmering.

There were *stars* in that pool. How ironic it was, thought Arrow Maker, that perhaps here at last he would find the stars of which old, mad Uvarov had dreamed.

The ghost-man – *Mark* – was still speaking to him, urgently; but the ghost was crumbling into cubes of light, which scattered in the air, shrinking and melting.

Arrow Maker barely noticed.

Suddenly, she thought she understood.

She spoke rapidly. 'Uvarov, listen. Please. The skydome above the forest *isn't truly transparent*. It's semisentient – it's designed to deconvolve the distorting effects of the flight, to project an illusion of stars, of normal sky. Garry, can you hear me? The skydome shows a *reconstruction* of the sky – and I think you've *forgotten* that it's a reconstruction. The forest people *can't* have seen the stars.' She tried to find words to reach this man, whom she'd first known a thousand years ago. 'I'm sorry, Garry. I truly am. But you *must* make him turn back.'

'Louise.' Mark's voice was clipped, urgent. 'Arrow Maker is not responding. I'm starting to break up; we're already within

189

the exoticity field of the Interface, and –'

Uvarov screamed, 'The Interface, Arrow Maker! You'll travel back across five million years – tell them we're here, that *we made it*. Arrow Maker!'

Now there were other voices on Uvarov's link: a man, a girl. 'Maker! Maker! Come back . . .'

Mark's voice faded out.

On Louise's desk, the gleaming, toylike images, of pod and Interface, converged.

The blue-white framework was all around him now, its glow flooding the cabin of the pod with shadowless light and banishing the spine and lifedome, as if they were insubstantial. The pod shuddered, its framework glowing blue-violet.

The voice of Spinner-of-Rope, his daughter, became indistinct.

He called to her: 'Look after your sister, Spinner-of-Rope.'

He couldn't make out her reply. Soon there was only the tone of her dear voice, pleading, pressing.

A tunnel – lined by sheets of light, shimmering, impossibly long – opened out before him.

He sank into the golden pool, and even Spinner's voice was lost.

Louise massaged her temples and closed her eyes. There was nothing more she could do. Not now.

She remembered how it had become clear – early in the flight, after a shockingly short time – that the *Northern's* fragile artificial society was going to collapse. Mark had helped her understand the cramped social dynamics going on inside the lifedome: the dome contained a closed system, he said, with positive socio-feedback mechanisms leading to wild instabilities, and . . .

But understanding hadn't helped them cope with the collapse.

The first rebellion had been inspired by one of Louise's closest allies: Uvarov, who had led his eugenics-inspired withdrawal to the forest. After that Superet – or rather, the Planners who had turned the original Superet philosophy into a bizarre ideology – had subverted whatever authority Louise had retained and imposed its will on the remaining inhabitants of the lifedome.

Louise and Mark had withdrawn to this place: to the converted, secure *Great Britain*. From here Louise had isolated the starship's essential systems – life support and control – from the inhabitants of the dome. During the long centuries since – long after Mark's death, long after the occupants of the dome had forgotten her existence – she had watched over the swarming masses within the lifedome: regulating their air, ensuring the balance of the small, enclosed ecologies was maintained, guiding the ship to its final destination.

What the people did to each other, what they believed, was beyond her control. Perhaps it always had been. All she strove to do was to keep as many as possible of them alive.

But now, if the wormhole was lost, it had all been for nothing. *Nothing.*

The kinetic energy of the pod shattered the spacetime flaw that was the wormhole. The portal behind it imploded at lightspeed, and gravitational waves and exotic particles pulsed around the craft.

Arrow Maker felt the air thicken in his lungs, cold settling over his bare skin. The pod jolted, and he was almost thrown out of his seat; calmly he unwrapped Spinner's liana-rope from his waist and tied it around his torso and the seat, binding himself securely.

He held his hands before his face. He saw frost, glistening on his skin; his breath steamed in the air before him.

The pod's fragile hull cracked and starred; one by one the craft's systems – its heating, lights, air – collapsed under the hammer-blows of this impossible motion.

Through a transient network of wormholes which collapsed behind him in storms of heavy particles and gravity waves, Arrow Maker fell across past and future, the light of collapsing spacetime playing over his shivering flesh.

Light flared from the Interface. It gushed from every face of the tetrahedron like some liquid, bathing the *Northern* in violet fire.

It was like a small sun.

The starship shuddered. The steady glow of the GUTdrive

flickered – actually flickered, for the first time in centuries. The *Britain*, old and fragile in its cradle, rocked back and forth, and Louise heard a distant clatter of falling objects, the incongruously domestic sound of sliding furniture.

All over the lifedome, lights flickered and died.

14

He was the last man.

He was beyond time and space. The great quantum functions which encompassed the Universe slid past him like a vast, turbulent river, and his eyes were filled with the grey light against which all phenomena are shadows.

Time wore away, unmarked.

And then –

There was a box, drifting in space, tetrahedral, clear-walled.

From around an impossible corner a human entered the box. He sat in a battered, fragile craft which tumbled through space. A rope was wrapped around his waist, and he was dressed in treated animal skins. He was gaunt, encrusted in filth, his skin ravaged by frost.

He stared out at the stars, astonished.

Spacetime-fire erupted into the box, finally engulfing the little craft.

Something had changed. History had resumed.

Michael Poole's extended awareness stirred.

PART III

EVENT: SOL

15

Louise Ye Armonk stood on the pod's short ladder. Below her, the ice of Callisto was dark, full of mysterious depths in the smoky Jovian ring-light.

She felt a starburst of wonder. For the first time in a thousand subjective years she was going to walk on the surface of a world.

She stepped forward.

Her feet settled to the ice with a faint crunch. Her boots left well-defined, ribbed prints in the fine frost which coated Callisto's surface.

The thick environment suit felt heavy, despite the easiness of Callisto's thirteen-per-cent-gee gravity. Louise lifted her hands and pressed her palms together; she was barely able to feel her hands within the clumsy gloves. The suit was a thousand years old. Trapped inside this thing she felt deadened, aged, as if she were forced to work within some glutinous fluid.

She looked around, peering through her murky faceplate, squinting to make out detail through the plate's degraded image-enhancement. As her sense of wonder faded, she felt irritation grow; she knew it was weak of her, but, damn it, she *missed* the crystal clarity of her Virtual dioramas.

Jupiter and Sol were both below the little moon's infinite-flat, icy horizon: but Jupiter's new rings arced spectacularly out of the horizon and across the sky. The ring system's far edge occluded the stars, razor-sharp, and the ice and rock particles of the rings sparkled milky crimson in the cool, distant sunlight.

The rings were like a huge artefact, she thought. Here, a mote on a plain of ice, she felt dwarfed to insignificance.

She tipped back her head and looked at the stars.

It had already been a year since the *Northern*'s speed had dropped sufficiently for the last relativistic effects to bleach from the Universe, a year in which they'd slowly coasted in from the outer System to Jupiter. The *Northern* had been in orbit around the Jovian moon for several days now, and Morrow had been working down here for most of that time. Preliminary scans from the *Northern* had told them that there was something buried inside the freshly frozen Callisto ice – something *anomalous*. Morrow, with his team of 'bots, was trying to find out what that was.

But this was Louise's own first trip down to the surface. And the experience of being immersed in a *sky* – a genuine, spread-out, distortion-free starry sky – was an unnerving novelty to Louise, after so long being surrounded by the washed-out starbow of near-lightspeed.

But what a sky it was – a dull, empty canopy of velvet, peppered by the corpses of stars: wizened, cooling dwarfs, the bloated hulks of giants – some huge enough to show a disc, even at interstellar distances – and, here and there, the traceries of debris, handfuls of spider-web thrown across the sky, which marked the sites of supernovas.

There was a grunt, and a diffuse shadow fell across the ice.

Louise turned. Spinner-of-Rope was making her slow, cautious way out of the pod after her. Spinner's small body, made bulky by the suit, was silhouetted against the pod lights. She placed each footstep deliberately on the surface, and she held her arms out straight.

Louise grinned at Spinner. 'You look ridiculous.'

'Oh, thanks,' Spinner said sourly. Through the dully reflective faceplate Louise could see the glint of Spinner's spectacles, the glare of face paint, the white of Spinner's teeth. Spinner said, 'I just don't want to go slip-sliding across this ice-ball of a moon.'

Louise looked down and scuffed the surface with her toe, leaving deep scratches. Within the ice she could see defects: planes, threads and star-shaped knots, imperfections left by the freezing process. 'This is ice, but it's not exactly smooth.'

Spinner waddled up to her and sniffed; the noise was like a scratch in Louise's earpiece. 'Maybe,' Spinner said. 'But it's a lot smoother than it used to be.'

'. . . Yes.'

'Look,' Spinner said, pointing. 'Here comes the *Northern*.'

Louise turned and peered up, dutifully. The *Northern*, trailing through its hour-long orbit, was a thousand miles above the surface. Subvocally she ordered her faceplate to enhance the image. The ship became a remote matchstick, bright red in the light of Sol; it looked impossibly fragile, like some immense toy, she thought. The asteroid ice which had provided reaction mass for so long was a dark, anonymous lump, barely visible now that the great blue flame of the GUTdrive had been stilled after its thousand-year service. The spine, with its encrustation of antennae and sensor ports, was like an organic thing, bony, coated by bleached parasites. Red sunlight pooled like blood in the antennae cups. Still fixed to the spine was the wreckage of the wormhole Interface – twisted so that its tetrahedral form was lost beyond recognition, the electric-blue sparkle of its exotic matter frame dulled.

And the lifedome itself – eggshell-delicate – was huge atop that skinny spine, like the skull of a child. Most of the dome was darkened – closed up, impenetrable – but the upper few layers still glistened with light.

Within those bland walls, Louise reflected, two thousand people still went about their small, routine lives. Beyond Louise and her close companions, there were very few within the lifedome's fragmented societies who even knew that the *Northern*'s immense journey was, at last, over.

'How are you doing down there?'

She winced. The sudden voice in her ear had been raucous, overloud – another problem with this damn old suit.

'Mark, I'm fine. How are you?'

'What can you see? What are you thinking?'

'Mostly I can see the inside of this faceplate. Couldn't you have got it cleaned up? It smells like something's been *living* in it for a thousand years.'

He laughed.

'...I see the stars. What's left of them.'

'Yes.' Mark was silent for a moment. 'Well, it's just as we suspected from the deconvolved reconstructions during the flight ... but never quite believed, maybe. It's the same picture all over the sky, Louise; we've found no exceptions. It's incredible. In the five million years of our flight, stellar evolution has been forced through at least five *billion* years. And the effect isn't limited to this Galaxy. We can't even *see* the Lesser Magellanic Cloud, for example.'

The sky was lowering, oppressive. She said, 'Superet got it about right, didn't they? Remember the projections they showed us in the Virtual dome in New York, when they recruited us?'

'Yes ... wizened stars, faded galaxies. Depressing, isn't it?'

She smiled. 'Maybe. But the sky's become an astrophysicist's dream lab.'

'But it can't have been much of a dream for anyone left alive here, in the Solar System, when those novae and supernovae started going off. The sleet of hard radiation and massive particles must have been unrelenting, for a million years ...'

'Yes. A hard rain indeed. That will have sterilized the whole damn place –'

'– if there had been anyone left alive here by then. Which we've yet to find evidence of. Well, we're still following up our four leads – the maser radiation coming out of the Sun, the *very* strange gravity waves coming from Sagittarius, the artefact in the ice, here on Callisto, and that weak beacon in transPlutonian space ... But we're no further forward understanding any of it.'

'I can see the forest,' Spinner murmured, her faceplate upturned.

Louise studied the lifedome more carefully, enhanced the image with artificial colours – and there, indeed, she could see a thin layer of Earth green at the leading edge of the lifedome, the layer of living things stained dark by the aged sunlight.

That pet forest, she thought suddenly, might be the only *green* left, anywhere in the Universe.

Absurdly, she felt her throat tightening; she found it difficult to pull her gaze away from that drifting particle of *home*.

There was a hand on her arm, its weight barely registering through the numbing, stiff fabric of the suit. Spinner smiled. 'I know how you feel.'

Louise peered through the faceplate at this odd girl-woman, with her glinting spectacles and her round, childish face.

After Spinner's father had wrecked the Interface – and with it, any chance of getting home again – Louise had offered Spinner and her people AS-treatment. And, looking at Spinner now, fifty years later, it was hard to remember that this was no longer a child, but a sixty-five-year-old woman.

'I *doubt* you know how I feel,' she said coldly. 'I doubt it very much.'

Spinner studied her for a few moments, her painted face expressionless behind her plate.

They climbed back into the pod.

The little ship rose to a height of a mile, then levelled off and coasted parallel to the surface. Louise looked back. Their landing jets had blown a wide, shallow crater in the ice; it marred a plain which stretched, seamless and featureless, to the close horizon.

Louise sat in her seat; surrounded by the disconcertingly transparent hull, she felt – as always, in these pods – as if she were suspended in space. Below them the Callisto plain was a geometrical abstraction; above them, *Northern* climbed patiently past the deep, gleaming rings of Jupiter, a spark against those smooth arcs.

The main activity on Callisto was centred around Morrow's excavation site on the far side of the moon, the Jupiter-facing side. The purpose of this jaunt was to have a general scout, and to give Spinner-of-Rope some more experience of working outside the ship, the *feel* of standing on a planet surface ... Even, Louise thought, a surface so featureless, and with a sky so bare, that the moon had become almost an abstract representation of a planet.

Still, Louise knew it did *her* good to get away from the ship that had been her home, and prison, for so many centuries – and which, barring a miracle, was going to have to sustain her and her people for the rest of her life. Callisto was – had been – Jupiter's eighth moon, one of the four big Galilean satellites. At the time of *Northern*'s launch Callisto had been a ball of water ice and rock, heavily cratered. Debris had been sprayed across the mysterious surface from the bright cores of the impact craters; from space, Callisto had looked like a sphere of glass peppered by gunshots. One basin – called Valhalla – had been four hundred miles across, an immense amphitheatre surrounded by concentric terrace-like walls.

Louise remembered how human cities, feeding on Callisto's

ancient water, had glinted in the shadows of Valhalla's walls, shining like multicoloured jewels.

Well, the craters had gone now – as had Valhalla, and all the cities. Gone without trace, it seemed. Callisto had been wiped smooth, unblemished save for her own footsteps.

During, or after, the depopulation, Callisto had been caused to *melt*. And, when the moon froze once more, something had been trapped in the ice ...

The pod skimmed around the smooth limb of the moon. They were heading over the moon's north pole, and soon, Louise realized, they would be passing over the sharp terminator and into daylight.

... Or what passed for daylight, in these straitened times, she thought.

Beside her, Spinner fitted her faceplate over her head, leaving it open below her mouth. She peered around, through the flimsy walls of the pod. From the absent, unfocused expression in her eyes, Louise could tell she was using the plate's enhancement and magnification features.

'I can see moons,' Spinner said. 'A sky full of moons.'

'Nice for you,' Louise said drily. 'There should be eight – there used to be eight beyond Callisto. Small, irregular: probably captured asteroids. The outer four of them were retrograde, moving backwards compared to the planet's own rotation.'

'I'm surprised *any* moons survived the destruction of the planet.'

Louise shrugged. 'The nearest of the outer moons was a hundred and fifty Jovian radii from the primary, before the planet imploded ... even Callisto survived, remember, and that was a mere twenty-six radii out.' The orbits of the surviving moons had been disturbed by the Jovian event, of course; the implosion had sent them scattering with a shock of gravity waves, and now they swooped around their shattered parent along orbits of high eccentricity, like birds disturbed by earth tremors.

Within the orbit of Callisto, nothing had survived.

Now, as the pod passed over the pole, the Jovian ring system unfolded like a huge floor before Louise, infinite-flat and streaked with shadows.

This new ring system, the debris of worlds, lay in what had been Jupiter's equatorial plane – the plane once occupied by the vanished moons. Callisto still lay in the equatorial plane, patiently circling the site of the giant planet just outside the ring system, so that the disc of ring material – if it had stretched out so far – would have bisected Callisto neatly.

The ring system didn't terminate at a sharp inner boundary, like Saturn's. Instead the creamy, smoothed-out material stretched inwards – this system was actually more a disc than a ring system, Louise realized slowly. As her eyes tracked in towards the centre the system's texture slowly changed – becoming more rough, Louise saw, with knots of high density locked into the churning surface, orbiting through tight circles, swirling visibly.

The whole assemblage was stained crimson by scattered sunlight.

The rings were almost featureless – *bland*, without the complex colours and braids which characterized Saturn's system. Louise sighed. The gravitational interaction of moons had provided Saturn's rings with their fantastic structure. The trouble was that Jupiter's remaining moons simply weren't up to the job of shepherding the rings. For poor, dead Jupiter, only a single dark streak marked the orbital resonance of Callisto itself.

Now, the centre of the ring-disc rose above Callisto's sharp horizon. Louise could clearly see inhomogeneities churning around the geometric centre of the disc, twisting through their crowded, tortured orbits. But the disc centre itself was unspectacular – just a brighter patch, spinning with the rest of the disc. It was somehow frustrating, as if there were something missing.

Spinner sounded disappointed. 'I can't see anything in the middle. Where the planet used to be.'

Louise grinned. 'You'd hardly expect to. A black hole with Jupiter's mass would have a diameter of just twenty feet or so . . .'

'There's plenty to see in higher frequencies,' Mark cut in. 'The X-ray, and higher . . .

'Towards the heart of the system we have a true accretion disc,' he went on, 'with matter being heated tremendously before falling into the black hole itself. It's small, but there's a lot of structure there, if you look at it in the right bands.'

Spinner, with apparent eagerness, adjusted her plate over her face, and Mark told her how to fix the settings. Soon, Spinner's eyes assumed that unfocused look again as they adjusted to the enhanced imagery.

Louise left her own visor in her lap; the black hole, and its huge, milky ring, depressed her enough in visible light.

Jupiter's new ring system, with its bland paleness, and the jostling, crowding swirl at the centre, was far from beautiful, on any wavelength. It was too obviously a place of wreckage, of *destruction* – a destruction which was visibly continuing, as the black hole gnawed at its accretion disc. And, to Louise's engineer's eye, with its empty centre the system had something of an unfinished, provisional look. There was no *soul* to this system, she thought, no balance to the scale of the rings: by comparison, Saturn's rings had been an adornment, a necklace of ice and rock around the throat of an already beautiful world.

Spinner turned to her, her bespectacled eyes masked by the faceplate. 'The whole thing's like a whirlpool,' she said.

Louise shrugged. 'I suppose so. A whirlpool surrounding a hole in spacetime.'

'A whirlpool of gas –'

– *gas, and rock and water ice: bits of smashed-up worlds* –

Louise started to tell Spinner-of-Rope about the vanished moons of Jupiter. She remembered Io with its volcano mouths and their hundred-mile-high vents, its sulphur-stained surface and its surrounding torus of volcano-fed plasma; she remembered Io's mineral mines, nestling in the shadow of the huge volcano Babbar Patera. She told Spinner of Ganymede: larger than Mercury, heavily cratered and geologically rich – the most stable and heavily populated of all the Jovian moons. And Europa, a ball of ice, with a bright smooth surface – constantly renewed by melting and tectonic stress – covering a liquid layer beneath. Europa had been a bright precursor of this smoothed-over corpse of Callisto, perhaps.

Worlds, all populated – all gone.

Louise hoped fervently that there had been time to evacuate the moons before the final disaster. If not, then – drifting through Jovian orbit among the fragments of rock and ice which comprised those rings – there would be bits of humanity:

shards of shattered homes, children's toys, corpses.

Spinner pushed up her faceplate and rubbed her eyes. 'I'd have liked to have seen Jupiter, I think, with its moons and all those cities ... Perhaps Jupiter could have been saved. After all, the implosion must have taken thousands of years, you told me.'

Louise bit back a sarcastic reply. 'Yes. But picking black holes out of the heart of a gas giant was evidently a bit too difficult, even for the humans of many millennia beyond my time.'

Jupiter had been wrecked by the actions of the Friends of Wigner.

The Friends were human rebels from a Qax-occupied future, who had fled back in time through Michael Poole's time-tunnel wormhole.

The Friends had had in mind some grand, impossible scheme to alter history. Their plan had involved firing asteroid-mass black holes into Jupiter.

The Friends' project had been interrupted by the arrival of Qax warships through Poole's wormhole – but not before the Friends had succeeded in spearing the giant planet with several of their tiny singularities.

The pinprick singularities had looped through the thick Jovian atmosphere like deadly insects, trailing threads of plasma. When the holes met, they had whirled around each other before coalescing, their event horizons collapsing into each other in Planck timescales.

The vibration of merging event horizons had emitted vicious pulses of gravity waves. Founts of thick, chemically complex atmosphere had been hurled out of the planet, bizarre volcanoes on a world of gas.

The Friends' ambitions had been far-reaching. Before the final implosion they'd meant to *sculpt* the huge planet with these directed gravity-wave pulses, produced by the complex interactions of their singularity bullets.

Louise now stared morosely at the bland, displeasing disc of glowing rubble. Well, the Friends had certainly succeeded in part of their project – the reduction of Jupiter. Quite a monument to such ambition, after five million years, Louise thought: a collapsed Jovian, and a string of crushed human worlds.

And all for what? A black hole of the wrong size ...

'It's getting brighter over there,' Spinner said, pointing.

Louise looked right, across Callisto. A dull, flat crimson light was spreading across the ice. The glow cast long, disproportionate shadows from the low irregularities in Callisto's smooth surface, turning the ice plain into a complex landscape of ruby-sparkling promontories and blood-red pools of shadow.

At the horizon, smoky tendrils of crimson gas were rising across the sky.

'Sunrise on Callisto,' Louise said sourly. 'Come on; let's land. We don't want to miss the full beauty of the Solar System's one remaining wonder, do we?'

On the surface of Callisto, standing beside Louise in her environment suit, Spinner held up her arms, framing the Sun with her outspread hands; standing there on the light-stained ice floor, with the swollen globe reflected, distorted, in her faceplate, Spinner-of-Rope looked more than ever like a child.

Sol, looming over the horizon, was a wall of blood-red smoke. It was transparent enough to see through to the distant stars for perhaps a quarter of the disc's radius – in fact, the material was so thin that Louise could make out the steadily deepening colour of the thicker layers towards the core.

The Sun didn't even *look* like a star any more, she thought tiredly. A star was supposed to be hard, bright, hot; you weren't supposed to be able to see *through* it.

'Another astrophysicist's dream,' Mark said drily. 'You could learn more about the nature of stellar evolution just by standing there and *looking*, than in all the first five millennia of human astronomy.'

'Yes. But what a price to pay.'

Once, from Jupiter's orbit the Main Sequence Sun would have been a point source of light – distant, hot, yellow. Now, the Sun's arc size had to be at least twenty degrees. Its bulk covered fully a fifth of Louise's field of view: twenty times the width of the full Moon, as seen from Earth.

Jupiter was five AU from the Sun's centre – an AU was an astronomical unit, the radius of Earth's orbit. For the Sun to subtend such an angle, it must be two AU across, or more.

Two astronomical units. In exploding out to become a giant, the

Sun had swallowed the Earth, and the planets within Earth's orbit – Venus, Mercury.

Spinner-of-Rope was studying her, concern mixing with curiosity behind those pale spectacles.

'What are you thinking, Louise?'

'This shouldn't have happened for five billion more years,' Louise said. Her throat was tight, and she found it difficult to keep her voice level. 'The Sun was only halfway to turnoff – halfway through its stable lifecycle, on the Main Sequence.

This shouldn't have happened. Somebody did this deliberately, robbing us of our future, our worlds – damn it, this was *our Sun* ...'

'Louise.' Mark's synthesized voice was brisk, urgent.

She breathed deeply, trying to put away her anger, her resentment, to focus on the present.

'What is it?'

'You'd better come back to the *Northern*. Morrow has found something ... Something in the ice. He thinks it's a spacecraft.'

16

'Uvarov. *Uvarov.*'

Garry Uvarov jerked awake. It was dark. He tried to open his eyes . . .

As always, in that first instant of wakefulness – even after all these years – he *forgot*. His blindness crowded in on him, a speckled darkness across his eyes, making every new waking a savage horror.

'Garry. Are you awake?'

It was the solicitous voice of that fake person, Mark Bassett Friar Armonk Wu. Uvarov swung his head around, trying to locate the source of the artificial voice. It seemed to be all around him. He tried to speak; he felt his gummy mouth open with a pop, like a fish's. 'Mark Wu. Where are you, damn it?'

'Right here. *Oh.*' There was a second of silence. Then: 'I'm here.'

Now the voice came from directly in front of him, from a precise, well-focused place.

'Better,' Uvarov growled.

'I'm sorry,' Mark said. 'I hadn't formed an image. I didn't think –'

'You didn't *bother*,' Uvarov snapped. 'Because I can't see you, you thought it was enough to float around me in the air like some damn spirit.'

'I didn't think it would be so important to you,' Mark said.

'No,' Uvarov said. 'To think of that would have been too much the *human* thing to do for an imprint like you, wouldn't it?'

'Do you need anything?' Mark asked, with strained patience. 'Some food, or –'

'Nothing,' Uvarov snapped. 'This chair takes care of it all. With me, it's in one end and out of the other, without even

208

having to swallow.' He stretched his lips and leered. 'As you know. So why did you bother to ask after my health? Just to make me feel dependent?'

'No.' Mark sounded cool, but more certain of himself. 'I thought to ask would be the *human* thing to do.'

Uvarov let himself cackle at that. 'Touché.'

'It's just that you sleep for such a long time, Uvarov,' Mark said drily.

'So would you, if you weren't dead,' Uvarov said briskly.

He could hear the rattle of his own breath, the subdued ticking of a huge old clock somewhere, here in the dining saloon of Louise's old steam ship. Hauling this useless relic five megayears into the future had been, of course, an absurd thing to do, and it showed a fundamental weakness in the character of Louise Ye Armonk. But still, Uvarov had to admit, the textures of the old material – the painted walls, the mirrors, the polished wood of the two long tables – *sounded* wonderful.

'I suppose you had a *reason* for waking me.'

'Yes. The Sun maser probes –'

'Yes?'

'We're starting to get meaningful data, Uvarov.' Now Mark sounded excited, but Uvarov never let himself forget that every inflection of this AI's voice was a mere artifice.

Still, despite this cynical calculation, Uvarov too began to feel a distinct stirring of interest – of wonder. *Meaningful data*?

The maser radiation was coming from hot-spots on the photosphere itself – patches of intense maser brightness, equivalent to tens of millions of degrees of temperature, against a background cooler than the surface of the yellow Sun had once been. The convection mechanism underlying the maser flares' coherent pathways fired the radiation pulses off tangentially to the photosphere. So the *Northern* had sent out small probes to skim the swollen, diffuse surface of the photosphere, sailing into the paths of the surface-grazing maser beams.

'Tell me about the data.'

'It's a repeating group, Uvarov. Broadcast on maser wavelengths, from within what's left of the Sun ... Uvarov, I think it's a *signal*.'

They hadn't learned much about the Solar System, in the year since their clumsy, limping arrival from out of the past. So many of the worlds of man simply didn't exist any more.

Still, in the quiet time before the arrival of the *Northern* at Jupiter, Uvarov and the AI construct had performed some general surveys of the Solar System – what was left of it. And they'd found a few oddities . . .

There was what looked like one solid artefact – Morrow's anomalous object buried in the ice of Callisto. And, apart from that, there were just three sources of what could be interpreted as intelligently directed signals: this maser stuff from the Sun, the fading beacon from the edge of the System, and – strangest and most intriguing of all, to Garry Uvarov – those strange pulses of gravity radiation from the direction of Sagittarius.

Uvarov had done a little private study, on the structure of the Universe in the direction of Sagittarius. Interestingly enough, he learned, the cosmic structure called the *Great Attractor* was to be found there, right at the place the photino beam was pointing. The Attractor was a huge mass concentration: the source of galactic streaming, for hundreds of millions of light-years' distance around. Could the Attractor be connected to the g-waves?

And then there was all that strange photino activity in and around the Sun.

The data was patchy and difficult to interpret – after all, dark matter was, almost by definition, virtually impossible to study . . . but there *was* something strange there.

Uvarov thought he'd detected a *streaming*.

There was a steady flow, of photino structures, out of the heart of the Sol giant . . . and on out of the Solar System. It was a beam of photinos aimed like a beacon, out of Sol – and straight towards the source of the anomalous gravity waves in Sagittarius.

Something was happening in Sagittarius – something huge, and wonderful, and strange. And, somehow, impossibly, it was connected to whatever was taking place in the heart of the poor, suffering Sun.

. . . The Virtual, Mark Armonk, was talking to him again. Or perhaps *at* him, Uvarov thought sourly.

'I wish you'd pay attention, Uvarov –'

'Without me to talk to, you'd lapse into non-sentience, devoid of independent will,' Uvarov pointed out. 'So spare me the lectures.'

Mark ground out, 'The *Sun*, Uvarov. The photosphere maser radiation is standard stuff – generated by silicon monoxide at 43 Gigahertz. There are natural mechanisms for generating such signatures. But in this case, we've found hints of *modulation* of the silicon monoxide stuff . . . deliberate modulation.

'We've found structure *everywhere*, Uvarov.' Again that fake excitement in Mark's voice; Uvarov felt his irritation grow. Mark went on, 'There is structure in the amplitude of the beams, their intensity, phasing, polarization – even in the Doppler shifting of the signals. Uvarov, someone – or something – is *in there*, trying to signal out with modulated natural masers, as hard as they can. I'm trying to resolve it, but . . .'

Uvarov strove to shift in his chair, vainly trying to find a more comfortable posture – a prize he'd been seeking for the best part of a thousand years, with as much assiduousness as Jason had once sought his Fleece, he thought. How *pathetic*, how limited he was!

He tried to ignore his body, to fix his analytical abilities – his imagination – on the concept of an intelligence within the Sun . . .

But it was so difficult.

His mind wandered once more. He thought of his forest colony. He thought of Spinner-of-Rope.

Sometimes Uvarov wondered how much better *young* people might have fared, if they'd been given this opportunity to study and learn, with this strange, battered Universe as an intellectual playground. How much more might youth have unearthed, with its fresh eyes and minds, than *he* could!

It had already been fifty years since – in his misguided, temporary lunacy – he had inspired his forest children to undertake their hazardous journey out of the lifedome. *Fifty years*: once most of a human lifetime, he thought – and yet, now, scarcely an interlude in his own, absurdly long life, stuck as he was in this mouldering cocoon of a body.

So even Spinner-of-Rope, Arrow Maker's wise-ass daughter, must be – what, sixty-five chronological? Seventy, maybe? An old woman already. But still, thanks to AS-freezing, she'd retained the features – and much of the outlook, as far as he could tell – of a child.

He felt a great sorrow weigh upon him. Of course his experiment was lost, now; his carefully developed gene pool was already polluted by interbreeding, no doubt, between the forest folk and the Superet-controlled Decks, and his immortal strain was overwhelmed by AS treatments.

But the progress he had made was still there, he thought; the *genes* were there, dormant, ready. And when – *if* – the inhabitants of the *Northern* got through this time of trouble, when they reached whatever new world waited for them, *then* the great experiment could begin anew.

But in the meantime . . .

He thought again of Spinner-of-Rope, a girl-woman who had grown up among trees and leaves, now walking through the wreckage of the Solar System.

Uvarov had made many mistakes. Well, he'd had *time* to. But he could be proud of this, if nothing else: that to this era of universal desolation and ruin, he – Garry Uvarov – had restored at least a semblance of the freshness of youth.

'. . . Uvarov,' Mark said.

Uvarov turned. The AI's synthesized voice sounded different – oddly flat, devoid of expression. *None of that damn fake intonation, then*, Uvarov thought with faint triumph. It was as if the Virtual's processing power had, briefly, been diverted somewhere else. Something had *happened*.

'Well? What is it?'

'I've done it. I've resolved the signal – the information in the maser pulses. There's an image, forming in the data desk . . .'

'An image? *Tell me*, damn you.'

It was a woman's face (Mark said), crudely sketched in pixels of colour. A *human* face. The woman was aged about sixty-five physical; she had short-cropped, sandy hair, a strong nose, a wide, upturned mouth, and large, vulnerable eyes.

Her lips were moving.

'*A woman's face* – after five million years, transmitted out on maser signals from the heart of a Sun rendered into a red giant? I don't believe it.'

Mark was silent for a moment. 'Believe what you want. I think she's trying to say something. But we don't have sound yet.'

'How very inconvenient.'

'Wait ... Ah. Here it comes.'

Now Uvarov *heard* it, heard the voice of the impossible image from the past. At first the timbre was broken up, the words virtually indecipherable, and, so Mark informed him, badly out of synchronization with the moving lips.

Then, after a few minutes – and with considerable signal enhancement from the data desk processors – the message cleared.

'Lethe,' Mark said. 'I even recognize the language ...'

My name is Lieserl. Welcome home, whoever you are. I expect you're wondering why I've asked you here tonight ...

Against the dull red backdrop of the ruined, inflated Sun, the accretion disc of the Jovian black hole sparkled, huge and threatening.

Once more a pod from the *Northern* carried Spinner-of-Rope – alone, this time – down to the surface of Callisto. Spinner twisted to look down through the glass walls of the little pod; as she moved, biomedical sensors within her suit slid over her skin, disconcerting.

The craft from within the ice, dug up and splayed out against the surface by a team of autonomous 'bots, was like a bird, with night-dark wings a hundred yards long trailing back from a small central body. The wing material looked fragile, insubstantial. The ice of Callisto seemed to show through the wings' trailing edges.

Louise and Mark had told her that the craft was alien technology. And it had a *hyperdrive*, they thought ...

She scratched at her shoulder, where one of Mark's damned biosensors was digging particularly uncomfortably into her flesh. When she landed, Louise was damn well going to have to tell her why she'd been buttoned up like this.

The craft was more like some immense, black-winged insect, resting on a sheet of glass, Spinner thought. Its elegant curves were surrounded by the stumpy, glistening forms of the *Northern*'s pods, and by other pieces of equipment. Spinner could see a small drone 'bot crawling across the surface of one nightdark wing, trailing twisted cable strands and scrutinizing the alien material with clusters of sensors. The Callisto ice around the craft was scarred and broken, pitted by the landing jets of the pods and criss-crossed by vehicle tracks.

The craft was *immense*. The activities of the humans and their machines looked utterly inadequate to contain the power of this artificial beast ... if it were to awake from its centuries-long slumber.

Spinner's fear seemed to rise in inverse proportion to her nearness to the craft. It was as if the sinister insectile form, pinned against the ice, radiated threat.

She shivered, pulling the fabric of her environment suit close around her.

The streets and houses around Morrow were empty. The endless, ululating cries of the klaxon echoed from the bare walls of the ruined buildings and the steel underbelly of the sky.

A grappling hook – a crude thing of sharpened, twisted partition-metal – sailed past Morrow's face, making him flinch. The hook caught in some irregularity in the floor of the Deck, and the rope it trailed stiffened, jerking. Within a few seconds Trapper-of-Frogs had come swarming along the rope, across the Deck floor; her brown limbs, glistening with sweat, were flashes of colour against the grey drabness of the Decks' sourceless light, and her blowpipe and pouch of darts bounced against her back as she moved.

Morrow sighed and dropped his face. In zero-gee, they were abseiling across the floor of Deck Two. The metal surface before his face was bland, incongruously familiar, worn smooth by countless generations of feet, including his own. He twisted his neck and took a glance back. His other companions were strung out across the surface of the Deck behind him, their faces turned to him like so many flowers: there was Constancy-of-Purpose with her powerful arms working steadily, and her dangling, attenuated legs, the Virtual Mark Wu, a handful of forest folk. The Virtual was trying to protect their sensibilities, Morrow saw, by making a show of climbing along the ropes with the rest of them.

The Temple of the Planners was a brooding bulk, outlined in electric blue, still hundreds of yards ahead, across the Deck.

Many of the houses, factories and other buildings were damaged – several quite badly. In one corner of Deck Two there was evidence of a major fire, a scorching which had even licked at the grey metal ceiling above.

Morrow tried to imagine what it must have felt like to have been here, in the cramped, enclosed world of the Decks, when the GUTdrive had finally been turned off – when *gravity* had faded out. He imagined walking along, on his way to another routine day at work – and then that strange feeling of lightness, *his feet leaving the Deck* ...

The klaxon had called out ever since they'd climbed down here, into the Decks, through the Locks from the forest; perhaps it had been wailing like this ever since the zero-gee catastrophe itself. The noise made it difficult even to *think*; he tried to control his irritability and fear.

Trapper twisted and grinned at him. 'Come on, Morrow, wake up. You climbed all the way down the elevator shaft with Spinner-of-Rope, once, didn't you? And that was under gravity. Zero-gee is *easy*.'

'Trapper, *nothing* is easy when you get to my age.'

Trapper laughed at him, with all the certainty of youth. And it was *genuine* youth, he reflected; Trapper was – what? Eighteen, nineteen? Children continued to be born, up in the forest, even all these decades after the opening-up of the Locks on Deck One, and the provision of AS treatment for the forest folk.

'You know,' he said, 'you remind me of Spinner-of-Rope.'

Trapper twisted easily, as if her small, bare body had all the litheness of rope itself; her face was a round, eager button. 'Really? Spinner-of-Rope's something of a hero up there, you know. In the forest. It must have taken a lot of courage to follow Uvarov down through the Locks, and –'

'Maybe,' Morrow said testily. 'What I meant was, you're just as *annoying* as she was, at your age.'

Trapper frowned; there was a sprinkling of freckles across her small, flat nose, he saw, and a further smattering that reached back across her dark-fringed patch of shaven scalp. Then her grin broke out again, and he felt his heart melt; her face reminded him of the rising of a bright star over the ice fields of Callisto. She craned her neck forward and kissed him lightly on the nose.

'All part of the package,' she said. 'Now come *on*.'

She scrambled up her rope again; within seconds she had reached her grappling hook and was preparing to throw the next one across the Deck, in preparation for the next leg of the trek.

Wearily, feeling even older than his five centuries, Morrow made his way, hand over hand, along his rope.

He tried to keep his eyes focused on the scuffed floor surface before his face. Why was he finding this damn jaunt so *difficult*? He was, after all, Morrow, Hero of the Elevator Shaft, as Trapper had said. And since then he had been out, beyond the ribbed walls surrounding the Decks, out into space. He had walked the surface of Callisto, and watched the rise of the bloated corpse of legendary Sol over the moon's ice plains; he had even supervised the excavation of that ancient alien spacecraft. He'd shown courage then, hadn't he? He must have done – why, he hadn't even *thought* about it. So why did he feel so different, now he was back here, inside the Decks once more – inside the metal-walled box which had been his only world for half a millennium?

He'd been apprehensive ever since Louise had asked him to lead this expedition in the first place.

'I don't *want* to go back in there,' he'd told Louise bluntly.

Louise Ye Armonk had come down to Callisto to congratulate him on his archaeology and to give him this new assignment. She had looked tired, old; she'd run a hand through grizzled hair. 'We all have to do things we don't want to do,' she said, as if speaking to a child, her patience barely controlled. When she'd looked at him, Morrow could detect the contempt in her eyes. 'Believe me, if I had someone else to send, I'd send 'em.'

Morrow had felt a sense of panic – as if he were being asked to go back into a prison cell. 'What's the point?' he asked, his desperation growing. 'The Planners closed off the Decks centuries ago. *They* don't want to know what's happening outside. Why not leave them to it?'

Louise's mouth was set firm, fine wrinkles lining it. 'Morrow, we can't afford to "leave them to it" any more. The Universe outside – *we* – are impinging on what's happening in there. And we've evidence, from our monitors, that the Planners are not – ah, not reacting well to the changes.

'Morrow, there are two thousand people in there, in the Decks. There are only a handful of us outside – only a few hundred, even including the forest on Deck Zero. We can't afford to abandon those two thousand to the Planners' deranged whims.'

Morrow heard his own teeth grind. 'You're talking about *duty*, then.'

Louise had studied him. 'Yes, in a way. But the most fundamental duty of all: not to me, or to the Planners, or even to the ship's mission. It's a duty to the *species*. If the species is to survive we have to protect the people trapped in there, with the Planners – as many as possible, to maintain genetic diversity for the future.'

'*Protect*,' he said sourly. 'Funny. That's probably just what the Planners believe they are doing, too . . .'

Now he looked around at the abandoned houses in their surreal rows, suspended from what felt like a vertical wall to him now, not a floor; he listened to the silence broken only by the plaintive cries of the klaxon. All the people had gone – taken, presumably into the Temples, by the Planners – leaving only this shell of a world; and now the elements of this oppressive place seemed to move around him, pushing at him like elements of a nightmare . . .

Perhaps it was the very *familiarity* of the place that was so uncomfortable. Coming back here – even after all these decades – it was as if he had never been away; the metal-clad walls and ceiling, the rows of boxy houses, the looming tetrahedral bulks of the Planner Temples all loomed closely around him, oppressing his spirit once more. It was as if the huge, remarkable Universe beyond these walls – of collapsing stars, and ice moons, and magical alien spacecraft with wings a hundred yards wide – had never existed, as if it had all been some bizarre, fifty-year fantasy.

In the old days, before his first encounter with Arrow Maker and Spinner, he'd thought himself something of a rebel. An independent spirit; a renegade – not like the rest of the drones around him. But the truth was different, of course. For centuries, the culture of the Planners had trained him into submission. If it hadn't been for the irruption of the forest folk – an event from outside his world – he'd never have had the courage, or the initiative, to break free of the Planners' domination.

In fact, he realized now, no matter what he did or where he went in the future – and no matter how this conflict with the Planners turned out – he never *would* be free of that oppression.

Now he reached the end of his rope. He let himself drift away from the Deck a little, and launched himself through the air across the few feet to the next rope Trapper had fixed. He glanced back again; the little party was strung along the chain of ropes which led all the way back to the ramp from the upper levels.

There was a rush of air above his head, a sizzling, hissing noise.

Instinctively he ducked down, pressing his body flat against the Deck; infuriatingly he bounced away from the scarred surface, but he grasped the edges of Deck plates and clung on.

The noise had sounded like an insect's buzz. But there were very few insects within the Decks . . .

Another hiss, a sigh of air above him. And it had come from the direction of the Temple which was – he sneaked a look up – still a hundred yards away. Another whisper above him – and another, and now a whole flock of them.

Someone behind him cried out, and he heard the clatter of metal against the Deck.

Trapper-of-Frogs came clambering back down the rope towards him; without inhibition she scrambled over his arms and snuggled against his side, a warm, firm bundle of muscle; her shaven patch of scalp was smooth against his cheek. She was no more than four feet tall, and he could feel her bony knees press into his thighs.

'It's the Planners,' she whispered into his ear. Her breath was sweet, smelling of forest fruit. 'They're *shooting* at us from the Temple.'

He felt confused. 'Shooting? But that's impossible. Why should they?'

She growled, and again he was reminded of a young Spinner-of-Rope, decades ago, who also had spent a lot of time getting annoyed at him. 'How should I know?' she snapped. 'And besides, *why* hardly makes a difference. What's important is that we get *out* of here before we get hurt.'

He clung to his rope, disoriented. Maybe he should have been prepared for this. Maybe the Planners really *had* gone that crazy.

But if that was true, what was he supposed to *do* about it?

Now someone else came clambering up behind him. It was Constancy-of-Purpose, pawing her way across the Deck with her huge, powerful right hand; she clutched something shiny and hard in her left. Those AS-wasted legs, Morrow thought irrelevantly, looked even slimmer than Trapper's; they clattered against the Deck, pale and useless.

'Morrow.' Constancy-of-Purpose opened her left hand. The object nestling within it was a piton: sharpened, the coarse, planed surfaces of its point glistening in the sourceless light. 'This look familiar? The Planners are using their damn crossbows on us again.'

'But why?'

Constancy-of-Purpose looked exasperated, even amused. '*Why* hardly matters, does it?'

Trapper punched Morrow in the ribs, lightly; he winced as her small, hard fist dug into the soft flesh. 'That's what I've been telling him, too,' she told Constancy-of-Purpose.

'At the moment they're hitting the Deck behind us,' Constancy-of-Purpose said urgently. 'They are shooting over our heads. Maybe they're trying to find their range. Or maybe they're just trying to warn us; I don't know. But as soon as they like, they'll be able to pick us off ... Come on. We have to retreat.'

Morrow, still confused, twisted his head to study the Temple ahead of him.

The building's tetrahedral form, with its outline of electric blue and triangular faces of golden-brown, was no longer a seamless whole. Windows had been knocked out of the nearest face, leaving black, gaping scars. He saw small figures in those windows: men and women, dressed in the drab, uniform coveralls he'd worn himself for so many centuries.

They were raising bows towards him.

'All right,' he said, wishing only that this were over. 'Let's move out of range. Come on; Constancy-of-Purpose, you lead the way ...'

The pod landed close to the stern of the night-dark craft.

Spinner climbed down onto the ice of Callisto.

Around her waist she'd tied a length of her own rope, and within her suit, suspended on a thread between her breasts, was one of her father's arrow-heads. She raised her hand to her chest and pressed the glove against the fabric of her suit; the cool metal of the arrow-head dug into her flesh, a comforting and familiar shape. She tried to regulate her breathing, looking for bits of comfort, of stability. Even the gravity here was wrong, of course; and the presence of the heavy suit over her flesh, with Mark's biostat probes inside, was a constant, scratching irritant.

Louise Ye Armonk walked up to the pod, leaving shallow footprints in the frost of Callisto. The engineer had turned up an interior light behind her faceplate.

'Spinner-of-Rope.' Louise held out her hand and smiled. 'Well, here we are again. Come on. I'll show you around the craft.'

Spinner took Louise's hand. Slowly, her feet crunching softly against the worn ice, she walked with Louise to the craft.

The rings of Jupiter arced across the sky, a plain of blood-stained, frozen smoke. The craft lay against the ice, dark, vital.

They drew to a halt perhaps ten feet from the edge of the nearest wing. The wing hovered a few feet above the ice, apparently unsupported; perhaps it was so light it didn't need support, apart from its join with the central trunk of the ship, Spinner thought. Beyond the leading edge the wing curved softly, like a slow, frozen billow of smoke; its form, foreshortened, was sharply delineated against the bland ice backdrop of Callisto, but its utter darkness made the scale of the wing's curves hard to judge. At the trailing edge of the wing, the material was so delicate that Spinner – bending, and peering upwards – could see *through* the fabric of the wing, to the wizened glow of the stars.

'In form the ship is like a sycamore seed.' Louise glanced across at Spinner. 'Do you have sycamores in your forest? ... Here are these lovely wings, which sweep back through a hundred yards. The small central pilot's cage sits on top of the "shoulders" of the ship – the base of the wings.'

Lovely, Louise had said. Well, Spinner reflected, perhaps there was a certain loveliness here – but it was a beauty that was utterly inhuman, and endlessly menacing.

'This isn't a human ship,' she said slowly. 'Is it, Louise?'

'No.' Louise set her shoulders. 'Damn it,' she said sourly. 'We find one reasonably complete artefact in the rubble of the Solar System, and it has to be alien ...

'Spinner, we think this is a *Xeelee* craft. We've checked the old Superet projections; we think this is what the Friends of Wigner – the people from the Qax occupation era – called a *nightfighter*. A small, highly mobile, versatile scout craft.'

The leading edge of a sycamore-seed wing was at a level with Louise's face; now she raised a gloved hand and made as if to pass a fingertip along that edge. Then, thoughtfully, she drew her hand back. 'Actually, we wouldn't advise that you touch anything, unless you have to. This stuff is *sharp*. The wings, and the rest of the hull, are probably made of Xeelee *construction material*.'

She ducked her head and sighted along the plane of the wing. Spinner had to stand on tiptoe to do the same. When she did manage to raise her eyes to the level of the wing, the Xeelee material seemed to disappear, such was its fineness. Even this close it was utterly black, returning no reflections from the ice, or the Jovian rings above. It wasn't like anything *real*, she thought; it was as if a slice had been taken out of the world, leaving this hole – this *defect*.

Louise said, 'This stuff resists analysis. Uvarov and Mark suggest that the construction material is a sheet of bound nucleons – bound together by the strong nuclear force, I mean, as if this was some immense, spun-out atomic nucleus.

'But I'm not so sure. The density doesn't seem right, for one thing. I have a theory of my own: that what we're looking at is something more fundamental. I think the Xeelee have found a way to suppress the Pauli Exclusion Principle, and so have found their way into a whole new regime of matter. Of course the problem with that theory is that there aren't supposed to *be* any loopholes in the Exclusion Principle. Well, I guess nobody told the Xeelee about that ...'

'How did they make this stuff?'

Louise smiled. 'If you believe the old Superet reconstructions, they *grew* it, from "flowers". Construction material simply sprouted like petals from the flowers, in the presence of radiant energy.

221

'It would be interesting to know how this ship got here, to Callisto, in the first place,' she said. 'Capturing a Xeelee craft must have been a great triumph, for humans of any era.

'Uvarov thinks this moon was used as a lab. This site, remote from the populated colonies, was a workshop – a safe place to study the Xeelee craft. There must have been research facilities here, built around the nightfighter, as the people of the time tried to pry out the secrets of its intrasystem drive, its hyperdrive, the construction material. But we've found little evidence of any human occupation, apart from close to this nightfighter. When the war came –'

'What war?'

Louise dropped her faceless, helmeted head. 'A war against the Xeelee, Spinner. One of many wars. More than that I doubt we'll ever know.

'In the final war, the human facilities – and any people here – were destroyed, all save a few scraps. But –'

'But the Xeelee nightfighter survived,' Spinner said.

Louise smiled. 'Yes. The Xeelee built to last. Whatever happened was enough to *melt Callisto's ice*. But the nightfighter sank into the new oceans, and was trapped in there when Callisto froze again.'

Spinner thought: *Trapped, dormant, for an immeasurable time – perhaps a million years.*

'And they never came back,' Louise said. 'The people, I mean. The humans. They never recovered, to return here to rebuild. Perhaps that really was the war to end all wars, as far as Sol was concerned ...

'Here's the pilot cage, Spinner-of-Rope ... Well, now you can see why I need your help.'

Spinner-of-Rope stared at the squat cage of construction material. *It was barely six feet across.*

She felt a prickly cold spread across her limbs.

17

A simple metal stepladder rested against the side of the cage; the ladder looked incongruously primitive, amid all this alien high technology.

Spinner looked at the ladder with dread. 'Louise,' she said. 'I have to climb in. Don't I?'

Louise, bulky and anonymous in her environment suit, stood close beside her. 'Well, that's the general idea. Look, Spinner-of-Rope, we need a pilot ...' Her voice trailed off; she shrugged her shoulders, uncertain.

Spinner closed her eyes and took deep breaths, trying to still the shuddering, deep in her stomach. *'Lethe.* So that's why I'm all wired up.'

'I'm sorry we didn't tell you before bringing you down here, Spinner. We didn't know what was best. Would telling you have made things any easier?'

'I don't get a choice, do I?'

Louise's face, through her plate, was hard. 'You're the best candidate we have, Spinner-of-Rope. We *need* you.'

Without letting herself think about it, Spinner grabbed the ladder and pulled herself up.

She looked into the pilot's cage. It was an open sphere made of tubes of construction material. The tubes were arranged in an open lattice which followed a simple longitude-and-latitude pattern. Inside the cage was a horseshoe-shaped console, of the black Xeelee material. Other devices, made of dull metal – looking crude by comparison, obviously human – had been fixed to the Xeelee console.

A human couch had been cemented into the cage, before the console. Straps dangled from it. To fit into the cramped cage, the couch had been made small – too small for any human from the Decks but a child ... or a child-woman from the forest.

223

'I'm going to climb in, Louise.'

'Good. But for Life's sake, Spinner-of-Rope, until I tell you, *don't touch anything.*'

Spinner swung her legs, easily in the light gravity, through the construction-material frame and into the cage.

The couch fitted her body closely – as it should, she thought resentfully, since it had obviously been *made* for her – but it was *too* snug. The couch – the straps across her chest and waist, the bulky, crowding console before her – *devoured* her. The cage was a place of shadows, criss-crossing and mysterious, cast by the Jovian ring and the ice below her. It pressed around her, barely big enough for the couch and console.

She looked out through her murky faceplate, beyond the construction-material cage, to the ice plains of Callisto. She saw the blocky forms of the *Northern*'s 'bots, the pod that had brought her here, the shadowy figure of Louise. It all seemed remote, unattainable. The only reality was herself, inside this suit, this alien craft – and the sound of her own breathing loud in her ears.

Spinner had got used to a lot of changes, in the few decades since she and her father had climbed down through the lifedome with Morrow. Just *not growing old* had been a challenge enough. Most of her compatriots in the forest had refused the AS treatments offered to them by Louise, and after a few years the physical-age differences had grown marked, and widened rapidly.

Spinner had a younger sister: Painter-of-Faces, Arrow Maker's youngest child. By the time the little girl had grown older than Spinner could remember her mother, Spinner had let her visits back to the forest dwindle away.

The life of the forest people carried on much as it always had done – despite the end of the *Northern*'s journey and the discovery of the death of the Sun. Because of her greater awareness – her wider understanding – Spinner felt shut out of that old, enclosed world.

Isolated by age and by her own extraordinary experiences, she had tried to grow accustomed to the bizarre Universe outside the walls of the ship. And, over the years, she'd learned a great deal; Louise Ye Armonk, despite the ghastly way she had of patronizing Spinner, had assured her often of the great strides she'd made for someone of her low-technology upbringing.

But now, she longed to be away from this bleak, threatening place – to be naked again, and moving through the trees of the forest.

'Spinner-of-Rope.' It was the voice of the artificial man, Mark, soft inside her helmet. 'You've got to try to relax. Your biostat signs are way up –'

'Shut up, Mark.' Louise Ye Armonk walked up to the Xeelee cage and pressed her body against the black bars, peering in; she'd turned on the light behind her faceplate, so Spinner could see her face. 'Spinner, are you all right?'

Spinner took a deep breath. 'I'm fine.' She tried to focus on her irritation: with patronizing Louise, the buzzing ghost Mark. She fanned her annoyance into a flame of anger, to burn away the chill of her fear. 'Just tell me what I have to do.'

'Okay.' Louise lifted her hands and stepped back from the cage. 'As far as we can tell, the cage you're in is the control centre of the nightfighter. You can see, obviously, that it's been adapted for use by humans. We put the couch in for you. You have waldoes –'

'I have *what*?'

'Waldoes, Spinner. The metal boxes on top of the horseshoe. See?'

There were three of the boxes, each about a foot long, one before Spinner and one to either side. There were touch pads – familiar enough to her now – illuminated across the tops of the boxes. She reached out towards the box in front of her –

'*Don't touch*, damn you,' Louise snapped.

Spinner snatched her fingers back.

With audibly strained patience, Louise said, 'Spinner-of-Rope, the controls in those boxes have been tied into what we believe are controls inside the horseshoe console – and *they* are the nightfighter's real controls, the Xeelee mechanisms. That's why we called the boxes waldoes ... By working the waldoes you'll be able to work the controls. The waldoes are reconstructions, based on fragments left from the destruction of the original lab.'

225

'All right.' Spinner ran a tongue over her lips; sweat, dried in a rim around her mouth, tasted of salt. 'I understand. Let's get on with it.'

Beyond the cage, Louise held up her hands. 'No. Wait. It's not as simple as that. We reconstructed the waldoes from clues left by the original human researchers. We believe they are going to work . . . But,' she went on drily, 'we don't know what they will make the nightfighter *do*. We don't know what will happen when you touch the waldoes.

'So we'll have to be patient. Experiment.'

'All right,' Spinner said. 'But the original researchers, before the war, must have known what they were doing. Mustn't they?'

Mark said, 'Not necessarily. After all, if they'd been able to figure out Xeelee technology, maybe they wouldn't have lost the war –'

'Shut up, Mark,' Louise said mildly. 'Now, Spinner. Listen carefully. You have three waldoes – three boxes. We believe – we *think* – the one directly in front of you is interfaced to the hyperdrive control, and the two to your sides connect to the intraSystem drive.'

'IntraSystem?'

'Sublight propulsion, to let you travel around the Solar System. All right? Now, Spinner, today we aren't going to touch the hyperdrive – in fact, that waldo is disabled. We just want to see what we can make of the intraSystem drive. All right?'

'Yes.' Spinner looked at the two boxes; the touch-pad lights glowed steadily, in reassuring colours of yellow and green.

'On your left hand waldo you'll see a yellow pad. It should be illuminated. See it?'

'Yes.'

Louise hesitated. 'Spinner, try to be ready. We don't know what to expect. There might be *changes* . . .'

'I'm ready.'

'Touch the yellow pad – once, and as briefly as you can . . .'

Spinner tried to put aside her fear. She lifted her hand –

Spinner-of-Rope. Don't be afraid.

Startled, she twisted in her couch.

It had been a dry, weary voice – a *man's* voice, sounding from somewhere inside her helmet.

Of course, she was alone in the cage.

It's just a machine, the voice said now. *There's nothing to fear . . .*

She thought, *Lethe. What now? Am I going crazy?*

But, strangely, the voice – the sense of some invisible presence, here in the cage with her – was somehow *comforting*.

Spinner held her right hand over the waldo. She pressed her gloved finger to the yellow light.

A subtle change in the light, around her. There was no noise, no sense of motion.

She glanced down, through the bars of her cage.

The ice was gone. *Callisto had vanished.*

She twisted in her seat, the straps chafing against her chest, and peered out of her cage. The rings of Jupiter and the Sun's swollen form covered the sky – unperturbed by the disappearance of a mere moon. She couldn't see the *Northern.*

She spotted a ball of ice, small enough to cover with her fist, off to her right, below the nightfighter.

Could that be Callisto? If so, she'd travelled thousands of miles from the moon, in less than a heartbeat – and felt nothing.

She looked behind her.

The Xeelee nightfighter had *spread* its sycamore-seed wings. From within their hundred-yard shells, sheets of night-darkness – *hundreds of miles long* – curled across space behind her, occluding the stars.

At her touch, the ancient Xeelee craft had come to life.

She screamed and buried her faceplate in her gloves.

Lieserl soared out from the core, out through the shell of fusing hydrogen, and inspected her maser convection loops. She sensed the distorted echoes of her last set of messages, as they had survived their cycles through the coherence paths of the convection loops.

She adjusted the information content of her maser links, and initiated new messages. She added in the latest information she'd gleaned, and restated – in as strong and simple a language as she could muster – her warnings about the likely future evolution of the Sun.

When she was done, she felt something within her relax.

Once more she'd scratched this itch to communicate; once more she'd assuaged her absurd, ancient feelings of guilt . . .

But it was only after she'd sent her communication that she studied, properly, the cycled remnants of her last signals.

She allowed the maser bursts to play over her again. The messages had *changed* – and this time it wasn't simple degradation. How was this possible? Some unknown physical process at the surface of the red giant, perhaps? Or – she speculated, her excitement growing as she began to see traces of structure within the changes – or was there someone *outside*: someone still alive, and recognizably human – and trying to talk to her?

Feverishly she devoured the thin information stream contained in the maser bursts.

Fifty thousand miles from Callisto, pods from the *Northern* hung in a rough sphere. At the centre of the sphere, the magnificent wings of the Xeelee ship remained unfurled, darkly shimmering – almost alive.

Spinner sat with Louise within the safe, enclosing glass walls of a pod. Louise, with a touch on the little control console before her, guided the pod around the Xeelee nightfighter; neighbouring pods slid across space, bubbles of light and warmth. The wings were immense sculptures in space, black on black. Spinner could hear Mark whispering in Louise's ear, and numbers and schematics rolled across a data slate on Louise's lap.

Spinner's faceplate dangled at her back, and she relished the feel of fresh air against her face. It was *wonderful* simply not to breathe in her own stale exhalations.

She'd dug her father's arrow-head out of her suit so that it dangled at her chest; she fingered it, rubbing her hands compulsively over its smooth lines.

Louise glanced at Spinner. 'Are you all right now?' She sounded apologetic. 'Mark got to you as quickly as he could. And –'

Spinner-of-Rope nodded, curtly. 'I wasn't hurt.'

'No.' Louise glanced down at her slate again; her attention was clearly on the data streaming in about the activated nightfighter. She murmured, 'No, you did fine.'

'Yeah,' Spinner grunted. 'Well, I hope it was worth it.'

Louise looked up from her slate. 'It *was*. Believe me, Spinner; even if it might be hard for you to see how. The very fact that you weren't harmed, physically, by that little jaunt has told us volumes.'

Now Mark's voice sounded in the air. 'You travelled tens of thousands of miles in a fraction of a second, Spinner. You should have been *creamed* against the bars of that cage. Instead, something protected you ...'

Louise looked at Spinner. 'He has a way of putting things, doesn't he?'

They laughed together. Spinner felt a little of the numbness chip away from her.

'Mark's right,' Louise said. 'Thanks to you, we're learning at a fantastic rate about the nightfighter. We know we can use it without killing ourselves, for a start ... And, Spinner, understanding is the key to turning *anything* from a threat into an opportunity.'

Louise took the pod on a wide arc around the unfurled wings of the Xeelee craft. The wings were like a star-free hole cut out of space, beneath Spinner-of-Rope; they retained the general sycamore-seed shape of the construction-material framework, but were vastly extended. Spinner could see 'bots toiling patiently across the wings' surface.

'This far out, the mass-energy of the wing system is actually attracting the pod, gravitationally,' Louise murmured. 'The wings have the mass equivalent of a small asteroid ... I can see from my slate that the pod's systems are having to correct for the wings' perturbation.

'Let's go in a little way.'

She took the pod on a low, sweeping curve over the lip of one wing and down towards its surface. The wing, a hundred miles across, was spread out beneath Spinner like the skin of some dark world; the little pod skimmed steadily over the black landscape.

Louise kept talking. 'The wing is *thin* – as far as we can tell its thickness is just a Planck length, the shortest distance possible. It has an extremely high surface tension – or, equivalently, a high surface energy density – so high, in fact, that its gravitational field is inherently non-Newtonian; it's actually *relativistic* ... Is this making any sense to you, Spinner?'

Spinner said nothing.

Louise said, 'Look: from a long way away, the pod was attracted to the wings, just as if they were composed of normal matter. *But they're not.* And, this close, I can detect the difference.'

She drew the pod to a stop, and allowed it to descend, slowly, towards the wing surface.

Spinner, gazing down, couldn't tell how far away the night-black, featureless floor was. Was Louise intending to land there?

The pod's descent slowed.

Louise, working her control console, caused the pod's small vernier rockets to squirt, once, twice, sending them down towards the wing surface once more. But again the pod slowed; it gradually drifted to a halt, then, slowly, began to rise, as if rebounding.

Louise's face was alive with excitement. 'Spinner, could you feel that? Do you see what's happening? This close, the wing surface is actually gravitationally *repulsive*. It's pushing us away!'

Spinner eyed her. 'I know you, Louise. You've already figured out how a discontinuity drive would work. You were *expecting* this antigravity stunt, weren't you?'

Louise smiled and waved a hand at the Xeelee craft. 'Well, okay. Maybe I made a few educated guesses. This ship isn't magic. Not even this antigravity effect. It's all just an exercise in high physics. Of course we couldn't *build* one of these.' Her eyes looked remote. 'Not yet, anyway ...'

'Tell me how it works, Louise.'

At extremes of temperature and pressure, spacetime became highly symmetrical (Louise told Spinner). The fundamental forces of physics became unified into a single superforce.

When conditions became less intense the symmetries were broken. The forces of physics – gravity, nuclear, electromagnetic – froze out of the superforce.

'Now,' Louise said, 'think of ice freezing out of water. Think back to what we saw on Callisto – all those flaws inside the ice, remember? The freezing of water doesn't happen in an even, symmetrical way. There are usually *defects* – discontinuities in the ice.

'And in just the same way, when physical forces freeze out of the unified state, there can be defects – but now, these are defects in spacetime itself.'

Space was three-dimensional. Three types of stable defects were possible: in zero, one or two dimensions. The defects were points – *monopoles* – or lines – *cosmic strings* – or planes – *domain walls*.

The defects were genuine flaws in spacetime. Within the defects were sheets – or points, or lines – of *false vacuum*: places where the conditions of the high-density, symmetrical, unified state still held – like sheets of liquid water trapped within ice.

'These things can form naturally,' Louise said. 'In fact, possibly many of them did, as the Universe expanded out of the Big Bang. And maybe,' she went on slowly, 'the defects can be manufactured artificially, too.'

Spinner stared out of the pod at the nightfighter. 'Are you saying –'

'I'm saying that the Xeelee can create, and control, spacetime defects. We think that the "wings" of this nightfighter are defects – domain walls, bounded about by loops of cosmic string.

'Spinner-of-Rope, the Xeelee use sheets of antigravity to drive their spacecraft . . .'

The domain walls were inherently unstable; left to themselves they would decay away in bursts of gravitational radiation, and would attempt to propagate away at speeds close to that of light. The Xeelee nightfighter must actually be stabilizing the flaws, actively, to prevent this happening, and then destabilizing the flaws to gain propulsion.

Louise believed the Xeelee's control of the domain-wall antigravity effect must be behind the ship's ability to shield the pilot cage from acceleration effects.

'All this sounds impossible,' Spinner said.

'There's no such word,' Louise said aggressively. 'Your trip was a real achievement.' Louise, clearly excited by the Xeelee's engineering prowess, sounded as alive and full of enthusiasm as Spinner had ever heard her. 'You gave us the first big break we've made in understanding how this nightfighter operates –

and, more significantly, how we can use it without destroying ourselves.'

Spinner frowned. 'And is that so important?'

Louise looked at her seriously. 'Spinner, I need to talk this out properly with you. But I suspect how well we use this nightfighter is going to determine whether we – the human species – survive, or perish here with our Sun.'

Spinner gazed out at the Xeelee craft, at the scores of drone 'bots which clambered busily across the face of its wings.

Perhaps Louise was right; perhaps understanding how something worked *did* make it genuinely less threatening. The Xeelee nightfighter wasn't a monster. It was a tool – a resource, for humans to exploit.

'All right,' she said. 'What next?'

Louise grinned. 'Next, I think it's time to figure out how to take this nightfighter on a little test jaunt around the Solar System. I'd like to see what in Lethe happened here. And,' she said, her face hardening, 'I want to know what's happening to our Sun . . .'

18

Milpitas put down his pen.

Annoyingly, it drifted away from the surface of his desk and up into the air, cart-wheeling slowly; Milpitas swiftly scooped up the offending item and swept it into a drawer, where it could drift about to its little insensate heart's content.

He climbed stiffly from his chair and made his slow way from the office.

Fine white ropes had been strung out along the Temple's warren of corridors. By judiciously sliding one's closed fists along the rope, one could quite easily maintain the illusion – for oneself and others – of walking, as normal. He passed another Planner, a junior woman with her tall, shaven dome of a scalp quite gracefully formed. Her legs were hidden by a long robe, so that – at first glance anyway – it could have been that she *was* walking. Milpitas smiled at the girl, and she nodded gravely to him as they passed.

Excellent, he thought. That was the way to deal with this ghastly, offensive situation of zero-gee, of course: by not accepting its reality, by allowing no intrusion into the normal course of things – into the usual, smooth running of their minds. By such means they could survive until gravity was restored. He moved through the corridors of his Temple, past Planner offices which had been hastily adapted to serve as dormitories and food stores. Beyond the closed doors he heard the slow, subdued murmur of the voices of his people, and beyond the Temple walls there continued the steady, sad wailing of the klaxon.

He worked his way out from the bowels of the building, out towards the glistening skin of the Temple. He had conducted an inspection tour like this every shift since the start of the emergency. His assistants formed a complex web of intelligence throughout the Temple, of course, and reports were ready for him whenever he requested them. Some contact had even been maintained with the other Temples, thanks to carefully selected runners. But, despite all that data, Milpitas still found there was no substitute for getting out of his office and *seeing* for himself what was going on.

And, he flattered himself to think, perhaps it comforted the people – the lost children he'd gathered here into his protection, in the midst of this, their greatest crisis – to be aware that he, Milpitas, their Planner, was among them.

But, he thought, what if gravity were never returned?

He pulled at his chin, his fingernails lingering on the network of AS scars they found there.

They would have to adjust. It was as simple as that. He evolved vague schemes for stringing networks of ropes across the Decks; there was really no reason why normal life – at least, a close semblance of it – should not resume.

The discipline of the Planners had already persisted for almost a thousand years. Surely a little local difficulty with the gravity wasn't going to make any difference to that.

Still, he thought, some events – however unwelcome – *did* force themselves into one's awareness. Such as the moment when the gravity had died. Milpitas remembered clinging to his own chair, watching in horror as the artefacts on his desk – the ordinary, humdrum impedimenta of everyday life – drifted away into the treacherous air.

In the Decks, there had been panic.

Milpitas had sounded the klaxon – and it still sounded now – calling the people to him, to the protection of the Temple.

Slowly, one by one, or in little groups clinging to each other fearfully, they had come to him. He had lodged them in offices, giving them the security of four stout walls about them.

People had been stranded helplessly in mid-air. Ropes had been slung between the Decks, huge nets pulled through the air to gather in the flopping human fish. All of them had been brought to him, some almost catatonic with fear, their old-young faces rigid and white.

He reached the tetrahedral outer hull of the Temple. The skin was a wall of golden glass which inclined gracefully over him, softening the harsh light of the Decks; the wall's framework cast long, soft-edged shadows across the outer corridors.

...But the light, today, had changed, he noticed now. He glanced up, quickly, above his head. Shafts of grey Deck daylight, raw and unfiltered, came seeping through holes in the golden wall. At each gap in the wall a sentry hovered, fixed to the glass wall by a loose sling of rope.

The holes had been punched out, in the last few minutes or hours, by the sentries; they must have seen someone, somehow, approaching the Temple.

The nearest sentry glanced down at Milpitas' approach. It was a woman, Milpitas saw; she held her cross-bow up against her chest, nervously.

He smiled at her and waved. Then, as soon as he felt he could, he dropped his eyes and moved on.

Damn. His composure, the gestalt of his mood, had been quite disrupted by the sight of the sentries and the knocked-out glass panes. Of course he himself had posted the sentries up there as a precaution (a precaution against *what*, he hadn't cared to speculate). He'd really hoped that the sentries wouldn't need to be used, that no more irruptions from *outside* would occur.

Evidently that hope hadn't yet been fulfilled. His plans to repopulate the Decks would have to be postponed for a while longer.

Well, there was still food and other essentials, here in the Temples. And when the supplies ran out, their AS nanobots could preserve them all for a long while; the nanobots would enable each antique human body to consume its own resources, digging deeper and deeper, to preserve the most vital functions.

And even the failure of *that* last fallback would, in the end, be irrelevant, of course.

The people would remain with him, Planner Milpitas, here in the Temple. Where they were safe. He had to protect the future of the species. That was his mission: a mission he had followed unswervingly for centuries. He had no intention of abandoning his duty to his charges now.

Not even if it meant keeping them in here forever.

The wings of the nightfighter loomed over the battered surface of Port Sol.

The relativistic effects of the flight – intense blue shift ahead, the hint of a starbow girdling the sky – faded rapidly from Spinner's sensorium. The Universe beyond her cage of construction material assumed its normal aspect, with the wizened stars scattered uniformly around the sky, and the blood-red bulk of the Sun an immense, brooding presence.

She took her hands from the control waldoes and lay back in her couch. She closed aching eyes, and tried to still the trembling in her hands.

She sucked apple-juice from the nipple inside her helmet. The juice tasted slightly odd – as usual, because of the nutrient supplements that had been added to it. Her legs and back felt stiff, her muscles like bits of wood, after two days in this box. The plumbing equipment she'd been fitted with was chafing again, and somewhere under her back there was a fold of cloth in her suit, a fold which dug enthusiastically into her flesh. Even the loop of rope at her waist felt tight, restricting.

'Spinner-of-Rope. Can you hear me?' It was Louise's voice, calling from the cosy shirtsleeve environment inside the life-lounge she'd fixed to the shoulders of the nightfighter. 'Are you all right?'

Spinner sighed. 'About as all right as you'd expect me to be.' She clenched her hands together and worked her fingers through the thickness of the gloves' material, trying to loosen up the muscles. Over-tension in her hands was probably going to be her biggest problem, she reflected. Her guidance of the ship was assisted by the processing power Louise had had installed inside the life-lounge, but still, and quite frequently, Spinner had to supply manual intervention.

'Spinner, do you want to close up the wings?'

Spinner stabbed at a button on the left-hand waldo. She didn't bother to look back to watch the controlled defects in spacetime heal themselves over; without the wings, the quality of light in the cabin changed a little, brightening.

'Okay. Would you like to come into the lounge for a while?'

Another damn spacewalk? She closed her eyes; her eyeballs prickled with fatigue. 'No thanks, Louise.'

'You've been in that couch for thirty-six hours already, Spinner. You need to be careful with yourself.'

'What are you worried about?' Spinner asked sourly. 'Bed-sores?'

'No,' Louise said calmly. 'No, the safety of the night-fighter . . .'

Spinner had quickly learned that journey times in the 'fighter were going to be *long*. Louise had worked out that the nightfighter's discontinuity drive could bring it to better than half lightspeed. Terrific. But most of the Solar System was empty space. It was a big place. During a 'fighter journey, little would change visibly, even from hour to hour – but that served to make the *worst* moments, when she came plummeting at some planet or moon, even more terrifying, with their sensations of such intense *speed*.

Spinner had felt no acceleration effects, and Louise assured her that her suit – and the action of the construction material cage around her – would protect her from any hard radiation, or heavy particles she might encounter . . . But still, she was forced to sit in this damn box, and watch the stars blue-shift towards her.

Maybe the Xeelee had never suffered from vertigo, but she'd quickly found that *she* sure did.

'Well, here we are at Port Sol. Louise, how long do you want to stay here?'

Louise hesitated. 'Not long, I don't think. I didn't expect to find anything here, and now that I'm here I still don't.'

'Then I'll stay in the pod. The sooner we can get away, the more comfortable I'll feel.'

'All right. I accept that. Spinner-of-Rope, tell me what you see.'

Spinner opened her eyes, with some reluctance, and looked beyond the construction material cage.

In contrast to the crowded sky of the ruins of the Jovian system, there was *emptiness* here.

The Sun was a ball of dull red, below the cage and to her right. Even here, on the rim of the System, Sol still showed a large disc, and sent bloody light slanting up through her cage.

To her left the worldlet Louise called Port Sol rotated, slowly. The little ice moon was scarred by hundreds of craters: deep, surprisingly regular. The tiny moon had supplied the ancient interstellar GUTships with ice for reaction mass. There were still buildings here, tight communities of them all over the surface; Spinner could see the remnants of domes, pylons and arches, spectacular microgravity architecture which must have been absurdly expensive to maintain.

But the buildings were closed, darkened, and thin frost coated their surfaces; the pylons and graceful domes were collapsed, with bits of glass and metal jutting like snapped bones.

'I recognize some of this,' Louise said. 'Some of the geography, I mean. I could even tell you place names. Can you believe that – after five megayears?

'. . . But I guess that's just telling us that Port Sol was abandoned not long after my time. Once the Squeem hyperdrive was acquired, the GUTship lines – even the wormhole route operators – must have become suddenly obsolete. There was no longer any economic logic to sustain Port Sol. I wonder what the last days were like . . . Perhaps the Port was kept going by tourism, for a while. And, thinking back, there would have been a few who wouldn't want to return to the crowded pit of the inner System. Perhaps some of them stayed here until their AS treatment finally failed them . . .

'Maybe that's how it was,' she said. 'But I think I'd rather imagine they closed the place up with one *major* party.'

'How did Port Sol survive the wars?'

'Who would want to come here?' Louise said drily. 'What is there to fight over? There's nothing that's even worth *destroying*. Spinner, Port Sol must have been abandoned for most of the five megayears since the *Northern*'s departure. It's drifted around the rim of the System, unremarked and never visited, while the tides of the Xeelee wars washed over the inner worlds. The System is probably littered with sites like this – abandoned, too remote to be worth tracking down for study, or exploitation, or even to destroy. All encrusted with bits of human history – and lost lives, and bones.'

Spinner laughed uneasily; she wasn't used to such reflection from the engineer.

She twisted her head, looking around the sky. 'I don't like it here, Louise,' she said. 'It's *barren*. Abandoned. I thought the Jupiter system was bad, but –'

Apart from the Sun and Port Sol, only the distant, dimmed stars shone here, impossibly remote. Spinner felt cowed by the dingy immensity all around her: she felt that her own spark of human life and warmth was as insignificant against all this darkness as the dim glow of the touchpad lights on her waldoes.

Empty. Barren. These were the true conditions of the Universe, she thought; life, and variety, and energy, were isolated aberrations. The *Northern* forest-Deck – the whole of that enclosed world which had seemed so huge to her, as a child – was nothing but a remote scrap of incongruous green, irrelevant in all this emptiness.

Louise said, 'I know how you're feeling. At least at Jupiter there was something in the sky. Right? Listen to me, Spinner; it's all a question of *scale*. Port Sol is a Kuiper object – a ball of ice travelling around the Sun about fifty AUs out. AUs – astronomical units – that means –'

'I know what it means.'

'Spinner, Jupiter is only *five* AUs from the centre of the Sun. So we're ten times further out from the heart of the System than *Northern* is ... so far out that we're on the edge of the Solar System, so far that the other bodies in the System – save Sol itself – are reduced to points of light, invisible without enhancement. Spinner, emptiness is what you have to expect, out here.'

'Sure. So tell me how it makes *you* feel.'

Louise hesitated. 'Spinner-of-Rope, five million years ago I came here to work – in the old days, while the *Great Northern* was being constructed ...'

Louise spoke of bustling, sprawling, vigorous human communities nestling among the ancient ice-spires of the Kuiper object. The sky had been full of GUTships and stars, with Sol a bright yellow gleam in Capricorn.

'But now,' Louise said, her voice tight, 'look at the Sun ... Spinner-of-Rope, even from this far out – even from fifty AUs – the damn thing is twice as wide as the Moon, seen from old Earth. It's *obscene* to me. It makes it impossible for me to forget, even for a moment, what's been done.'

Spinner sat silently for a moment. Memories of Earth meant nothing to her, but she could feel the pain in Louise's voice.

'Louise, do you want to land here?'

'No. There's nothing for us down there ... It was only an impulse that brought me out here in the first place; we had no evidence that anything had survived. I'm sorry, Spinner.'

Spinner sighed. 'Where to now?'

'Well, since we're out here in the dark, let's stay out. We're still picking up that remote beacon.'

'Where's the signal coming from?'

'Further out than we are now – about a hundred AUs – *and* a goodly distance around the equatorial plane from Port Sol. Spinner-of-Rope, we're looking at another few days in the saddle, for you. Can you stand it?'

Spinner sighed. 'It's not getting any easier. But it's not going to get any worse, is it?' ... And, she thought, it wasn't as if the base they had established amid the ruins of the Jupiter system was so fantastically inviting a place to get back to. 'Let's get it over.'

'All right. I've already laid in your course ...'

There could be no true dialogue, Garry Uvarov thought, between Lieserl – the strange, lonely exile in the Sun – and the crew of the returned *Great Northern*.

The corpse of Jupiter was only just over a light-hour from the centre of the Sol-giant, but Lieserl's maser messages took far longer than that to percolate out of the Sun along the flanks of their immense convection cells. So communications round-trips – between the *Northern* and the antiquated wormhole terminus that supported Lieserl's awareness – took several days.

Still, once contact was established, a prodigious amount of information flowed, asynchronously, back and forth across the tenuous link.

'Incredible,' Mark murmured. 'She dates from our own era – she was placed within the Sun at almost exactly the same time as our launch.'

It sounded as if Mark were speaking from somewhere inside Uvarov's own head. Uvarov swivelled his sightless face about the dining saloon. 'You're forgetting your spatial focus again,' he snapped. 'I know you're excited, but –'

There was a soft concussion; Uvarov pictured Virtual sound-sources reconfiguring throughout the saloon. 'Sorry,' Mark said, from a point in the air a few feet before Uvarov's head.

'As far as I can tell, she's human,' Mark said. 'A human ana-logue, anyway. The woman's been in there, alone, for *five million years*, Uvarov. I know that subjectively she won't have endured all that time at a normal human pace, but still . . .

'She's another Superet project – just as we are. Which is why there's such a coincidence in dates. We must both date from Superet's most active period, Uvarov.'

Uvarov smiled. 'Perhaps. And yet, what has resulted of all the grand designs of those days? Superet was planning to adjust the future of mankind – to ensure the success of the species. But what is the outcome? We have: one half-insane relic of a woman-Virtual, wandering about inside the Sun, one broken-down GUTship, the *Northern* . . . and a Sun become a giant in a lifeless Solar System.' He worked his numb mouth, but there was no phlegm to spit. 'Hardly a triumph. So much for the abilities of humans to manage projects on such timescales. So much for Superet!'

'But Lieserl has followed a lot of the history of the human race – in patches, and from a distance, but she knows more than we could ever hope to have uncovered otherwise. She lost contact with the rest of the race only as humans entered a late period called the Assimilation, when mankind was moving into direct competition with the Xeelee.'

Uvarov couldn't wrench his imagination away from the plight of Lieserl. 'But, I wonder, are these few, pathetic scraps of data sufficient compensation for a hundred thousand lifetimes of solitude endured by this unfortunate *Lieserl*, in the heart of a dying star?'

Mark synthesized a sniff. 'I don't know,' he said frankly. 'Maybe you're a better philosopher than I am, Uvarov; maybe you can come to judgements on the moral value of data. At this moment I don't really *care* where this information has come from.'

'No,' Uvarov said. 'I don't suppose you do.'

'I'm simply grateful that, because Lieserl exists, we've managed to learn something of humanity's five-megayear past . . . *and* of the photino birds.'

'*Photino birds?*'

The timbre of Mark's voice changed; Uvarov imagined his stupid, pixel-lumped face splitting into a grin. 'That's Lieserl's phrase. She found what she was sent in to find – dark matter energy flows, sucking the energy out of the core of the Sun. But it wasn't some inanimate process, as her designers had expected:

Lieserl found *life*, Uvarov. She's not alone. She's surrounded by photino birds. And I think she rather enjoys the company ...'

'*Lieserl* ...' Uvarov rolled the name around his mouth, savouring its strangeness. 'An unusual name, even a thousand years ago.' Uvarov's patchy, unreliable memory fired random facts into his tired forebrain. 'Einstein had a child called Lieserl. I mean Albert Einstein, the –'

'I know who he was.'

'His wife was called Mileva,' Uvarov said. 'Why do I remember this? ... They bore a child, Lieserl – but out of wedlock: a source of great shame in the early twentieth century, I understand. The child was adopted. Einstein had to choose between his child, and his career in science ... all that beautiful science of his. What a choice for any human to have to make!

'So this woman has the name of a bastard,' he said. 'A name redolent of isolation. How appropriate. How *lonely* she must have been ...

'And now she enjoys the company of dark matter life forms,' he mused. 'I wonder if she still remembers she was once *human*.'

Port Sol was twenty light-hours from the source of the beacon, Louise estimated. The nightfighter would be able to complete the trip in fifty hours.

Spinner-of-Rope, working her rudimentary controls with growing confidence, opened up the sail-wings of the nightfighter. She glanced over her shoulder to watch the wings. Her view was partially obscured by Louise's life-lounge, an improvised encrustation which sat, squat, on the thick construction material shoulders of the ship's wing-mountings, just behind her own cage. One of the *Northern*'s small, glass-walled pods had been fixed there too.

The nightfighter used its domain wall antigravity effect to protect the lounge, with Louise in it, from its extremes of acceleration. After a lot of experimentation they had found that securely attaching the lounge, and other artefacts, to the structure of the Xeelee nightfighter was enough to fool the craft into treating the enhancements as part of its structure.

But still, despite the human obstructions, Spinner could see the sparkle of the cosmic-string rims of the wings as they wound out across hundreds of miles of space, hauling open the night-blackness of the domain wall wings themselves. As they unfurled, the wings curved over on themselves with a grace and delicacy astonishing, Spinner thought, in artefacts so huge – and yet those curves seemed imbued with a terrific sense of vigour, of power.

She touched the waldoes.

The wings pulsed, once.

There was an instant in which she could see Port Sol recede from her, a flashbulb impression of squat human buildings and gaping ice-wounds which imploded to a light-point with a terrifying, helpless velocity.

And then the worldlet was gone. Within a heartbeat, Port Sol had become too dim even to show up as a point – and there was no longer a frame of reference against which she could judge her speed.

Then, with slow sureness as her speed built up, blue shift began to stain the stars ahead of her once more. For a few hours relativistic effects would spuriously restore those agèd lights to something like the brilliance they had once enjoyed.

...And again she had the sense, almost undefinable, of someone *here* with her, inside the cage – a presence, surely human, staring out wistfully at the blue shifted stars as she did.

She wondered whether she should tell Louise about this. But – real or not, external to her own, fuddled mind or not – her companion wasn't *threatening*.

And besides, what would Louise make of it? What could she do about it?

As the starbow coalesced around her once more, Spinner-of-Rope opaqued her faceplate, wriggled in her couch until an irritating wrinkle of cloth behind her back had smoothed itself out, and tried to sleep.

The slow, wide orbits of Port Sol and the beacon source had left them ninety degrees apart, as seen from the centre of the Sun. Louise had laid in a course which took the nightfighter on a wide, high trajectory high above the plane of the System, arcing across its outer regions. The nightfighter's path was like a fly hopping across a plate, from one point on the plate's rim to another.

The Sun sat like a bloated, grotesque spider at the heart of its ruined System. All of the inner planets – Mercury, Venus, Earth/Luna – were gone ... save only Mars, which had been reduced to a scorched cinder, surely barren of life, its orbit taking it skimming through the outer layers of the new red giant itself.

In a few more millennia that fragile orbit would erode, pitching Mars, too, into the flames.

Of the outer gas giants – Jupiter, Saturn, Uranus, Neptune – all had survived with little change, save imploded Jupiter. But the outermost planet of all – the double world Pluto/Charon – had disappeared.

Spinner listened to Louise describe all this. 'So where did Pluto go?'

'I've no idea,' Louise said. 'There's not a trace to be seen, anywhere along its old orbital path. Maybe we'll never know.

'Spinner, a lot of the minor bodies of the System seem to have taken a real beating. Some of that is no doubt due to the Sun's new, extreme state ... but maybe some of it has been deliberate, too.'

Once, the Solar System had served as host to billions of minor bodies. The Oort-Opik Cloud was – had once been – a swarm of a hundred billion comets circling through an immense, sparse shell of space, between four light-months and three light-years from the Sun. Now, that cloud was denuded.

Louise said, 'Many of the comets must have been destroyed by the growth of the Sun – flashed to steam by its huge out-pouring of heat energy, in one last, extravagant fling ... They would have been visible from other systems, actually; they'd have inserted water lines, briefly, in the spectrum of the Sun: a kind of spectral Last Post for the Solar System, if there was anybody left, anywhere, to see.'

Further in towards the Sun, there were the Kuiper objects, like Port Sol: icy worldlets, orbiting not far outside the widest planetary orbits. And throughout the System there were more rings of small objects – like the asteroids, shepherded into semi-stable orbits by the gravitational interaction of the major planets.

'But *all* those worldlet rings are depleted,' Louise said. 'Now, some of that depletion must be due to the Sun's forced evol-

244

ution, not to mention the loss of three of the inner planets. But many of the small objects *must* have been populated, by the era of the Xeelee wars.'

'So the objects might have been deliberately destroyed – more casualties of war.'

'Right.'

Spinner swilled apple-juice around her mouth, wishing she had some way to spit it out – or better still, to clean her teeth.

Spinner had learned of the Solar System only through Louise's bookslates and records, but she'd gained an impression of an immense, bustling, prosperous world-system. There had been huge orbital habitat-cities, heavily populated worlds laced together by wormhole transit routes, and ships like immense, extravagant diamonds crossing the face of the yellow-gold Sun. Somewhere inside her – despite all the dire warnings of Superet – she'd hoped to arrive here and find it all just as she'd read.

Instead, there was only this decayed Sun and its ruined worlds ... even the wormhole routes, it seemed, had been shut down. And here *she* was, stuck inside the pilot-cage of an alien craft, chasing across tens of billions of miles in search of one, sad, isolated beacon.

She began to take her body through a simple regime of callisthenics, exercises she could get through without climbing out of her couch. 'So, Louise. You're telling me that Sol is dead. The System is dead. And you sound ... upset about it. But what else did you expect to find?'

'I expected nothing. I *hoped* for more,' Louise said. 'But I guess the slow destruction of the Sun, coupled with the Xeelee assaults, were together enough to wipe the System clean ... '

Spinner felt, suddenly, profoundly depressed, as if the weight of all those lost years, those hundreds of billions of lives which had resulted in nothing but this cosmic rubble, was bearing down on her.

'Louise, I don't want to hear any more.'

'All right, Spinner. I –'

Spinner shut her off.

She blanked out her faceplate, and filled its inner side with a soothing, cool green light, the light which had filtered through leaves from an artificial Sun to illuminate her childhood. She immersed herself in the warm feel of her muscles, as she pushed through her exercises.

Immersed in the cries of the klaxon, Morrow's party held a council of war.

'I've been scouting,' Mark said. 'And as far as I can tell it's the same all over the Decks. No people, anywhere. The same emptiness ... Everyone has been taken into the Temples. And it's not going to be easy to get them out.'

'Let's leave them in there, then,' Trapper-of-Frogs said practically. 'If that's what they want.'

Morrow studied her round, unmarked face. 'Unfortunately, that isn't an option,' he said gently. 'We have to protect them.'

'From themselves?'

'If necessary, yes. At any rate, from the Superet Planners.'

Trapper thrust her face up at his. 'Why?'

Morrow started to feel impatient. 'Because we have to. Look, Trapper, I didn't want to come on this jaunt into the Decks any more than you did. It's not *my* fault we're being shot at –'

'Starve them,' Trapper said simply.

Morrow turned to her. 'What?'

'Starve them.' She turned to study the Temple with an appraising eye, as if assessing its capacity. 'There must be hundreds of people in there – and in the other Temples. They can't have that much food and water; there just isn't room in there. I say we wait here, until they get starved out. Simple.'

Constancy-of-Purpose grinned, maliciously. 'We could block the sewage outlets. I know where the outlets are; it would be easy. That would be fun. And a lot faster acting.'

Mark hovered before her, his artificial face drawn into stern disapproval. 'And cause plague, illness and death on a massive scale? Is that really what you're proposing?'

Constancy-of-Purpose looked doubtful; she passed a massive hand over her scalp.

'Listen to me,' Mark said slowly. 'This is my field – I'm a socio-engineer, after all. Was, whatever. The last thing we want is a siege, here. Do you understand? I'm not sure if we have the resources to break a siege. If we tried, the fall-out – the illness and death – would put an immense strain on the *Northern*'s infrastructure.

'Besides –' He hesitated.

Morrow said, 'Yes?'

'Besides, I'm not certain that breaking a siege is even *possible*.'

'What do you mean?'

'Look: the Planners see themselves as messianic. They, and only they, can save "their" people. If we besiege them, the Planners simply won't respond the way a rational person would – by studying their resources, by assessing the chances of a successful break-out, and so on. Worse still, we – the besiegers – would become part of the fabric of their delusion, an embodiment of the external threats which assail their people.'

Morrow frowned. 'I don't understand.'

Mark, evidently forgetting there was no drive-induced gravity, started pacing around the Deck, his Virtual feet soundlessly missing the floor by a fraction of an inch. 'You have to understand things from the point of view of the people in control in there: *the Planners*.' He turned a frank gaze on Morrow. 'I've been studying you, Morrow. I know you're still intimidated – by this place, by the nearness of the Planners. Aren't you? – despite all your experiences outside here, beyond these walls.'

Morrow said nothing.

'This culture has a lot of power,' Mark said. 'Almost all of it is concentrated in the hands of the Planners, with the mass of people dumbly acquiescing. Morrow, the Planners have taken the species-survival logic of Superet – the logic which lay behind the whole of the *Northern*'s mission, after all – and extrapolated it into something more – something almost religious.

'We're dealing with a powerful concept, folks; one that seems to touch buttons wired deep into our human psyches. People on these Decks have followed where the Planners have led for nearly a millennium – including you, Morrow.

'When Louise and I saw this tendency developing, quite early in the flight, we decided we couldn't overcome it – and it would be wastefully destructive to try.

'So we withdrew, to the *Great Britain*, leaving enough of a physical control infrastructure in place for us to ensure the ship could run smoothly.

'Well, maybe we were wrong to do that; because now the

Planners' messiah complex is leading us to a crisis ...'

Morrow found he intensely disliked being analysed in this way by a Virtual construct. 'But what are we to *do*?' he snapped. 'How are we to use these staggering insights of yours?'

'The situation is unpredictable,' Mark said bluntly. 'But it's possible that the Planners would *destroy* their people – and themselves – rather than let us win.'

The little party exchanged shocked glances.

Trapper said, 'But that's *insane*. It even contradicts their conscious goals – to protect their people.'

Mark's smile was thin. 'Nobody said it had to make sense. Unfortunately, there are plenty of precedents, right through human history.'

Constancy-of-Purpose said, 'With flaws like that hard-wired into our heads, it's a wonder we ever got into space in the first place.' She let herself drift a little way from the Deck, her legs dangling beneath her, and studied the Temple, eyes squinting. 'Well, if we can't break the siege, we're going to have trouble. For a start, there are more of them than us. And, second, their cross-bows have a much greater range than these blowpipes wielded by Trapper and her friends –'

'Maybe,' Trapper-of-Frogs said slowly, 'but I've been thinking about that. I mean, the Planners could have killed us earlier, when we were strung out along the Deck. Couldn't they?'

Mark frowned. 'They fired *over* us. Maybe they were trying to warn us.'

'Maybe.' Trapper-of-Frogs nodded grudgingly. 'Or maybe they *were* trying to hit us – but couldn't. Watch this.'

She pulled a dart from the pouch at her waist and raised her blowpipe to her lips. She spat the dart harmlessly into the air, on a flat trajectory parallel to the Deck.

Morrow, bemused, tracked the little projectile. It rapidly lost most of its initial speed to the resistance of the air, but its path continued flat and even, still parallel to the Deck. Eventually, Morrow supposed, it would slow up so much that it would fall to the Deck, and ...

No, it wouldn't, he realized slowly. The GUTdrive was shut off: there was no gravity. Even if air resistance stopped the dart completely, it still wouldn't fall.

'When the gravity first disappeared,' Tracker said, 'I couldn't hit a damn thing. I seemed to aim too high, every time. I quickly worked out why: even over quite short distances, gravity will pull a dart – or a cross-bow bolt – down a little way. I've grown up compensating for that, allowing for it unconsciously when I aim at something.

'In the absence of gravity the dart just sails on, in a straight line, until it hits something.' She hefted the blowpipe. 'It took me hours of practice before I felt confident with this thing in zero-gee; it was like learning from scratch all over again.'

Mark was nodding slowly. 'So you think the Planners' bowmen *meant* to hit us.'

'I'm sure of it. But they shot too high. They haven't learned to adjust to zero-gee; they certainly didn't allow for it when they shot at us.'

Constancy-of-Purpose cupped her chin. 'Maybe you're right. But I don't see how that helps us. Even if their aim is a little off, there are enough of them to blanket us with bolts if we try to get too close.'

'Yes,' Mark said, some excitement entering his artificial voice, 'but maybe we can use Trapper's insight in another way. She's right; the Planners – everyone in that building – are failing to learn how to cope with the absence of gravity. In fact, they seem to be denying that the absence even exists.' He glanced around, staring at the tracery of ropes they'd laid from the access ramps as if seeing them for the first time. 'And *so have we*. Look at the way we've travelled – abseiling across the floor, sticking to the familiar two dimensions to which gravity restricts us.'

Morrow frowned. 'What are you suggesting?'

Mark raised his face to the iron sky. 'That we try a little lateral thinking ...'

At the origin of the weak, ancient signal Louise and Spinner found a worldlet. It was a dirty snowball three hundred miles across, slowly turning in the outer darkness.

When Louise bathed the worldlet with spotlights from her life-lounge, broken ice shone, stained with splashes of colour: rust-brown, grey.

This lost little fragment followed a highly elliptical path, each of its distorted journeys lasting a million years or more. Its closest approach to the Sun came somewhere between the orbits of Saturn and Uranus, while at its furthest it got halfway to the nearest star – two light-years from the inner worlds.

'Bizarre,' Louise mused. 'It's got the *orbital* characteristics of a long-period comet – but none of the *physical* characteristics. In morphology it's more like a Kuiper object, like Port Sol. But then it should be in a reasonably circular orbit . . .'

Spinner-of-Rope peered out of her cage at the dark little world, wondering what might still be living down there.

Here and there, in pits in the ice, metal gleamed.

'*Artefacts*,' Louise said. 'Can you see that, Spinner? Artefacts, all over the surface.'

'Human?'

'I'd guess so. But I don't recognize anything. And I doubt if there's much still working . . .

'I'm taking radar scans. There are hundreds of chambers in there, in the interior. And our beacon's somewhere inside: still broadcasting on all wavelengths, with a peak in the microwave range . . . Life knows what's powering it.'

'Is this ice-ball *inhabited*? Is there anyone here?'

'I don't know.' Spinner heard Louise hesitate. 'I guess I'm going to have to go down to find out.'

The pod's small jets flared across the worldlet's uneven surface as Louise descended. Spinner watched; the pod was the only moving thing in all of her Universe.

'I'm close to the surface now,' Louise reported. 'I'll level off. They certainly made a mess of this surface. I think these artefacts are sections of *ships*, Spinner. Not that I can label much of it – so much of this technology must be tens of millennia beyond us . . . Lethe, I wish we had the time to spend here, to study all this stuff.

'But at least it's *human*.' Her voice sounded strained. 'The first traces of humanity we've found in the whole damn System, Spinner.

'I think people landed here, and broke up their ships for raw materials to occupy the interior.

'I'm going to land now. I see what looks like a port.'

Louise couldn't find any way to open the wide, hatch-like port to the interior. Instead, she had to erect a plastic bubble to serve as an airlock over the port, and cut her way through, working slowly in the microgravity.

'All right, I'm in.' Her breath was scratchy, shallow – almost as if she were whispering, Spinner thought. 'It's *dark* here, Spinner. I have lamps; I'm going to leave a trail of them, as I go through.'

Spinner, listening in her cage, prayed that nothing bad happened to Louise down there. If it did, what could she – Spinner – do? Would she have the courage even to try a landing on the ice worldlet?

Doubt flooded her, a feeling of inadequacy, of being unable to cope ...

You'll manage, Spinner-of-Rope.

That same dry, sourceless voice.

Strangely, her fears seemed to subside. She glanced around; of course, she was alone in the cage, with the nightfighter suspended passively over the ice worldlet. But still – again – she had had the impression that someone was *here* with her. She couldn't see him, or her – but somehow she knew there was nothing to fear; she sensed a massive, comforting presence similar to her own, lost father.

But still – hearing voices? *What in Lethe is going on inside my head*?

'... Lots of chambers,' Louise said a little breathlessly. 'They are boxes, carved out of the ice and plated over with metal and plastic. A bit cramped ... There is air here, but foul; I won't be breaking my suit seal. This was definitely a human colony, Spinner. But it's all – neat. Tidy; abandoned in an orderly way.

'I guess they took a long time to die. They had time to clear up after themselves – to bury their dead, maybe, even, as they withdrew. I guess they went deeper as their numbers dwindled, towards the centre of the world ... It's kind of dignified, don't you think? There are no signs of panic, or conflict. I wonder how *we* would behave, in the same circumstance. Spinner, I'm going on now.'

Later: 'I'm in a deeper layer of chambers. I think I've found the source of the signal.' She was silent for a while. Then, 'They sure built this to last.'

'Well, they got that right.'

'I still can't identify what's powering it ... I guess one of the

251

ship's GUTdrive plants on the surface. I think they used nanobots to maintain the beacon, Spinner. Maybe they adapted AS nanobots from their medical stores.' Her tone of voice changed, subtly, and Spinner imagined her smiling. 'They were determined to enable this to survive. But it's been millions of years ... and the 'bots have made a few cumulative mistakes. The damn thing looks as if it's *melted*, Spinner. But it's still pumping out its signal, so we can't criticize too much ...'

'Louise,' Spinner asked slowly, 'why were these people here? What were they trying to do?'

Louise thought for a while. 'Spinner, I think they were trying to *escape*.'

This ice-world was typical of the small, subplanetary bodies which could once have been found throughout the Solar System, Louise said, shepherded into orbital clusters by the major planets.

'But,' Louise said, 'the orbits of many of those little bodies were only *semi-stable*. Their orbits were intrinsically chaotic, you see ... That means, over a long enough time period the minor bodies could move out of their stable pathways. They could even fall into the gravity wells of the major planets and be flung out of the System altogether. It's a form of *evaporation* – an evaporation of worlds and moons out of stellar systems. In fact, over a long enough scale – and I'm talking tens of billions of years now – the same thing would happen to the major planets too – and to stars, which could evaporate out of their parent galaxies ... If,' she went on sourly, 'they had ever been given the chance.'

'So you think this little world just evaporated away from Sol, gravitationally?'

'No ... not necessarily.'

Louise speculated about the closing stages of the Xeelee conflicts. She imagined mankind trapped within its home System, sliding towards the final defeat. Towards the end, even communication between the worlds might have broken down. Humanity would have been reduced to isolated pockets, cowering under the Xeelee onslaughts.

But some might have seen a way out – a way to try to escape the final investing of the System by the Xeelee.

Louise said, 'Imagine this little worldlet following its

semi-stable path – say, between the orbits of Saturn and Uranus. It wouldn't have taken much to push it far enough out of its orbit to bring on orbital instability. And once equilibrium was lost, the drift away from the standard orbital elements could have been quite rapid – say, within a few orbits – and the decay wouldn't have required any further deliberate – and observable – impulses, perhaps.'

Silently, all but invisibly to anyone watching, the little world, with its precious cargo of cowering, fearful humans, had looped through its increasingly perturbed orbit, falling at last – after many orbits, perhaps covering centuries – into the gravitational field of one of the major planets.

Then, finally, the worldlet was slingshot out of the Solar System.

'If they'd got it right,' Louise said, 'maybe it would have been a viable plan. *If*. These people were going to the stars, by the lowest-tech way you can imagine. It would have taken tens of thousands of years to get to even the nearest star – but so what? They *had* tens of thousands of years to play with, thanks to AS – or the equivalent they'd developed by then. And locked up in the ice of the worldlet there was probably as much water as in the whole of the Atlantic Ocean ... Going to the stars in an ice moon was certainly a better chance than staying here to be creamed by the Xeelee with the rest – it was a viable way to get out of all this, all but undetectable.

'The scheme obviously attracted support. You can see the bits of ships, littering the surface ... People must have fled here, quietly, from all over the collapsing System. The mission was a beacon of hope, I guess.

'But –'

'But what?'

'But *they got it wrong*.

'I'm going to go deeper now, Spinner.'

'Be careful, Louise.'

There was a long silence, broken only by the sound of Louise's shallow breath. Spinner filled her faceplate once more with cool, green leaf-light and stared into it, trying not to imagine what Louise was finding, down there inside the little tomb-world.

At length, Louise said: 'Well, that's it. I guess I'm here: the last place they occupied ... the one place they couldn't tidy up after themselves.'

Spinner stared into green emptiness. 'What can you see?'

'Abandoned clothes.' Hesitation. 'Dust everywhere. No bones, Spinner; no crumbling corpses ... you can put your imagination away.'

After five megayears, there *would* only be dust, Spinner thought: a final cloud, of flakes of bone and crumbled flesh, settling slowly.

'If they left records, I can't find them,' Louise said. She sounded as if she were trying to be unconcerned – to maintain control – but Spinner thought she could hear fragility in that level voice. 'Perhaps there's something in the electronics. But that would take years of data mining to dig out, even if we could restore the power. And we're probably looking at technology a hundred thousand years beyond ours anyway ...'

'Louise, there's nothing you can do in there. I think you should come out.'

'... Yes. I guess you're right, Spinner-of-Rope. We don't have time for this.'

Spinner thought she heard relief in Louise's tone.

The little *Northern* pod clambered up from the worldlet's shallow gravity well, towards the Xeelee craft.

Louise, safe inside her life-lounge, said: 'They couldn't control the slingshot well enough. Or maybe the Xeelee interfered with their plans.

'They weren't thrown out of the System as they'd planned, on an open-ended *hyperbolic* trajectory; instead they were put into this wide, and deadly, *elliptical* orbit – an orbit which was closed, taking them nowhere, very slowly.

'I guess they tried to stick it out. Well, they'd broken up their ships; they had no choice. Maybe if we had time for a proper archaeological study here we could work out how long they lasted. Who knows? Hundreds of thousands of years? Maybe they were hoping for rescue, for all that time, from some brave new future when humans had thrown out the Xeelee once more.

'But it was a future that never came.

'By the time they set up their beacon, their final plea for help, they must have known they were through – and that there *was* nobody to come to their aid.'

'Nobody except us.'

'Yes,' Louise growled. 'And what can we offer them now?'

'What about the beacon?'

'I shut it down,' Louise said softly. 'It's served no purpose … not for five million years.'

Spinner sat in her Xeelee-crafted cabin, watching the grim little tomb of ice turn beneath her prow. 'Louise? Where to now?'

'The inner System. I think I've had it with all this bleakness and dark. Spinner-of-Rope, let's go to Saturn.'

19

Surrounded by swooping photino birds, Lieserl sailed around the core of the Sun. She let hydrogen light play across her face, warming her.

The helium core, surrounded by the blazing hydrogen shell scorching its way out through the thinning layers, continued to grow in the steady hail of ash from the shell. Inhomogeneities in the giant's envelope – clouds and clumps of gas, bounded by ropes of magnetic flux – moved across the face of the core, and the core-star actually cast shadows *outwards*, high up into the expanding envelope.

The photino birds swept, oblivious, through the shining fusion shell and on into the inert core itself. Lieserl watched as a group of the birds broke away and sailed off and out, to their unknowable destination beyond the Sun. She studied the birds. Had their rate of activity *increased*? She had the vague impression of a greater urgency about the birds' swooping orbits, their eternal dips into the core.

Maybe the birds knew the ancient human spacecraft, the *Northern*, was here. Maybe they were reacting to the humans' presence ... It seemed fanciful – but was it possible?

The processes unfolding around the Sun were quite remarkably beautiful. In fact, she reflected now, every stage of the Sun's evolution had been beautiful – whether accelerated by the photino birds or not. It was too anthropomorphic to consider the lifecycle of a star as some analogy of human birth, life and death. A star was a construct of physical processes; the evolution it went through was simply a search for equilibrium stages between changing, opposing forces. There was no life or death involved, no loss or gain: just *process*.

Why *shouldn't* it be beautiful?

She smiled at herself. Ironic. Here she was, an AI five million years old, accusing herself of too much anthropomorphism ...

But, she thought uneasily, perhaps her true fault lay in *not enough* anthropomorphism.

The sudden communication from the humans outside – the whispers of maser light which had trickled down the flanks of the huge, dumb convection cells – had shaken her to her soul.

She'd undertaken her cycle of messages, she suspected strongly, because she was driven to it by some sinister bit of programming, buried deep within her: not out of choice, or because she believed she might actually get a *reply*. So she'd packed her data with pictures of herself, and small, ironic jokes – all intended, she supposed, to signal to herself that this wasn't real: that it was all a game, unworthy of being taken seriously because there was no one left out there to hear.

Well, it seemed now, she'd been wrong. These people – of her own era, roughly, preserved by relativistic time dilation in their strange ship, the *Great Northern* – had returned to the Solar System.

And they were – she'd come to believe – *people who didn't approve of her*.

They hadn't said as much, explicitly. But she suspected an inner coldness was there, buried in the long communications they exchanged with her.

They thought she'd lost her objectivity – forgotten the reason she was placed in here in the first place. They thought she'd become an ineffectual observer, seduced by the rhythmic beauty of the photino birds.

Lieserl was some form of traitor, perhaps.

For the truth was – in the eyes of the men and women of the *Northern* – the photino birds were deadly. The birds were anti-human. They were killing the Sun.

They couldn't understand how Lieserl could not be *aware* of this stark enmity.

She closed her eyes and hugged her knees; the hydrogen shell, fusing at ten million degrees, felt like warm summer Sunlight on her Virtual face. She'd watched the photino birds do their slow, patient work, year after year, leaching away the Sun's fusion energy in slow, deadly, dribbles. She'd come to understand that the birds were killing the Sun – and yet she'd never thought really to wonder what was happening *outside* the

257

Sun, in other stars. Had she vaguely assumed that the photino birds were somehow native to the Sun, like a localized infection? – But that couldn't be, of course, for she'd seen birds fly away from here, and come skimming down through the envelope to join the core-orbiting flock. So there *must* be birds beyond the Sun – significant flocks of them.

She realized now, with chilling clarity, that her unquestioned assumption that the birds were contained to just one star, coupled with her intrigued fascination with the birds themselves, had led her to *justify* the birds' actions, in her own heart. It hadn't even mattered to her that the result of the birds' activity would be the death of *Sol* – perhaps, even, the extinction of man.

She quailed from this unwelcome insight into her own soul. She had once been human, after all; was she really so clinical, so *alien*?

The murder of Sol would have been bad enough. But in fact – the crew of the *Northern* had told her, in brutal and explicit detail – all across the sky, the stars were dying: ballooning into diseased giants, crumbling into dwarfs. The Universe was littered with planetary nebulae, supernovae ejecta and the other debris of dying stars, all rich with complex – and useless – heavy elements.

The photino birds *were* killing the stars: and not just the Sun, man's star, but *all* of the stars, out as far as the *Northern*'s sensors could pick up.

Already, there was nowhere in the Universe for humans to run to.

And she, Lieserl – the *Northern* crew seemed to believe – should be doing more than leaking out wry little messages via her maser convection cells. She should be screaming warnings.

Through her complex feelings, a mixture of self-doubt and loneliness, anger erupted. After all, what right did the *Northern* crew have to criticize her – even implicitly? She'd had no choice about this assignment – this immortal exile of hers in the heart of the Sun. She'd been allowed no *life*. And it wasn't *her* who had shut down the telemetry link through the wormhole, during the Assimilation.

Why, after millions of years of abandonment, should *she* offer any loyalty to mankind?

And yet, she thought, the arrival of the *Northern*, and the fresh perspective of its crew, had made her take a colder, harder look at the birds – and at herself – than she had for a *long* time.

She pictured the shadow universe of dark matter: a universe which permeated, barely touching, the visible worlds men had once inhabited ... And yet that image was misleading, she thought, for the dark matter was no shadow: it comprised most of the Universe's total mass. The glowing, baryonic matter was a mere glittering froth on the surface of that dark ocean.

The photino birds – and their unknowable dark matter cousins, perhaps as different from the birds as were the Qax from humanity – slid through the black waters like fish, blind and hidden.

But the small, shining fraction of baryonic matter seemed vital to the dark matter creatures. It was a catalyst for the chains of events which sustained their species.

For a start, dark matter could not form stars. And the birds seemed to *need* the gravity wells of baryonic stars.

When a clump of baryonic gas collapsed under gravity, electromagnetic radiation carried away much of the heat produced – it was as if the radiation *cooled* the gas cloud. The residual heat left in the cloud eventually balanced the gravitational attraction, and equilibrium was found: a star formed.

But dark matter could not produce electromagnetic radiation. And without the cooling effect of the radiation, a dark matter cloud, collapsing under gravity, trapped much more of *its* heat of contraction. As a result, much larger clouds – larger than galaxies – were the equilibrium form for dark matter.

So the early Universe had been populated by immense, cold, bland clouds of dark matter: it had been a cosmos almost without structure.

Then the baryonic matter had gathered, and the stars began to implode – to shine. Lieserl imagined the first stars sparking to life across the cosmos, tiny pinprick gravity wells in the smooth oceans of dark matter.

The photino birds lived off a trickle of proton-photino interactions, which fed them with a slow, steady drip of energy. And to get a sufficient flow of energy the birds needed *dense* matter – densities which could not have formed without baryonic structures.

And the birds' dependence on baryonic matter extended further. She knew that the birds needed templates of baryonic material even to reproduce.

So baryonic-matter stars had given the photino birds their very being, and now fed them and enabled them to reproduce.

Lieserl brooded. A fine hypothesis. But *why*, then, should the birds be so eager to kill off their mother-stars?

Once more the chatter of the humans from the *Northern* passed through her sensorium, barely registering. They were asking her more questions – requesting more detailed forecasts of the likely future evolution of the suffering Sun.

She sailed moodily around the core, thinking about stars and the photino birds.

And her mind made connections it had failed to complete before in millions of years.

At last, she saw it: the full, bleak picture.

And, suddenly, it seemed urgent – terribly urgent – to answer the humans' questions about the future.

She hurried to the base of her convection cells.

The shower's needle-sharp jets of water sprayed over Louise's skin. She floated there at the centre of the shower cubicle, listening to the shrill gurgle of the water as it was pumped out of the booth. She lifted her arms up and let the water play over her belly and chest; it was hot enough, the pressure sufficiently high, to make her battered old skin tingle, as if it were being worked over by a thousand tiny masseurs.

She hated being in zero-gee. She always had, and she hated it still; she even loathed having to have a pump to suck the water out of her shower for her. She'd insisted on having this shower installed, curtained off in one corner of the life-lounge, as her one concession to luxury – *no, damn it*, she thought, *this is no luxury; the shower is my concession to what's left of my humanity*.

A hot shower was one of the few sensual experiences that had remained *vivid*, as she'd got so absurdly old. High-pressure, steaming water could still cut through the patina of age which deadened her skin.

There was hardly anything else left. Since her sense of smell had finally packed up, eating had become a process of basic refuelling, to be endured rather than enjoyed. And, apart from her Virtuals, nothing much stimulated her mentally; it would take more than a thousand-year life to exhaust the libraries of mankind, but she'd long since wearied of the ancient, frozen thoughts of others, rendered irrelevant by the death of the Sun.

She turned off the spigot. Hot air gushed down around her, drying her rapidly. When the droplets had stopped floating off her skin she pulled back the shower curtain.

The lounge was basic – it contained little more than this shower, a small galley, a sleeping cocoon and her data desk with its processor bank. Lashed up in haste from sections of the *Northern*'s hull material, the lounge was a squat cylinder five yards across, crouched on the shoulders of the Xeelee craft like a malevolent parasite – utterly spoiling the lines of the delicate nightfighter, Louise had thought regretfully. The walls of the lounge were opaqued to a featureless grey, making the lounge rather dingy and claustrophobic. And the place was a mess. Bits of her clothing drifted around in the air, crumpled and soiled, and she was conscious of a stale smell. She really ought to clean up; she knew she utterly lacked the obsessive neatness needed to survive for long in zero gee.

She reached for a towel drifting in the air close by. She rubbed herself vigorously, relishing the feeling of the rough fabric on her skin. A mere blast of air never left her feeling really *dry*.

The feel of the warm towel on her skin made her think, distantly, about sex.

She'd always had a sour public persona: people saw her as an engineer obsessed with her job, with building things *out there*. But there was more to her than that – there were elements which Mark had recognized and treasured during their marriage. Sex had always been important to her: not just for the physical pleasure of it but also for what it symbolized: something deep and old within her, an echo of the ancient sea whose traces humans still carried, even now. The contrast of that oceanic experience with her work had made her more complete, she thought.

After she and Mark had reconciled – tentatively, grudgingly, in recognition of their joint isolation in the *Northern* – they had revived their vigorous sex life. And it had been good, remaining vital for a long time. Longer than either of them had a right to expect, she supposed. She wrapped the towel around her back and began to rub at her buttocks. Maybe if Mark had stayed alive –

The lounge walls snapped to transparency; space darkness flooded over her.

Louise cried out and pulled the towel around her body.

From her comms desk came the sound of laughter.

She scrambled in a locker for fresh clothes. The door of the jury-rigged locker jammed and she hauled at it, swearing, aware of the towel slipping around her.

'By Lethe's waters, Spinner, what do you think you're doing?'

Louise could just make out Spinner's cage, a box of winking lights at the prow of the nightfighter. A shadow moved across the lights – Spinner, probably, twisting in her couch to take a mocking look at her. 'I'm sorry. I *knew* you'd be embarrassed.'

Louise had found a coverall; now she thrust her legs into it. 'Then why,' she said angrily, 'did you invade my privacy by doing it?'

'What difference does it make? Louise, there's no one to see; we're a billion miles from the nearest living soul. *And* you're a thousand years old. You really ought to rid yourself of these taboos.'

'But they're *my* taboos,' Louise hissed. 'I happen to like them, and they make a difference to *me*. If you ever get to my age, Spinner-of-Rope, maybe you'll learn a little tolerance.'

'Well, maybe. Anyway, I didn't de-opaque your walls just to catch you with your pants off.' She sounded mischievous.

Suspiciously, Louise asked, 'Why, then?'

'Because –' Spinner hesitated.

'Because what?'

'Look ahead.'

There was a point of light, far ahead, beyond Spinner's cage: a point that ballooned, now, exploding at her face –

Saturn, plummeting out of emptiness at her.

Louise cried out and buried her face in her hands.

'Because,' Spinner said softly, 'we're there. I thought you'd enjoy watching our arrival.'

Louise opened her fingers, cautiously.

Steady, orange-brown light shone into her cabin: the light of a planet, illuminated by the bloated body of its Sun.

Spinner was laughing softly.

Louise said slowly, 'Spinner – if this is Saturn – *where are the rings*?'

'Rings? What rings?'

The planet itself was the same swollen mass of hydrogen and helium, with its core of rock twenty times as massive as Earth intact, deep within it. Elaborate cloud systems still wound around the globe, like watercolour streaks of brown and gold, just as she remembered. And the largest moon, Titan, was still there.

But the *rings* had gone.

Louise hurried to her data desk.

'...Louise? Are you all right?'

From the surface of the city-world of Titan, the rings had been a line of light, geometrically precise, vivid against the autumn gold of Saturn ...

Louise made herself reply. 'I think I'm mourning the rings, Spinner. They were the most beautiful sight in the Solar System. Who would smash up such harmless, magnificent beauty? And, damn it, they were *ours*.'

'But,' said Spinner, 'there *is* a ring here. I can see it. Look ...'

Following Spinner's directions, Louise studied her data desk.

The ring showed up as a faint band across the stars, a shadow against the swollen, imperturbable bulk of the planet itself.

Once, three ice moons had circled outside the orbit of Titan: Iapetus, Hyperion and retrograde Phoebe. All that was left of those three moons was this trail of rubble. Thin, colourless, with no evidence of structure, the ring of ice chunks, glowing red in the light of the dying Sun, circled the planet at about sixty planetary radii, a pale ghost of its glorious predecessor.

And where were the other moons?

Louise paged through her data desk. Once, Saturn had had seventeen satellites. Now – as far as she could tell from their orbits – only Titan and Enceladus remained. And there wasn't much left of Enceladus at all; the little moon still swung through an orbit around four planetary radii from Saturn, but its path was much more elliptical than before. Its surface – always broken, uneven – had been left as rubble. There was no sign of the small human outposts which had once sparkled against the shadows of its curved ridges and cratered plains.

The rest of the moons – even the harmless, ten-mile-wide islands of water ice – had gone.

Louise remembered the ancient, beautiful names. *Pan, Atlas, Prometheus, Pandora, Epimetheus* ... Names almost as old, now, as the myths from which they had been taken; names which had outlived the objects to which they'd been assigned.

'Louise?'

'I'm sorry, Spinner.'

'Still mourning?'

... *Janus, Mimas, Tethys, Telesto* ...

'Yes.'

'I guess somebody has to.'

'Spinner, what *happened* here?'

'A battle,' Spinner said quietly. 'Obviously.'

Calypso, Dione, Helene, Rhea, Hyperion, Iapetus, Phoebe ...

The nightfighter spread its hundred-mile wings, eclipsing the debris of the shattered moons.

Milpitas sat in his office. From throughout the Temple, there were the sounds of shouting, of screams, of yelled words too indistinct for him to hear.

The shouting seemed to be coming closer.

He cleared his magnetized desk top, putting his paper, pens, data slates away into drawers. He folded his hands and held them over the desk.

The door to his office was opened.

The renegade from – *outside* – hovered there in the air. He was almost horizontal from Milpitas' point of view: as if he were defying the Planner to fit him into his orderly, gravity-structured Universe.

The renegade spread his empty hands. 'I'm not going to hurt you.'

'I know you,' Milpitas said slowly.

'Perhaps you do.' The renegade was tall, quite well-muscled; he wore a practical coverall equipped with a dozen pockets which were crammed with unidentifiable tools. He wore his hair short, but not shaven-clean; his look was confident, even excited. Milpitas tried to imagine this man without the hair –

and with a little less of that damnable confidence, too – in standard, drab Superet coveralls, and with a more appropriate posture: stooped shoulders, perhaps, hands folded before him ...

'My name's Morrow. You had a certain amount of – trouble – with me.' The renegade glanced around at the office, as if recalling some sour experience. 'I was in here several times, as you tried to explain to me how wrong I was in my thinking ...'

'*Morrow.* You disappeared.'

Morrow frowned. 'No. No, I didn't disappear. Milpitas, you sound like a child who believes that as soon as an object is out of sight, it no longer exists ...'

Milpitas smiled. 'What do *you* know of children?'

'Now, a lot,' Morrow said. He smiled, in turn, quite in control. 'I didn't disappear, Milpitas. I went somewhere else. I've done extraordinary things, Planner – seen wonderful sights.'

Milpitas folded his hands and settled back in his chair. 'How did you get in?'

'Past your sentries?' Morrow smiled. '*We came in from above.* It took seconds, and we were quite silent. Your sentries were positioned to watch for an approach across the Deck; they didn't imagine anyone would come in over their heads. They didn't even know we were in the building, before we took them out.'

'"Took them out"?'

'They're unconscious,' Morrow said. 'The forest people use a certain type of frog sweat, which ... well, never mind. The sentries are unharmed.'

Milpitas tried to think of something to say – some words with which he could regain control of the situation. He felt a rising panic; suddenly, his orders had failed to be executed. He felt as if he were at the heart of some immense, dying machine, poking at buttons and levers which were no longer linked to anything.

Morrow's voice was gentle. 'It's over. I know you believe what you're doing is right, for the people. But this is for the best, Milpitas. More deaths would have been – inexcusable. You see that, don't you?'

'And the *mission*?' Milpitas asked bitterly. 'The goals of Superet? What of that?'

'That's not over,' Morrow said. 'Come back with me, Milpitas. There are remarkable things out there. The mission is still alive ... I want you to help me – help us – achieve it.'

Milpitas closed his eyes again; suddenly he felt immensely old, as if the energy which had sustained him for the best part of a thousand years were suddenly drained away.

'I don't know if I can,' he said honestly.

Someone, in the depths of the Temple, stilled the klaxon at last; the final, chilling echoes of its wail rattled from the close, claustrophobic metal sky.

20

The pod slid, smooth and silent, down towards Titan.

Louise clutched at her seat. The hull was quite transparent, so that it felt as if she – swathed in her environment suit, with a catheter jammed awkwardly inside her – were suspended helplessly above the pale brown clouds of Titan.

Above her, the Xeelee nightfighter folded its huge wings.

Titan, Saturn's largest satellite, was a world in itself: around three thousand miles across, larger than Earth's Moon. As she descended, the cloudscape took on the appearance of an infinitely flat, textured plane. Huge low pressure systems in the photochemical smog spiralled around the world, and small, high clouds scudded across the stratosphere.

The first thin tendrils of air curled around the walls of the pod. Overhead, the stars were already misting out.

Suddenly the pod dropped, precipitously. She was jarred down into her seat. Then the little craft was yanked sideways, rocking alarmingly.

'Lethe,' Louise said ruefully, rubbing her spine.

Louise had left Spinner in the lounge, to follow the pod's progress on the data desk. 'Are you all right?' Spinner asked now.

'I've been better . . . I'm not hurt, Spinner-of-Rope.'

'You knew you had to expect this kind of treatment. Titan's atmosphere is a hundred miles thick: plenty of scope for generating a lot of weather. And there are high winds, up there at the top of the atmosphere.'

It was quite dark in the cabin now; the opaque atmosphere had enfolded the pod completely, leaving only the cabin lights to gleam from the transparent walls.

Spinner went on, 'And did you know Titan has seasons? It's spring; you've got to *expect* a lot of turbulence.'

As the pod dropped further it shuddered against a new

onslaught; this time Louise thought she actually heard its structure creak.

'Spring,' murmured Louise. '"Where are the songs of Spring? Ay, where are they?"'

'Louise?'

'John Keats, Spinner-of-Rope. Never mind.'

Now the buffeting of the little ship seemed to lessen; she must have passed through the high-wind stratosphere. She pulled out a little slack in the restraints which bound her to the seat. Beyond the hull, the cabin lights illuminated flakes of ammonia ice, and fine swirls of murky gas shot up past the pod and out of sight.

'It's bloody dark,' she muttered.

'Louise, you're dropping into a mush of methane, ethane and argon. It's a smog of photochemical compounds, produced by the action of the Sun's magnetosphere on the air – I can see a lot of hydrogen cyanide, and –'

'I know all that,' Louise growled, gripping her seat as the pod lurched again. 'Don't read out the whole damn data desk to me. Photochemical compounds aren't what I came down here to find.'

'What, then?'

'. . . *People*, Spinner.'

Once, this had been the most populous world outside the orbit of Jupiter: Titan had cradled mankind's most remote cities. Surely – Louise had thought – if anywhere had survived the devastation that had struck the inner worlds it would be here.

She needed to *see* what was going on. Louise punched at the control pad before her. The walls of the pod faded to pearly opacity. She called for a Virtual image, an amalgam constructed of radar and other data.

Below her, in the pod's Virtual windows, the landscape of Titan assembled itself, as if from elements of a dream.

She banked the pod and took it skimming over the crude Virtual representation, fifty miles above the surface.

Titan had a core of rock at its heart, clad by a thick mantle of frozen water-ice. Beneath the obscuring blanket of atmosphere, eighty per cent of the solid ice surface was covered by oceans of liquid methane and ethane, richly polluted by hydrocarbons.

The remaining fraction of 'dry' ice-land was too sparse to form into sizeable continents; instead, ridges of water-ice, protruding above the methane, formed strings of islands and long peninsulas.

Well, the oceans were still here. Louise let the ancient, familiar names roll through her head: there was the Kuiper Sea, Galilei Archipelago, the Ocean of Huygens, James Maxwell Bay . . .

But, of the humans who had once named this topography, there was no sign. In fact, it was as if they had never been.

Once, huge factory ships had sailed across these complex oceans, trailing high, oily wakes; enough food had been manufactured in those giant ships to feed all of Titan, and most of the other colony-moons in the Saturn system as well. There were no ships here now. Maybe, if she looked hard enough, she would find traces of huge metal carcasses, entombed in the ice floors of the chemical seas.

. . . But now there seemed to be something approaching over the tight-curving horizon: a feature which didn't chime with her memory. She leaned forward in her seat, trying to see ahead more clearly.

It was a ridge of ice, looming over the oceans, stretching from side to side of her field of view as it came over the edge of the world.

'Spinner – *look*.'

'I can't quite make it out – it doesn't seem to fit the maps . . .'

'Maps?' Louise muttered. 'We may as well throw the damn things out.'

It was the rim of a crater – a crater so huge it sprawled like an immense scar around the curve of the planet. Within the mile-high walls of the crater, a new sea, deep and placid, lapped its huge low-gravity waves.

'Well, that wasn't here before,' Spinner said. 'It's wiped out half the surface of the moon.'

Louise had Spinner download projections of the crater's overall shape, the deep profile hidden from view by the circular methane ocean it embraced.

Beneath the ocean surface the crater was almost cylindrical, with sharp, vertical walls and a flat base.

'Volcanic, do you think?' Spinner asked.

'It doesn't look like any volcano mouth I've ever seen,' Louise said slowly. 'Anyway, Titan is inert.'

'Then what? Could it be an impact crater? Maybe when the moons got broken up –'

'Look at it, Spinner,' Louise said impatiently. 'The shape's all wrong; this was no impact.'

'Then what?'

Louise sighed. 'What do you think? We've come all this way to find another relic of war, Spinner-of-Rope. Now we know what happened to the people. When whatever caused *that* struck Titan, the whole surface of the moon must have convulsed. No wonder the cities were lost ...'

She imagined the ice-ground cracking, becoming briefly liquid once more, swallowing communities whole; there must have been mile-high tidal waves in the low gravity methane seas, overwhelming the food ships in moments.

Spinner was silent for a while. Then, 'You're saying this was done deliberately?'

Louise smiled. Superet, reconstructing the future from the glimpses left by Michael Poole's encounter with the Qax, had come across the concept of a *starbreaker*: a planet-smashing weapon wielded by the Xeelee – a weapon based on focused gravity waves. Superet had even had evidence that a starbreaker of limited power had been deployed inside the Solar System itself: by the Qax invaders from the future, during their failed onslaught on the craft of the Friends of Wigner.

She said to Spinner, 'You ought to be getting used to this by now. We know the Xeelee had weaponry sufficient to destroy worlds. For some reason they spared Titan. Instead – *they wiped it clean*. Just as they did Callisto.'

Louise took the pod down to one of the largest individual islands, close to the rough rim of the Kuiper Sea. There was a soft crunch when she landed, as the pod crushed the friable-ice surface.

A small airlock blistered out of the side of the pod's hull, and Louise climbed through it.

Instantly she was enclosed by a shell of darkness. In the murk of photochemical smog, her suit lights penetrated barely a few feet. Looking down she could only just make out the surface.

Under a layer of thick frost, which creaked as it compressed under her boots, the ground was firm, flat. She lifted herself on her toes, trying her weight; she felt light, springy, under Titan's thirteen per cent gee. There was a soft wind which pushed at her chest.

Snow, drifting down from the huge atmosphere, began to lace across her faceplate; it was white and stringy, and – when she tried to wipe it off with her glove – it left clinging remnants. It was a snow of complex organic polymers, drifting down from the hundred-mile-thick chemical soup above her head.

'Louise? Can you still hear me?'

'I hear you, Spinner.'

She took a few steps forward, away from the gleaming pod; soon, its lights were almost lost in the polymer sleet.

'You know, we terraformed Titan,' Louise told Spinner. 'There were ships to extract food and air from the seas. You could walk about on the surface in nothing more than a heated suit. We got the atmosphere *clear*, Spinner-of-Rope. You could see Saturn, and the rings. And the Sun. You knew you weren't alone down here – that you were part of the System . . .'

Now, the terraforming had collapsed. Titan had reverted. It was as if humans had never walked Titan's surface.

'There used to be a city here, Spinner. *Port Cassini*. Huge, glittering caverns in the ice; igloos on the surface . . . A hundred thousand people, at least.

'Mark was born here. Did you know that?' She looked around, dimly. 'And as far as I can remember this was the site of his parents' home . . .'

She tried to imagine how it must have been to stand here as the final defence around Titan fell, and the Xeelee onslaught began. *The starbreaker beams – cherry-red, geometrical abstractions – burned down, through the hydrocarbon smog, from the invisible nightfighters far above the surface. Methane seas flash-evaporated in moments – and the ancient water-ice of the mantle flowed liquid for the first time in billions of years . . .*

'Louise? Are you ready to go home, now?'

'Home?' Louise raised her face to the hidden sky and allowed the primeval, polymeric snow to build up over her faceplate; for a moment, tears, ancient and salty, blinded her. 'Yes. Let's go home, Spinner-of-Rope.'

271

'Helium flash,' Mark said.

Uvarov had been dozing; his dreams, as usual, were filled with birds: ugly carrion-eaters, with immense black wings, diving into a yellow Sun. When Mark spoke the dreams imploded, leaving him blind and trapped in his chair once more. He felt a thin, cold sensation in his right arm: another input of concentrated foodstuffs, provided by his chair.

Yum, he thought. *Breakfast.*

'Mark,' he whispered.

'Are you all right?'

'All the better for your cheery questioning, you – *construct.*' He spoke with a huge effort, fighting off his all-encompassing tiredness. 'If you're so concerned about my health, plug yourself into my chair's diagnostics and find out for yourself. *Now.* Tell me again what you said. And what in Lethe it means . . .'

'Helium flash,' Mark repeated.

Uvarov felt old and stupid; he tried to assemble his scattered thoughts.

'We've heard from Lieserl. Uvarov, the birds are continuing to accelerate the evolution of the Sun.' Mark hesitated; his intonation had gone flat, a sign to Uvarov of his distraction. 'I've put together Lieserl's observations with a little extrapolation of my own. I think we can tell what's going to come next . . . Uvarov, I wish I could show you. In pictures – a Virtual simulation – it would be easy.'

'Well, you can't,' Uvarov said sourly, twisting his face from side to side. 'Sorry to be so *inconvenient.* You're just going to have to hook up a few more processor banks to enhance your imagination and tell me, aren't you?'

'. . . Uvarov, the Sun is *dying.*'

For millions of years, the photino birds had fed off the Sun's hydrogen-fusing core. Each sip of energy, by each of Lieserl's birds, had lowered the temperature of the core, minutely.

In time, after billions of interactions, the core temperature had dropped so far that hydrogen fusion was no longer possible. The core had become a ball of helium, dead, contracting. Meanwhile, a shell of fusing hydrogen burned its way out of the Sun, dropping a rain of helium ash onto the core.

'The inert core has steadily got more massive – contracting,

272

and heating up. Eventually the helium in the collapsing core became degenerate – it stopped behaving as a gas, because –'

'I know what degenerate matter is.'

'All right. But you have to be clear about why that's important, for what comes next. Uvarov, if you heat up degenerate matter, it doesn't *expand*, as a gas would ... Degenerate matter is *not* a gas; it doesn't obey anything like the gas laws.'

'So we have this degenerate, dead core of helium, the burning shell around it. What next?'

'Now we start speculating. Uvarov, in a conventional giant, when the core mass is high enough – about half a Solar mass – the temperature becomes so high, a hundred million degrees or more, that a *new* fusion chain reaction starts up: the triple-alpha reaction, which –'

'The fusion of the helium ash into carbon.'

'Yes. Suddenly the "dead" core is flooded with helium fusion energy. Now remember what I told you, Uvarov: the core is degenerate. So it doesn't expand, to compensate for all that heat ...'

'You turn condescension into an art form,' Uvarov growled impatiently.

'*Because* it can't expand, the core can't cool off. There is a runaway fusion reaction – a *helium flash* – lasting no more than seconds. After that, the core starts to expand again, and eventually a new equilibrium is reached –'

'All right. That's the standard story; now let's get back to the Sun. Sol isn't a conventional giant, whatever it is.'

'No. But it's approaching its helium flash point.'

'Won't the action of the birds suppress this helium runaway – the helium flash – just as they've suppressed hydrogen fusion, all this time?'

'No, Uvarov. They're not taking out enough energy to stop the flash ... Maybe they don't intend to. And, of course, the fact that the core of Sol is so unusually hydrogen-rich is going to make a difference to the outcome. Perhaps there will be some hydrogen fusion in there as well, a complex multiple reaction.'

'Mark. You said a new *equilibrium* will be reached, after the helium flash.' Uvarov didn't like the sound of that. He wondered if it would be healthy to be around, while an artificially induced red giant struggled to find a new stability after the explosion of its core ... 'What will happen, after the helium flash?'

'Well, the pulse of heat energy released by the flash will take time – some centuries – to work its way through the envelope. The envelope will expand further, seeking a new balance between gravity and radiation pressure. And the energy released in the flash will be immense, Uvarov.'

'Immense?'

'Uvarov, there will be a superwind.'

Superwind ...

The helium flash would blow away half the mass of the Sun, into an expanding shell ballooning outwards at hundreds of miles a second.

The core – exposed, a shrunken thing of carbon-choked helium – would become a *white dwarf star*: cooling rapidly, with half the mass of Sol but just a few thousand miles across, no larger than old Earth. The flocks of photino birds, insubstantial star-killers, would continue to swoop around the heart of Sol's diminished gravity well.

At present – before the flash – Sol was a red giant around two astronomical units across. After the superwind the envelope would be blown into a globe *twenty thousand times* that size, a billowing, cooling cloud three hundred light-days across.

The furthest planet from the heart of old Sol was only forty astronomical units out – six light-hours. So the swelling envelope would, at last, smother all of Sol's children.

Then, when the superwind was done, the dwarf remnant would emit a new wind of its own: a fizz of hot, fast particles which would blow at the expanding globe, pushing out the inner layers. The globe would become a *planetary nebula* – a huge, cooling, hollow shell of gas, fluorescing in the light of the dying dwarf at its heart.

Mark said, 'At last, of course, the fusing helium in the core will be exhausted. Then the core will shrink once more, until the temperature of the regions around the core becomes high enough for helium fusion to start – in a shell *outside* the core, but *within* the hydrogen-burning shell. And the helium fusion will deposit carbon ash onto the core, growing in mass and heating it up – until the fusion of carbon begins ...

'The cycle repeats, Uvarov. There will be carbon flashes – and, later, flashes of oxygen and silicon ... At last, the giant might have a core of almost pure iron, with an onion-shell structure of fusing silicon, oxygen, carbon, helium and hydrogen around it. But iron is a dead end; it can only fuse by *absorbing* energy, not liberating it.'

'And all this will happen to the Sun?'

Mark hesitated. 'Our standard models say that the reactions go all the way to iron only in stars a lot more massive than the Sun – say, twelve Solar masses or more.' He sighed, theatrically. 'Will we get onion-shell fusion in the heart of the Sun? I don't know, Uvarov. We may as well throw out our theoretical models, I guess. If the photino birds are as widespread as they seem to be, there may not be a single star in the Universe which has followed through a "standard" lifecycle.'

'*Superwind*,' Uvarov breathed. 'How soon is Sol's helium flash?'

'Lieserl's observations are sketchy on this. But, Uvarov, the conditions are *right*. The flash may even have happened by now. The superwind could already be working its way out ...'

'How soon, damn you?'

'We have a few centuries. No more.'

Uvarov swept his blind face around the saloon. He pictured the ruined Jovian system beyond these walls, the bloated star dominating the sky outside.

'Then *we can't stay here*,' he said.

21

By the time she'd climbed to the top of the giant kapok tree her hand-grips were slick with sweat, and her lungs were pumping rapidly. Spinner-of-Rope took off her spectacles and wiped the lenses on a corner of her loincloth. Zero-gee or not, it still took an effort to haul her bulk around this forest ... an effort that seemed to be increasing with age, despite all the AS treatment in the world.

She was at the crown of the kapok. The great tree was a dense, tangled mass of branches beneath her. Seeds drifted everywhere, filling the rippling canopy with points of light – like roaming stars, she thought. Somewhere a group of howler-monkeys shrieked out their presence. Their eerie ululations, rising and falling, reminded her of the klaxon which had once called the Undermen to their dreary work ...

She put that thought out of her mind with determination. She pulled some dried meat from her belt and chewed on it, relishing the familiar, salty taste. She felt *tired*, damn it; she'd come here, alone, because she wanted – just for a few hours – to put all of the strangeness below the forest Deck, and beyond the skydome, out of her mind, to immerse herself once more in the simple world in which she'd grown up.

In the distance a bird flapped, shrieking, its colours gaudy against the bland afternoon blue of the skydome.

The bird was flying upside down.

'Spinner-of-Rope.'

The voice was close to her ear. Still chewing her meat, Spinner turned, slowly.

Louise Ye Armonk hovered a few feet away, standing on the squat, neat platform of a zero-gee scooter. Louise grinned. 'Did I make you jump? I'm sorry for cheating with this scooter; I'm not sure I would have managed the climb.'

Spinner-of-Rope glared at her. 'Louise. Never – *never* – sneak up on someone at the top of a tree.'

Louise didn't look too concerned. 'Why not? Because you might lose your grip, and drift off the branch a couple of feet? What a disaster.'

Spinner tried to maintain her anger, but she started to feel foolish. 'Come on, Louise. I'm trying to make a point.'

Louise, skilfully, brought her scooter in closer to Spinner; without much grace she clambered off the scooter and onto the branch beside Spinner. 'Actually,' she said gently, 'so am I.' She breathed deeply of the moist forest air, and looked around the sky. 'I saw you watching that bird.'

Spinner pushed her spectacles up the bridge of her nose. 'So what?'

Louise picked at the tree bark. 'Well, the bird seems to be doing its best to get by, in zero-gee.'

'Maybe. Not everyone here is doing so well,' Spinner said heavily. The loss of gravity was, slowly but surely, devastating the forest biota. 'The higher birds and animals seem to be adapting okay ... The monkeys quickly learned to adjust the way they climb and jump. But otherwise, things are falling apart, in a hundred tiny ways.' She thought of spiders which could no longer spin webs, of tree-dwelling frogs which found their tiny leaf-bound ponds floating away into the air. 'We're doing our best to keep things working – to save whatever we can,' she said. 'But, damn it, even the rain doesn't fall right any more.'

Louise reached out and took her hand; the old engineer's skin was cold, leathery. 'Spinner, we have to re-establish all of this. Permanently.' Louise lifted her face; the diffuse light of the dome softened the etched-in age lines. 'I *designed* this forest Deck, remember. And this is the only fragment of Earth that's survived, anywhere in the Universe – as far as we know.'

Spinner-of-Rope pulled her hand away. 'I know what your little parable about the bird was about, Louise. I should adapt, just like the plucky little bird. Right? You want me to come back to the nightfighter.'

Louise nodded, studying her.

'Well, it was a dumb parable. The bird is the *exception*, not the rule. And –'

'Spinner, I know you needed a break. But you've been climbing around these trees for a long time, now. I need you to come back – we all do. I know it's difficult for you, but you're the only person I have who can do the job.'

Spinner watched her face, sceptically. 'But we're not talking about mere discontinuity-drive jaunts around the Solar System now. Are we, Louise?'

'No.' Louise wouldn't meet her eyes.

Spinner felt a hollowness in her chest – as if it had expanded, leaving her heart fluttering like a bird in some huge cavity. *Hyperdrive* ...

'Spinner, we need the hyperdrive. You understand that, don't you? *The Sun is dying*. Perhaps we could attempt to establish some sort of colony here, in the Solar System. But we need to find out what's happening beyond the System. Are there any people left, anywhere? Maybe we can join them – find a better place than the Solar System has become.

'But, without the hyperdrive, journeys like that would take millennia, more – even with the discontinuity drive. And I don't think we *have* millennia ...'

Spinner took a deep breath. 'Yes, but ... Louise, what will happen when I throw the switch? How will it feel?'

Louise hesitated. 'Spinner, *I don't know*. That's the truth; that's what we want to find out from the first flight. We aren't going to know for sure until we try it in anger. Mark and I have only just begun to put together theories on how the damn hyperdrive works ... Spinner, all we know is it's something to do with *dimensionality*.'

A conventional craft (Louise said) worked in a 'three-plus-one' dimensional spacetime – three spatial dimensions, plus one of time. And within those dimensions nature was described by a series of fundamental constants – the charge on the electron, the speed of light, the gravitational constant, Planck's constant, and others.

But – humans believed – physics was governed by the *Spin(10)* theory, which described symmetries among the forces of nature. And the symmetries needed to be expressed in *higher* dimensions than four.

'So, Spinner-of-Rope, there are more than three spatial

dimensions,' Louise said. 'But the "extra dimensions" are compactified –'

'They're what?'

'Collapsed down to the smallest possible scale – to the Planck scale, below which quantum physics and gravitation merge.'

Once – just after the initial singularity – the forces of physics were one, and the Universe was fully multi-dimensional. Then the great expansion started.

'Three of the spatial dimensions expanded, rapidly, to the scales we see today. The other dimensions remained compactified.'

'Why did *three* dimensions expand? Why not four, or two, or one – or none at all?'

Louise laughed. 'That's a good question, Spinner. I wish I had a good answer.

'Geometrically, three-dimensional spaces have some unique attributes. For instance, only in three dimensions is it possible for planets to have stable orbits governed by the central forces exerted by stars. Did you know that? Planets in a *four*-dimensional cosmos would drift into space, or spiral into their suns. So if life needs billions of years of a stable planetary environment, three dimensions are the only possibility. Matter isn't *stable* in higher dimensions, even: the Schrodinger wave equation would have no bound solutions ... And waves can propagate without distortion, only in three dimensions. So if we need high-fidelity acoustic or electromagnetic signals to be able to make sense of the world, then again, three dimensions is the only possibility.

'Spinner, maybe there are alternate universes, out there somewhere, where more than three dimensions ballooned up after the initial singularity. But as far as we can see, life – our kind of life – couldn't have evolved there; the fundamental geometry of spacetime wouldn't have allowed it ...

'Remember, though, the extra dimensions are here, still, but they're rolled up very tightly, into high-curvature tubes a Planck length across.'

'So we can't see them.'

'No. But – and here's the trick we think the Xeelee have exploited, Spinner – the extra dimensions *do* have an impact on our Universe. The curvature of these Planck tubes *determines the value of the fundamental constants of physics.* So the *way* the tubes are folded up determines things like the charge of an electron, or the strength of gravity.'

Spinner nodded slowly. 'All right. But what has this to do with the hyperdrive?'

'Spinner-of-Rope, we think the Xeelee found a way to *adjust* some of those universal numbers. By changing the constants of physics – in a small region of space around itself – the hyperdrive can make spacetime unfurl, just a little.' Louise lifted her face. 'Then the nightfighter can move, a short distance, through one of the higher dimensions.

'Think of a sheet of paper, Spinner. If you're confined to two dimensions – to crawling *over* the paper – then it will take you a long time to get from one side to the other. But *if* you could move through the third dimension – *through* the paper – *then* you could move with huge apparent speed from one place to another ...'

Spinner frowned. 'I think I see that. Is this something like wormhole travel?'

Louise hesitated. 'Not really. Wormholes are defects in our three-plus-one-dimensional spacetime, Spinner; they don't involve the higher collapsed dimensions. And wormholes are fixed. With a wormhole you can travel only from one place to another, unless you drag the termini around with you. With the Xeelee drive – we think – you can travel *anywhere*, almost at will. It's like the difference between a fixed rail route and a flitter.'

Spinner thought it over. 'It sounds simple.'

Louise laughed. 'Believe me, it's not.' She turned, distracted. 'Hey. Look,' she said, pointing to the skydome.

Spinner looked up, squinting through her spectacles against the glare of the dome. 'What?'

Louise leaned closer so that Spinner could sight along her outstretched arm. 'See? Those shadows against the dome, over there ...'

The shadows, ten or a dozen forms, clambered across a small corner of the skydome, busy, active.

Spinner smiled. 'Howler-monkeys. They've colonized the skydome. I wonder how they got up there.'

'The point is,' Louise said gently, 'they've adapted, too. Just like that parrot.'

'Another *parable*, Louise?'

Louise shrugged, looking smug.

Spinner felt, she decided, like one of Morrow's Undermen. She was no longer free; she was bowed down by the need to serve Louise's vast, amorphous project.

'All right, Louise, you've made your point. Let's go back to the nightfighter.'

For the first time, Lieserl *understood* the photino birds.

She thought of novae, and supernovae.

As the newly shining stars had settled into their multi-billion-year Main Sequence lifetimes, the Universe must have seemed a *fine* place to the photino birds. The stars had appeared stable: eternal, neat little nests of compact gravity wells and fusion energy.

Then had come the first *instabilities*.

Red giant expansions and novae must have been bad enough. But even a nova was a limited explosion, which could leave a star still intact: survivable, by the infesting birds. A supernova explosion, however, could *destroy* a star in seconds, leaving behind nothing more than a shrivelled, fast-spinning neutron star.

Lieserl tried to see these events from the point of view of the photino birds. The instabilities, the great explosions, must have devastated whole core-flocks. Perhaps, she speculated now, the birds had even evolved a civilization in the past; she imagined huge, spinning cities of dark matter at the heart of stars – cities ripped apart by the first star-deaths.

If she were a photino bird, she wouldn't *tolerate* this.

The birds didn't *need* spectacular, blazing stars. They certainly didn't need instability, novae and supernovae, the disruption of dying stars. All they demanded from a star was a stable gravity well, and a trickle-source of proton-photino interaction energy.

She thought of Sol.

When the birds were finished with the Sun – after the superwind had blown through the wrecked System – a white dwarf would remain: a small, cooling lump of degenerate matter smaller than the Earth. The Sun's story would be over. It could expect no change, except a slow decline; there would certainly be no cataclysmic events in Sol's future . . .

But the dwarf would retain over half the Sun's original mass. And there would be plenty of dense matter to interact with, and energy from the slow contraction of the star.

The Sun would have become an ideal habitat for photino birds.

Lieserl saw it all now, with terrifying clarity.

The photino birds were not prepared to accept a Universe full of young, hot, dangerous stars, likely to explode at any moment. So they had decided to get it over with – to manage the ageing of the stars as rapidly as possible.

And when the birds' great task was done, the Universe would be filled with dull, unchanging white dwarfs. The only motion would come from the shadowy streams of photino birds sailing between their neutered star-nests.

It was a majestic vision: an engineering project on the grandest possible of scales – a project which could never be equalled.

But it was making the Universe – *the whole of the Universe* – into a place inimical to humans.

She studied the swelling core of the Sun. Its temperature climbed higher almost daily; the helium flash was close – or might, indeed, already have occurred.

The humans seemed to have assimilated the data she had sent them. A reply came to her, via her tenuous maser-light pathways.

She translated it slowly. A smiling face, crudely encoded in a binary chain of Doppler-distorted maser bursts. Words of thanks for her data. And – an invitation.

Join us, the human said.

Once again, Spinner-of-Rope sat in the cage of the Xeelee nightfighter. Arcs of construction material wrapped around her; beyond them the bloated bulk of the Sun loomed, immense and pale, like some vast ghost.

She tried to settle into her couch. Between each discontinuity-drive jaunt she'd had Mark adjust the couch's contours, but still it didn't seem to fit her correctly. Maybe it was because of the biostat sensors with which she continued to be encrusted, for each flight . . .

Or maybe, she thought dispiritedly, it was just that she was so *tired* of this bombardment of strangeness.

She fingered her chest, against which – under her suit – lay her father's arrow-head. Before her was the black horseshoe of the Xeelee control console, with its three grafted-on waldoes. She stared at the waldo straight ahead of her – the one which controlled the hyperdrive. Superficially the waldo was just another box of metal and plastic, its telltale lights glowing warmly; but now it seemed to loom large in her vision, larger even than the corpse of the Sun ...

'Spinner. Can you hear me?'

'Yes, Louise. I'm here.'

'Are you all right? You're in your couch?'

Spinner allowed herself a sigh of exasperation. 'Yes, I'm in my couch, just where you saw me not five minutes ago.'

Louise laughed. 'All right, Spinner, I'm sorry. I'm in the life-lounge. Look – whatever risks you take in this, I'll be right here sharing them ...'

Now Spinner laughed. 'Thanks, Louise; that's making me feel a lot better.'

Louise was silent for a moment, and Spinner imagined her lopsided, rather tired grin. 'I never was much of a motivator. It's amazing I ever got as far as I did in life ... Are you ready to start?'

Spinner took a deep breath; her throat was tight, and she felt light, remote – as if this were all some Virtual show, not connected to anything real.

'I'm ready,' she said.

There was silence; Louise Ye Armonk seemed to be holding her breath.

'Spinner-of-Rope, if you need more time –'

'I said, I'm ready.' Spinner opened her eyes, settled into her crash couch, and flexed her gloved fingers. Before her, the touchpads on the hyperdrive waldo glowed.

'Tell me what to do, Louise.'

The Sun was a brooding mass to her right hand side, flooding the cage with dull red light.

There were three touchpads in a row, all shining yellow.

Without thinking about it, Spinner stabbed her forefinger at the middle touchpad.

The ambient light – *changed*.

She was aware that she had stopped breathing; even her pulse, loud in her ears inside this helmet, seemed to have slowed to a crawl.

She was staring at her gloved hand, the outstretched forefinger still touching the surface of the waldo; beyond that, in her peripheral vision, she could see the ribs of the construction-material cage. It was all just as it had been, a heartbeat before.

... Except that the shadows which her hand cast across the waldo box had altered, subtly.

Before, the diffuse globe of the Sun had flooded her field of view with a crimson, bloody glow, and her cage was filled with streaky, soft-edged shadows. But now the shadows had moved around, almost through a hundred and eighty degrees. As if the Sun – or whatever light source was acting now – had moved around to her left.

She lifted her hand and turned it over before her face, studying the way the light fell across her fingers, the creases in the glove material. The *quality* of the light itself had changed, too; now it seemed more diffuse – the shadows still softer, the light pinker, brighter.

She dropped her hand to her chest. Through layers of suit material she could feel the hard edges of her father's arrow blade, pressing against her chest. She pushed the point of the head into her body, feeling her skin break; the tiny pinpoint of pain was like a single, stationary point of reality amid this Universe of wheeling light.

She turned her head, slowly.

The Sun had gone. Where its immense bulk had coated the sky with crimson smoke, there was only emptiness – blackness, a smearing of wizened stars.

And to her left there had appeared a wall of pinkish gas, riven by lanes of dark, its edges diffusing into blackness. It was a cloud full of stars; it must be light-years across.

She must have travelled hundreds – perhaps even *thousands* of light-years. And she'd felt *nothing*. A mere touch of a button ...

She folded forward, dropping her head into her lap. She

clutched the arrow-head to her chest, stabbing at her skin, over and over; she spread one hand against her faceplate and scrabbled at it, seeking her face. She felt her bladder loosen; warm liquid gushed through her catheter.

'Spinner-of-Rope. *Spinner ...*'

Hands on her shoulders, shaking her; a distant voice. Her thumb was crammed into her mouth. The pain in her chest had become a dull ache.

Someone pulled her hand away from her mouth, gently.

Before her there was a square, weary face, concern showing through an uneven smile, a crop of grey, stiff hair.

'Louise ... ?'

Louise's smile broadened. 'So you're with us again. Thank Life for that; welcome back.'

Spinner looked around. She was still in her cage; the waldoes still sat on their jet-black horseshoe of construction material before her, their touchpad lights burning. But a dome of some milky, opaque material had been cast around the cage, shutting out the impossible sights outside.

Louise regarded her gravely. She hovered beyond the cage, attached by a short length of safety rope; reaching through the cage bars she held out a moistened cloth. 'Here. You'd better clean yourself up.'

Spinner glanced down at herself. Her helmet lay in her lap. Her hands were moist with spittle – and she'd *dribbled* down her chin – and where Louise had opened Spinner's suit at the chest, there was a mass of small, bleeding punctures.

'What a mess,' Spinner said. She dabbed at her chest.

Louise shrugged. 'It's no great trouble, Spinner. Although I had to move fast; I needed to get the air-dome up around you before you managed to open your faceplate.'

Spinner picked up her helmet; reaching through the faceplate, she found an apple-juice nipple. 'Louise, what happened to me?'

Louise grinned and reached through the construction-material bars; with her old, leathery hand she touched Spinner's cheek. 'The hyperdrive happened to you. You've nothing to be ashamed of, Spinner. I knew this wouldn't be easy, but I had no idea how traumatic it would be.'

Spinner frowned. 'There was no sensation of movement *at all*. It seemed like magic, impossible. Even with the discontinuity drive there are visual effects; you can see the planets looming up at you, and the blue shift, and –'

Louise sighed and rubbed her face. 'I know. Sometimes, I think I forget that this is a Xeelee ship. It's just not designed for human comfort ... I guess we can conclude that the Xeelee are a little tougher, psychologically, than we are.'

'But did it *work*, Louise?'

'Yes. Yes, it worked, Spinner. We crossed over *two thousand light-years* – in a time so brief I couldn't even measure it ...'

Louise took her hand from Spinner's cheek and rested it on her shoulder. 'Spinner, I can de-opaque this dome. If you feel you want me to.'

Spinner didn't want to think about it. 'Do it, Louise.'

Louise picked up her helmet and whispered instructions into its throat mike.

The Trifid Nebula, from Earth, had once been a faint glow in the constellation of Sagittarius – as broad as the full Moon in the sky, but far dimmer; at over two thousand light-years from Earth, powerful telescopes had been needed to reveal its glorious colours. Light took fully thirty years to cross its extent.

Louise and Mark had chosen the Trifid as the first hyperdrive target. Even if the nightfighter's trajectory was off by hundreds of light-years, the Nebula should surely be an unmistakable landmark.

But the waldo had worked. Louise's programming had brought the nightfighter to within sixty light-years of the rim of the Nebula.

The Nebula was a wall, sprawled across half of Spinner's sky. It was a soft-edged study in pinks and reds. Dark lanes cut across the face of the Nebula in a rough Y-shape, dividing the cloud into three parts. The material seemed quite smooth, Spinner thought, like some immense watercolour painting. Stars shone through the pale outer edges of the Nebula – and shone, too, from within its bulk.

'This is an emission nebula, Spinner,' Louise said abstractedly. 'There are stars within the gas; ultraviolet starlight ionizes hydrogen in the Nebula, making the gas shine in turn ...' She

286

pointed. 'Those dark rifts are empty of stars; they're dozens of light-years long. The Nebula is called the Trifid because of the way the lanes divide the face into three … see? And – can you see those smaller, compact dark spots? They're called Bok globules … the birth places of new stars, forming inside the Nebula.'

Spinner-of-Rope turned to Louise; the engineer sounded flat, distant.

'Louise? What's wrong?'

Louise glanced at her. 'I'm sorry, Spinner. I should be celebrating, I guess. After all, the hyperdrive delivered us just where I expected to be. And I was only using the Trifid as a landmark, anyway. But – damn it, the Trifid used to be so much *more*, Spinner. The colours, all the way through the spectrum from blue, and green, all the way to red … There were hot, bright young stars in there which made it *blaze*.

'But now, those stars are gone. Snuffed out, or exploded, or rushed through their lifecycles; like every other star in the damn Galaxy.

'I just find it hard to accept all this. I try, but every so often something like this comes along, and hits me in the eye.'

Spinner turned to the Nebula again, trying to lose herself in its light.

Louise smiled, her face outlined by the Nebula's soft light. 'And what about you? … Why, Spinner, you're *crying*.'

Surprised, Spinner raised the heel of her wrist to her cheeks. There was moisture there. She brushed it away, embarrassed. 'I'm fine,' she said. 'It's just –'

'Yes?'

'It's so *beautiful*.' Spinner stared at the eagle wings of the Nebula, drinking in its pale colours. 'Louise, I'm so lucky to be here, to *see* this. Uvarov might have sent someone else through the Locks, that first time; not me and Arrow Maker. You might have asked someone else to learn to run your nightfighter for you – and not me.

'Louise, I might have *missed* this. I might have died without seeing it – without ever even knowing it existed.' She looked at Louise uncertainly. 'Do you understand?'

Louise smiled. 'No.' She reached into the cage and patted Spinner's arm. 'But once I would have felt the same way. Come

287

on, Spinner. We've done what we came to do. Let's go home.'

Spinner-of-Rope picked up her helmet. As she fastened up her suit, she kept her eyes fixed on the impossible beauty of the Trifid.

22

Lieserl walked into the dining saloon of the *Great Britain*.

She hesitated, uncertain, in the low doorway. She was stunned by the antique beauty of the place: by its fine pillars and plasterwork, the mirrors glimmering on the walls. She was the last to arrive for this strange dinner; there were six people – three men and three women – already seated, facing each other at the centre of one of the long tables. The only light came from candles (real candles, or Virtuals?) set on the table between them. As the people talked, their faces, and the fine cutlery and glass, shone in the flickering, golden light; shadows stretched across the rest of the old saloon, turning it into a place of mystery – even romance.

One of the men turned as she came in. He rose, pushing back his chair, and walked towards her, smiling. His blue eyes were bright in a dark face.

She felt an odd, absurd, flutter of nervousness in her throat; she raised her hand to her mouth, and felt the coarseness of her flesh, the lines etched deep there. This was her first genuine human interaction in five million years ... But how ludicrous to suffer adolescent nerves like this! She was an AI, *geologically* old, yet within mere subjective days of returning to the company of humans she had become immersed once more in the complex, impossibly difficult world of human interactions.

She felt a sudden, intense, nostalgic desire to return to the clean, bright interior of the Sun. All those millennia, orbiting the core with the photino birds, seemed like a long, fantastic dream to her now: an interval within this, the true human reality ...

The man reached out and *touched* her arm. His flesh was firm, warm.

She cried out and stumbled backwards.

Five faces, bright with candlelight, turned towards her, and the conversation died.

No one had *touched* Lieserl in megayears.

The man leaned towards her, his blue eyes bright and mischievous. 'I'm sorry,' he said. 'I couldn't resist that. I'm Mark Bassett Friar Armonk Wu.'

She straightened herself up, primly, and glared at him. The sudden touch had left a trembling, deep in her stomach, and she was sure a flush was spreading over her cheeks, despite her age of physical-sixty. She was vividly aware – *too* aware, distractingly so – of Mark's presence beside her.

He took her arm again, more delicately, and escorted her towards the dinner party. 'I won't startle you again, I promise. And I'm the only Virtual here – other than you, of course.'

'These Virtual illusions are just too damn good sometimes,' she said. Her voice sounded feathery – weak, she thought. It was going to take her a long time to forgive Mark Wu for that trick.

He led her to a seat and pulled it out for her – *so that was Virtual, too* – and she sat with the rest.

The woman opposite her leaned forward and smiled. Lieserl saw a square, strong face, tired eyes, a thatch of grizzled hair. 'I'm Louise Ye Armonk,' she said. 'You're welcome here, Lieserl.'

'Ah,' Lieserl said. 'Louise. The leader.'

One of the men – grotesquely blind, bald, wrapped in a blanket – allowed his head to rock back on its spindle of a neck, and bellowed laughter.

Louise looked weary. 'Lieserl, meet Garry Uvarov ... You've spoken with him before.'

Louise introduced the rest: Morrow, a spindly, reticent man who, with Uvarov, had supervised her downloading through the maser link from the Interface carcass (now abandoned) inside the Sun; and two tiny, young-looking women with strange names – Spinner-of-Rope, Trapper-of-Frogs – their bare flesh startlingly out of place in the formal surroundings of the saloon. Their faces were painted with vivid, intimidating splashes of scarlet, and patches of their scalps were shaven bare. The older-looking one of the pair wore glinting spectacles and carried a crude arrow-head on a thong tied around her neck.

Lieserl was still new enough to all this to be intensely aware of her own appearance. Her hands cast soft shadows, and her brooch – of intertwined snakes and ladders – glittered in the candlelight. Looking out from the twin caverns of her eyes, she saw how the flickering of the light was reflected, with remarkable accuracy, on the blurred outlines of her own face; she knew she must look quite authentic to the others.

She smiled at Louise Ye Armonk. 'You've invested a great deal of processing power in me.'

Louise looked a little defensive; she pulled back slightly from the table. 'We can afford it. The *Northern*'s on idle. We've plenty of spare capacity.'

'I wasn't criticizing. I was *thanking* you. I can see you're trying to make me welcome.'

Mark, sitting beside Lieserl, leaned towards her. 'Don't mind Louise. She's always been as prickly as a porcupine . . .'

Spinner-of-Rope, the girl with the spectacles, said: 'A *what*?'

'. . . and that's why I divorced her.'

'*I* divorced *him*,' Louise Ye Armonk said. 'And still couldn't get rid of him.'

'Anyway,' Mark said to Lieserl, 'maybe you should reserve your thanks until you've seen the food.'

The meal was served by autonomic 'bots. A 'bot – presumably a Virtual – served Mark and Lieserl.

The meal was what Louise Ye Armonk called 'traditional British' – just what somebody called 'Brunel' would once have enjoyed, on an occasion like this, she said. Lieserl stared at the plates of simulated animal flesh doubtfully. Still, she enjoyed the wine, and the sensation of fresh fruit; with discreet subvocal commands she allowed herself to become mildly drunk.

The conversation flowed well enough, but seemed a little stilted, stale to Lieserl.

During the meal, Trapper-of-Frogs leaned towards her. 'Lieserl . . .'

'Yes?'

'Why are you so *old*?'

Uvarov, the crippled surgeon, threw back his head and bellowed out his ghastly laughter once more. Trapper looked confused, even distressed. Watching Uvarov, Lieserl felt herself start to incubate a deep, powerful dislike.

She smiled at Trapper, deliberately. 'It's all right, dear.' She spread her hands, flexing the thin webbing between thumb and forefinger, immersing herself in the new reality of the sensation. 'It's just that this is how I remember myself. I chose this Virtual shell because it reflects how I still feel inside, I suppose.'

'It's how you were before you were loaded into the Sun?' Spinner-of-Rope asked.

'Yes ... although by the time I reached my downloading I was quite a bit *older* than my aspect now. You see, they actually let me die of old age ... I was the first person in a long time to do so.'

She began to tell them of how that had felt – of the blights of age, of rheumy eyes and failing bladders and muscles like pieces of old cloth – but Spinner-of-Rope held her hand up. Spinner smiled, her eyes large behind her glasses. 'We *know*, Lieserl. We'll take you to the forest sometime; we'll tell you all about it.'

The meal finished with coffee and brandy, served by the discreet 'bots. Lieserl didn't much care for the brandy, but she loved the flavour of the coffee, Virtual or not.

Mark nodded at her appreciation. 'The coffee's authenticity is no accident. I spent *years* getting its flavour right. After I got stranded in this Virtual form I spent longer on replicating the sensations of coffee than anything.' His blue eyes were bright. 'Anything, except maybe those of sex ...'

Disconcerted, Lieserl dropped her eyes.

Mark's provocative remark made her think, however. *Sex.* Perhaps that was the element missing from this gathering of antique semi-immortals. Some had been preserved better than others – and some, like Spinner-of-Rope, were even genuinely (almost) young – but there was no *sexual tension* here. These people simply weren't aware of each other as human animals.

She knew of Uvarov's eugenics experiments on the forest Deck, inspired by a drive to improve the species directly. Maybe this gathering, with its mute testimony to the limitations of AS technology, was a partial justification of Uvarov's project, she thought.

Louise Ye Armonk gently rapped her empty brandy glass with a spoon; it chimed softly. 'All right, people,' she said. 'I guess it's time for us to get down to business.'

Uvarov grinned towards Lieserl, showing a mouth bereft of teeth. 'Welcome to the council of war,' he hissed.

'Well, perhaps this *is* a war,' Louise said seriously. 'But at the moment, we're just bystanders caught in the crossfire. We have to look at our options, and decide where we're going from here.

'We're in – a difficult situation.' Louise Armonk looked enormously tired, worn down by the responsibilities she had taken on, and Lieserl felt herself warm a little to this rather intimidating engineer. 'Our job was to deliver a wormhole Interface to this era, to the end of time, and then travel back through the Interface to our own era. Well, we know that didn't work out. The Interface is wrecked, the wormhole collapsed – and we've become stranded here, in this era.

'What I want to decide here is how we are going to preserve the future of our people. Everything else – *everything* – is subordinate to that. Agreed?'

For a moment there was silence around the table; Lieserl noticed how few of them were prepared to meet Louise's cold eyes.

Morrow leaned forward into the light. Lieserl saw, with gentle amusement, how his bony wrists protruded from his sleeves. 'I agree with Louise. We have one priority, and one only. And that's to protect the people on this ship: the two thousand of them, on the Decks and in the forest. *That's* what's *real*.'

Louise smiled. 'Morrow, you have the floor. *How*, exactly?'

'It's obvious,' Morrow said. 'For better or worse, we're now the custodians of a thousand-year-old culture – a culture which has evolved in the conditions which were imposed on it during the flight. The confined space, the limited resources ... and the constant, one-gee gravity.

'But now the flight is over. *And we took away the gravity*, virtually without notice. You know we managed to break up the Temple sieges, without much injury or loss of life. But, Louise, I can't tell you that life in the Decks has gone back to normal. How could it? Most people are barely retaining their *sanity*, let alone returning to work. No one's producing any food. At the moment we're working our way through stores, but that's not going to last long.'

Trapper pushed her face forward. 'And in the forest, too, the biota are –'

Louise held up her hands. 'Enough. Morrow has made the point. Give me a suggestion, please.'

Morrow and Trapper exchanged glances. 'If there was an Earth to return to,' Morrow said slowly, 'I'd say return there.'

'But there isn't,' Uvarov said acidly. His voice was a rasp, synthesized by some device in his throat. 'Or had you missed the point?'

Morrow was clearly irritated, but determined to make his case. 'I *know* there's no Earth.'

'So?' Louise asked.

'So,' Morrow said slowly, 'I suggest we stay in the ship. We overhaul it, quickly, and retrieve more reaction mass. Then we send it on a one-gee flight.'

'Where?' Mark asked.

'Anywhere. It really doesn't matter. We could loop around the Sun in some kind of powered orbit, for all I care. The point is to restart the drive: to restore acceleration-induced gravity inside the ship. Let us – let the people in there – get back to normal again, and start *living*.'

There was silence for a moment. Then Spinner-of-Rope said, 'Actually, in this scenario, it surely *would* be better to stay in the Solar System, on a powered orbit. The new chunk of reaction mass would be used up, in time; wouldn't it be better to stay close enough to the Sun to be assured of being able to refuel later? ... Even if that's not for another thousand years from now.'

'Perhaps.' Louise rubbed her nose thoughtfully. 'But I'm not sure it's going to be viable to stay in the ship. Not in the long term.' She sighed. 'The dear old *Northern* did her job superbly well – she exceeded all her design expectations. And maybe she *could* last another thousand years.

'But, in the end, she's going to fail. It may not be for *ten* thousand years, but failure will come. And then what?' She frowned. 'Then, *we* might not be around to oversee any transition to another environment.'

'There's a more fundamental point,' Mark said seriously. 'The engineering – the nuts and bolts – may have survived the trip, but the *social* fabric of the *Northern* didn't stand the strain so well. Consider the behaviour of the Planners, towards the end; their messianic visions, which had had a thousand long years to incubate, became psychotic delusions, virtually.' He looked pointedly at Uvarov. 'And we had one or two other little local difficulties along the way.'

'Yes.' Louise's tiredness was etched into her face. 'I guess, in the end, we didn't do a very good job of preserving our rationality, across the desert of time we've traversed . . .'

Mark looked around the table. 'People, we aren't Xeelee. We aren't *designed* to live with each other for centuries, or millennia. We just don't know how to build a society that could survive, indefinitely, in a cramped, enclosed box like the ship. We've already failed to do so.'

'Do you have an alternative?' Louise asked.

'Sure. We stay in the System. But we get out of the damn ship. We could try to colonize some of the surviving moons. They can give us raw materials for habitats, at least. We could break up the *Northern* to give the new colonies a start . . . Louise, what I'm advocating is giving ourselves *space*, before we kill each other.'

Uvarov turned his face towards the Virtual; his blind smile was like a snake's, Lieserl thought. 'A nice romantic thought,' he said. 'But not viable, I'm afraid.'

'Why not?'

'Because of *the helium flash*.' Uvarov turned, disconcertingly, straight to Lieserl; his eyes were shadowed pits. 'The flash: the coming gift from Lieserl's cute dark matter chums inside the Sun. Our best predictions are that it will blossom from the Sun within – at the most – a few centuries.' He swivelled his head towards Louise. 'And after that we can expect the carbon flash, and the oxygen flash, and . . . My friends, thanks to the photino birds the Solar System is, in practical terms, uninhabitable.'

Mark glared at the old surgeon. 'Then come up with a better idea.'

Louise held up her hands. 'Wait. Let's talk around the photino birds a little.' She glanced at Lieserl. 'You know more about the birds than any of us. Uvarov's projections are right, I suppose.'

'About the continuing forced evolution of the Sun? Oh, yes.' Lieserl nodded, feeling uncomfortable to be at the centre of attention; she was aware of the flickering candlelight playing around her nose and eyes. 'I've watched the birds for five million years. They've maintained their behaviour pattern for all of that time; I've no reason to believe they are going to change now. And your observations show that every other star, as far as we can tell, is inhabited –'

Uvarov scowled. '*Infested*. These birds of yours – these creatures of dark matter – they are our true enemy.'

Louise regarded Lieserl. 'Do you think he's right about that, too?'

Lieserl thought carefully. 'No. Not exactly. Louise, I don't think the birds really know we are *here*. After all, we're as marginally visible to them as they are to us.' She closed her eyes; the illusion of inner eyelids was remarkably accurate, she thought absently. 'I think they became aware of me, quite early ... I've told you I think they tried to find ways to keep me alive. But they never showed any inclination to go seeking more of my kind. And they never tried to communicate with me ... Still,' she said firmly, 'I don't think it's true that the photino birds are an *enemy*.'

Uvarov laughed. 'Then what in Lethe's waters are they? They fit most of the criteria I can think of.'

Lieserl quailed from the harshness of the ruined man's tone, but she pressed on. 'I just don't think it's helpful to think of them in that way. They're doing what they're doing – wrecking our Sun – because that's what they *do*. By accelerating the stars through their lifecycles they're building a better Universe for themselves, and their own offspring, their own future.' She groped for an image. 'They're like insects. Ants, perhaps.' She glanced around the table. 'Do any of you know what I'm talking about? The birds are following their own species imperatives. Which just happen to cut across ours, is all.'

Mark nodded. 'I think your analogy is a good one. The birds don't even have to be *alive*, in our sense of the word, to accomplish enormous things – changes on a cosmic scale. From the way you've described their lifecycles, they sound like classic von Neumann self-replicating machines ...'

Uvarov leaned forward; his head seemed to roll at the top of his thin neck. 'Listen to me. Alive or not, conscious or not, the photino birds *are* our eternal, true enemy. Because *they* are of dark matter, *we* are of baryonic matter.'

Louise drained her brandy snifter and poured herself a fresh measure. 'Maybe so. But for most of human history – as far as we can tell from the old Superet projections, and from the accounts Lieserl has provided us – the enemy of man was seen as the *Xeelee*.'

Uvarov smiled, eerily. 'I don't deny that, of course. Why should you be surprised at such a monumental misapprehension? My friends, even the comparatively few millennia of human history before our departure from the time streams in the *Northern* were a litany of ghastly errors: the tragi-comic working out of flaws hard-wired deep into our psyches, a succession of ludicrous, doomed enterprises fuelled by illusions and delusions. I refer you to the history of religious conflict and economic ideology, for a start. And I see no reason to suppose that people got any wiser after we left.' He turned his head to Mark. 'You were a socio-engineer, before you dropped dead,' he said bluntly. 'You'll confirm what I say. It seems to me that the Xeelee war – or wars – were no more than still another ghastly, epochal *error* of mankind. We know that the Xeelee inhabited a higher plane, intellectually, than humans ever could: you only have to consider that remarkable craft, the nightfighter, to see that. But humans – being humans – could never *accept* that. Humans believed they must challenge the Xeelee: overthrow them, become petty kings of the baryonic cosmos.

'This absurd rivalry led, in the end, to the virtual destruction of the human species. And – worse – it blinded us to the true nature of the Xeelee, and their goals: *and* to the threat of the dark matter realm.

'It is clear to me now that there is a fundamental conflict in this Universe, between the dark and light forms of matter – a conflict which has, at last, driven the stars to their extinction. Differences among baryonic species – the Xeelee and ourselves, for instance – are as nothing compared to that great schism.'

Louise Ye Armonk frowned. 'That's a fairly gloomy scenario, Uvarov. Because if it's true –'

'If I'm correct, we face more than a simple search for safety beyond this imperilled Solar System. We may not be able to find a place to hide in this *cosmos*. Even if we were able to found some viable colony, the birds would come to seek it out, and destroy it. *Because they must.*'

Mark, the Virtual, seemed to be suppressing a laugh. '*This*

Universe ain't big enough for the both of us ... Let me sum up: everyone's dead, and the whole Universe is doomed. Well. How are we supposed to cope with an emergency like that?' He grinned.

Lieserl studied his face curiously. After their brief physical contact, she felt intensely *aware* of Mark. And yet, it disquieted her that he could speak so flippantly.

For if Uvarov was right, then it could be that the humans in this fragile old ship were the *only* people left alive in an implacably hostile Universe.

Lieserl seemed to shrink in on herself, as if cowering inside this recently rediscovered shell of humanity; she looked around at the serious, young-old faces in the candlelight. Could it be true? Was this – she wondered with a stab of self-pity – was this the final ironic joke to be played on her by a vicious fate? She had been born as an alien within her own species. Now she had returned – been welcomed, even – and was it only to find that the story of man was finished?

'I'm sorry,' Mark was saying; he seemed deliberately to calm down. 'Look, Uvarov, what you're saying sounds absurd. Impossibly pessimistic.'

'Absurd? Pessimistic?' Uvarov swivelled his blind eyes towards Mark. 'You have sight; I do not. Show me a part of the sky free from the corruption wrought by these dark-matter crows.'

Mark's grin grew uncertain. 'But we can't escape the *cosmos*.'

Now Uvarov smiled, showing the blackness of his toothless mouth. 'Can't we?'

Lieserl watched Uvarov with interest. His analysis of the *Northern*'s situation had a devastating clarity. He seemed to be prepared to address issues with unflinching honesty – more honestly than any of the others, including herself.

Perhaps this was why Louise Armonk kept Uvarov around, Lieserl speculated. As a human he was barely acceptable, and his sanity hung by a thread. But his *logic* was pitiless.

Spinner-of-Rope folded her bare arms on the tablecloth. 'So, Doctor, you know better than all the generations of humans who ever lived.'

Uvarov sighed. 'Perhaps I do, my dear. But then I have the benefit of hindsight.'

'Then tell us,' Louise said. 'You said humans were blind to the goals of the Xeelee. What *were* the Xeelee up to, all this time?'

'It's obvious.' Uvarov swept his empty eyes around the table, as if seeking a reaction. 'The Xeelee are the dominant baryonic species – the *baryonic lords*. And they have led the fight, the climactic battle for the Universe, against these swarms of dark-matter photino birds. They have been striving to preserve *themselves* in the face of the dark matter threat.'

'And the human wars with the Xeelee –'

'– were no more than an irritation to the Xeelee, I should judge. But a dreadful, strategic error by humanity.'

The group fell into silence; Lieserl noticed that the eyes of Trapper-of-Frogs had become huge with wonder, childlike. She stared into the candle flames, as if the truth of Uvarov's words could be found there.

'All right,' Louise said sharply. 'Uvarov, what I need to understand is where this leaves us. What should we actually *do*?'

There was a gurgling sound from within Uvarov's wrapping of blankets; Lieserl, uneasily, realized that his chair was feeding him as he spoke.

'What we should do,' he said, 'is obvious. We cannot possibly defend ourselves against the photino birds. Therefore we must throw ourselves on the mercy of our senior cousins – we must seek the protection of the baryonic lords, the Xeelee.'

Mark laughed. 'And how, exactly, do we do that?'

'We have evidence that the Xeelee are constructing a final redoubt,' Uvarov said. 'A last defence perimeter, within which they must intend to fall back. We must go there.'

Louise looked puzzled. 'What evidence? What are you talking about?

Mark thought for a moment. 'He means the Great Attractor ...' He summarized the findings of the anomalous gravity-wave emissions from the direction of the Attractor.

Louise frowned. 'How do you know that's anything to do with the Xeelee?'

'Well, it could make sense, Louise; from the gravity waves we've picked up, we know *something* is going on at the Attractor site. Some kind of activity ... something *huge*. And there's no sign of life anywhere else ...'

Uvarov nodded, his head jerking. 'The Attractor is an immense construction site, perhaps: the last great baryonic project. We can even guess at its nature.'

'Yes?' Louise snapped.

'We know their technology was based on the manipulation of spacetime,' Uvarov said. 'We have the evidence of the starbreaker – gravity-wave weapons – and the domain wall defect drive of the nightfighter. I believe the object in Sagittarius, whatever it is, is a construct.'

'A construct of what?'

'Manipulated spacetime,' Uvarov said.

'It's logical, Louise,' Mark said. 'Think about it. Only through spacetime effects, including gravitation, can the Xeelee interact with the photino birds. So they've evolved weapons and artefacts based on the manipulation of spacetime: the nightfighter domain-wall drive, the starbreaker . . .'

'*The Ring,*' Lieserl breathed. 'Perhaps this – the Great Attractor – is the Ring. The Xeelee's greatest, final Project . . .' *Is it possible*? 'Dr Uvarov, have you found the Ring?'

Garry Uvarov turned to her. 'Perhaps.'

Mark was nodding. 'Maybe you're right . . . We've evidence that the dark matter creatures know about the activity in Sagittarius, too.' To Lieserl he said, 'We've seen streams of them coming and going from the Sun and heading in the direction of the Attractor . . . as if that is the focus of *their* activities, as well.'

Uvarov smiled. 'It is the final battlefield.'

'How far?' Lieserl asked.

Louise grimaced, her mouth twisting. 'To the Great Attractor? Three hundred million light-years . . . It's no walk around the block.'

'But we could get there,' Mark said. Lieserl noticed that his tone was flat, more distant than before. 'We have the nightfighter hyperdrive. We've no evidence that the hyperdrive is distance-limited. Spinner's flights have already man-rated it . . .'

Lieserl saw how Spinner-of-Rope shrank, subtly, away from the table, and dropped her small hands into her lap, her round face expressionless.

Louise Ye Armonk was frowning. 'We'd have to find a way of transporting our people, obviously.'

Mark spread his hands. 'Surely that's possible. We may have to detach the lifedome from the *Northern*, fix it to the nightfighter somehow . . .'

Louise nodded. 'We'd have to strengthen the dome internally, though . . . Obviously we'll need co-operation from the Decks. Morrow – will we get it?'

Morrow leaned forward, into the light, to reply.

Lieserl folded her hands on the table and tried to stop them trembling. She let the rest of the conversation, as it delved into detail, wash over her.

The decision seemed to have been made, then, almost by default. She examined it in her own mind.

Had there been any alternative? Given Uvarov's devastating logic, probably not.

But Uvarov's logic implied that she – Lieserl – was going to end her own long, strange life at the centre of all myths – myths which had persisted for most of mankind's sad history.

She was going to the Ring . . .

PART IV

TRAJECTORY: SPACELIKE

23

From the upper forest Deck to the loading bay at the base, lights blazed from the *Northern*'s battered lifedome. The human glow flooded over impassive Xeelee construction material, evoking no reflection.

Spinner-of-Rope sat in her cramped pilot's cage. Her helmet was filled with urgent chatter relayed from the lifedome.

Her hands fidgeted, plucking at the seams of her gloves; they looked like nervous, fluttering birds, she thought. She rested the hands deliberately against the material of her trousers, stilling them. The crew *still* weren't ready. How much of this waiting did they think she could endure?

Behind her, the smooth lines of the nightfighter's discontinuity-drive wings swept across space, outlined in blood-red by the bloated hulk of the Sun. The lifedome of the *Great Northern* – severed from its columnar spine – had been grafted crudely onto the shoulders of the nightfighter, pinned within a superstructure of scaffolding which embraced the lifedome and clasped it to the nightfighter. Behind the dome a GUTdrive power source, cannibalized from the abandoned *Northern*, sat squat on the nightfighter, cables snaking from it and into the dome. And, cradled within the attaching superstructure, Spinner could see the short, graceful profile of the *Great Britain*: the old sea ship, preserved from abandonment once more by the sentimentality of Louise Ye Armonk, was a dark shadow against the lifedome, like some insect clinging to its glowing face.

The lifedome was a mile-wide encrustation on the cool morphology of Xeelee technology; it dwarfed the Xeelee ship which carried it, looking like a grotesque parasite, she thought.

Spinner closed her eyes, trying to shut out the surrounding, pressing universe of events. She listened to the underlying wash of her own, rapid, breathing. Under her helmet her spectacles pinched the bridge of her nose with a small, familiar discomfort, and she could feel the cool form of her father's arrow-head against her chest. Clinging biostat telltales clung to her flesh, sharp and cold, but the little probes had at least become familiar: not nearly as uncomfortable as she'd found them at first. The environment suit smelled of plastic and metal, and a little of herself; but there was also a sparkle of orange zest, from one of the helmet nipples.

'...Spinner-of-Rope.'

The voice emerged from the background lifedome babble like the clear voice of an oboe within an orchestra. (And *that*, she thought, was a metaphor which wouldn't have occurred to her in the days before she'd poked her head out of the forest.)

'I hear you, Louise.'

'I think we're ready.'

Spinner laughed. 'Are you joking? I can't imagine you all sounding *less* ready.'

Louise sighed, clearly irritated. 'Spinner, we're as ready as we're ever going to be. We've been working on this for a year now. If we wait until every bolt is tightened – and until every damn jobsworth in the Decks, every antique anal-retentive on every one of Morrow's damn launch committees, is prepared to give his or her grudging acquiescence – we'll still be sitting here when the Sun goes cold.'

'It's a little different from your old days, Louise,' Spinner said ruefully. Spinner had seen images of the *Northern's* first launch – the extravagant parties that had preceded it, the flotilla of intraSystem craft that had swirled around the huge GUTship as it had hauled itself out of the System.

Louise grunted. 'Yeah, well. I guess those days are gone. Things are a little more seat-of-the-pants now, Spinner.'

Yes, Spinner thought resentfully, *but the trouble is it's my seat; my pants*.

Louise said, 'We're ready technically, anyway, according to all of Mark's feedbacks. We've laid the co-ordinates of the flight into your waldo systems ... all we can do now is see if they work.'

'Right.' Sourly, Spinner asked, 'Shall I do a countdown? You could relay it through the Decks; it might be fun. *Ten – nine –*'

306

'Come on, Spinner. Don't play games. It's time to *do* it. And, Spinner –'

Spinner stared at the Sunlight. 'Yes?'

'. . . Be *prepared*.'

Spinner's resentment grew. She knew what *that* meant. If anything went badly wrong with this first, full hyperdrive flight – so bad that it hadn't been predicted by the endless Virtual scenarios, so bad that the automatics couldn't cope – then it was going to be up to her, Spinner-of-Rope, and her famous seat-of-the-pants. And that was why she was still here, in this damn open cage: because Louise and Mark had failed to find a way to automate out that human element.

On her reactions and quick thinking, she knew, could depend – not just her own life, and the lives of her friends, the safety of the forest – but the future of the species.

I should have stuck to rope-spinning, she thought gloomily.

She reached out towards her hyperdrive waldo. She found herself staring at her own hand and arm, becoming aware of the enormity of the action she was about to take. The light of the dying Sun flooded the cage in shades of blood-red; gaudy golden highlights glimmered from the material of her glove.

She was filled, suddenly, with a profound sense of melancholy. She stifled a cry; the mood was so powerful it was almost overwhelming . . .

And the flood of emotion was coming from outside her. It came from her *companion*, she realized; her silent, invisible companion, here in the cage . . .

Louise sounded tense, almost unbearably so. 'Spinner? We're waiting.'

Spinner-of-Rope looked around at the empty sky of the Solar System: at the ruin of the Sun, the glistening Jovian accretion disc. Despite the alienating devastation, it was strange to think that she would be the last human to witness this aching, echoing, cathedral of space and history. 'Louise – no one's ever going to come back here, are they?'

'To the Solar System? No,' Louise replied briskly.

'It doesn't seem right,' she said slowly.

'What doesn't?'

'That we should simply *leave* like this. Louise, we're the last humans. Shouldn't we –'

Louise laughed. 'What? Nail a plaque to Callisto? Make a speech?' "Last one to leave, turn off the lights"?'

'I don't know, Louise. But –'

'Spinner.' It was always very obvious when Louise was forcing herself to be patient. *It's over.* Just push the damn button.'

Spinner-of-Rope closed her hand around the waldo.

Sunlight imploded.

Spinner-of-Rope was switched into darkness, into a sea of shadows which flooded the cage. She glanced down at her lap. The only illumination was a dim crimson glow – far less brilliant than Sol's – which barely revealed the outlines of her own body.

The hyperdrive transit was as sudden and seamless as the test runs. There was no internal sense of motion at all: merely a *lighting change*, as if all of this were no more than some shallow Virtual stunt.

She twisted in her couch. Behind her, the lifedome still sat on the frail-looking shoulders of the Xeelee craft, apparently undamaged; yellow human light, aping lost Sol, still blazed from a hundred sources, pale against the emptiness of space.

And beyond the lifedome there was a star, near enough to show a globe – as red as Sol but evidently much dimmer, cooler. The star provided the little light available. Beyond the star's glowing limb, six distant stars – a little brighter than the average – trailed across the sky in a zigzag shape. The star at one end of the compact constellation, ruby red, shone *through* the tenuous outer atmosphere of the nearby star globe.

The more remote constellations were an array of crimson and yellow spread across the sky. They were unchanged, as far as she could tell. Well, that was no surprise: she knew Louise hadn't planned to come far on this first jaunt.

'How are you, Spinner-of-Rope?'

'Fine,' Spinner said briskly. 'As I'm sure you know better than I do, thanks to Mark's tell-tales.'

Louise laughed. 'I've learned never to trust these damn gadgets. How did the trip feel?'

'As good as ever. As bad as ever ... I take it we all survived.'

'I'm just checking my summaries. No structural damage, as

far as I can see. One case of shock –' She snorted. 'A man who fell out of your big kapok tree, Spinner-of-Rope, when the Sun disappeared. The fool floated around until he could be snagged and hauled in. As we hoped, the nightfighter's domain-wall inertial shielding protected the whole of the lifedome from any side-effects of the jump ... Spinner, I don't think many people in the Decks have even *realized* we've jumped.'

'Good. I guess it's better that way.' Spinner-of-Rope stared around the sky. 'Louise, I thought the Solar System was depressing enough. But this system is a *tomb*.'

'I know, Spinner. I'm sorry. But it is in our flightpath. Spinner, we're going to head out of the plane of the Galaxy, in the direction of the Centaurus constellation: towards the Great Attractor ...'

'The Xeelee Ring.'

'If that's what it is, yes. And this star lies in Centaurus also.'

The main stars of the Centaurus constellation were ranged over distances from four light-years to five hundred light-years from the Sun. *Northern*, piggy-backing the Xeelee nightfighter, was going to move, in a rough straight line, out through this three-dimensional layout – and then beyond, out of the Galaxy and towards the Great Attractor itself.

'Spinner, would you believe I decided we should come here, on the first hop, for sentimental reasons?'

'Sentimental? About this place? Are you kidding?'

'Spinner, that dull globe is Proxima Centauri: the nearest star to the Sun, less than four light-years out. When I was a kid, growing up on Earth, we'd barely reached the stars with the first GUTships. Systems like Proxima were places of wild romance, full of extraordinary adventure and possibility. Superet's sombre warnings of implacably hostile alien species Out There Somewhere just added to the allure for kids like me ... I felt I had to get out here and see for myself.'

The *presence*, in the cage with her, seemed amused at this – even satisfied, Spinner thought.

Spinner grunted and picked at the material of her suit. 'Well, you made it to Proxima at last. And I'm touched by these childhood reminiscences,' she said sourly.

You're too harsh on her, Spinner-of-Rope ...

Spinner went on, 'This Proxima looks like a red giant. So I

guess the photino birds have already done their work here ...'

'No,' Louise said. 'Actually, Spinner, Proxima is a red *dwarf* ... It's a Main Sequence star, quite stable.'

'Really?' Spinner-of-Rope twisted in her seat and stared into the dull disc of Proxima. 'You mean it's *always* been like this?'

Louise laughed. 'I'm afraid so, Spinner. It's just a lot less massive than the Sun, and so has always been much dimmer – twenty thousand times less luminous than the Sun, in fact. The photino birds didn't need to turn it cool and red, like the Sun; Proxima has *always* been a dwarf. Stable, and harmless – and quite useless.'

'Useless for us. For baryonic life. But maybe not for the birds.'

'No,' Louise said. 'I guess a red dwarf is the ideal stellar form, for them: the model towards which they are guiding every damn star in all the galaxies. Of course Proxima has its moments: it's quite a brilliant flare star – a UV Ceti type. It can vary in brightness by up to a magnitude ...'

'It can?' For a few seconds Spinner studied the bland crimson disc. 'You want we should wait around and see if it does something exciting?'

'No, Spinner. Anyway, I suspect the photino birds will have put a stop to such frivolities by now ... *Oh.* One thing. Spinner-of-Rope, turn around.'

Loosening her restraints, Spinner twisted in her seat. 'What now?'

'Spinner, do you see that constellation just to the right of Proxima's disc?'

Louise must mean the jagged row of six stars behind Proxima, Spinner decided. 'Yes. What about it?'

'From Earth, that constellation used to be called Cassiopeia: named after the queen of Cepheus, the mother of Andromeda ...'

'Save the fairy tales, Louise,' Spinner growled.

'But from here, the constellation looks different. From here, the pattern's distinctive W-shape is spoiled a bit – by the addition of that bright red star at the left hand end of the row.'

Spinner stared; the star was a ruby jewel glimmering through the hazy outer layers of Proxima.

'The first colonists of Proxima – or rather, of the Alpha

system, of which Proxima is a part – called the new constellation the Switchback.

'Spinner, that extra star is the Sun. *Our* Sun, seen from Proxima. Another jump and Sol will be invisible; Spinner-of-Rope, yours are the last human eyes ever to look at Sunlight . . .'

Giant Sol glowed through the crimson velvet of Proxima; Spinner stared at it, trying to make out a disc, until her eyes began to ache.

At last she tore her gaze away. 'Enough,' she said. 'Come on, Louise; no more of the past.'

'All right, Spinner . . .'

Spinner closed her hand around the waldo once more.

. . . And the brooding globe of Proxima was replaced, abruptly, without any internal feeling of transition, by a new star system. This was another red star – huge, ragged-edged – but this time with a companion: a smaller yellow star, a point of light, barely a diameter away from the red globe. The giant was pulled into an elliptical shape by the dwarf companion, and Spinner thought she could see a dim bridge of material linking the two stars, an arc of red-glowing star stuff pulled out of the giant.

'. . . Spinner?'

'Yes, Louise. I'm still here. You're really showing me the sights, aren't you?'

'This is *Menkent* – Gamma Centauri. We're further through the Centaurus constellation: a hundred and sixty light-years from Sol, already. Menkent used to be a glorious A-class binary . . . But the photino birds have been at work. Now, one of the companions is going through its giant stage, and the other has already been reduced to a dwarf. Disgusting. Depressing.'

Spinner-of-Rope studied the twin stars, the lacy filaments of crimson gas reaching out of the giant to embrace its dwarf twin. 'Depressing? I don't know, Louise . . . It's still beautiful.'

Yes, Spinner-of-Rope. And this is the last star we'll visit that was significant enough to be named by Earth-bound astronomers, before spaceflight. Another gloomy little milestone . . .

'Don't you get morbid too,' Spinner said.

'Spinner?'

'Nothing. Sorry, Louise.'

'All right, Spinner, we've established everything is functioning well enough. I'm going to cut in the main navigation sequence now, and we'll try some major jumps ... Do you think you're ready?'

Spinner closed her eyes. 'I'm ready, Louise.'

'Now, I know it's going to be hard, but it will help if you keep in mind an understanding of what you're going to see. We're heading out of the Galaxy, at around twenty degrees below the plane of the disc. We're going to attempt thirty-five light-years every jump – and we'll be trying for a jump every second. At that rate, we should cover the hundred and fifty million light-years to the Attractor in –'

'– in around fifty days. I *know*, Louise.'

'I'm in the forest, Spinner. I'm looking out through the skydome, with Morrow and Uvarov, Trapper-of-Frogs, a few of the others. So you're not alone, out there; we can see what you can see, Spinner –'

'Another pep-talk? I know, Louise. I *know*.' She sighed. 'Louise, you're a great engineer, and a strong human being. But you're a damn awful *leader*.'

'I'm sorry, Spinner. I –'

'Let's *do* it.'

Impulsively, Spinner slapped her hand down on the waldo.

– and the brooding coupled stars of Menkent were replaced, instantaneously, by another binary pair. This time the stars – twin red giants – seemed more equally matched, and a bridge of cooling, glowing material linked them. A wide, spreading spiral of dim gas was curled tightly around the giants, and –

– before she had time to think about it here was still another binary pair, this time much further from the ship, with a bright, hot blue star traversing the decaying hulk of a dim red giant. She saw how the giant hung behind the blue star like smoke behind a diamond –

– when she was whisked away yet again and now, before her, hung a softly shimmering globe of light: a planetary nebula, she recognized, the expanding corpse of a red giant, blown apart by its bird-induced superwind, but before –

– she could wonder if Sol would one day look like this, the nebula had gone to be replaced by an anonymous, distant star field which –

– vanished, because now she was surrounded by a dim, red smog; she was actually *inside* a giant star, she realized, *inside* its cooling outer flesh and –

– that was gone too, replaced by a huge, ragged nebula – *a supernova site?* – which –

– imploded and –

– a star loomed at her, swollen, ruddy, achingly like Sol, but not Sol, and –

– *and – and – andandand –*

The stars were a huge, celestial barrage around her head. Beyond the immediate battering of light, the more distant constellations slid across space, elegant, remote, like trees in a forest.

Spinner sat rigidly in her crash-couch, letting the silent explosions of starlight wash across her cage.

...And, abruptly as it had begun, the barrage of starfields thinned out, diminished, vanished. Before the nightfighter now was only a uniform, restful darkness; a soft pink light, from some source behind her, played over the surfaces of the cage.

It's over.

Spinner-of-Rope felt herself slump in her couch. She felt as if her bones had turned to water. She cradled her visor in her glove, shutting out the Universe, and sucked on an orange juice nipple; the sharp, homely taste seemed to fill up her head.

She felt herself retreat into the small cosmos of her own body once more, into the recesses of her own head. *It's comfortable in here,* she thought groggily. *Maybe I should never come out again ...*

'Spinner-of-Rope.' Louise's voice, sounding very tender. 'How are you feeling?'

Spinner sucked resentfully on her orange juice. 'About as good as you'd expect. Don't ask stupid questions, Louise.'

'You did bloody well to withstand that.'

Spinner grunted. 'How do you know I *did* withstand it?'

'Because I didn't hear you scream. And because my telltales are showing me that you aren't chewing the inside of your helmet. And –'

'Louise, I knew what to expect.'

'Maybe. But it was still *inhuman*. A Xeelee might have enjoyed that ride ... People, it seems, need to work on a smaller scale.'

313

'You're telling me.'

'... When you're ready, take a look behind you.'

Spinner lifted her face from the nipple. The pinkish light from the source behind her still played over the surfaces of the waldoes, the crumpled suit fabric over her thighs.

She loosened her restraints, carefully, and turned around.

There was a *ceiling* of light above her. It was an immense plane of curdled smoke: lurid red at its heart and with violent splashes of colours – yellow and orange and blue – further out. The plane was foreshortened, so that she stared across ridged lanes of gas towards the bulging, pregnant centre. Smoky gas was wrapped around the core in lacy spirals of colour.

The plane of light receded, almost imperceptibly slowly, from the ship. The plane was a cathedral roof, and the nightfighter – with its precious burden of people, and all the hopes of humanity – was a fly, diving down and away from that immense surface.

'Louise, it's *beautiful*. I had no idea ...'

'Do you understand what you're seeing, Spinner-of-Rope?' Louise's voice sounded fragile, as if she were struggling with the enormity of what she was saying. 'Spinner, you're looking up at our Galaxy – *from the outside*. And that's why that barrage of stars has finished ... Our Galaxy's disc is only around three thousand light-years thick. Travelling obliquely to the plane, we were out of it in just a couple of minutes.'

The nightfighter had plunged out of the Galaxy at a point about two-thirds of the way along a radius from the centre to the rim. The ship was going to pass under the centre of the disc; that bloated bulge of crimson light would look like some celestial chandelier, thousands of light-years across, hanging over her head. Spiral arms – cloudy, streaming – moved serenely over her head. There were blisters of gas sprinkled along the arms, she saw, bubbles of swollen colour.

'Spinner, the disc is a hundred thousand light-years across. It will take us just fifty minutes to traverse its width ...'

Spinner heard Louise turn away and mumble something.

'What was that?'

'Your kid sister. Painter-of-Faces. She asked why we aren't seeing relativistic distortion.'

Spinner grinned. 'Tell her not to bother us with such stupid questions.'

'We aren't all hardened space pilots like you, Spinner-of-Rope ...'

There was no relativistic distortion – no starbow, no red or blue shift – because the nightfighter wasn't moving *through* the Universe. The 'fighter was hopping from point to point – like a tree frog, Spinner thought, leaping between bromeliads. And at the end-point of each jump, the ship was stationary – just for a second – relative to the Galaxy.

So, no blue shift.

But the nightfighter was falling out of the Galaxy at an effective velocity of millions of times lightspeed. It was the *frequency* of the jumps which gave Spinner this illusion of constant, steady motion.

It was working out, just as planned.

'We're *making* it, Louise,' Spinner said. 'We're making this *happen*.'

'Yes ... But –'

Spinner let out a mock groan. 'But now you're going to tell me how things just ain't what they used to be, *again*, aren't you?'

'Well, it's true, Spinner,' Louise said angrily. 'Look at it ... Even from this distance, outside the Galaxy, you can see the handiwork of those damn photino birds.'

The Galaxy contained two main classes of stars, Louise told Spinner. *Population I* stars, like the Sun, had evolved in the hydrogen-rich spiral arms, away from the centre. Some of these – like the blue supergiants – had been hundreds of times larger than the Sun, blazing out their energy in a short, insanely profligate youth. Population I stars tended to explode, enriching the interstellar medium – and later generations of stars – with the complex products of their nucleosynthesis.

By contrast, *Population II* stars had formed in regions where hydrogen fuel was in scarce supply: in the old regions close to the core, or in the clusters outside the main disc. The II stars were more uniform in size, and – by the era of the earliest human astronomy – had already been old, characterized by jostling herds of red giants.

'Look at that disc,' Louise snapped. 'I don't suppose the damn birds had to do much to the dull, stable Population IIs;

those things were half-dead already. But look – oh, look at the spiral arms ...'

Spinner saw how ragged the spirals were, disrupted by the blisters of yellow-red light which swelled across the lanes of dust.

'Those blisters are supernova remnants,' Louise said bitterly. 'Spinner, not every star would respond as peacefully to the photino birds' engineering as did our poor old Sun. A lot of the more spectacular, and beautiful, Population I stars would simply explode, tearing themselves apart ... Probably the birds set off chain reactions of supernovae, with the wreckage of one star destabilizing another.'

Spinner stared up at the wreckage of the disc, the muddled spiral arms.

... We're already forty thousand light-years below the disc, Spinner, her companion said. *The light you're seeing now left the stars forty millennia ago ... Think of that. Forty thousand years before my birth, humans were still shivering on the edges of glaciers, making knives out of bits of stone. And the further we travel, with every second, the light is getting older: Spinner-of-Rope, you're taking us through a hail of ancient light ...*

Spinner laughed. 'You should have been a poet.'

'What?'

'... Tell me what's coming next, Louise.'

'All right. Spinner, do you know what a *globular cluster* is?'

Spinner frowned. 'I think so.' She closed her eyes. 'A stable ball of stars – perhaps a hundred thousand of them – orbiting around the main disc, in the Galactic halo.'

'Right,' Louise said. 'They are Population II stars. And one particular cluster, called Omega Centauri, was one of the brightest clusters visible from old Earth.'

Spinner thought that over. '*Omega Centauri.* That name means it was in the line-of-sight of the Centaurus constellation.'

'Right.'

'You mean –'

'We're heading right for it. Keep your eyes tight shut, Spinner-of-Rope.'

Spinner turned, and looked ahead.

Beyond the fragile cage, giant stars ballooned at her, dazzling her with their billowing silence.

24

Upright on their zero-gee scooters, Lieserl and Milpitas descended into the deep loading bay at the base of the *Northern*'s lifedome. Above Lieserl the maintenance bulkhead at the base of Deck Fifteen spread out, an improbable tangle of ducts, cables and tree roots.

From the corner of her eye, Lieserl watched Milpitas curiously. He looked down at the drop beneath his feet with undisguised dread. Milpitas had been a starship traveller for a thousand years, but he was so obviously a gravity-well dweller. He visibly suffered in this zero-gee environment, his instincts quite unadapted to the fact that even if his scooter failed completely he'd simply drift through the air, perfectly safely.

Beneath the thick layer of dank, empty air into which she was descending, the base of the *Northern*'s lifedome had been turned transparent. The base appeared to Lieserl as a pool of cool darkness – and there, pinned against the underside of the lifedome base, like some immense insect immersed in a pond, was the slender form of the Xeelee nightfighter which bore them through space. Its sycamore-seed wings looked somehow darker even than the emptiness between stars.

The Planner turned to her stiffly and smiled. 'You look – uncomfortable – on that scooter.'

She suppressed a grin. *Me*? 'Uncomfortable? Not really.' She clicked her fingers and her scooter disappeared. She smiled at Milpitas, feeling mischievous. She did a back flip in the air, rolling twice; the clear floor beneath her wheeled across her vision.

She finished up falling alongside Milpitas once more. 'I don't feel uncomfortable,' she said. 'Just – well, a little foolish. Sometimes I feel these Virtual masks Mark sets up for me are a little forced.'

Milpitas had turned away from her antics, his face pale; he gripped the handles of his scooter so hard his knuckles were white.

Hastily she called subvocally for the return of her Virtual scooter. 'I'm sorry,' she said, sincerely. 'I guess I shouldn't have done that.'

She saw how the sweat glistened on the patchwork scars of his brow, but he determinedly held himself erect on his scooter. 'Don't apologize,' he said primly. 'We're here on an inspection tour ... to consider the disposition of *the ship*, not my well-being.'

So, after that brief moment of human frailty, Milpitas was back in his shell. She turned away, vaguely disappointed.

They were approaching the base of the loading bay, now. Lieserl could see the twin small jets of her scooter reflected in the clear floor; like attracting stars, she converged with her own image – in fact it was an image of an image, she thought wryly; the processors which sustained her were doing a good job with their Virtual reality creation today.

Milpitas, with a tense flick of his bony, scarred wrist, levelled off and began to sail parallel to the surface. Lieserl followed, a few feet behind.

Beneath the dome base, the Xeelee nightfighter spread its construction-material wings, huge, dormant.

'Good morning, Spinner-of-Rope,' Louise said.

Spinner stretched. Allowing herself to wake up slowly, she sucked fortified fruit juice from her helmet nipples and let the environment suit clean her skin with blasts of ultrasonics; she felt a warm trickle of urine enter her catheter.

She grunted in reply to Louise.

It was Spinner's tenth day in the nightfighter cage.

She loosened her restraints and looked around – and found herself staring into intergalactic emptiness. In the distance were patches of muddy light which could have been galaxies, or clusters of galaxies – so remote that even at the 'fighter's immense speed of three million light-years a day, she could make out no discernible movement.

Spinner slumped back into her couch. 'Lethe. Another day in the middle of this grey, lifeless desert,' she said sourly.

Louise – watching, Spinner knew, from her encampment on the *Northern*'s forest Deck – laughed, sounding sympathetic. 'But today should be a little more interesting than most, Spinner-of-Rope. We've reached a milestone. Or rather, a *mega-light-year-stone* ...'

'We have?'

'After ten days, we've come thirty million light-years from Sol. Spinner, we've reached the centre of the Virgo Cluster – the supercluster of galaxies of which our Galaxy is a member. Way behind you is a little patch of light: that's the Local Group – three million light-years across, the small cluster dominated by our Galaxy and the Andromeda galaxy. And to your left, at about eleven o'clock, you'll see the centre of the Virgo Cluster itself: that massive group of several thousand bright galaxies. They *used* to be bright, anyway ...'

Spinner made out the central galaxy group. It was a grey, grainy cloud of light. 'Fascinating.'

'Oh, come on, Spinner. Look, we're making an epic journey here – we're travelling so *far* we're making progress through the large-scale structure of spacetime. You can't fail to be – well, *uplifted*.'

'But I can't *see* any of it, Louise,' Spinner said fretfully.

Louise was silent for a moment. Then she said, 'All right, Spinner. I'll *show* you where you are.'

A ball of brilliant white light, expanding rapidly to about a foot across, appeared a few yards in front of the 'fighter cage.

Spinner slouched in her couch and folded her arms. 'Another educational Virtual display, Louise?'

'Bear with me, Spinner-of-Rope. Look at this. Here's the Universe, expanding from the Big Bang – as it was after perhaps three hundred thousand years. The cosmos is a soup of radiation and matter – a mixture of the dark and light variants.

'The temperature is still too high for atoms to form. So the baryonic matter forms a plasma. But plasma is quite opaque to radiation, so the pressure of the radiation stops the matter from clumping together. There are no stars, no planets, no galaxies.'

Abruptly the Virtual Universe expanded to double its size, and turned clear; a flash of light flooded out over Spinner's face, making her blink.

'Now the temperature has fallen below three thousand

degrees,' Louise said. 'Suddenly the electrons can combine with nuclei, to form atoms – and atoms *don't* interact strongly with photons. So the Universe is transparent for the first time, Spinner. The radiation, free to fly unhindered across space, will never interact with matter again. And in fact we can still see the primordial radiation today – if we care to look, its wavelength greatly stretched by the expansion of the Universe – as the cosmic background microwave radiation.

'But the key point is, Spinner, that after this decoupling the radiation could no longer stop the matter from clumping together.'

The model Universe was now a cloud of swarming, jostling particles.

'It looks like a mist,' Spinner said.

'Right. Think of it as like a dew, Spinner. It's spread out thin and uniform: on average there's one hydrogen atom in a space the size of one of our transport pods. And at this point the expansion of the Universe is pushing the dewdrops still further apart. But now, the structures of matter – the galaxies, the clusters and superclusters of galaxies – are ready to coalesce; they'll condense out like dewdrops on a spider web.'

Spinner smiled. 'Some spider. But where's the web?'

The ball of mist was filled, now, by a fine tracery of lines; the toy Universe looked like a cracked, glass sphere. *'Here's* the web, Spinner,' Louise said. 'You're looking at *cosmic strings*. Strings are defects in spacetime –'

'I know about string,' Spinner said. 'The Xeelee used strings – and domain walls – in the construction of the nightfighter.'

'Right. But *these* strings formed naturally. They are remnants of the phase transitions of the early Universe, remnants left over after the decomposition of the GUT unified superforce which came out of the singularity . . . Cosmic strings are residual traces of the ultrahigh, symmetric vacuum of the GUT epoch, embedded in the "empty space" of our Universe – like residual lines of liquid water in solid ice. And the strings are superconducting; as they move through the primordial magnetic fields, huge currents – of a hundred billion billion amps or more – are induced in the strings . . .'

The strings writhed, like slow, interconnected snakes, across space. The particles of mist, representing the uniform matter distribution, began to drift towards the strings. They coalesced in narrow columns around the strings, and in thin sheets in the wake of the strings.

'It's beautiful,' Spinner said.

'The strings are moving at close to lightspeed,' Louise said. 'They leave behind them flat wakes – planes towards which matter is attracted, at several miles a second. Structure starts to form in the wakes, so we get a pattern of threads and sheets of baryonic matter surrounding voids ...'

Now the baryonic matter, coalescing around the string structure, imploded under its own gravity. Tiny Virtual galaxies – charming, gem-like – twinkled to life, threaded along the webbing of cosmic string.

'And there's more,' Louise said. 'Look at this.'

Now there was a *loop* of cosmic string, twisting in space and oscillating wildly.

'String loops can form, when strings cross each other,' Louise said. 'But they're unstable. When loops form they decay away rapidly ... unless they are stabilized, as the Xeelee have made stable their nightfighter wings. Now: remember I told you that the strings are superconducting threads, carrying immense electrical currents? When the strings decay, all that electromagnetic energy has to go somewhere ...'

Abruptly the loop shrank, precipitately, and once again light blasted into Spinner's face.

Spinner lifted her hand to her faceplate. 'I wish you'd stop doing that,' she said.

'Sorry. But *watch*, Spinner. See what's happened?'

Spinner dropped her hand and blinked dazzled eyes.

The explosion of the loop of string had blown out a huge hole, in the middle of the mesh of galaxy threads.

Spinner nodded. 'I get it. There's a pulse of electromagnetic energy, which blows a bubble in the clouds of matter.'

'Not quite,' Louise said. 'Spinner, remember that dark matter is *transparent* to photons – to electromagnetic radiation. So the loop's electromagnetic pulse blows out just the *baryonic* matter; it leaves a hole, filled by dark matter but scoured clean of star stuff.

'Spinner, all this cosmic engineering induced by the strings – the primordial seeds – has left us with a *fractal* structure. *Fractal*

321

means the foam has the same general structure at all scales. It *looks* the same, no matter how far out or how close in you study. Our Galaxy is part of a small cluster – the Local Group – which, together with several other clusters, is part of a supercluster called the Virgo Cluster ... which in turn –'

'I get the idea,' Spinner said.

'The baryonic matter is clustered in filaments and sheets, around huge voids filled only with dark matter. It's like a froth, Spinner – and it's a very active froth, like an ocean's surface, perhaps; the strings are whipping through space at near lightspeed, and so there are huge movements, currents in the foam.'

'Louise, you said you'd show me where *I* am.'

'All right, Spinner ...'

Below the glistening glass the curves of the nightfighter rippled like some immense sculpture. There was Xeelee construction material only feet away from her now, and Lieserl had an urge to reach out and stroke it, as if the 'fighter were some immense, caged animal. But the material was separated from her both by the base of the lifedome and by a layer of hard vacuum – and, she thought ruefully, by a layer of unreality which only Mark Wu and his gadgets could breach.

'You're thoughtful,' Milpitas said.

She rubbed her chin. 'I was thinking how very *alive* this Xeelee ship looks. Not like a piece of technology at all. This is like some immense ocean beast, trapped beneath a frozen surface; it's as if I can see *muscles* beneath that skin of construction material.'

Milpitas grunted. 'It's an attractive image,' he said drily. 'Although I'm not entirely sure how helpful it is.'

Lieserl glanced up at the maintenance layer, a fifth of a mile above her, with its tangle of tree roots and plumbing conduits. 'Look at that primitive mess up there, by contrast ... Lethe's waters, Milpitas, this was a starship designed to last a thousand years. Some of that design looks as if it predates the Romans.' She sighed. 'You know, I caught a few glimpses of human technology, as we advanced over the years after the *Northern*'s launch. Obviously, we got better with time. But we always – *always* – ended up carrying our damn plumbing with us. I don't think humans ever, in their long history, *ever* came close to matching the simple perfection of this one Xeelee artefact, this nightfighter.'

Milpitas dipped closer to the transparent base surface and peered through it, intent. 'Perhaps you are right. But does that imply we should bow down and worship the Xeelee and all their works?'

'No,' she said coldly. 'But it *does* imply that the Xeelee were smarter than we ever were, or could have become.'

She saw his eyebrows rise, through a fraction of an inch; otherwise he didn't reply.

Now they were close to the rim of the base, near the transparent, curving wall of the loading bay. Here, the broad shoulders of the fighter nestled against the underside of the base; thick bands curled from the base around the 'fighter's curves and out of sight, hugging the 'fighter against the lifedome.

Milpitas leaned over the control bar of his scooter, peering at the attaching bands. He seemed quite fearless, Lieserl thought with some amusement, now that he was only a few feet above the lifedome base: close to the floor of his rigid, gravity-dominated mental universe.

She allowed herself to sail smoothly along the lines of the Xeelee ship. *Shoulders* – yes, that was a good label for this part of the 'fighter, at the root of the wings; here, so close to the ship, she had a real sense of being *carried*, on the broad, strong shoulders of some giant of construction material.

Milpitas straightened up from his inspection.

'So how's the engineering?' she asked.

'Fine,' he said, without looking up. 'That is, within tolerance limits ... The creep is minimal today.'

'*Creep?*'

He studied her. 'Perhaps you're not aware of the problems we faced, fixing the lifedome to this nightfighter. Lieserl, Xeelee construction material is effectively frictionless, and it is harder than any material substance known to us. It's impervious even to exotic matter ... You know we've speculated its manufacture may have violated the Pauli Exclusion Principle –'

'I heard about that.'

'So when we came to attach the lifedome, we couldn't simply

323

nail a superstructure to the nightfighter. No known adhesive would adhere to the construction material either. So, instead, we constructed a loose cage around the 'fighter.'

Governed by the *Northern*'s processors, 'bots had drawn in the straps comprising the cage, slowly and steadily tugging the lifedome against the nightfighter.

'So,' the Planner said, 'the strap arrangement hugs the nightfighter tightly against us, without *fixing* us to it. But that's obviously enough to persuade the 'fighter to carry the lifedome safely through hyperspace.'

'And – creep?'

'Because the cage is not fixed to the 'fighter – and because we are subject to various stresses – the cage's bands sl p over the construction-material surface. They creep. But we have nanobots out there working continually, readjusting the straps and compensating for stress.'

Lieserl nodded. 'It's a smart solution, Milpitas.'

He bowed, sardonically. 'Perhaps. But I can't take the credit for it. I merely implemented the design which –'

Suddenly she felt a stab of pity for this scarred, *stunted* man. 'Don't underestimate yourself,' she said on impulse. 'Believe me, you've achieved so much . . .'

'For a madman?' he asked disarmingly. He smiled at her. 'I know you think I'm a rather foolish, rigid person, Lieserl.'

Startled, she opened her mouth to deny this, but he held up his hand.

'Well, perhaps I am. But I *was* responsible, in large part, for the teams of 'bots which constructed this frame for the nightfighter. I know that our sensors could tell us much more about the state of the infrastructure which fixes us to this nightfighter than my naked gaze ever could. And yet –'

'And yet, you feel you want to see it for yourself?' She smiled. 'You're wrong, Planner. You're not the easiest person I've ever had to get along with, but I don't think you're a fool to follow your instincts.'

He studied her, coolly appraising. 'You believe so?'

'I know so,' she said firmly. 'After all, that was the whole point of my stay in the Sun – in fact, the point of my very *existence*. Plenty of probes were dropped into the Sun ahead of me, and after me. I was sent in so that – at least through a surrogate –

human eyes could *see* what was happening in there.'

He grunted. 'Although, it seems, we made precious little use of the insights you gained.'

'That's as may be.' She laughed. 'But I couldn't control that.'

He studied her. 'You may be a surrogate,' he said. 'But, Lieserl, despite that your humanity is powerful and obvious.'

That left her confused. She kept her face straight, determinedly. She issued subvocal commands, overriding the autonomic simulation of her face; she was adamant that her cheeks shouldn't show a hint of colouring. 'Thank you,' she said lightly. 'Although I'm not sure you *need* thanks. You're not proffering compliments, are you? I suspect you don't praise, Planner; you *ap*praise,' she said.

'Perhaps.' He turned away, closing the subject.

She studied his battered profile. Milpitas gave the impression of a man in control, but maybe he gave away more than he bargained for. With Milpitas, the communication of information was only one function – and a subsidiary one at that – of speech. The real purpose of conversation, for Milpitas, was *control*. She felt he was constantly fencing with her – testing her sharpness, and strength of will.

This was a man who was used to power, and used to exerting it, even in the most trivial conversation. But what type of person was this who – after centuries of subjective existence – would bother to fence with a tired old Virtual like her?

Milpitas continued his inspection, slowly, methodically.

Perhaps he was a little less than human – less, even, than *her*, she thought. Still – she conceded warily – there was a core of strength in Milpitas she had to admire.

Milpitas had been forced to watch his world – a world he'd *controlled* – fall apart, before his eyes. And he'd fought hard to preserve it. But then he'd *stopped* fighting, when he realized his old world was gone – that his beliefs were actually indefensible.

And *that* was the hard part. *That*, she reflected, was the point from which the endless strings of martyrs strewn across mankind's bloody history had failed to return. And since then he'd kept functioning – contributing to the mission.

She grinned. 'I think you're tougher than you look, Planner Milpitas. I mean, you have managed to break out of the prison of your past ...'

He turned. 'But the past is *not* a prison,' he said softly. 'The past is altered, constantly, by our actions in the present. Every new act revalues the meaning of the past ...'

She was surprised. 'That sounds like the surface of a deep philosophy.'

'Deep, and old,' he said. He eyed her, the tracery of scars over his scalp vivid in the flat light of the loading bay. 'We in Superet were never one-dimensional oppressors, Lieserl. We saw ourselves as preserving the best of humanity's wisdom, and we sought constantly to interpret our present and future in history's light ...'

She grunted. 'Hmm. Interesting. Perhaps the notion of a fluid past, recast in the light of our changing assumptions, is the only philosophy which will allow a race of immortals to stay sane. Maybe I'm still underestimating you, Milpitas.'

He touched his control bar and, gently, rose into the air. His face was impassive. 'Perish the thought,' he said drily.

The Universe-image expanded, focusing on a comparatively small volume; Spinner studied a nondescript chunk of cosmic foam, a collection of threads, voids and sheets of shining matter.

'Okay, Spinner-of-Rope: here's a three-dimensional map of our neighbourhood. The voids are around a hundred million light-years across, on average.

'Now here's a local landmark – a famous void called the Hole in Boötes, two hundred million light-years across – and, look, here's the *Great Wall*: the largest coherent structure in the Universe, a sheet of galaxies *five hundred million* light-years long.' Louise paused, and when she spoke again her voice was darker, tinged with the resentment and half-suppressed anger Spinner had come to recognize. 'Of course the Wall isn't quite the tourist site it was when I was a girl,' she said sourly. 'The damn photino birds have been active there as well ... All across the Wall, as far as we can observe, there's evidence of bird degradation.'

Spinner allowed herself to smile. She could imagine what Louise was thinking. *Damn it, it's our Wall!*

Louise was saying, 'This cloud' – a mist fragment the size of Spinner's hand, labelled by a small red arrow – 'is the Virgo Cluster. Our local supercluster.' A small region within the

Virgo cloud began to flash yellow, and a straight blue line snaked out of the yellow clump, piercing the heart of the Virgo. 'The little yellow volume is the Local Group, where Sol is,' Louise said, 'and the line represents our journey so far with the nightfighter: right through the middle of the Virgo super-cluster.'

Spinner grunted. 'Not very far.'

'Oh, come on, Spinner; think about the scale of this picture!

'Now look at this,' Louise said. Small, lime-green vector arrows appeared, bristling over the dusty surface of the Virgo Cluster. 'See that? The whole of our supercluster is moving through space – and it's at a significant speed, a million miles an hour or more. So fast that the motion was even observable from Earth – it imposed a Doppler shift on the whole Universe, Spinner: on the microwave background radiation itself.'

Now more velocity arrows appeared on another massive cluster close to the Virgo Cluster. 'There's another supercluster, called Hydra-Centaurus,' Louise said. 'And guess what: *that's* streaming in the same direction as the Virgo.'

Velocity arrows bristled now all over the foamy region of space ... and all the arrows, Spinner saw, pointed *inwards*, to an anonymous region at the heart of the three-dimensional diagram.

And the projected blue line of the nightfighter's voyage reached towards the centre of the immense implosion.

'I know what that is,' Spinner breathed. 'At the centre of the implosion. That's the Great Attractor.' *The place all the galaxies are falling to* ...

'Yes. There seems to be a mass concentration there, attracting galaxies across hundreds of millions of light years. The Attractor is a hundred and fifty million light-years from Sol, and with the mass of ten thousand galaxies ...'

Staring into the toy Universe, Spinner-of-Rope felt her heart flutter. 'And if it really is an artefact –'

'If it is, then it's an artefact so massive it's drawing in superclusters like moths, Spinner; so massive it's actually counteracting the expansion of the Universe, in this part of space ... It's an artefact beyond our imagination.'

Yes, thought Spinner. *Beyond imagination. And that's where we're heading* ...

25

'I don't know why you had to drag me up here, into the forest,' Louise grumbled. 'Not *now*. Couldn't you wait until you were sure of your data?'

Mark said, 'But the data –'

'Is partial, and incomplete, and hardly conclusive. What have you got – just two double images?'

'But the spectral match of the double galaxy images is almost perfect, in each case. I tell you it *must* be string,' Mark insisted.

'And I'm telling you that's impossible,' Louise growled. She felt her irritation rise. 'How could there be cosmic string in the middle of a void like this?'

Uvarov raised his skull-like face and cackled, relishing the conflict.

The three of them were suspended just below the forest skydome. Louise was on a zero-gee scooter, and Uvarov had been strapped into a stripped-down life support chair attached to three of the flexible little scooters.

Mark, irritatingly, was choosing to manifest himself as a disembodied head, twice life-size, hovering in the air. 'How's Spinner-of-Rope?' he asked Louise.

She grunted. 'Bearing up. We're thirty-three days into the mission, now – thirty-three days for Spinner in that couch. And the last ten of them inside this damn hole in the sky.'

'Well, this is really a pretty exciting part of the journey,' Mark said. 'We're crossing the edge of the greatest cosmological void ever detected: more than two hundred million light-years across. As far as we can tell, we're the only scrap of baryonic matter in all that immensity. That's an exciting thought even without my evidence of cosmic string ...'

'Not exciting for Spinner,' Louise said drily. 'For her this void is nothing but sensory deprivation.'

'Hmm,' said Uvarov. *'The Universe as an immense sensory deprivation tank* ...maybe that's a good image to sum up the photino birds' cosmic handiwork.'

Now schematic graphics of remote galaxies – sheets of them, at the boundary of the huge void – peppered the dome with splashes of false colour; here and there fragments of text and supplementary images were interspersed amid the insect-like galactic swarms.

Mark's head swivelled around towards Louise. 'Look, I'm sorry you don't think it's appropriate for me to have dragged you up here. Maybe I *should* have waited for *proof* of the string's existence. Well, I didn't realize we were out here to do *science*. I thought we were trying to find ways to stay alive – to anticipate what we're up against. And that means reacting – *and thinking*, Louise – as quickly and as flexibly as possible. All right, maybe I'm guessing. But – what if it *is* cosmic string out there? Have you thought about that?'

Louise turned her face, uncertainly, up to the dome. 'If it is string – *here* – then, perhaps, we're heading into something even more extraordinary than we've anticipated.'

Uvarov chuckled. 'Perhaps we should stick to the *facts*, my dear Mark.'

'There are *no* facts,' Louise said. 'Only a handful of observations. And – across distances measured in hundreds of millions of light-years, and taken from a platform moving through a hyperdrive journey – they're damned imprecise observations at that.'

Uvarov turned his head to the Virtual. 'Tell me about your observations, then. Why are these double images so all-fired important?'

'I've been taking observations of the far side of the void,' the Virtual said. 'I've been looking for evidence of gravitational lensing ... The distortion of light from distant objects by the gravitational field of some huge, interposed mass. I wasn't looking for *strings* specifically. I was trying to see if I could detect any structure within the void – any concentrations of density.'

'Are the strings so massive, then, that they can distort light so far?'

Louise said, 'It isn't really as simple as that, Uvarov. Yes, strings are massive: their width is only the Planck length, but their density is enormous – a one-inch length would have a mass of around ten million *billion* tons ... a string stretching from Sol to Saturn, say, would have around one Solar mass. We expect strings to be found either in loops thousands of light-years across, or else they will be *endless* – stretched right across the Universe by the expansion from the singularity.'

Uvarov nodded. 'Therefore, if they are so massive, their gravitational fields are correspondingly huge.'

'Not quite,' Louise said. 'Strings are very exotic objects. They aren't like stars, or planets, or even galaxies. They simply aren't Newtonian objects, Uvarov. The relativistic gravitational fields around them are *different*.'

Uvarov turned to her. 'Are you telling me the strings are antigravitational, like the domain walls of the nightfighter's discontinuity-drive wings?'

'No ... '

Far enough from a loop – a finite length of string – the mass of the string would attract other bodies, just as would any other massive object. But an observer *close* to a string, either a loop or part of an infinite string, would *not* experience the gravitational effects to be expected from such massive concentrations of matter.

Louise said, 'Uvarov, gravitational attraction works by distorting spacetime. Spacetime is flat if no heavy objects are present; an object will sail across it in a straight line, like a marble across a tabletop. But the spacetime close to a Newtonian object, like a star, is distorted into a well, into which other objects fall. But close to a string, spacetime is locally *flat* – it's what's called a Minkowski spacetime. Objects close by *aren't* attracted to the string, despite the huge mass ... '

'But,' Mark said, 'the spacetime around a string *is* distorted. It is *conical*.'

Uvarov frowned. 'Conical?'

'Imagine spacetime as a flat sheet. The presence of the string removes a slice from that sheet – like a slice of a pie, cut out of spacetime. What's left of the spacetime is joined up – the hole left by the missing slice is closed up – so that the spacetime is like a cone. Still flat, but with a missing piece.

'If you were to draw a circle around a string, you would find its circumference shorter than you would expect from its radius – it's just like drawing a circle around the apex of a cone.'

'And this small spacetime defect is sufficient to cause the double images you speak of?'

'Yes,' Mark said.

A cosmic string wasn't visible directly. But its path *could* be made visible, by a track of double images of remote objects, separated by about six arc seconds, along the length of the string.

Louise said, 'Uvarov, imagine two photons setting off towards us from a remote galaxy, beyond a string. One of them comes to us directly. The second, passing on the far side of the string, travels through the conical defect. The second photon actually has less distance to travel to reach us, thanks to the defect; its journey time is less than the first's by around ten thousand years. Hence, the double images.'

Uvarov grunted. 'Louise, you have explained to me how the network of strings was the web around which the galaxies coalesced. I do not understand how this can be, if the gravitational effects of these strings are so slight.'

Louise sighed. 'The strings are primeval objects: they were formed within an invisible fraction of a second after the Big Bang itself, during the symmetry loss caused by the decomposition of the unified superforce. Since then, the expansion of the Universe has *stretched* the strings. So the strings are under great tension – a tension caused by the expansion of the Universe itself . . . The strings whip through space, at close to the speed of light.

'Where the strings pass, their conical defects cause them to leave a *wake*. Matter falls in towards the two-dimensional, sheet-like path swept out by the string. And it's this infalling that caused the formation of the baryonic matter structures we observe now: clusters of galaxies, in threads and sheets.'

'In fact,' Mark said, 'the wake is itself observable. Or should be. It imposes a slight Doppler shift on the microwave background radiation. I should be able to see a slightly brighter sky on one side of the invisible string than on the other . . .'

'And have you seen this?' Uvarov snapped.

'No,' Mark admitted. 'Damn it. The *Northern* couldn't be a much worse platform for this kind of measurement; the microwave Doppler is below my level of resolution.'

'But you do think you've found some image pairs,' Uvarov persisted.

'Yes,' Mark said, sounding excited again. 'Two pairs so far, and a few other candidates. The two pairs are aligned, just as you'd expect them to be if a string is the cause ...'

'Enough,' Uvarov snapped. He raised his chair into the air above them and prowled across the underside of the skydome, his ravaged profile silhouetted against the false colours of the galaxies. 'Now tell me what this means. Let us accept, Louise, that your Virtual lover has found a fragment of this – *string*. So what? Why should we care?'

'We're in a *void*, Uvarov,' Louise said patiently. 'We'd expect to find string at the heart of huge baryonic structures – like the Great Wall, for instance, a sheet of clusters half a billion light-years long, which –'

'But we are *not* at the heart of such a huge baryonic structure. Is that your point, Louise?'

'Yes. That's the point. There's no reason why we should find string *here*, in this void, away from any concentrations of matter.'

'I see. There is nothing out there but dark matter,' Uvarov growled quietly. 'Nothing but the photino birds, and their even more exotic cousins – and whatever they've chosen to build, here at the heart of their dark empire, far from any baryonic structure.'

Uvarov wheeled to face Louise, his scooters spurting puffs of reaction gas. 'If it exists, will the string have any effect on the photino birds?'

'Possibly,' Mark said. 'Strings are gravitational defects. Dark matter is influenced by gravity ...'

Uvarov nodded. 'So perhaps the string is here to do damage to the photino birds. Is that possible? Perhaps the string has been moved here *deliberately*.'

'I hadn't thought of that, but I guess it's possible.' Mark peered up into the dome, his eerie, disembodied head looking bizarre. 'Yes. If someone is waging war on the photino birds, then maybe they are using lengths of cosmic string as weapons. Think of that. And more: who in this Universe is capable of such an act, but the Xeelee themselves?

'Lethe – fighting wars with bits of cosmic string. How have

they the audacity to even *imagine* such weapons?'

Louise looked up into the dome's sketchy, gaudy rendering of the Universe. Suddenly these scraps of data seemed pathetic, their understanding hopelessly limited. Were the final wars for the destiny of the Universe being played out between Xeelee and photino birds, somewhere in this huge void, even now, as she stared up in her blindness and ignorance?

'Keep gathering your data, Mark,' she said. 'In another few days we'll be out of this damn void.'

'We're like rats, crossing the rim of some huge war zone,' Mark said, his huge face expressionless. 'We can barely comprehend the visions around us. And we're heading for the final battlefield ...'

Suspended between Decks, in the middle of a cloud of floating chickens, Mark and Lieserl made love.

Afterwards, Lieserl rested her head against Mark's bare chest. His skin, under her cheek, was rough, covered in short, tight-curled dark hairs, and slick with sweat – in fact she could taste the sweat, smell its salty tang. She felt a pleasant, moist ache in her thighs.

'I still feel breathless. Maybe I'm too old for this,' she said.

Mark nuzzled her hair. 'Then make yourself younger.'

'No.' She pressed her face against his chest. 'No, I don't want to change anything. Let's keep it just the same, Mark; let's keep it *real*.'

'Sure.'

She was silent for a moment. Then, despite herself, she added, 'And it *is* bloody real, you know. A magnificent illusion.'

She felt him smile.

'I told you. I've put a lot of time into getting it right,' he said. 'This and coffee.'

She laughed, and pulled herself away; her skin parted from his with a soft, moist sucking sound. 'I wonder if anyone was watching us.'

Mark stretched; the chickens, fluttering and clucking, swam clumsily through the air away from his arms. He glanced around. 'I don't see anyone. If there was, do you care?'

'Of course not. It might have done them good, in fact. Shaken them up a bit more.'

Lieserl rolled in the air, reached behind her back and began to straighten her hair. The Decks wheeled slowly around her, an immense box of green-furred walls. After the surrender of the Temples, the coming of zero-gee had, slowly, made inroads into the life of the people – the Undermen, as Spinner-of-Rope still called them – who lived here between the Decks. The most noticeable was the cultivation of *all* of the available surfaces of the Decks; now, the walls and ceilings were coated with meadows, patches of forests, fields of wheat and other crops. The trees grew a little haphazardly, of course, but they were being trained to emerge straight. And, without the pressure of walking feet, the grass in the parks and other areas was beginning to look a little wild.

A huddle of people had gathered under what had been the roof of Deck Two – the underside of Deck One. Mark – or rather a second projection of him – was taking the hesitant, young-old people through a literacy and Virtual usage programme. And elsewhere, Lieserl knew, the infrastructure of the Decks was being upgraded to remove the Decks' enforced reliance on pictograms.

These initiatives gladdened Lieserl. She remembered the world of her brief childhood, drenched in Sunlight and data and Virtuals and sentience: perhaps the most information rich environment in human history. The contrast with the stunted, data-starved environment of the Decks was poignant.

In one spot, close to the surface, she saw Milpitas and Morrow, toiling together. The two old men were constructing a sphere of water, bound together in a frame of wood and reeds: *a zero-gee water garden*, Morrow had called it. Lieserl remembered his smile. 'All part of Milpitas' therapy,' he'd said.

The whole environment made for a charming prospect: the Decks had evolved away from the bleak, iron-walled prison they'd been under the Planners during the long flight, and turned into a green-lined sylvan fantasy. There were trees growing at you out of the *sky*, for Life's sake. And some inspired soul had liberated boxes of wild flower seeds from the *Northern*'s long-term stores; now the inverted meadows were, more often than not, peppered with bluebells.

The old floors were still coated with the old, boxy homes and factories, of course. But many of the homes had been abandoned; they sat squat on the surface like empty shells. Instead, new homes had been established in the air: rangy, open dwellings, loosely anchored to whichever surface was nearest, or fixed on thin, impossibly fragile spindles.

She held Mark's hand and drifted through the chicken cloud, drinking in the fowls' childhood, farmyard smell (... or at least a Virtual, cleaned-up version of it). 'You know,' she said, 'maybe zero-gee was the best thing that could have happened to this society. Slowly the Decks are turning into a decent place to live.'

Mark grunted. 'But it's taken a *long* time. And sometimes I think this is all a little unreal.'

'What is?'

He waved a hand. 'The strange, aerial society that's been established here. I mean, beyond these walls of grass there is *nothing* – nothing but an intergalactic desert, across which we're fleeing in search of protection from an alien species with whom man has been at war for megayears ...'

Across the Universe we flee, Lieserl thought, *with chicken eggs and bluebells ...*

'Maybe that's true,' she said. 'But so what? Is it a bad thing? What can the people here do, but live their lives and maintain the lifedome's infrastructure? An awareness of what's outside – of the Universe as megayear celestial battlefield, across which we're fleeing – is like a morbid, paralysing awareness of death, it seems to me. Mark, we're bystanders in the middle of a war. I suspect the last thing any of us needs is a sense of perspective.'

He grinned, and laid his hands on her bare hips. His eyes were alive, vibrant blue, within his coffee-dark face. 'You're probably right.' He pulled her to him, and she could feel the firmness of a new erection against her own pad of pubic hair. 'What can any of us do, but follow our instincts?'

She felt a small, contained part of herself open up in his warmth. Sex – even this Virtual reconstruction of it – was *wonderful*, and, remotely, she was reminded once more of how much had been kept from her during her brief, engineered life. She'd gained five million years of sentience, but had been deprived of her ancient, human heritage.

She lifted her arms and wrapped them around Mark's neck. 'You should be careful with me,' she said. 'I'm an old lady, you know . . .'

He bent his head to hers and kissed her; she ran her tongue over the sharpness of his teeth.

Around them, the chickens rustled softly, detached feathers drifting through the air like snow.

26

It was a *good* day for Spinner-of-Rope.

She found a large hive high in a tree. The bees buzzed in alarm as she approached, but she circled the trunk warily, keeping away from their vicious stings. She set a small fire in a notch in the bark a little below the fat, lumpy form of the hive, and piled the flames high with moist leaves; she let the thick smoke waft up and over the hive. The bees, disoriented and alarmed, come flooding out into the smoke and scattered harmlessly.

Spinner, whooping in triumph, clambered back to the abandoned hive, broke it open with her axe of Underman metal, and dug out huge handfuls of comb, dripping with thick honey. She feasted on the rich, golden stuff, cramming it into her mouth; the honey smeared over her face and splashed her round spectacles. There would be more than enough to fill the two leather sacks she carried at her waist.

... Then, sitting on her branch, eating the honey, she found herself shivering. She frowned. Why should she be *cold*? It wasn't even noon yet.

She dismissed the odd sensation.

In a nearby tree, a hundred yards from Spinner, a man sat. He wore a battered coverall, and his face looked tired, lined, under a thatch of grey hair. He was eating too: a fruit, a yam, perhaps. He smiled and waved at her.

He was a friend. She waved back.

She rinsed her face in a puddle of water inside a fat bromeliad, and climbed down to the ground.

She ran lightly across the level, leaf-coated floor of the forest. Arrow Maker would be tending his bamboo clumps, she knew; there were only a few groves of the species which provided the six-feet-long straight stems Arrow Maker needed to manufacture his blowpipes, and Maker cultivated the clumps with loving care, guarding them jealously from his rivals. Spinner would run up to him and show him the honey treat she'd found, and then –

Spinner-of-Rope. I know you're awake.

... and then ...

Come on, Spinner, talk to me.

Spinner slowed to a halt.'

With regret she glanced down once more at the honey she would not be able to enjoy, and issued a soft, subvocal command.

Out of the air, the environment suit congealed over her limbs like some web made of silvery cloth, and the bulky couch materialized around her body. Like a skull poking through decaying flesh, the darkness of space, the harsh telltale lights of her waldoes, emerged through the forest dream.

'Spinner-of-Rope. *Spinner*.'

Her heart beat as rapidly as a bird's. 'Yes, Louise.'

'I'm sorry I had to dig you out of your Virtual like that. You, ah, you didn't want to come back to us, I don't think.'

Spinner grunted as the suit went into its daily sonic bath routine. 'Well, can you blame me for wanting to escape?' She let the bleakness outside the cage flood into her mind. How *wonderful* it had been to be ten years old again, to have no greater horizon than a day's frog-hunting with her father! But she *wasn't* ten years old; more than five decades had worn away since those honey-hunting days, and since then immense responsibilities had descended on her. The renewed awareness of *who she was* settled over her like a tangible weight: a weight she'd been carrying around for all this time – but which she'd forgotten to notice.

She shivered again – and became suddenly, sharply suspicious. She hissed out brief subvocal commands and called up a display of her environment suit air temperature. It was around eighteen degrees Celsius. Not exactly ice-cold, but still noticeably cool. She called up a faceplate-graphic of how her suit temperature had varied over the last few days.

The coldness she'd felt in her dream had been real. The suit temperature had been *changed*. For more than a week it had been maintained at twenty-five degrees – fully seven degrees warmer than today.

'Louise,' she said sternly.

She heard Louise sigh. 'I'm here, Spinner-of-Rope.'

'What in Lethe is going on? What have you been trying to do, cook me to death?'

'No, Spinner. Look, we've come to understand – a bit belatedly, maybe – how hard this trip is for you. I wish, now, we'd found some other solution: someone else to relieve you, perhaps. But it's too late for that. We've got ourselves into a situation in which we're very dependent on you, and your continued good functioning out in that cage, Spinner.'

'And the heat?'

'Heat acts as a mild sedative, Spinner-of-Rope. As long as your fluid balance isn't affected – and we're monitoring that – it's quite harmless. I thought it was a good solution to the problem . . .'

Spinner rubbed her cheek against the lining of her helmet. 'Right. So you were sedating me, without my consent. Louise Ye Armonk, engineer of human bodies and souls . . .'

'I guess I should have discussed it with you.'

'Yes, I guess you should,' Spinner said heavily. 'And now?'

Louise hesitated. 'It was becoming harder and harder to dig you out of your fantasies, Spinner. I was afraid we might lose you altogether . . . lose you to a dream of the forest.'

A dream of the forest.

With a sigh she straightened her posture in her couch. 'Don't worry, Louise. I won't let you down.'

'I know you won't, Spinner.' Louise sounded nervous, excited – uncharacteristically so. 'Spinner-of-Rope . . . *it's the fifty-first day.* Look around you.'

Spinner loosened her restraints; she glared around at her surroundings, at first seeing only emptiness. Irritated, she snapped out subvocals, and the faceplate began to enhance her naked-eye images.

'Spinner, we've travelled a hundred and fifty million light-years. We're reaching the end of the programmed hyperdrive jumps . . .

'It's nearly over, Spinner-of-Rope. We're almost there.'

As the faceplate worked, dim forms emerged – the moth-like

forms of galaxies, far away, all around her. She saw spirals, ellipticals, gigantic irregulars: huge clusters of galaxies in their characteristic threads and sheets, the whole vision looking impossibly fragile.

But there was something *odd* about the pale images.

'We've arrived, Spinner-of-Rope,' Louise said. 'We are at the centre of things.'

Blue shift, Spinner-of-Rope. Blue shift, everywhere . . . Can you see it?

Yes. The galaxies – all around her sky – were tinged *blue*, she realized now. *Blue shift.*

She had come, at last, to the place all the galaxies were falling into.

PART V

EVENT: RING

27

The nightfighter – with its fragile cargo of humans, and travelling thirty-five light-years with every hyperdrive jump – arced down towards the disc of the scarred galaxy. Spinner-of-Rope sat in her cage, letting the waldoes run through their program; in the corner of her eye, telltales winked reassuringly.

This galaxy was a broad spiral, with multiple arms tightly wrapped around a compact, glowing core. The star system was a pool of rust red, punctuated with the gleam of novae and supernovae: thus, she saw, the galaxy had not escaped depredation at the hands of the photino birds. And the gleaming disc was disfigured by one stunning feature: a huge gouge of a scar, a channel of dust and glowing star-stuff that cut right across the disc, from rim to core.

Now the nightfighter, flickering through hyperspace, neared the rim of the disc, close to the termination of the scar.

This might have been the original Galaxy of humans, Spinner thought, and she wondered if Louise Armonk was sitting under the skydome over the forest, peering out at this freight of stars. Maybe this nostalgic similarity was the reason Louise and the rest had chosen this particular galaxy, out of hundreds of thousands around the cavity, for a closer study.

Suddenly the plane of the disc loomed up at her – and the nightfighter slid neatly into the notch gouged out of the disc.

'Good navigation, Louise,' she said. 'Right down the channel.'

'Well, it wasn't so hard to hit. The channel is over two thousand light-years wide, and as straight as one of your blowpipes. The channel was cut so recently that the galaxy's rotation hasn't had time to distort it too far – although, in another few hundred thousand years there will be barely a trace of this feature left . . . '

The 'fighter plunged along the gouge, and the view was

spectacular. Above her was the gaunt, galaxy-stained sky of the Attractor; below and around her was an open tunnel of stars, hurtling past her. Looking ahead, it seemed she could see all the way to the gleaming core of the galaxy. It was difficult to remember that this neat star-walled valley was no less than fifty thousand light-years long ...

At thirty-five light-years a second, the ship would reach the core in under thirty minutes.

Now the 'fighter dived into a bank of opaque dust – and then exploded out again, the stars gleaming crimson and gold in the walls of the galaxy-spanning tunnel.

Spinner punched her fist into her palm and whooped.

She heard Louise laugh. 'You're enjoying the ride, Spinner-of-Rope?'

There were voices behind Louise Armonk. 'I see it.' Excited, shouting. 'I see it –'

I see it, too.

Spinner turned in her chair, the restraints riding up awkwardly across her chest. The voice had sounded as if it had come from her left.

It had been the voice of the man from her forest dreams, of course. She almost expected to see that slim, dark form, sitting out there beyond the cage: that sixty-year-old face, the hair of grey pepper-speckled with black, the vulnerable brown eyes ...

Somehow, she felt he was coming closer to her. He was *emerging*.

But there was nobody there. She felt disappointed, wistful.

'That was Morrow, butting in,' Louise was saying. 'I'm sorry, Spinner. Do you want me to patch you into the conversation? ... Spinner? Did you hear me? I said –'

'I heard you, Louise,' she said. 'I'm sorry. Yes, patch me in, please.'

'... straight ahead of us, at the end of this gouge,' Morrow was saying. 'There ... *there* ... See?'

'Spinner, I'll download our visuals to you,' Louise said.

Spinner's faceplate image was abruptly overlaid with false colours: gaudy reds, yellows and blues, making detail easy to discriminate.

The glowing walls of the star valley dwindled into a dull mist at infinity. And at the end of the valley – almost at the vanishing point itself – there was a structure: a sculpture of thread, colour-ed false blue.

'I see it,' Spinner breathed. Subvocally, she called for magnification.

'Do you know what you're looking at, Spinner?' Louise's flat voice contained awe, humility. 'It's what we suspected must have gouged out this valley. It's a fragment of cosmic string ...'

At the centre of an immense cavity, walled by crowded galaxies, Lieserl and Mark rotated slowly around each other, warm human planets.

The sky was peppered with the dusty spirals of galaxies, more densely than the stars in the skies of ancient Earth. But the cavity walls were ragged and ill-defined, so that it was as if Lieserl was at the centre of some immense explosion. And every one of the galaxies was tinged by *blue shift*: the light from each of these huge, fragile star-freights was compressed, visibly, by its billion-year fall into this place.

Mark took her hand. His palm was warm against hers, and when he pulled gently at her arm, her body slowly rotated in space until she faced him.

'I don't understand,' Lieserl said. 'This – cavity – is empty. *Where's the Ring?*'

The light of a hundred thousand galaxies, blue-shifted, washed over his face. Mark smiled. 'Have patience, Lieserl. Get your bearings first.

'Look around. We've arrived at a cavity, almost free of galaxies, ten million light-years across: a cavity right at the site of the Great Attractor. The whole cavity is awash with gravita-tional radiation. Nothing's visible, but we know there's some-thing here, in the cavity ... It just isn't what we expected.'

Lieserl raised her face to stare around the crowded sky, at the galaxies embedded in the walls of this immense cave of sky. One galaxy with an active nucleus – perhaps a Seyfert – emitted a long plume of gas from its core; the gas, glowing in the search-light beam of ionizing radiation from the core, trailed behind the infalling galaxy like the tail of some immense comet. And *there* was a giant elliptical which looked as if it was close to disintegration, rendered unstable by the fall into the Attractor's monstrous gravity well; she could clearly see the elliptical's multiple nuclei, orbiting each other within a haze of at least a thousand billion stars.

Some of the galaxies were close enough for her to make out individual stars – great lacy streams of them, in disrupted spiral arms – and, in some places, supernovae glared like diamonds against the paler tapestry of lesser stars. She picked out one barred-spiral with a fat, gleaming nucleus, which trailed its loosening arms like unravelling bandages. And there was a spiral – heartbreakingly like her own Galaxy – undergoing a slow, stately collision with a shallow elliptical; the galaxies' discs had cut across each other, and along the line where they merged exploding stars flared yellow-white, like a wound.

It was, she thought, as if the Universe had been wadded up, compressed into this deep, intense gravity pocket.

Everywhere she caught a sense of motion, of activity: but it was motion on an immense scale, and frozen in time. The galaxies were like huge ships of stars, Lieserl thought, voyaging in towards *here*, to the centre of everything – but they were ships caught suspended by the flashbulb awareness of her own humanity. She longed for the atemporal perspective of a god, so that she could run this immense, trapped diorama forward in time.

'It's all very beautiful,' she said. 'But it almost looks artificial – like a planetarium display.'

Mark grunted. 'More like a display of trapped insects. Moths, maybe, drawn in to an invisible gravitational flame. We're still sifting through the data we're gathering,' he said softly. 'I wonder if any astronomers in human history have ever had such a rich sky to study ... even if it does mark the end of time.

'But we've found one anomaly, Lieserl.'

'An anomaly? Where?'

He raised his arm and pointed, towards an anonymous-looking patch of sky across the cavity. 'Over there. A source in the hydrogen radio band. As far as we can tell it's coming from a neutron star system – but the neutron star is moving with an immense velocity, not far below lightspeed. Anomalies all round, right? The source is difficult to pick out against all this galactic mush in the foreground. But it's undoubtedly there ...'

'What's so special about it?'

He hesitated. 'Lieserl, it seems to be a signal.'

'A *signal*? From who?'

'How should I know?'

'Maybe it's a freak; an artefact of our instruments.'

'Quite possibly. But we're thinking of checking it out anyway. It's only a million light-years away.' He smiled ruefully.
'That's all of eight hours' travel, if you hitch a ride on a
nightfighter ...'

A signal, here at the end of space and time ... Was it possible
the motley crew of the *Northern* wasn't alone after all?

The hair at the base of her skull prickled. At the end of this
long, long life, she'd thought there was nothing left to surprise
her.

Evidently, she was wrong.

Mark said, 'Lieserl, what you're looking at here is visible
light: the Virtual display we're drifting around inside is based
on images from right at the centre of the human visible
spectrum. You're seeing just what any of the others would see,
with their unaided vision. But the image has been enhanced by
blue shift: red, dim stars have been made to look blue and
bright.'

'I understand.'

Now the blue stain faded from the galaxy images, seeping out
like some poor dye.

A new colour flooded the galaxy remnants, but it was the colour of decay – dominated by flaring reds and crimsons, though
punctuated in places by the glaring blue-white of supernovae.
And without the enhancement offered by the blue shift, some of
the galaxies faded from her view altogether.

The galaxies had turned into ships of fire, she thought.

Mark's profile was picked out, now, in colours of blood. 'Take
a good look around, Lieserl,' he said grimly. 'I've adjusted out
the blue shift; this is how things *really* are.'

She looked at him curiously; his tone had become hostile,
suddenly. Though he still held her hand, his fingers felt stiff
around hers, like a cage. 'What are you saying?'

'Here's the result of the handiwork of your photino bird pets,'
he said. 'In the week since we arrived, we've been able to
catalogue over a *million* galaxies, surrounding this cavity. In
every one of those million we see stars being pushed off the
Main Sequence, either explosively as a nova or supernova or via

347

expansion into the red-giant cycle. Everywhere the stars are close to the end of their lifecycles – and, what's worse, there's no sign of new star formation, anywhere.'

Suddenly she understood. 'Ah. *This* is why you've set up this display for me. You're *testing* me, aren't you?' She felt anger build, deep in her belly. 'You want to know how all this makes me *feel*. Even now – even after we've been so close – you're still not sure if I'm fully *human*.'

He grinned, his red-lit teeth like drops of blood in his mouth. 'You have to admit you've had a pretty unusual life history, Lieserl. I'm not sure if any of us can empathize with you.'

'Then,' she snapped, 'maybe you should damn well try. Maybe that's been the trouble with most of human history. Look at all this: we're witnessing, here, the death of *galaxies*. And you're wondering how it makes *me* feel? Do you think all this has somehow been set up as a test of my *loyalty* to the human race?'

'Lieserl –'

'I'll *tell* you how I feel. I feel we need a sense of perspective here, Mark. So what if this – this cosmic discontinuity – is *inconvenient* for the likes of you and me?' She withdrew from him and straightened her back. 'Mark, this is the greatest feat of cosmic engineering our poor Universe will ever see – the most significant event since the Big Bang. Maybe it's time we humans abandoned our species-specific chauvinism – our petty outrage that the Universe has unfolded in a way that doesn't suit us.'

He was smiling at her. 'Quite a speech.'

She punched him, reasonably gently, beneath the ribs, relishing the way her fist sank into his flesh. 'Well, you deserve it, damn it.'

'I didn't mean to imply –'

'Yes, you did,' she said sharply. 'Well, I'm sorry if I've failed your test, Mark. Look, you and I – by hook or by crook – have survived the decline and destruction of our species. I know we're going to have to fight for survival, and I'll be fighting right alongside you, as best I can. But that doesn't remove the *magnificence* of this cosmic engineering – any more than an ant-hill's destruction to make way for the building of a cathedral would despoil the grandeur of the result.'

Still holding her hand within his stiff fingers, he turned his face to the galaxy-stained sky. His offence at her words was tangible; he must be devoting a great deal of processing power to this sullen rebuke. 'Sometimes you're damn cold, Lieserl.'

Lethe, she thought. *People.* 'No,' she said. 'I just have a longer perspective than you.' She sighed. 'Oh, come on, Mark. Show me the Ring,' she said.

The sculpture of string, driving itself into the heart of the scarred galaxy, was not symmetrical. It was in the form of a rough figure-of-eight; but each lobe of the figure was overlaid with more complex waveforms – a series of ripples, culminating in sharp, pointed cusps.

'Do you see it, Spinner?' Mark asked. 'That is a loop of string nearly a thousand light-years wide.'

Spinner smiled. 'That's not a loop. That's a *knot*.'

'It's moving towards the galactic core at over half the speed of light. It's got the mass of a hundred billion stars ... Can you believe that? It's as massive as a medium-size galaxy itself. No wonder it's cutting this swathe through the stars; the damn thing's like a scythe, driving across the face of this galaxy.'

Louise laughed. '*A knot*. Knot-making is a skill, up there in the forest, isn't it, Spinner? I'll bet you'd have been proud to come up with a structure like that.'

'Actually,' Mark said, 'and I hate to be pedantic, but that *isn't* a knot, topologically speaking. If you could somehow stretch it out – straighten up the cusps and curves – you'd find it would deform into a simple loop. A circle.'

Spinner heard Garry Uvarov's rasp. 'And I hate to be a pedant, in my turn, but in fact a simple closed loop *is* a knot – called the trivial knot by topologists.'

'Thank you, Doctor,' Louise said drily.

Spinner frowned, peering at the detailed image of the string loop; in the false colours of her faceplate it was a tracery of blue, frozen against the remote background of the galaxy core. She realized now that she was looking at one projection of a complex three-dimensional object. Subvocally she called for a depth enhancement and change in perspective.

The loop seemed to loom towards her, lifting away from the starry background, and the string was thickened into a three-dimensional tubing, so that she could see shadows where one strand overlaid another.

The image rotated. It was like a sculpture of hosepipe, rolling over on itself.

Mark commented, 'But the string isn't stationary, of course. I mean, the whole loop is cutting through this galaxy at more than half lightspeed – but in addition the structure is in constant, complex motion. Cosmic string is under enormous tension – a tension that increases with curvature – and so those loops and cusps you see are struggling to straighten themselves out, all the time. Most of the length of the string is moving at close to lightspeed – indeed, the cusps are moving *at* lightspeed.'

'Absurd,' Spinner heard Uvarov growl. 'Nothing material can reach lightspeed.'

'True,' Mark said patiently, 'but cosmic string isn't truly *material*, in that sense, Uvarov. Remember, it's a defect in spacetime ... a flaw.'

Spinner watched the beautiful, sparkling construct turn over and over. It was like some intricate piece of jewellery, a filigree of glass, perhaps. How could something as complex, as *real* as this, be made of nothing but spacetime?

'I can't see it move,' she said slowly.

'What was that, Spinner?'

'Mark, if the string is moving at close to lightspeed – how come I can't *see* it? The thing should be writhing like some immense snake ...'

'You're forgetting the scale, Spinner-of-Rope,' Mark said gently. 'That loop is over a thousand light-years across. It would take *a millennium* for a strand of string to move across the diameter of the loop. Spinner, it *is* writhing through space, just as you say, but on timescales far beyond yours or mine ...

'But watch this.'

Suddenly the three-dimensional image of the string came to life. It twisted, its curves straightening or bunching into cusps, lengths of the string twisting over and around each other.

Mark said, 'This is the true motion of the string, projected from the velocity distribution along its length. The motion is actually periodic ... It resumes the same form every twenty thousand years or so. This graphic is running at billions of times true speed, of course – the twenty-millennia period is being covered in around five minutes.

'But the graphic is enough to show you an important feature of this motion. It's *non-intersecting* ... The string is not cutting itself at any point in the periodic trajectory. If it did, it would bud off smaller sub-loops, which would oscillate and cut themselves up further, and so on ... the string would rapidly decay, shrivelling through a thousand cuts, and leaking away its energy through gravitational radiation.'

Spinner wished, suddenly, that she wasn't *human*: that she could watch the motion of this loop unfold, without having to rely on Mark's gaudy projections. How wonderful it would be to be able to step out of time!

... Close your eyes, Spinner.

'What?'

You can step out of time, just as you desire. Close your eyes, and imagine you are a god.

... And here, in her mind's eye – so much more dramatic than any Virtual! – came the knot of string, sailing out of space. The knot wriggled like some huge worm, closed on itself as if swallowing its own tail.

The knot struck the rim of this defenceless galaxy and scythed towards the core, battering stars aside like blades of grass.

It was a disturbing, astonishing image. She snapped open her eyes, dispelling the vision; fear flooded her, prickling over her flesh.

She wasn't normally quite so imaginative, she thought drily. Maybe her *companion* had had something to do with that brief, vivid vision ...

She returned her attention to the harmless-looking Virtual display. Now Mark showed Spinner the loop's induced magnetic field, a yellow glow of energy which sleeved the fake blue of the string itself.

'As it hauls through the galaxy's magnetic field, that string is radiating a lot of electromagnetic energy,' Mark said. 'I see a *flood* of high-energy photons ...'

Cosmic string wasn't actually one-dimensional; it was a Planck length across, a fine tube containing charged particles: quarks, electrons and their antiparticles, gathered into superheavy clusters. As a result, string acted as a superconducting wire.

The string knot was cutting through this galaxy's magnetic field. As it did so immense electrical currents – of a hundred billion billion amps or more – were induced in the string. These currents generated strong magnetic fields around the string.

The string's induced field was stronger than a neutron star's, and dominated space for tens of light-years around the knot.

Mark said, 'The string has a maximum current capacity. If it's overloaded, the string starts to shed energy. It *glows* with gamma radiation. And the lost energy crystallizes into matter: ions and electrons, whispering into existence all along the length of the string.' Spinner saw representations of particles – out of scale, of course – popping into existence around the string image. 'So the string is glowing as brightly as a star.'

'Yes,' Louise put in. 'But the distribution of the radiation is odd, Mark. Look at this. The radiation is beamed *forward* of the loop's motion – parallel to that forward spike of gravitational radiation.'

'Like a searchlight,' Morrow said.

Or a spear . . . .

She heard Morrow saying, 'Mark, what is *driving* the string? What is impelling it through space, and into this galaxy?'

'Gravitational radiation,' Mark said simply.

Louise said, 'Morrow, gravity waves are emitted whenever large masses are moved through space. Because the loop is asymmetrical it's pushing out its gravitational radiation in particular directions – in spikes, ahead of and behind it. It is pushing out momentum . . . It is a *gravitational rocket*, using its radiation to drive through space.'

Mark said, 'Of course the gravitational radiation is carrying away energy – the string is shrinking, slowly. In the end it will collapse to nothing.'

'But not fast enough to save this galaxy,' Uvarov growled.

'No,' Louise said. 'Before it has time to decay away, the string is going to reach the core – and devastate the galaxy.'

Close your eyes.

Spinner-of-Rope shivered. Once again the voice had come from her left – from somewhere outside her suit. She stared at the Virtual image in her faceplate, not daring to look around.

*Close your eyes. Think about your vision again – of the string loop,
cutting through the stars. It frightened you, didn't it? What did that
image mean, Spinner-of-Rope? What was it telling you?*

Suddenly she saw it.

'Mark,' she said. 'This is *not* just a gravitational rocket.'

'What?'

'Think about it. The string knot must be a *missile*.'

The galaxy images dimmed, leaving Mark and Lieserl suspended in a crimson-tinged darkness. Then, against that
background, new forms began to appear: speckles of light,
indistinct, making up the ghostly outline of a *torus*, its face
tipped open towards her.

'Of course this is a false colour representation,' Mark said.
'The images have been reconstructed from gravity wave and
gamma ray emissions . . .'

The torus as a whole reminded her, distantly, of Saturn's
rings; it was a circle which spanned the galaxy-walled cavity.

At first she thought the component speckles were mere
points of light: they were like stars, she thought, or diamonds
scattered against the velvet backdrop of the faded galaxy light.
But as she looked more closely she could see that some of the
nearer objects were not simple points, but showed structure of
some kind.

So these weren't stars, she thought, and nor was this some
attenuated galaxy: there were only (she estimated quickly) a
few thousand of the shining forms, as opposed to the billions of
stars in a galaxy . . . And besides, this cavity-spanning torus was
immense: she could see how the blood-dark corpses of galaxies
sailed *through* its sparse structure.

She knew that the Galaxy of humans had been a disc of stars a
hundred thousand light-years in diameter. This torus must be
at least *a hundred times as broad* – more than ten million light-
years across.

She turned to Mark; he studied her face, a certain kindness
showing in his eyes now. 'I know how you're feeling. It's
magnificent, isn't it?'

'It can't be the Ring,' she said slowly. 'Can it? As far as we
know, Jim Bolder reported a solid object – a single, continuous
artefact.'

'Look more closely, Lieserl. Cheat a little; enhance your vision. What do you see?'

She turned her head and issued brisk subvocals. A section of the torus exploded towards her; the fragments, rushing apart, gave her a brief, disorienting impression of sudden velocity.

Her view steadied. Now, it was as if she was within the torus itself, and the sparkling component objects were all around her.

The fragments weren't simple discs – or ellipses, or any of the shapes into which a star or galaxy might be distorted by the presence of others. She could see darkness *within the heart* of these objects.

The fragments were *knots*.

'Mark –'

'You're looking at loops of cosmic string,' he said calmly. 'This immense torus is made up of string knots, Lieserl – ten thousand of them, each a thousand light-years across.'

She was aware of her hand convulsing closed around his. 'I don't understand. This is – fantastic. *But it isn't the Ring Bolder described.*'

He looked distant, wistful. 'But it *must* be. We know we've come to the right place, Lieserl. This is undoubtedly the site of the Great Attractor: the loops, together, have sufficient mass to cause the local streaming of galaxies.

'And we know this assemblage must be artificial. Primeval string loops could have formed during the formation of the Universe, after the singularity. But there should have been no more than a million of them – *in the entire Universe*, Lieserl – spaced tens of millions of light-years apart. It simply isn't possible for a collection of ten thousand of the damn things to have gathered spontaneously within a cavity a mere ten million light-years across . . .'

'But,' Lieserl said patiently, 'but Bolder said the Ring was solid. If he was right –'

'If he was right then the Ring has been destroyed, Lieserl. These loops are – rubble. We're looking at the wreckage of the Ring. The photino birds have won.' He turned to her, his face a sculpture, expressionless, obviously artificial. 'We're too late, Lieserl.'

She felt bewildered. 'But if that's true – where are we to go?'

Mark had no answer.

Louise said, 'What are you talking about, Spinner?'

'Can't you see it?' She closed her eyes and watched, once again, as the string loop punched through the fragile superstructure of the galaxy. 'Mark – Louise – this string loop was *aimed*, quite precisely. It's a weapon. It is blasting through this galaxy with its gravitational rockets, destroying all in its path with focused beams of electromagnetic and gravitational energy . . . '

Louise snapped, 'Mark?'

Mark hesitated. 'We can't prove she's right, Louise. But the chances of the loop hitting such a precise trajectory at random are tiny . . . '

'It seems crazy,' Morrow said. 'Who would *dare* use a thousand-light-year loop of cosmic string as a weapon of war?'

Uvarov grunted. 'Isn't that obvious? The very entities we have come all this way to seek, from whom we hope to obtain shelter – *the Xeelee*, Morrow; the baryonic lords.'

'But why?' Mark asked. 'Why destroy a galaxy like this?'

'In defence,' Uvarov snapped.

'What?'

'Isn't that clear too? The Xeelee were masters of the manipulation of spacetime. Their weaponry consisted of these immense structures of spacetime flaws. And the flaws have been used against the weapons of their enemies – *like this galaxy*.'

There was silence for a moment. Then Morrow said, 'Are you insane, Uvarov? You're saying that this *galaxy* has been hurled like some rock – deliberately?'

'Why not?' Uvarov replied calmly. 'The photino birds are creatures of dark matter – which attracts baryonic matter gravitationally. We can easily imagine some immense dark chariot hauling at this fragile galaxy, hurling it hard through space . . .

'Think of it. The photino birds must have begun to engineer the deflection of this galaxy's path many millions of years ago – perhaps they were intent on launching this huge missile at the Ring long before men walked on the Earth. And the Xeelee must have been preparing their counter, this loop of string, over almost as great a timescale.'

Now Spinner-of-Rope felt a bubble of laughter, wild, rise in her own throat. She had an absurd image of two giants,

355

bestriding the curving Universe, hurling galaxies and string loops at each other like lumps of mud.

'We are truly in the middle of a war zone,' Uvarov said coldly. 'This galaxy, with the bullet of cosmic string aimed so accurately at its heart, is merely one incident among ten million in a huge battlefield. To our fleeting perceptions the field is frozen in time – we buzz like flies around the bullet as it hurtles *into* the chest of its target – and yet the battle rages all around us.'

Don't be afraid.

Spinner closed her eyes and thought of the forest dream man, smiling at her from his tree and eating his fruit . . .

I know who this is, she realized suddenly. *I've seen his face, in Louise's old Virtuals . . .*

'I know you,' she told him.

Yes. Don't be afraid, said Michael Poole.

28

Louise Armonk asked Spinner to take the nightfighter to the source of Mark's anomalous hydrogen-band signal.

She showed Spinner some data on the signal. 'Here's a graphic of the main sequence, Spinner-of-Rope.' A barchart, in gaudy yellow and blue, marched across Spinner's faceplate. 'We're getting pretty excited about this. For one thing it's periodic – the same pattern recurs every two hours or so. So we're pretty sure it has to be artificial. And look at *this*,' Louise said. A sequence of thirty bars, buried among the rest, was now highlighted with electric blue. 'Can you see that?'

Spinner looked at the ascending sequence of bars, trying hard to share Louise's excitement. 'What am I looking for, Louise?'

She heard Louise growl with impatience. 'Spinner, the amplitude of these pulses is increasing, *in proportion with the first thirty prime numbers.*'

The electric-blue bars were split into discrete blocks, now, to help Spinner see the pattern. She counted the blocks: one, two, three, five, seven . . .

She sensed an invisible smile. *Just like a child's puzzle, isn't it?*

'Oh, shut up,' she said easily.

'What was that?'

'Nothing . . . I'm sorry, Louise. Yes, I see it now.'

'Look – what's exciting about finding this sequence of primes is that it means the signal is almost certainly *human.*'

'How do you know that, just from this pattern?'

'We don't know for sure, of course,' Louise said impatiently. 'But it's a damn good clue, Spinner-of-Rope. We've reason to believe the prime numbers are of unique significance to humans.

'The primes are fundamental structures of arithmetic – at least, of the discrete arithmetic which seems to come naturally to humans. We are compact, discrete creatures: I'm here, you are out there somewhere. One, two. Counting like this seems to be natural to us, and so we tend to think it's a fundamental facet of the Universe. But it's possible to imagine other types of mathematics.

'What of creatures like the Qax, who were diffuse creatures, with no precise boundaries between individuals? What of the Squeem, with their group minds? Why should simple counting be *natural* to them? Perhaps *their* earliest forms of mathematics were continuous – or perhaps the study of infinities came naturally to them, as naturally as arithmetic to humans. With us, Cantor's hierarchy of infinities was quite a late development. And –'

Spinner barely listened. *Humans? Here, at the edge of time and space?* 'Louise, have you decoded any of the rest of it?'

'Well, we can figure some of it out,' Louise said defensively. 'We think, anyway. But remember, Spinner, we may be dealing with humans from a culture far removed in time from our own – by millions of years, perhaps. The people of such a distant future could be almost as remote from *us* as an alien species. Not even Lieserl has been able to help us work this out . . .'

'But you've made some progress. Right?'

Louise hesitated. 'Yes. We think it's a distress call.'

'Oh, great. Well, we're certainly in a position to help out god-humans from five million years after our birth.'

'Who knows?' Louise said drily. 'Maybe we are. Anyway, that's what we're going to find out.'

. . . There was motion at Spinner's left. She turned.

Suddenly, the forest-dream man was *visible*. He was sitting there, quite casually – *outside* the cage – on the construction-material shoulder of the nightfighter. He wore no environment suit, nothing but a plain grey coverall. His hands were folded in his lap. Light – from some unseen source – caught the lines around his mouth, the marks of tiredness in his eyes.

At last he had emerged. Gently, he nodded to her.

She smiled.

'. . . Spinner?'

'I'm here, Louise.' She tried to focus her attention on her tasks; she reached for the hyperdrive waldo. 'Are you ready?'

'Yes.'

*　　*　　*

The nightfighter flickered through hyperspace. Travelling at more than a hundred thousand light-years per hour, the *Northern* edged around the torus of fragmented string loops, like a fly around the rim of a desert.

The journey took ten hours. As it neared its end Spinner-of-Rope took a brief nap; when she woke, she had her suit's systems freshen her skin, and she emptied her bladder.

She checked a display on her faceplate. Twenty jumps to go. Twenty more seconds, and –

Something vibrant-blue exploded out of space at her, ballooning into her face.

She cried out and buried her faceplate in her arms.

It's all right, Poole said softly.

'I'm sorry, Spinner-of-Rope,' Louise Armonk said. 'I should have warned you ...'

Spinner lowered her arms, cautiously.

There was *string*, everywhere.

A tangle of cosmic string, rendered electric blue by the faceplate's false colouring, lay directly ahead of the ship. Cusps, moving at lightspeed, glittered along the twisted lengths. She leaned forward and looked up and down, to left and right; the threads of string criss-crossed the sky as far as she could see, a textured wall across space. Looking deeper into the immense structure, Spinner saw how the individual threads blurred together, merging into a soft mist at infinity.

The string loop was a barrier across the sky, dividing the Universe in two. It was quite beautiful, she thought – but *deadly*. It was a cosmic web, with threads long enough to span the distances between stars: a web, ready to trap her and her ship.

And, she knew, this was just one thousand-light-year fragment, among thousands in the torus ...

'Lethe,' she said. 'We're almost *inside* this damn thing.'

'Not quite,' Louise said. Her voice, nevertheless, was tight, betraying her own nervousness. 'Remember your distance scales, Spinner. The string loops in this toroidal system are around a thousand light-years across. We're as far from the edge of that loop as the Sun was from the nearest star.'

'Except,' Mark Wu cut in, 'that the loop *has* no easily definable edge. It's a tangle. Cosmic string is damn hard to detect; the display you're looking at, Spinner, is all Virtual reconstruction;

it's just our best guess at what lies out there.'

'Then are we at risk by being here?' Spinner asked.

Of course, Michael Poole said.

'No,' Louise said.

'Yes,' Mark said. 'Come on, Louise. Spinner, we're working to minimize the risks. But the danger is there. Spinner, you need to be ready to react – to get us out of here, quickly. We have escape routines laid into the waldoes, for both hyperdrive and discontinuity drive.'

'I'll be ready,' she said calmly. 'But *why* are we here? Is the human signal coming from somewhere in there – inside the string?'

'No,' Louise said. 'Thankfully. Spinner, the signal is coming from the system of a neutron star – just a few light-hours away from here. We've laid in –'

'– a discontinuity-drive sequence into the waldoes,' Spinner said drily. 'I know.' She reached for her controls. 'Tell me when you're ready, Louise.'

Poole looked tired, his brown eyes deep in a mesh of wrinkles. *You know, I worked with Louise Armonk,* he said. He smiled. *And here we are, together again. Small world, isn't it? She was a good engineer. I guess she still is.*

'I know you decided to close your wormhole time bridge,' Spinner said. 'Tell me what happened to you.'

Poole sat, apparently relaxed, on the 'fighter shoulder; his eyes were closed, his head bent forward. *I remember the lifedome of my GUTship entering the Interface,* he said slowly. *There was light – like fire, blue-violet – from all around the lip of the dome. I knew that was the flesh of the Spline, burning up against the Interface's exotic-matter framework. I remember – a sense of loss, of alienation.*

'Loss?'

I was passing out of my time frame. Spinner-of-Rope, each of us – (he raised translucent hands) *– even I – is bound into the world by quantum functions. I was linked non-locally to everything I had touched, seen, tasted … Now, all those quantum bonds were broken. I was as alone as any human had ever been.*

I engaged the hyperdrive.

Bits of the wormhole seemed to fall away. I remember streams of blue-white light ... I almost believed I could feel those hard photons, sleeting through the lifedome.

Spacetime is riddled with wormholes: it is like a sheet of flawed glass, crazed by cracks. When Poole set off his hyperdrive inside the wormhole, it was as if someone had smashed at that flawed glass with a hammer. Cracks exploded out from the point of impact and widened; they joined up in a complex, spreading network of cracks, a tributary pattern that continually formed and reformed as spacetime healed and shattered anew.

The spacetime cracks opened up like branching tunnels, leading off to infinity ... Poole smiled, self-deprecating. *I started to wonder if this had been a good plan, after all.*

The pod sailed down from the *Northern*'s lifedome.

Lieserl sat in a Virtual projection of a pod couch beside Mark Wu; ahead of them blind Uvarov was swathed in his blankets, his cavern of a mouth gaping, his breath a rattle. The huge discontinuity-drive wings of the nightfighter spread over the pod like the vaulted roof of some immense church.

Far below the pod revolved the bleak, airless planet to which they were descending. Staring down as the small island of solidity loomed out of the glowing fog, Lieserl had a sudden – and quite absurd – feeling of vertigo. She felt as if she were suspended, in this couch, without protection far above the planet's surface; she had an impulse, which she suppressed with determination, to grip the sides of her couch.

Vertigo ... After all her experiences inside the Sun, and despite her perfect knowledge that she couldn't be harmed even if the pod exploded here and now – since she was little more than a Virtual projection from the *Northern*'s main processors, with augmentation from the pod's processor banks – after all that, she had vertigo.

Still, she thought, it was comforting to know that she'd retained enough humanity to be just a *little* scared. Maybe she should tell Mark; it might make him think a little better of her.

Beyond the pod's clear hull, the neutron star system was a huge tableau all around them.

The neutron star itself was a tiny, fierce yellow-red ball. It had a companion – a normal star – and it was surrounded by a ring of gas, which glowed softly. And there were several planets, orbiting the neutron star, inside the smoke ring.

In fact, the anomalous signal was coming from one of the planets, the little world towards which Lieserl was now descending.

The nightfighter had dropped them *into* the ring of smoke which orbited the star. It was like descending into fog. Close to the pod Lieserl could see dense swirls of the ring gas – clumps and eddies of turbulent stuff – and, beyond that, the rest of the ring was a band of pale light bisecting the Universe. She could see the neutron star itself, a small, hard coal glowing yellow-red at the heart of this ring of smoke. Beside it hung its companion star – huge, pale, distorted into a squat egg-shape by the neutron star's fierce gravitational field. Tendrils of gas led from the carcass of the companion and reached blindly towards the neutron star.

And beyond *that*, tilted crazily compared to the gas torus, was a starbow.

This neutron star was moving with extraordinary speed: it plummeted across space at close to the speed of light. As a result of this high velocity, the neutron star and its system were the only visible objects in Lieserl's Universe. *All* of the rest – the blue-shifted galaxies, the nearby wall of cosmic string – was compressed into that pale starbow, a band of light around the equator of the star's motion. And away from the starbow, there was only darkness.

Uvarov tilted his head, and the pod's internal lights cast shadows across his imploded eye-sockets. 'Tell me what you see,' he hissed.

'I see a neutron star,' Mark said. 'An unexceptional member of its species. Just ten miles across, but with a mass not much less than Sol's ... What has made this one unusual is the fact that it has a companion, which is – was – a normal star.'

Before Mark, a Virtual diorama of the neutron star system glittered into existence; the globes of the neutron star and its companion were criss-crossed by lines of false colour, showing – Lieserl suspected – gravitational gradients, lines of magnetic flux, and other observables. Bits of text and subsidiary graphics drifted in the air beside the glowing objects.

'Once,' Mark said, 'these stars were a binary pair – a

spectacular one, since the neutron star must have been a brilliant giant. Somehow, the companion survived the giant's supernova explosion. But the remnant of that explosion – the neutron star – is killing its companion, just the same.' He pointed. 'The neutron star's gravity well is sucking out material from the companion . . . Look at it, Lieserl; those delicate-looking tendrils of smoke could swallow Jupiter. Some of the companion's lost matter is falling onto the neutron star itself. And as the mass down there increases, the rotation of the neutron star will glitch – the neutron star must suffer starquakes, quite regularly. The rest of the gas is drifting off to form this ring we're in, orbiting the neutron star.'

'Do you think the birds caused the supernova explosion, Mark?' Lieserl asked.

He shook his head. 'No. The system is too stable . . . I think the explosion took place long before the birds took an interest.'

'And the companion?'

He smiled, peering up at the complex sky. 'Lieserl, that is one star the birds don't *need* to kill. The neutron star is doing their work for them.'

The Virtual representation of the neutron star expanded before his face, expelling the companion and the other features from the diorama. Mark peered into a complex knot of light at what looked like one of the star's magnetic poles.

Lieserl looked away. The planet wasn't far below, now; slowly it was turning from a ball of rock, suspended in emptiness, into a landscape – bare, bleak, riven by cracks.

'What about the planets?' Lieserl asked. 'How could *they* have survived the supernova?'

'My guess is they didn't,' Mark said, still staring at the star's pole. 'I think they probably formed *after* the explosion: coalesced from material in the gas ring, and from debris left over from the explosion itself – maybe from the previous planetary system, if there was one . . . *Lieserl*. Lethe. Look at this.'

'What?'

The neutron star Virtual representation swept across the cabin towards her; the little knot of light at the pole was thrust in her face. Lieserl flinched, but stared gamely into the glowing, complex image.

Mark was grinning, his voice animated by excitement. 'Do you see it?'

'Yes, Mark,' she said patiently, 'but you're going to have to tell me *what* I'm seeing.'

'There's a major disturbance in the gravitational gradients at that magnetic pole.' Arrows clustered around the star's pole, forming themselves into a two-dimensional plane. 'Can you see it?'

'What about it?'

Mark sounded impatient. 'Lieserl, I think there's a sheet discontinuity down there. A two-dimensional defect. *A domain wall*, inside the star ...'

Lieserl frowned. 'That's impossible.'

'Of course it is.' He grinned. 'How could a domain-wall defect form within the structure of a neutron star? Impossible ... unless it's been put there.'

Uvarov's ruined mouth stretched into a smile. '*Put* there?'

'We wondered how come this neutron star was out here on its own – away from any galaxy, and moving so bloody fast. Well, now we know.'

Lieserl found herself laughing. 'This is *outrageous*. Are you suggesting –'

'Yes,' he said seriously. 'I think someone, maybe human, installed a discontinuity drive at the magnetic pole of this neutron star, and used it to hurl the whole system across space at close to lightspeed.'

'But that's absurd,' she said. 'Why should anyone *do* such a thing?'

Now Uvarov laughed, at her. 'Still the rationalist, Lieserl, after all our experiences? Well, perhaps we will soon learn the answer to such questions. But of this I'm sure – that it has some connection to this endless, bloody war in Heaven we've wandered into.'

The pod's descent bottomed out, now, and the little ship sailed over the planet's battered landscape.

At length, Mark said, 'We're over the source of the signals ... *There*,' he said suddenly. 'Can you see it?'

Uvarov tilted his head on its thin neck.

Lieserl peered down.

'A structure,' Mark said. 'There on the surface ... Some kind of building. Come on; I'll take us down.'

I fell into the future, Spinner-of-Rope, through a network of transient wormholes that collapsed after me. My instruments were smashed, but I knew my lifedome must have been awash with high-energy particles and gravity waves. I was as helpless as a new-born babe.

Poole sat in raw vacuum on the shoulder of the nightfighter with his legs tucked beneath him, lotus-style, his hands resting comfortably, palms-up, on his knees. Spinner could see a grooved pattern, moulded mundanely into the soles of his shoes.

He said, *I fell across five million years ...*

Mark Wu – or rather, one of his Virtual consciousness foci, on the *Northern* – peered at the loop of cosmic string through the hundred eyes of the ship's sensors. He wasn't happy: his multi-faceted view was muddy, imprecise.

The trouble was, the ship was in orbit around this damn neutron star planet, which was falling through space so fast the observable Universe was relativity-shifted into a skinny, pale starbow. It was like being taken back to the *Northern*'s thousand-year flight. Mark had to deconvolve out the effects of the near-lightspeed motion: to unsmear the Universe back out of the starbow once more.

Mark had subroutines to achieve this. But it was, he thought uneasily, a little like unscrambling an egg. The resulting images weren't exactly *clear*.

Inside his box of processors, Mark Wu worked on nanosecond timescales. He could process data at several millions of times the rate achievable by humans, and it sometimes took an effort of will to come back out of there and return to the glutinous slowness of the human world.

It was seven centuries since his physical death and downloading into the AI banks of the *Northern*, and he'd steadily got more proficient at non-human operation. Right now, for instance, he was maintaining a conventional human-Virtual on the pod with Lieserl and Uvarov, and another with Louise in the *Great Britain*, in parallel with his direct interfacing with the *Northern*'s systems.

Running these multiple consciousness foci felt odd, but he'd grown used to enduring minor discomforts when the need arose.

And there was need now.

Maybe he should have tried to veto this trip to the neutron star, he thought. It had brought the *Northern* close – too damn close – to this loop-cloud of cosmic string. When dealing with an object a thousand light-years across, he thought sourly, a separation of a mere handful of light-years didn't seem nearly sufficient.

Mark split off a series of more subordinate foci, and set to scanning overlapping sectors of the sky.

His image of the Universe was a mosaic, constructed of the fragments supplied to him by the sensors; he imagined it was a little like looking out through the multi-faceted eyes of a fly. And the Universe was criss-crossed, *everywhere*, by string double-image paths – it was as if the sky were some huge dome of glass, he thought, marred by huge cracks.

By studying the double images of stars and galaxies, Mark was able to check on the near-lightspeed velocities of the string segments; he constantly updated the internal model he maintained of the local string dynamics, trying to ensure the ship stayed a safe distance away from –

A watchful subroutine sounded an alarm. It felt to Mark like a prickling of vague unease, a shiver.

. . . *There was movement*, in the field of view of one sensor bank. He swivelled his consciousness, fixing most of his attention on the anomaly picked up by that sensor bank.

Against a background provided by a beautiful, blue-stained spiral galaxy, he saw a *double* track of multiple stellar images.

There had to be *two* lengths of string there, he realized: two arcs of this single, huge loop of string, no more than light-hours apart. And he could see from the melting flow of the star images that the arcs were sliding past each other in opposite directions; maybe eventually they would intersect.

In some places there were *three* images of single stars. Light from each of those stars was reaching him by three routes – to the left of the string pair, to their right, and straight through the middle of the strings.

The cause of the alert was obvious. All along the double tracks, he saw, star images were sliding, as if slipping across melting spacetime. These strings must be *close* – maybe even within the two-light-year limit he'd imposed on himself as a rough safety margin.

He ran a quick double-check on the routines he'd set up to monitor the strings' distance from the ship. He wondered if he ought to tell Louise and Spinner about this . . .

Now, suddenly, alarm routines shrieked warnings into his awareness. It was like being plunged into an instant panic; he felt as if adrenaline were flooding his system.

What in Lethe –

He interrogated his routines, briskly and concisely. It took only nanoseconds to figure out what was wrong.

The pair of string arcs were closer than he'd thought at first. His distance-estimation routines had been thrown by the interaction of the two strings, by the way the pair jointly distorted star images.

So the strings were closer than his monitoring systems had told him. The trouble was, he couldn't tell how close; maybe they were a *lot* closer.

Damn, damn. I should have anticipated this. Feverishly he set off a reprogramming routine, ensuring that for the future he wouldn't be fooled by multiple images from pairs of string lengths like this – or, indeed, from any combination.

But that wasn't going to help now.

He ran through a quick hack procedure, trying to get a first-cut estimate of the strings' true distance . . .

He didn't believe the answer. He modified the procedure and ran it again.

The answer didn't change.

Well, so much for my two-light-year safety zone.

The string pair was only around ten million miles from the *Northern* – less than a light-minute.

One of the pair of strings was receding – but the other was heading straight for the ship.

He ran more checks. There was no error.

In fifty seconds, that encroaching string would hit the *Northern*.

He burst out of the machinery and back into the world of

humans. With impatience he waited for pixels to congeal out of
the air, for his face to reassemble; he felt his awareness slow
down to the crawl of humans.

29

Five million years after the first conflict between humans and
Qax, the wreckage of a Spline warship had emerged, tumbling,
from the mouth of a wormhole that blazed with gravitational
radiation. The wormhole closed, sparkling.

The wreck – dark, almost bereft of energy – turned slowly in
the stillness. It was empty of life.

Almost.

*I'm still not sure how I survived. But I remember – I remember how
the quantum functions came flooding over me. They were like
rain-drops; it was as if I could see them, Spinner-of-Rope. It was
painful. But it was like being born again. I was restored to time.*

It hadn't taken Poole long to check out the status of the
derelict his craft had become. There had been power in the
lifedome's internal cells, sufficient for a few hours, perhaps. But
he had no motive power – not even a functioning data link out
of the lifedome to the rest of his ship.

*I remember how dead the Universe looked. I couldn't understand
how the stars had got so old, so quickly; I knew I couldn't have fallen
more than a few million years.*

But I knew I was alone. I could feel it.

I made myself a meal. I drank a glass of clear water . . . His face,
softly translucent, was thoughtful. *Do you know, I can remember
the taste of that water even now. I had a shower . . . I was thinking of
reading a book.*

But the lights went out.

*I felt my way back to my couch. I lay there. It started getting colder.
I wasn't afraid of death, Spinner-of-Rope. Strangely, I felt renewed.*

'But you didn't die,' she said. 'Did you, Michael?'

No. No, I didn't die, said Poole.

And then, a ship had come.

Poole, dying, had stared up in wonder.

369

It was something like a sycamore seed wrought in jet-black. Night-dark wings that spanned hundreds of miles loomed over the wreck of Poole's GUTship, softly rippling.

'A nightfighter,' Spinner breathed.

Yes. I got colder. I couldn't breathe. But now I didn't want to die. I wanted to live just a little longer – to understand what this meant.

And then –

'Yes?'

And then, something had plucked Poole from the wreck. It was as if a giant hand had cupped his consciousness, like taking a flame from a guttering candle.

And then it spun me out . . .

Poole had become discorporeal. He no longer even had a heartbeat.

He felt as if he had been released from the cave of bone that had been his head.

I believe I became a construct of quantum functions, he said. *A tapestry of acausal and nonlocal effects . . . I don't pretend to understand it. And my companion was still there. It was like a huge ceiling over me.*

'What was it?'

Perhaps it was Xeelee. Or perhaps not. It seemed to be beyond even the Xeelee – a construct by them, perhaps, but not of them . . .

Spinner-of-Rope, the Xeelee were – are – masters of space and time. I believe they have even travelled back through time – modified their own evolutionary history – to achieve their huge goals. I think my companion was something to do with that programme: an anti-Xeelee, perhaps, like an anti-particle, moving backwards in time.

I sensed – amusement, Poole said slowly. *It was amused by my fear, my wonder, my longing to survive.* She heard the faded ghost of bitterness in his voice.

After a time, it dissolved. I was left alone. And, Spinner, I found I could not die.

At first, I was angry. I was in despair. He held up his glowing hand and inspected it thoughtfully, turning it round before his face. *I couldn't understand why this had been done to me – why I'd been preserved in this grotesque way.*

But – with time – that passed. And I had time: plenty of it . . .

He fell silent, and she watched his face. It was blank, expressionless; she felt a prickle of fear, and wondered what experiences he had undergone, alone between the dying stars.

'Michael,' she said gently. 'Why did you speak to me?'

His bleak expression dissolved, and he smiled at her. *I saw a human being*, he said. *A man, dressed in skins, frost-bitten, in a fragile little ship ... He came plunging through a wormhole Interface, uncontrolled, into this hostile future.*

It was an extraordinary event ... So I – returned. I was curious. I probed at the wormhole links – and found you, Spinner-of-Rope.

Spinner nodded. 'He was Arrow Maker. He was my father,' she said.

Michael Poole closed his eyes.

'...Spinner-of-Rope,' Louise Armonk said. She sounded urgent, concerned.

'Yes, Louise.'

'I don't know what in Lethe is happening in that head of yours, but you'd better get it clear fast.' Spinner heard Louise issue commands over her shoulder. '... We've got a problem.'

'What kind of problem?'

'Listen to me, Spinner. Here's what you must –'

Louise's voice died, abruptly.

'Louise? Louise?'

There was only silence.

Spinner twisted in her couch. Behind her, the bulk of the lifedome loomed over the clean lines of the nightfighter, a wall of glass and steady light.

But now a soft webbing, a mesh of barely visible threads, lay over the upper levels of the lifedome.

'Lethe,' Spinner hissed. 'That's *string*.'

For the first time in several years, the Decks were filled with the wail of the klaxon.

Morrow, hovering in the green-tinged air close to Deck Two, straightened from his work. His back ached pleasurably, and there was warm dirt and water on his hands; he felt a fine slick of sweat on his forehead.

He looked around vaguely, seeking the source of the alarm.

Milpitas, his sleeves rolled up and the deep scars of his face running with sweat, studied him. The Planner fingered a handful of reeds which protruded from the spherical pond. 'Morrow? Is something wrong? Why the klaxon?'

371

'I don't know, Planner.'

The sound of the klaxon was deafening – at once familiar and jarring, making it hard to think. Morrow looked around the Decks, at the tranquil, three-dimensional motion of people and 'bots as they went about their business; in the distance the shoulders of the Temples loomed over the grass-covered surfaces. It all looked normal, placid; he felt relaxed and safe.

Morrow was working with Milpitas within what had once been Poole Park. They were still trying to establish their zero-gee water feature. Milpitas and Morrow had set a ball of earth on a fine pole, attached it to the Deck surface, and surrounded it with a globe of water five feet across, restrained by a fine skin of porous plastic. Reeds and lilies were planted in the ball of earth, and were already growing out of the water surface. Their vision was that the reeds and lilies – perhaps plaited in some way – together with the water's natural surface tension would eventually suffice to hold the pond together, and they could abandon the plastic membrane.

Then, at last, they could populate the pond, with fish and frogs.

It was a small, almost trivial project. But it had actually been Milpitas' idea, and Morrow had been glad to offer to work on it with him, as part of what he thought of as Milpitas' rehabilitation to zero-gee. Anything that got the Planner – and those he influenced – thinking and working in zero-gee conditions was a good thing, in Morrow's view.

'Morrow.' Louise Armonk's voice emerged from a point in the air. It was loud, urgent in his ear. '*Morrow*. Can you hear me?'

Morrow looked down to the grass-coated floor of the Deck; he knew that Louise was somewhere below his floor in her old steam-ship, studying the neutron star system. 'What is it, Louise?'

'Morrow, you have to get away from there.'

'But, Louise –'

'*Move*, damn it. *Anywhere*.'

Milpitas was studying him. 'Well? *Is* there a problem?'

'Milpitas. *Come*.'

Morrow grabbed the Planner's robe at the shoulder. He flexed his knees, planted his feet squarely against the Deck surface, and pushed himself into the air, dragging Milpitas after him. Looking down, he saw the spherical pond recede below them.

Air resistance brought them to a stop in mid-air, five yards above the Deck surface.

Morrow released the Planner. Milpitas' arms were still wet to the elbow, and his bony legs protruded from beneath his robe.

'Louise? All right, we've moved. *Now* will you tell me what's wrong?'

'We're in trouble.' Morrow heard panicky shouting behind Louise's voice, and flat, even commands being issued by Mark. 'We're in the path of a section of string ... If our projections are correct, it's going to pass right through Poole Park.'

Morrow stared around at the Decks. Suddenly the metal walls of this place, coated with plants and people, seemed impossibly fragile. 'But how can that be? I thought that loop was light-years away.'

'So did we, Morrow. We're trying to confirm the string's trajectory so we can program the discontinuity-drive waldoes, and –'

But Louise's voice was gone.

Lieserl and Mark stood on the surface of the neutron star planet, in Virtual mockups of environment suits. They looked at each other uncertainly.

'Something's wrong,' Lieserl said.

'I know.' Through his sketch of a faceplate, Mark's expression was lifeless, cold; Lieserl knew that meant he was diverting processing power to higher priorities.

The surface under Lieserl's feet was pumice-grey and looked friable. Beside them, waiting patiently, was a 'bot, a fat-wheeled trolley fitted with a few articulated arms and sensors. The dust of the planet had smeared the 'bot's wheels with grey, Lieserl saw.

A few yards away their pod was a fat, gleaming cylinder; within the pod's clear walls Lieserl could see Uvarov, wrapped in his blanket.

The sky was fantastic. The gas ring was a belt of smoke which encompassed the world, all the way to the horizon. The far side of the ring was a pale strip of white, bisecting the sky. She could just make out the neutron star itself, a tiny, baleful blood-pearl threaded onto the line of smoke; and its huge companion was an attenuated ball of yellow-grey mist, bleeding gas onto its malevolent twin.

The starbow was a crack across the emptiness away from the plane of the ring; high above her head, Lieserl could see the gleaming lights of the *Northern*'s lifedome, in the ship's remote orbit around the planet.

The building they had detected from orbit was a tetrahedron, twenty feet tall, sitting impassively on the surface.

Lieserl felt frustrated. Had they come so far, approached this astonishing mystery, so closely, only for their comms links to fail?

She tapped her helmet. 'I feel as if I've gone deaf,' she said.

'Me too.' Mark smiled thinly, some of the expression returning to the waxy image of his face. 'Well, we've certainly lost the voice links from the *Northern*.' He looked up uneasily. 'I wonder what in Lethe is happening up there.'

'Maybe they are trying to recall us.'

Mark shrugged. 'Or maybe not.' He looked at her. 'Lieserl, do you *feel* any different? As far as I can tell the links to the central processors back on the *Northern* are still functioning – although I'm working read-only at the moment.'

She closed her eyes and looked inwards. 'Yes. It's the same for me.' Read-only meant she couldn't pass her impressions – the new memories she was laying down – back to the processors on the *Northern* which were now the core of her awareness. She looked up at the *Northern*'s steady yellow light. 'Do you think we should go back?'

Mark hesitated, looking back at the pod.

Uvarov stirred, like an insect in some glass cocoon, Lieserl thought. 'I'm the only one of us who's in genuine danger here,' he rasped. 'The two of you are just projections. Virtual phantasms. You are only wearing those damn suits as crutches for your psyches, in Lethe's name. Even if this planet exploded now, all you'd lose would be a few hours of *data input*.' He snarled the last words like an insult.

'What's your point, Uvarov?' Mark said.

'Get on with your search,' Uvarov snapped. 'Stop wasting time. There is nothing you can do about whatever problems are occurring at the *Northern*. For Life's sake, look at the bigger picture. The baryonic Universe is coming to an end. What can happen to make things worse than that?'

Mark laughed, a little grimly. 'All right, Doctor. Come on, Lieserl.'

They trudged over the surface towards the structure.

The klaxon died. The sudden silence was shocking.

Morrow tapped his ear – he thought self-deprecatingly, as if *that* would restore the Virtual projection of Louise's voice.

Milpitas had left his side. With surprising agility the Planner had *swum* down through the air, away from Morrow and back towards the pond.

There was a grind of metal, high above him.

He heard a single scream – an unearthly sound that echoed from the walls, rattling through the silence of the Decks. And now there was another scream – but this time, Morrow realized, it was the product of no human voice; the shriek was of air escaping from a breached hull.

He peered up into the shining air, looking for the breach.

There. Against one wall, mist was gathering over a straight-line gash which sliced through a field of dwarf wheat. A literacy-recovery class had been working there; now, people scrambled through the air, away from the billowing fog, screaming.

He heard Milpitas grunt. Morrow looked down.

Milpitas stared down at his midriff and clasped his hands over his belly. His scarred face was creased into an expression of disapproving surprise, and – in that final instant – Morrow was reminded of Planner Milpitas as he had once been: tough-minded, controlling, forcing the world to bend to his will.

Then Milpitas folded forward, around a line just below his solar plexus. For the first fraction of a second it looked as if he were doubling over in pain – but, Morrow saw with mounting horror, *Milpitas kept on folding*, bending until Morrow could hear the crackle of crushed ribs, the deeper snap of vertebrae.

There was nothing visible, nobody near Milpitas; it was as if he were inflicting this unimaginable horror on himself, or as if the Planner's body had been crumpled in some huge, transparent fist.

Then, it seemed that that same huge fist – powerful, irresist-
ible, invisible – grabbed Morrow himself and hurled him down
towards the Deck.

He screamed and wrapped his arms around his head.

He smashed into the spherical pond, so lovingly constructed
by himself and Milpitas. Reeds and lilies slapped at his face and
arms, and brackish water forced itself into his eyes and mouth.

Then he was through the pond, and the Deck surface hurtled
up to meet him, unimaginably hard.

The tetrahedron was liberally coated with dust. Mark had the
'bot roll forward and wipe the building's surface, tentatively.
Beneath a half-inch thickness of the dust, the material of the
tetrahedron's construction was milky-white, seamless. The triangular faces gave the structure the look of something flimsy, or
temporary, Lieserl thought – like a tent of cloth.

It had been Mark's suggestion for them to approach this
structure in human form. 'We want to know – among other
things – if *people* built this thing, and why,' he had argued. 'How
else are we going to get a genuine feel for the place, unless we
look at it through human eyes?' Lieserl hadn't been sure. To
restrict themselves to human form – more than was necessary to
interface with Uvarov – had seemed inefficient. But, staring at
the structure now, Lieserl realized what a good idea it had been.

'It's a tetrahedron,' Lieserl observed. 'Like an Interface
portal.'

'Well, that's a characteristic signature of human architecture,'
Mark murmured. 'Doesn't mean a thing, by itself, though. And
from the thickness of that dust, I guess we know this place has
been abandoned for a long time.'

'Hmm. The door looks human enough.'

The door was a simple hatchway seven feet tall and three
wide, set at the base of one of the tetrahedron's triangular walls.
There was a touchpad control, set at the waist height of an
average human.

Mark shrugged. 'Let's try to open it.'

The 'bot rolled forward silently, bouncing a little on the
rough surface despite its fat, soft wheels. It extended an arm
fitted with a crude mechanical grab, tapped cautiously at the
door, and then pushed at the control pad.

The door slid aside, into the fabric of the tetrahedron. A puff of air gushed out at them. A few scraps of dust tumbled out, and, when the air had dispersed, the dust fell in neat parabolae to the surface.

Beyond the door there was a small rectangular chamber, big enough for four or five people. The walls were of the same milky substance as the outer shell, and were unadorned. There was another door, identical to the first, set into the far wall of the chamber.

'At least we know there's still power,' Mark said.

'This is an airlock,' Lieserl said, looking inside the little chamber. 'Plain, functional. Very conventional. Well, what now? Do we go in?'

Mark pointed.

The 'bot was already rolling into the airlock. It bumped over the lip, and came to a halt at the centre of the lock.

Lieserl and Mark hesitated for a few seconds; the 'bot waited patiently inside the lock.

Mark grinned. 'Evidently, we go in!'

He held out his arm to Lieserl. Arm in arm, they trooped after the robot into the lock.

The lock, containing the 'bot and the two of them, was a little cramped. Lieserl found herself shying away from the 'bot's huge, dusty wheels, as if she might get her environment suit smeared.

The 'bot reached out and pushed the control to open the next door. There was a hiss of pressure equalization.

The 'bot exposed an array of chemical sensors, and Mark cracked open his faceplate and sniffed elaborately.

'Oh, stop showing off,' Lieserl said.

'Air,' he said. 'Earth-normal, more or less. A few strange trace elements. No unusual smells – and quite sterile. We could breathe this stuff if we had to, Lieserl.'

The lock's inner door swung open, revealing a larger chamber. The 'bot pushed a lamp, magnesium-white, into the chamber, and light flared from the walls. Lieserl caught a glimpse of conventional-looking furniture: beds, chairs, a long desk. The chamber's walls sloped upwards to a peak; this single room looked large enough to occupy most of the tetrahedral volume of the building.

The 'bot rolled forward. Mark stepped briskly out of the lock and into the chamber; Lieserl followed.

'Mark Wu? Lieserl?' Uvarov's rasp was loud in her ear.

'Yes, Doctor,' Lieserl replied. 'We hear you. You don't need to shout.'

'Oh, *really*,' Uvarov said. 'Unlike you, I didn't simply assume that our transmissions would carry through whatever those walls are made of.'

Lieserl smiled at Mark. 'Were you worried about us, Uvarov?'

'No. I was worried about the 'bot.'

Lieserl stepped towards the centre of the main chamber and looked around.

The walls of the tetrahedral structure sloped up around her, coming to a neat point fifteen feet above her head. She could see partitioned sections in two of the corners. Bedrooms? Bathrooms? A galley, perhaps?

The 'bot scurried around the edge of the room, its multiple arms probing into corners and edges. It left planet-dust tracks behind itself.

The main piece of furniture was a long desk, constructed of what looked – for all the world – like wood. Lieserl could see monitors of some kind inlaid into the desk surface. The monitors were dead, but they looked like reasonably conventional touch-screens. Lieserl reached out a gloved hand, wishing she could feel the wood surface.

There were *chairs*, in a row, before the desk – four of them, side by side. These were obviously of human construction, with upright backs, padded seats, and two arms studded with controls.

'Mark, look at this,' she said. 'These chairs would fit either of us.'

Mark had found something – two objects – at the end of the desk; he had the 'bot roll across and pick the objects up. Mark's face was lit with wonder; he bent to inspect the first object, held before him in the 'bot's delicate grab. 'This is some kind of stylus,' he said. 'Could be something as simple as an ink pen . . .' The 'bot held up the second object. 'But this thing is unmistakable, Lieserl. Look at it. It's a *cup*.' His hands on his knees, he looked up at her. 'The builders of this place must have been gone a million years. But it's as if they just stepped outside.'

Uvarov rasped, 'Who? I wish you'd speak to me, damn it. What have you found?'

Mark and Lieserl looked at each other.

'People,' Lieserl said. 'We've found people, Uvarov.'

Mark sat with Louise in her oak-panelled bedroom inside the *Great Britain*. Mark had called up a Virtual schematic of the *Northern*'s lifedome; the schematic was a cylinder three feet tall, hovering over her bed. The schematic showed a lifedome which sparkled with glass and light, and the greenery of the forest Deck glowed under the skydome at the crown.

Louise felt something move inside her; the lifedome looked so beautiful – so fragile.

She stared around at the familiar polished walls of her room – it was actually two of the old ship's state rooms, knocked together and converted. Here was the centre of her world, if anywhere was; here were her few pieces of old furniture, her clothes, her first, antique data slate – which still contained the engineering sketches of the *Great Britain* she'd prepared during her first visit to the old ship as a teenager, five million years and half a Universe away. If only, she thought, if only she could pull this room around her like some huge wooden blanket, never to emerge into the complex horrors of the world ...

But here was Mark, politely sitting on the corner of her bed and watching her face. And now he said quietly: 'Here it comes, Louise.'

She forced herself to look at the Virtual of the lifedome.

Mark pointed at the mid-section of the lifedome. A horizontal line of blue-white light appeared; it shimmered balefully against the clear substance of the lifedome, like a sword blade.

'The string has sliced into us from this side. I guess we can be grateful the relative velocity was actually quite low ...'

The string cut easily into the substance of the dome, like a hot wire into butter.

Louise, watching in the silence of her room, felt as if the string were cutting into her own body; she imagined she could hear the shriek of lost air, the screams of her helpless human charges.

Mark looked blank as his processors worked. He said rapidly, 'The wake took a slice out of the hull tens of yards thick.

Lethe. We're losing a lot of air, Louise, but the self-repair systems are working well ... A lot of our infrastructure has gone down quickly – too damn quickly; I think we need to take a look at our redundancies again, if we make it through this ...'

'And the Decks? What's happening in there?'

He hesitated. 'I can't tell, Louise.'

She felt useless; the control panels in the room mocked her with their impotence. She felt the blame for this ghastly accident fall on her shoulders, like a tangible weight. *I'm responsible for bollixing up those distance-evaluation routines. I'm responsible for insufficient redundancy – and for losing touch with Spinner-of-Rope in the cage, just when we need her most. If only I could talk to Spinner, maybe she could get us out of here. If only –*

'The geometry of the string is just as theory predicted,' Mark said. 'I'm getting measurements of pi in the regions around the string ... 3.1402, compared to the flat-space value of 3.1415926 ... The conical space has an angle deficit of four minutes of arc.

'At this moment we have a quarter-mile length of string, actually inside the lifedome, Louise. That's a total mass of four hundred billion *billion* tons.' Mark looked bemused. 'Life, Louise, think about that; that's the mass of a fair-sized moon ...'

Her introspection was futile. The destruction of the lifedome could be – suddenly – mere seconds away. And, in the end, she was helpless. *All I could do, in those last, frantic moments, was sound the damn klaxon ...*

There was a whisper of spider-web light above Spinner. She could *see* how the string made the stars slide across the sky, just above the lifedome. The encroaching string was like the foregathering of some huge, supernatural storm around the *Northern*.

Don't be afraid ...

She twisted in her couch and tightened her restraints. 'What in Lethe do you expect me to be?' she yelled at Poole. 'We've been hit by a length of cosmic string, damn it. This could finish us off. I have to get us out of here.' She placed her hands on the waldoes. *'But I don't know what to do.* Louise? Louise, can you hear me?'

You know she can't.

Feverishly, Spinner said, 'Maybe we're already hit; maybe

that's why the connection went down. But what if she managed to program a routine into the waldoes before we lost the connection? Maybe –'

Come on, Spinner-of-Rope. You know that's not true.

'But I have to move the ship!' she wailed. The thump of her heartbeat sounded impossibly loud in the confined space of the helmet. 'Can't you see that?'

Yes. Yes, I see that.

'But I don't know *how* – or *where* – without Louise . . .'

A hand rested over hers. Despite the thickness of her glove fabric, she could feel the warm roughness of Michael Poole's palm.

I will help you. I'll show you what you must do.

The invisible fingers tightened, pushing her hands against the waldoes. Behind her, the nightfighter opened its wings.

Morrow, crumpled against the Deck beside the crushed body of Planner Milpitas, stared up into the wake of the cosmic string.

The structure of the middle Decks was fragile; it simply imploded into the string wake. Morrow saw homes which had stood for a thousand years rip loose from the Deck surfaces as if in the grip of some immense tornado; the buildings exploded, and metal sheets spun through the air. The newer structures, spun across the air in zero-gee, crumpled easily as the wake passed. Much of the surface of Deck Two was torn loose and tumbled above him, chunks of metal clattering into each other. Morrow saw patterns of straight lines and arcs on those fragments of Deck: shards of the soulless circular geometry which had dominated the Deck's layout for centuries.

People, scattered in the air like dolls, clattered against each other in the wake. The string passed through a Temple. The golden tetrahedron – the proudest symbol of human culture – collapsed like a burst balloon around the path of the string, and shards of gold-brown glass, long and lethal, hailed through the air.

And now the string passed through another human body, that of a hapless woman. Morrow heard the banal, mundane sounds of her death: a scream, abruptly cut off, a moist, ripping sound, and the crunch of bone, sounding like a bite into a crisp apple.

The woman's body, distorted out of recognition, was cast aside; tumbling, it impacted softly with the Deck.

The wake of a cosmic string ... The wake was the mechanism that had constructed the large-scale structure of the Universe. It was the seed of galaxies. *And we have let it loose inside our ship,* Morrow thought.

Once the string passed through the lifedome completely, the *Northern* would die at last, as surely as a body severed from its head ...

Morrow, immersed in his own pain, wanted to close his eyes, succumb to the oblivion of unconsciousness. Was this how it was to end, after a thousand years?

But the quality of the noise above him – the rush of air, the screams – seemed to change.

He stared up.

The string, still cutting easily through the structure, had slowed to a halt.

'Mark,' Louise hissed. 'What's happening?'

The string had cut a full quarter-mile into the lifedome. For a moment the blue-glowing string hovered, like a scalpel embedded in flesh.

Then the Virtual display came to life once more. The electric-blue string executed a tight curve and sliced its way back out of the lifedome, exiting perhaps a quarter-mile above its entry point.

Louise wished there was a god, to offer up her thanks.

'It's done a lot more damage on the way out – but we are left with an intact lifedome,' Mark said. 'The 'bots and autonomic systems are sealing up the breaches in the hull.' He looked up at Louise. 'I think we've made it.'

Louise, floating above her bed, hugged her knees against her chest. 'But I don't understand *how*, Mark.'

'Spinner-of-Rope saved us,' Mark said simply. 'She opened up the discontinuity-drive and took us away from there at half lightspeed – and in just the right direction. See?' Mark pointed. 'She pulled the ship backwards, and away from the string.'

She looked into his familiar, tired eyes, and wished she could hug him to her. 'It was Spinner-of-Rope. You're right. It must have been. But the voice link to Spinner was one of the first things we lost. And we certainly didn't have time to work up routines for the waldoes.'

'In fact, we're *still* out of touch with Spinner,' Mark said.

'So how did she know?' Louise studied the scarred Virtual lifedome. 'The trajectory she chose to get us out of this was almost perfect, Mark. *How did she know?*'

Spinner-of-Rope buried her faceplate in her gloves; within her environment suit she trembled, uncontrollably.

It's over, Spinner. You did well. It's time to look ahead.

'No,' she said. 'The string hit the ship. The deaths, the injuries –'

Don't dwell on it. You did all you could.

'Really? And did *you*, Michael Poole?' she spat.

What do you mean?

'Couldn't you have helped us more? Couldn't you have *warned* us that the thing was coming?'

He laughed, softly and sadly. *I'm sorry, Spinner. I'm not superhuman. I didn't have any more warning than your people. I'm pretty much bound by the laws of physics, just as you are . . .*

She dropped her hands and thumped the side of the couch. There was still no link – voice or data – to Louise, and the rest of the crew. She was isolated out here – stuck in the pilot's cage of an alien ship, with only a five-million-year-old ghost for company.

She felt a swelling of laughter, inside her chest; she bit it back. *Spinner-of-Rope?*

'I'm scared, Michael Poole. I'm even scared of you.'

I don't blame you. I'm scared of me.

'I don't know what to do. What if Louise can't get back in touch?'

He was silent for a moment. Then:

Look, Spinner, your people can't stay here. In this timeframe, I mean.

'Why not?'

Because there's nothing for you here. The Ring – which you came to find – is ruined. This rubble of string fragments can't offer you anything.

'Then what?'

You have to move on, Spinner. You have to take your people to where they can find shelter and escape. His hands, warm and firm, closed invisibly over hers once more. *I'll show you. Will you trust me?*

'Where are we going?'

In search of the Ring.

'But – but the Ring is here. And it's destroyed. You said so yourself.'

Yes, he said patiently. *But it wasn't always so ...*

30

The 'bot rolled fussily across the floor, its fat wheels crunching over the dust it had brought in from the surface of the neutron star planet. It held a bundle of sensors out before it on a flexible arm. Light, brilliant white, glared from the sensor arm. The way the 'bot held out its sensor pack was rather prissy, Lieserl thought, as if the 'bot didn't quite approve of what it was being forced to inspect in here.

The 'bot rolled up to one of the four chairs and sniffed at it cautiously.

'There's exotic matter here,' Mark said suddenly.

'What?'

'The 'bot has found exotic matter,' Mark repeated evenly. 'Somewhere inside the building.'

Uvarov growled from the pod, 'But we've seen no evidence of wormhole construction here. And that structure is too small to house a wormhole Interface.'

'I'm just reporting what the 'bot's telling me,' Mark snapped, letting his irritation show. 'Maybe we should gather a few more facts before wasting our time speculating, Uvarov.'

The 'bot was still lingering close to one of the chairs – the second from the left of the row of four, Lieserl noted irrelevantly. As she watched, the 'bot extended more arms, unfolded more packages of sensor equipment; it loomed over the chair menacingly, like some mechanical spider.

Mark walked up to the 'bot, his face expressionless. 'It's somewhere inside the chair. The exoticity ...'

'*Inside the chair*?' Lieserl felt like laughing, almost hysterically. 'What happened, did someone drop exotic matter down behind the cushion while watching a Virtual show?'

He glared at her. 'Come on, Lieserl. There *is* a construct of exotic matter embedded in this chair. It's tiny – only a few fractions of an inch across – but it's there.' He turned to the 'bot. 'Maybe we can cook up some kind of magnified Virtual image ...'

Pixels swirled before Lieserl's face, brushing her cheeks intangibly; she stepped back.

The pixels coalesced into a crude sketch, suspended in the air. It looked like a jewel – clear, complete and seamless – hanging before her. There were hints of further structure inside, not yet resolved by the 'bot's imaging systems.

She recognized the form.

'*Lethe*. Another tetrahedron,' she said.

'Yes. Another tetrahedron ... The form seems to have become a badge of humanity, doesn't it? But this one is barely a sixteenth of an inch across.'

Pixels of all colours hailed through the interior of the little tetrahedron, as if scrambling for coherence. Lieserl caught elusive, tantalizing hints of structure. At one point it seemed that she could see another, smaller tetrahedron forming, nested inside the first – just as this construct was nested inside the tetrahedral form of the base as a whole. She wondered if the whole of this structure was like a Russian doll, with a series of tetrahedra snuggled neatly inside each other ...

The magnified image was rather pleasing, she thought. It reminded her of the toy she'd had during her lightning-brief childhood: a tiny village immersed in a globe of water, with frozen people and plastic snowflakes ... Thinking that, she felt a brief, incongruous pang of regret that her childhood, even as unsatisfactory as it had been, was now so *remote*.

'Well, my exotic matter grain is in there somewhere,' Mark said. 'But the 'bot is having trouble getting any further resolution.' He looked confused. 'Lieserl, there's something very strange inside that little tetrahedral box.'

She kept her face expressionless; at times it was quite convenient to be a Virtual – it gave her such control. *Strange. Right. But what could be stranger than to be here: on the planet of a neutron star hurtling at lightspeed across the battlefield at the end of time? What can make things stranger than that?*

'There's a droplet of neutron superfluid in there,' Mark said. He peered into the formless interior of the tetrahedron, as if by sheer willpower he might force it to give up its secrets. 'Highly dense, at enormous temperatures and pressures ... Lieserl, the tetrahedron contains matter at conditions you'd expect to find deep in the interior of a neutron star – in a region beneath the solid crust, called the mantle. That's what the 'bot is trying to see into.'

Lieserl stared at the swirling mists inside the tetrahedron. She knew that a neutron star had the mass of a normal star, but compressed into a globe only a few miles in diameter. The matter was so dense that electrons and protons were forced together into neutrons; this superfluid of neutrons was a hundred billion *billion* times as dense as water.

'If that's so, how are the pressures contained? This construct is like a bomb, waiting to go off.'

He shook his head. 'Well, it looks as if the people who built this place found a way. And the construct may have been stable for a long time – millions of years, perhaps. You know, I wish we had more time to spend here. We don't even know how old this base is – from how many years beyond our time this technology dates.'

'But *why* construct such a thing?' She stared into the tetrahedron. '*Why* fill a little box with reconstructed neutron star material? Mark, do you think this was some kind of laboratory, for studying neutron star conditions?'

Uvarov's ruined voice brayed laughter into her ears. 'A laboratory? My dear woman, this is a war zone; I think basic science was unlikely to be on the agenda for the men and women who built this base. Besides, this neutron star is hardly typical. The people who came here placed discontinuity-drive engines at the star's pole, and drove it across space at close to lightspeed. Now, what research purpose do you think *that* served?'

Mark ignored him. He squatted down on his haunches before the image and peered up at it; the glow of the shifting pixels inside the tetrahedron cast highlights from his face and environment suit. 'I don't think the stuff in there *was* reconstructed, Lieserl.'

'What do you mean?'

'Think about it.' He pointed at the image. 'We know there is exotic matter in there ... and as far as we know the primary purpose of exotic matter is the construction of spacetime wormholes. I think there's a wormhole Interface in there, Lieserl.'

She frowned. 'Wormhole mouths are hundreds of yards – or miles – across.'

He straightened up. 'That's true of the Interfaces *we* can construct. Who knows what will be possible in the future? Or rather –'

'We know what you mean,' Uvarov snapped from the pod.

'Let's suppose there *is* a wormhole mouth inside this tiny construct,' Mark said. 'A wormhole so fine it's just a thread ... but it leads across space, to the interior of the neutron star. Lieserl, I think the neutron superfluid in here isn't some human reconstruction – I think it's a sample of material *taken from the neutron star itself.*'

Lieserl, involuntarily, glanced around the chamber, as if she might see the miniature wormhole threading across space, a shining trail connecting this bland, human environment with the impossibly hostile heart of a neutron star.

'But *why*?'

'Isn't it obvious?' Uvarov snapped.

Mark was smiling at her; evidently he had worked it out too. She felt slow, stupid, unimaginative. 'Just tell me,' she said dully.

Mark said, 'Lieserl, the link is there so the humans who built this base could reach the interior of the neutron star. I think they downloaded equipment into there: nanomachines, 'bots of some kind – maybe even some analogue of humans.

'They populated the neutron star, Lieserl.'

Uvarov rumbled assent. 'More than that,' he rasped. 'They *engineered* the damn thing.'

Closed timelike curves, Spinner-of-Rope.

The nightfighter arced through the muddled, relativity-distorted sky; the neutron star system wheeled around Spinner like some gaudy light display. Behind her, the huge wings of the Xeelee nightfighter beat at space, so vigorously Spinner almost imagined she could hear the rustle of immense, impossible feathers.

She felt her small fingers tremble inside gloves that suddenly seemed much too big for her. But Michael Poole's hands rested over hers, large, warm.

The ship surged forward.

We are going to build closed timelike curves . . .

Ignoring the protests of her tired back, Louise straightened up and pushed herself away from the Deck surface. She launched into the air, the muscles of her legs aching, and she let air resistance slow her to a halt a few feet above the Deck.

Once this had been a park, near the heart of Deck Two. Now, the park had become the bottom layer of an improvised, three-dimensional hospital, and the long grass was invisible beneath a layer of bodies, bandaging, medical supplies. A rough rectangular array of ropes had been set up, stretching upwards from the Deck surface through thirty feet. Patients were being lodged loosely inside the array; they looked like specks of blood and dirt inside some huge honeycomb of air, Louise thought.

A short distance away a group of bodies – unmoving, wrapped in sheets – had been gathered together in the air and tethered roughly to the frame of what had once been a greenhouse.

Lieserl approached Louise tentatively. She reached out, as if she wanted to hold Louise's hand. 'You should rest,' she said.

Louise shook her head angrily. 'No time for that.' She took a deep breath, but her lungs quickly filled up with the hospital's stench of blood and urine. She coughed, and ran an arm across her forehead, aware that it must be leaving a trail there of blood and sweat. 'Damn it. Damn *all* of this.'

'Come on, Louise. You're doing your best.'

'No. That isn't good enough. Not any more. I should have designed for this scenario, for a catastrophic failure of the lifedome. Lieserl, we're overwhelmed. We've converted *all* the AS treatment bays into casualty treatment centres, and we're *still* overrun. Look at this so-called hospital we've had to improvise. It's like something out of the Dark Ages.'

'Louise, there's nothing you could have done. We just didn't have the resources to cope with this.'

'But we *should* have. Lieserl, the doctors and 'bots are operating triage here. *Triage*, on my starship.'

. . . And it didn't help that I diverted most of our supply of medical nanobots to the hull . . . Instead of working here with the people – crawling through shattered bodies, repairing broken blood

389

vessels, fighting to keep bacterial infection contained within torn abdominal cavities – the nanobots had been press-ganged, roughly – and on *her* decision – into crawling over the crude patches applied hurriedly to the breached hull, trying inexpertly to knit the torn metal into a seamless whole once more.

She clenched her hands into fists, digging her nails into her palms. 'What if the Xeelee are studying us now? What will they think of us? I've brought these people across a hundred and fifty million light years – and five million years – only to let them die like animals . . .'

Lieserl faced her squarely, her small, solid fists on her hips; lines clustered around her wide mouth as she glared at Louise. 'That's sentimental garbage,' she snapped. 'I'm surprised at you, Louise Ye Armonk. Listen to me: what is at issue here is not *how you feel*. You are trying to survive – to find a way to permit the race to survive.'

Lieserl's stern, lined face, with the strong nose and deep eyes, reminded Louise suddenly of an overbearing mother. She snapped back, 'What do you know of how I feel? I'm a human, damn it. Not a – a –'

'An AI?' Lieserl met her gaze evenly.

'Oh, Lethe, Lieserl. I'm sorry.'

'It's all right, Louise. You're quite right. I *am* an artefact. I have many inhuman attributes.' She smiled. 'For instance, at this moment I have *two* foci of consciousness, functioning independently: one here, and one down on the planet. But . . .' She sighed. 'I *was* once human, Louise. If briefly. So I do understand.'

'I know, Lieserl. I'm sorry.' Louise had never found it easy to express affection. With a struggle, she said: 'In fact, you're one of the most *human* people I've ever met.'

Lieserl looked around at the makeshift hospital, following the soft cries of the wounded. 'Louise,' she said slowly, 'I have a long perspective. Think of the story of the race. Our timelines emerged from the oceans, and for millions of years circled the Sun with Earth. Then, in a brief, spectacular explosion of causality, the timelines erupted in wild scribbles, across the Universe. Humanity was everywhere.

'But now, our possibilities have reduced.

'Louise, all the potential paths of the race – all the timelines, running from those ancient oceans of the past, through millions of years to an unknown future – *all* of them have narrowed to a single event in spacetime: *here*, on this ship, *now*. And that event is under *your* control.'

Lieserl's face loomed before Louise now, filling her vision; Louise looked into her soft, vulnerable eyes, and – for the first time, really – she had a sudden, deep insight into Lieserl's personality. *This woman really is ancient – ancient, and wise.*

'Louise, you are not a woman – or rather, you are *more* than a woman. You are a survival mechanism: the best to be found, for this crucial instant, by our genes, and our culture, and our minds. If you didn't have the strength within you now, to deliver us through this causal gateway to the future, you would not have been chosen. But you *do* have the strength to continue,' Lieserl said. '*To find a way through*. Look within yourself, Louise. Tap into that strength . . .'

There was a deep, almost subsonic groan, all around Louise. It sounded like thunder, she thought.

It was the sound of metal, under immense stress.

She pulled away from Lieserl and twisted in the air. She looked across at the section of hull breached by the arc of string. The patch that had been applied across the string damage gleamed brightly, fresh and polished, at the centre of the grass-coated hull surface. A stress failure – another breach of the lifedome – would kill them all. But the patch *looked* as if it was holding up okay . . . not that a visual inspection from this distance meant anything.

As if on cue, a projection of Mark's head materialized before her. 'Louise, I'm sorry.'

'What is it?'

'Come with me. We need to talk.'

'No,' she said. Suddenly, she felt enormously weary. 'No more talk, Mark. I've done enough damage already.'

Behind her, Lieserl said warningly: 'Louise . . .'

'I heard what you said, Lieserl.' Louise smiled. 'But it's all a little too mystical for a tired old engineer like me. I'm going to stay here. Help out in the hospital.'

Lieserl frowned at her. 'Louise, you're an engineer, not a doctor. Frankly, I wouldn't want you treating *me*.'

Mark smiled. 'Besides, we don't have time for all this

391

self-pity, Louise. This is *important*.'

She sighed. 'What is?'

He whispered, in a surprisingly unrealistic hiss, 'Didn't you hear the hull stress noise? Spinner is moving the ship again.'

Think of spacetime as a matrix, Michael Poole whispered. *A four-dimensional grid, labelled by distance and duration. There are events: points in time and space, at nodes of the grid. These are the incidents that mark out our lives. And, connecting the events, there are* trajectories.

The starbow across the sky broadened, now. That meant her speed had reduced, since the relativistic distortion was lessened. Spinner called up a faceplate display subvocally. Yes: the ship's velocity had fallen to a fraction over half lightspeed.

Trajectories are paths through spacetime, Poole said. *There are* timelike *trajectories, and there are* spacelike *trajectories. A ship going slower than light follows a timelike path. And, Spinner, we – all humans, since the beginning of history – work our snail-like way along timelike trajectories into the future. At last, our world-lines will terminate at a place called* timelike infinity *– at the infinitely remote, true end of time.*

But 'spacelike' means moving faster than light. A tachyon – a faster-than-light particle – follows a spacelike path, as does this nightfighter under hyperdrive.

She twisted in her seat. Already the neutron star system had vanished, into the red-shift distance. And directly ahead of her there was a cloud of cosmic string; space looked as if it were criss-crossed by fractures, around which blue-shifted star images slid like oil drops.

Poole's hands, invisible, tightened around hers as the ship threw itself into the cloud of string.

We know at least three ways to follow spacelike paths, Spinner-of-Rope: three ways to travel faster than light. We can use the Xeelee hyperdrive, of course. Or we can use spacetime wormholes. Or, Poole said slowly, *we can use the conical spacetime around a length of cosmic string . . .*

Think of the gravitational lensing effect that produces double images of stars around strings. A photon coming around one side of the string can take tens of thousands of years longer to reach our telescopes than a photon following a path on the other side of the string.

So, by passing through the string's conical deficit, we could actually outrun a beam of light ... There was string all around the ship, now, tangled, complex, an array of it receding to infinity. A pair of string lengths, so twisted around each other they were almost braided, swept over her head. She looked up. The strings trailed dazzling highways of refracting star images.

Behind her the huge wings spread wide, exultant.

This damn nightfighter was made for this, she thought.

Under Poole's guidance, Spinner brought the craft to a dead halt; the discontinuity wings cupped as they tore at space. Then Spinner turned the craft around rapidly – impossibly rapidly – and sent it hurtling at the string pair once more. The nightfighter soared upwards, and this time the two strings passed *underneath* the ship's bow.

...And if you can move along spacelike paths, Spinner-of-Rope, you can construct closed timelike curves.

The neutron star system was *old*.

Once the system had been a spectacular binary pair, adorning some galaxy lost in the sky. Then one of the stars had suffered a supernova explosion, briefly and gloriously outshining its parent galaxy. The explosion had destroyed any planets, and damaged the companion star. After that, the remnant neutron star slowly cooled, glitching as it spun like some giant stirring in its sleep, while its companion star shed its life-blood hydrogen fuel over the neutron star's wizened flesh. Slowly, too, the ring of lost gas formed, and the system's strange, spectral second system of planets coalesced.

Then human beings had come here.

The humans soared about the system, surveying. They settled on the largest planet in the smoke ring. They threw microscopic wormhole mouths into the cooling corpse of the neutron star, and down through the wormholes they poured devices and – perhaps – human-analogues, made robust enough to survive in the neutron star's impossibly rigorous environment.

The devices and human-analogues had been *tiny*, like finely jewelled toys.

The human-analogues and their devices swarmed to a

magnetic pole of the neutron star, and great machines were erected there: discontinuity-drives, perhaps powered by the immense energy reserves of the neutron star itself.

Slowly at first, then with increasing acceleration, the neutron star – dragging its attendant companion, ring and planets with it – was forced out of its parent galaxy and thrown across space, a bullet of stellar mass fired at almost lightspeed.

'A bullet. Yes.' In the pod, Uvarov mused. 'An apt term.'

Lieserl stared at the swirling, unresolved pixels inside the Virtual image's clear tetrahedral frame. 'I wonder if there are still people in there,' she said.

Mark frowned. 'Where?'

'People-analogues. Inside the neutron star. I wonder if they've survived.'

He shrugged, evidently indifferent. 'I doubt it. Unless they were needed for maintenance, they would surely have been shut down after their function was concluded.'

Shut down . . . But these were *people.* What if they *hadn't* been 'shut down'? Lieserl closed her eyes and tried to imagine. How would it be, to live her life as a tiny, fish-like creature less than a hair's-breadth tall, living inside the flux-ridden mantle of a neutron star? What would her *world* be like?

'A bullet,' Uvarov said again. 'And a bullet, fired by our forebears – *directly at the heart of this Xeelee construct.*'

She opened her eyes.

Mark was frowning. 'What are you talking about, Uvarov?'

'Can't you see it yet? Mark, what do you *imagine* the purpose of this great engineering spectacle was? We already know – from the Superet data, and the fragments provided to us by Lieserl – that the rivalry between humanity and Xeelee persisted for millions of years. More than persisted – it *grew* in that time, becoming an obsession which – in the end – consumed mankind.'

Lieserl said, 'Are you saying that all of this – the discontinuity engines, the hurling of the neutron star across space – all of this was intended as an assault on the Xeelee?'

'But that's insane,' Mark said.

'Of course it is,' Uvarov said lightly. 'My dear friends, we've plenty of evidence that humanity isn't a particularly intelligent species – not compared to its great rivals the Xeelee, at any rate.

And I have never believed that humanity, collectively, is entirely *sane* either.'

'You should know, Doctor,' Mark growled.

'I don't understand,' Lieserl said. 'Humans must have known about the photino birds – damn it, *I* told them! They must have seen what danger the birds represented to the future of all baryonic species. And they must have seen that the Xeelee – if remote and incomprehensible – were at least baryonic too. So the goals of the Xeelee, if directed against the birds, had to be in the long-term interests of mankind.'

Uvarov laughed at her. 'I'm afraid you're still looking for rational explanations for irrational behaviour, my dear. Lieserl, I believe that the Xeelee grew into the position in human souls once occupied by images of gods and demons. But here, at last, was a god who was finite – who occupied the same mortal realm as humans. A god who could be *attacked*. And attack we did: down through the long ages, while the stars went out around us, all but ignored.'

'And so,' Mark said grimly, 'we fired off a neutron star at the Ring.'

'A spectacular gesture,' Uvarov said. 'Perhaps humanity's greatest engineering feat … But, ultimately, futile. For how could a mere neutron star disrupt a loop of cosmic string? And besides, the Xeelee starbreaker technology was surely sufficient to destroy the star before –'

'But it didn't work,' Lieserl said slowly.

Mark had been staring at the sensor 'bot; the squat machine had come to a halt before the chair, its sensor arms suspended in the air. 'What do you mean?'

'Think about it,' she said. 'The neutron star is heading *away* from the site of the Ring. And it's clearly not been disrupted by starbreakers.'

'Yes. So something went wrong,' Uvarov said. 'Well, the precise sequence hardly matters, Lieserl. And –'

It happened in a heartbeat.

The light died. The ancient structure was flooded with darkness.

Louise and Mark left the improvised hospital and found an abandoned house. The house was bereft of furniture, its owners gone to live in the zero-gee sky (but, of course, the zero-gee dwellings were gone now, Louise noted morosely, swept out of the sky by the cosmic string incursion).

Mark quickly created a Virtual diagram in the air: a geometrical sketch of lines and angles, lettered and arrowed.

Louise couldn't help but smile. 'Lethe, Mark. At a time like this, you give me a diagram Euclid would have recognized.'

He looked at her seriously. 'Louise, working out the spacetime geometry of a cosmic string is a hard problem in general relativity. But, given that geometry, all the rest of it is no more than Pythagoras' theorem . . .

'As near as I can figure out, this is what Spinner is up to.' There was a pair of tubes in the air, glowing electric blue, like neon. 'We are flying around a pair of cosmic strings. Now, here are the angle deficits of the strings' conical spacetimes.' Wedges of air, like long cheese slices, were illuminated pale blue; one wedge trailed each string length.

'Okay. Here comes the *Northern*.' The ship was represented by a cartoon sketch of a sycamore seed in black. 'You can see we're travelling on a curving path around the string pair, going against the strings' own rotation.'

Now the seed arced into the wedge-shaped angle deficit glow of one of the strings. As soon as it had entered the boundary it vanished, to reappear instantly at the far side of the deficit.

Mark snapped his fingers. 'See that? Faster-than-light travel: a spacelike trajectory right across the deficit.'

Now the little ship-model came arcing back and flickered through the second string's angle deficit. 'Louise, the strings are travelling just under the speed of light – within three decimal places of it, actually. Spinner has the *Northern* travelling at a little over half lightspeed. The turning curves, and the accelerations, are incredible . . . The domain wall inertial shielding seems to be working pretty well, although there's a little leakage.'

Louise nodded. 'Right. Which is why the *Northern* is complaining.'

'Yeah. Louise, the *Northern* wasn't designed for this – and neither was our bastardized lash-up of *Northern* and night-fighter. But there's nothing we can do. We'll just have to pray the whole mess holds together until Spinner-of-Rope finishes her joy-riding ...

'Anyway, the trajectory she's following is quite precisely machined ... We're passing from side to side of the string pair in light-minutes, but we're crossing light-*years* thanks to the spacelike savings. Louise, I think Spinner-of-Rope is assembling closed timelike curves, from these spacelike trajectories.'

Louise stared at the seed-craft; she felt an impulse to reach out and pluck it from the air. 'But why, Mark? And *how*?'

'I *know* what a closed timelike curve is,' Spinner said. Again she dragged the ship to a halt and whirled its nose around towards the string; although she was still shielded from the impossible accelerations she felt herself gasp as the Universe lurched around her. 'The original mission of the *Great Northern*, with its wormhole, was to follow a segment of a closed timelike curve ...'

Yes. A closed timelike curve is a circle in time. By following a closed timelike curve all the way to its starting point, you would at last meet yourself, Spinner-of-Rope ... Closed timelike curves allow you to travel through time, and into the past.

Again the nightfighter hurled itself at the cosmic string pair; again Spinner hauled at the waldoes, dragging the ship around. The huge wings beat at spacetime.

She screamed, 'How much longer, damn it?'

Spinner, each traverse around the string pair is taking us a thousand years into the past. But we need to travel back through a hundred millennia, or more ...

'A hundred traverses,' she whispered.

Can you do it, Spinner? Do you have the strength?

'No,' she said. 'But I don't think I have much choice, do I?'

Lieserl looked around the darkened chamber, confused. The 'bot's brilliant lantern had been extinguished. Suddenly the walls were dim grey sheets, closing over her head, claustrophobic.

'Lieserl.' Mark's face loomed before her, erupting out of the darkness; his blue eyes, white teeth where vivid. He moved with nanosecond speed, the slowness of humanity finally abandoned.

Dimly, she was aware of poor Uvarov sitting in the pod. He was frozen in human-time, and unable to follow their high-speed insect-buzz. 'What is it? What's happened?'

'The 'bot has failed. Lieserl, it was controlled by the ship's processors. The download link from the ship must have gone down . . .'

Immediately, she *felt* that loss of processor support. She felt as if her mind had been plunged into a twilight cavern, echoing; she felt *herself* drift away.

'They've abandoned us.'

'Probably they had no choice, Lieserl.'

I am to experience death, then. But – so suddenly?

Lieserl would survive, of course – as would Mark, as projections on board the *Northern*. But this projection – *she*, this unique branch of her ancient consciousness – couldn't be sustained solely by the limited processors on the pod.

She felt a spasm of regret that she would never be able to tell Louise and Spinner-of-Rope about the wonderful little people embedded inside the neutron star flux.

She reached for Mark. Their environment suits melted away; desperately they pressed their bodies against each other. With deep, savage longing, she sought Mark's warm mouth with her lips, and –

'Lethe. And we can't even *talk* to her.' Louise looked out of the house and across the lifedome, in the vague direction of the nightfighter cage. 'Mark, Spinner is a smart woman, but she's no expert on string dynamics. And she's out there without significant processor support. I don't see how she's even calculating the trajectories we're following.'

Mark frowned. 'I – wait.' He held up a hand, and his expression turned inward, becoming blank.

'What is it?'

'We've stopped. I mean, the traverses around the string pair have been halted.' He thought for a moment. 'Louise, I counted a hundred and seven complete circuits . . .'

'Louise? Mark?'

The voice sounded out of the air close to Louise's ear. 'Yes, Trapper-of-Frogs. I hear you. Where are you?'

'I'm in the forest. I –'

'Yes?'

'I think you'd better get up here.'

Louise looked at Mark; he was frowning, and no doubt some sub-projection of him was already with Trapper.

'Why?' Louise asked. 'What's wrong, Trapper?'

'Nothing's wrong. Not exactly. It's just – *different* ...'

Michael Poole's invisible ghost-touch evaporated. Spinner-of-Rope lifted her hands from the waldoes.

Her job was done, then. She pulled her fingers inside the body of her gloves and balled her stiff hands into fists, digging her nails into the palms of her hands. She felt herself shudder, from fear and exhaustion. There was a stabbing in the small of her back, and across her shoulder blades, just below her neck; she twisted in her couch and flexed her spine, trying to work out the stiffness.

Then she looked out, beyond the construction-material cage, for the first time.

31

'Dr Uvarov. Dr Garry Uvarov.'

The voice, flat and mechanical, roused him from a broken sleep.

He opened his mouth to reply, and ropy saliva looped across his lips. 'What is it now?'

'Is there anything you require?' The voice, generated by the pod's limited processors, didn't even bear a semblance of humanity, and it came – maddeningly! – from all around him.

'Yes,' he said. He felt himself shivering, distantly; he felt *cold*. Was the power in here failing already?

How long had it been, since his abrupt abandonment by Lieserl and Mark Wu?

'Yes,' he told the pod again. 'Yes, there is something I require. Take me back to the *Northern*.'

The pod paused, for long seconds.

Uvarov felt the cold settle over his bones. Was this how he was to die, suspended in the thoughts of an idiot mechanical? Was he to suffer a final betrayal at the hands of technology, just as the AS nanobots had been slowly killing him for years?

Well, if he was to die, he would take with him one deep and intense regret: that he had not lived to see the conclusion of his grand design, his experiment at extending the natural longevity of his race. He knew how others had seen him: as *obsessed* with his eugenics objectives, as a monomaniac perhaps. But – ah! What an achievement it would have been! What a monument . . .

Ambition burned within him still, intense, almost all-consuming, betrayed by the failure of his body.

His thoughts softened, and he felt himself grow more diffuse, his awareness drifting off into the warm, comfortable caverns of his memory.

The pod spoke again. 'I'm unable to comply with your request, Doctor. I can't obtain a fix on the *Northern*. I'm sorry. Would you like me to –'

'Then kill me.' He twisted his head from side to side, relishing the stabs of pain in his neck. 'I'm stranded here. I'm going to die, as soon as my supplies run out. Kill me now. Turn off the damn power.'

'I can't comply with that, either, Dr Uvarov.'

But Uvarov was no longer listening. Once more he felt himself falling into a troubled – perhaps final – sleep, and his ruined lips moved slowly.

'*Kill me, you damn mechanical . . .*'

32

The torus of ragged, fragmented string loops was gone. Now, cosmic string crossed the cavity: great, wild, triumphant whorls of it, shining a false electric blue in the skydome's imager.

This one, tremendous, complex, multiple loop of string filled the cavity at the bottom of the gravity well. This was – astonishingly, unbearably – a single object, an *artefact*, at least ten million light-years across.

Louise Ye Armonk – with Mark, Lieserl and Morrow – hovered on zero-gee scooters, suspended beneath the crown of the skydome. Beneath Louise – she was distantly aware – the layers of forest were filled with the rich, comforting noises: the calls of birds and monkeys and the soft burps of frogs, sounds of busy life which persisted even here at the end of time . . .

Beyond the clear dome, string filled the Universe.

Here, a hundred thousand years into the past, the galaxies still fell, fragmenting and blue-shifted, into the deepest gravity well in the Universe. And the *Northern* had emerged from its jaunts through the string loop's spacetime defects to find itself once more inside a star-walled cavity, at the bottom of this Universal well.

There the similarity ended, though, Louise thought. The cavity walls were much *smoother* than in the future, containing rather fewer of the ragged holes she'd noted . . . The walls looked almost *artificially* smooth here, she thought uneasily.

And, of course, there was the *Ring*, whole and magnificent.

The Ring was a hoop woven from a billion-light-year length of cosmic string. The *Northern* was positioned somewhere above the plane of the Ring. The near side of the artefact formed a tangled, impenetrable fence over the lifedome, twisted exuberantly into arcs and cusps, with shards of galaxy images glittering through the morass of spacetime defects. And the far side of the object was visible as a pale, hard band, remote across the blue-shifted sky.

The rough disc of space enclosed by the Ring – a disc no less than ten million light-years across, Louise reminded herself – seemed virtually empty. Perhaps, she mused, in this era the Xeelee were actively working to keep that central region clear.

... Clear, Louise saw as she looked more carefully, save for a single, glowing point of light, right at the geometric centre of the Ring. She saw how Lieserl was staring into that point of light, her mouth half-open.

Spinner-of-Rope's precipitate action had delivered them, back through time, to another snapshot-timeslice of this war in Heaven ... and this was, it seemed, an era not far removed from the Ring's final fall.

She was aware of their eyes – Mark's, Lieserl's, Morrow's – resting on her, expectantly. On *her*.

Remember what Lieserl said, she told herself. *I'm a survival mechanism. That's all. I have to keep functioning, for just a little while longer* ... She reached deep inside her.

She clapped her hands. 'All right, people – Mark, Lieserl. Let's do some work. I think it's obvious we've delivered ourselves right into the middle of a war zone. We know that, at this moment, the photino birds must be hitting this Ring from all sides – because, within a hundred thousand years, we know that the Ring is going to be destroyed. That gives me the feeling that we don't have much time, before one side or other notices we're here ...'

'I think you're right, Louise,' Mark said. Both the Virtuals, on high-capacity data links to the central processors, were working on different aspects of the situation. 'I don't think we should be fooled by the fact that most of the action in this incredible war seems to be occurring at sublight velocities, so that – on this scale – it has all the pace of an ant column crossing the Sahara. Let's not forget the Xeelee have a hyperdrive – which we've stolen – and, for all we know, so do the photino birds. We could be discovered at any time.'

'So give me a summary of the environment.'

Mark nodded. 'First of all, our position in *time*: Spinner-of-Rope constructed enough closed timelike paths for us to have travelled a hundred thousand years into the past, back from the era to which our first journey brought us.' He raised his face to the skydome and rose into the air by a few feet, absently forgetting to take his Virtual-scooter with him. 'The Ring is complete in this era, as far as we can tell. Its mass is immense – in fact we're suffering inertial drag from it. Kind of a lot of drag, in fact ... We're being hauled around, through space, by the Ring. Spinner-of-Rope seems to be compensating ...'

'Lieserl. Tell me what you have.'

Lieserl seemed to have to tear her eyes away from that tantalizing point of light at the heart of the Ring. She looked down at Louise.

'I have *the Ring*, Louise. We have been restored to an era before its destruction. Bolder's Ring is a single loop of cosmic string ... but an immense one, no less than ten million light-years across and with the mass of tens of thousands of galaxies, united into one seamless whole. The string is twisted over on itself like wool wrapped around a skein; the Ring's topography is made up of string arcs moving at close to lightspeed, and cusps which actually *reach* lightspeed. The motion is complex, but – as far as I can tell – it's non-intersecting. The Ring could persist forever.

'Louise, there is no way this monster could have formed naturally. Our best theories say that any natural string loops should be a mere thousand light-years across.' She looked up, and the blue false colour of the string images caught her profile, picking out the lines around her eyes. 'Somehow –' she laughed briefly '– somehow the Xeelee found a way to drag cosmic string across space – or else to manufacture it on a truly heroic scale – and then to knit it up into this immense *artefact*.'

Louise stared up at the Ring, tracing the tangle of string around the sky, letting Lieserl's statistics pour through her head. *And I might have died without seeing this. Thank you. Oh, thank you ...*

'The cosmology here is ... spectacular,' Lieserl said, smiling. 'We have, essentially, an extremely massive torus, rotating very rapidly. And it's *devastating* the structure of spacetime. The sheer mass of the Ring has generated a gravity well so deep that matter – *galaxies* – is being drawn in, towards this point, across hundreds of millions of light-years. Even our original Galaxy, the Galaxy of mankind, was drawn by the Ring's mass. So we know that the Ring was indeed the "Great Attractor" identified by human astronomers.

'And the *rotation* has significant effects. Louise, we're on the fringe of a Kerr metric – the classic relativistic solution to the gravitational field of a rotating mass. In fact, this is what's called a *maximal* Kerr metric: because the torus is spinning so fast the angular momentum far exceeds the mass, in gravitational units . . .

'As Mark said, the Ring's rotation is exerting a large torque on the ship. This is *inertial drag*: the twisting of spacetime around the rotating Ring.'

Morrow frowned. 'Inertial drag?'

Lieserl said, 'Morrow, naive ideas of gravity predicted that the *spin* of an object wouldn't affect its gravitational field. No matter how fast a star rotated, you'd be attracted simply towards its centre, just as if it wasn't rotating at all.

'But relativity tells us that isn't true. There are nonlinear terms in the equations which couple the rotating mass to the external field. In other words, a spinning object drags space around with it,' she said. '*Inertial drag*. And that's the torque the *Northern* is experiencing now.'

'What else?' Louise asked. 'Mark?'

He nodded. 'The first point is, we're *drowning* in radio-wavelength photons –'

That was unexpected. 'What are you talking about?'

'I mean it,' he said seriously, turning to face her. 'That's the single most significant difference in our gross physical environment, compared to the era we came from: we're now immersed in a dense mush of radio waves.' He looked absent for a moment. 'And the intensity of it is increasing. There's an *amplification* going on, slow, but significant on the timescales of this war; the doubling time is around a thousand years. Louise, none of this shows up in the future era. By then, the radio photons will be gone.'

Louise shook her head. 'I can't make sense of this. What's causing the amplification?'

He shrugged, theatrically. 'Beats me.' He glanced around the sky. 'But look around. The Ring is contained in a shell of galactic material, Louise. The frequencies of the radio waves are below the plasma frequency of the interstellar medium. So the waves are *trapped* in this galaxy-walled box. We're inside an immense resonant cavity, ten million light-years across, with reflecting walls.'

Morrow looked beyond the skydome uncertainly. 'Trapped? But what happens when –'

Lieserl cut in, 'Mark, I think I've figured it out. The cause of the radio-wave amplification.'

He glanced at her. 'What?'

'It's the inertial drag. We're seeing superradiant scattering from the gravitational field. A photon, falling into the Ring's gravity well, is coupled to the Ring by the inertial drag, and is then thrown out with additional energy –'

'*Ah*. Right.' Mark nodded, looking distant. 'That would give an amplification of a few tenths of one per cent each traverse ... just about fitting my observations.'

Morrow frowned. 'Did I understand that? It sounds as if the photons are doing gravitational slingshots around this Ring.'

Louise smiled at him, sensing his fear. 'That's right. The inertial drag is letting each photon extract a little energy from the Ring; the radiation is amplified, and the Ring is left spinning just a fraction slower ...

'Lieserl. Tell us more about the spacetime metric.' She looked up, at the point of light at the heart of the Ring. 'What do we see, there, at the centre?'

Lieserl looked up, her face composed. 'I think you know, Louise. It is *a singularity*, at the centre of the Ring itself. The singularity is hoop-shaped, a circular flaw in space: a rip, caused by the rotation of the immense mass of the Ring. The singularity is about three hundred light-years across – obviously a lot smaller than the diameter of the material Ring ...

'If the Ring were spinning more slowly, the Kerr metric would be quite well-behaved. The singularity would be cloaked in *two* event horizons – one-way membranes into the centre – and, beyond them, by an *ergosphere*: a region in which the inertial drag is so strong that *nothing* sublight can resist it. If we were in an ergosphere, we'd have no choice but to rotate with the Ring. In fact, if it weren't rotating at all, the Kerr field would collapse into a simple, stationary black hole, with a point singularity, a single event horizon and no ergosphere.

'But the Ring *is* spinning ... and too rapidly to permit the formation of an event horizon, or an ergosphere. And so . . . '

Louise prompted, 'Yes, Lieserl?'

'And so, the singularity is *naked*.'

Michael Poole sat with his legs crossed comfortably on the shoulder of the nightfighter. His gaze was on Spinner's face, steady, direct.

The Ring is a machine, whose sole purpose is to manufacture that naked singularity. Don't you see? The Xeelee constructed this huge Ring and set it spinning – in order to tear a hole in the Universe.

Spinner-of-Rope enhanced the false-colour of the central singularity in her faceplate imager. The flaw looked like a solid disc – a coin, perhaps – almost on edge towards her, but tipped slightly so that she could see its upper surface.

In that surface, white starlight swam. (*White?*)

She said to Poole, 'The Xeelee built all of this – they modified history, disrupted spacetime, drew in galaxies to their destruction across hundreds of millions of light-years – just for *this*?'

Poole lifted his eyebrows. *It is the greatest baryonic artefact, Spinner-of-Rope. The greatest achievement of the Xeelee . . .*

The singularity was like a jewel, surrounded by the undisciplined string-scribble of the Ring itself.

'It's very beautiful,' she conceded.

Poole smiled. *Ah, but its beauty lies in what it does . . .*

He turned his gaunt, tired face up to the singularity. *Spinner-of-Rope, humans have imputed many purposes to this artefact. But the Ring is not a fortress, or a last redoubt, or a battleship, or a base from which the Xeelee can reclaim their baryonic Universe,* he said sadly. *Spinner, the Xeelee know they have lost this war in Heaven. Perhaps they have always known that, even from the dawn of their history.*

'I don't understand.'

Spinner, the singularity is an escape hatch.

Lieserl and Mark turned to each other, inhumanly quickly. They stared into each other's eyes, as if exchanging data by some means invisible to humans, their blank expressions like mirror images.

'What is it?' Louise asked. 'What's happened?'

Pixels, defects in the Virtual projection, crawled across Mark's cheek. 'We need Spinner-of-Rope,' he snapped. 'We can't wait for the repairs to the data links. We're trying to find bypasses – working quickly –'

Louise frowned. 'Why?'

Mark turned to her, his face expressionless. 'We're in trouble, Louise. The cops are here.'

Spinner-of-Rope asked, 'How do you *destroy* a loop of cosmic string ten million light-years across?'

It isn't so difficult … if you have the resources of a universe, and a billion years, to play with, Spinner-of-Rope. Poole, perched on the shoulder of the nightfighter, pointed at a hail of infalling galaxies swamping a nearby section of the Ring. *If the Ring tangles – if cosmic string self-intersects – it cuts itself,* he said. *It intercommutes. And a new subloop is formed, budding off the old. And perhaps that subloop, too, will self-intersect, and split into still smaller loops … and so on.*

Spinner nodded. 'I think I understand. It would be an exponential process, once started. Pretty soon, the Ring would decay into the torus of debris we found – will find – a hundred thousand years from now …'

Yes. No doubt the motion of the Ring has been designed by the Xeelee so that it does not cut itself. But all one need do is start the process, by disrupting the Ring's periodic behaviour. And that is evidently what the photino birds are endeavouring to do, by hurling galaxies – like thrown rocks – at the Ring.

Spinner sniffed. 'Seems kind of a crude technique.'

Poole laughed. *Baryonic chauvinism, Spinner-of-Rope? Besides, the birds have other mechanisms. I –*

'… Spinner. *Spinner-of-Rope.* Can you hear me?'

Spinner sat bolt upright in her couch and clutched at her helmet. 'Lieserl? Is that you?'

'Listen to me. We don't have much time.'

'Oh, Lieserl, I was beginning to think I'd never –'

'*Spinner*! Shut up, damn you, and *listen*.'

Spinner subsided. She'd never heard Lieserl use a tone like that before.

'Use the waldoes, Spinner. You have to get us out of here. Take us straight up, with the hyperdrive, over the plane of the Ring. Have you got that? Use the longest jump distance you can find. We'll try to patch subroutines into the waldoes, but –'

'Lieserl, you're scaring the pants off me. Can't you tell me what's wrong?'

'No time, Spinner. Please. Just do it ...'

The Universe *darkened*.

For a bleak, heart-stopping instant Spinner thought she was going blind. But the telltales on the waldoes still gleamed at her, as brightly as ever.

She looked up. There was something before the ship, occluding the blue-shifted galaxy fragments, hiding the Ring.

She saw night-dark wings, spread to their fullest extent, looming over the *Northern*.

Nightfighters.

She twisted in her seat. There were *hundreds* of them – impossibly many, dark lanterns hanging in the sky.

They were Xeelee. The *Northern* was surrounded.

Spinner screamed, and slammed her fists against the hyperdrive waldo.

The 'fighters moved through electric-blue cosmic string like birds through the branches of a forest. There were so *many* of them in this era. They were cool and magnificent, their nightdark forms arrayed deep into space all around her. Lieserl stared at the swooping, gliding forms, willing herself to see them more clearly. Had any humans ever been closer to Xeelee than this?

The Xeelee moved in tight formation, like bird-flocks, or schools of fish; they executed sudden changes of direction, their domain wall wings beating, in squads spanning millions of miles – absolutely in unison. Now Lieserl saw how 'fighters *should* be handled, in contrast to Spinner's earnest, clumsy work. The nightfighters were sculptures of spacetime, with a sleek beauty that made her shiver: this was baryonic technology raised to perfection, to a supreme art, she thought.

She was struck by the contrast between this era and the age of devastation – of victory for the photino birds – to which the *Northern* had first brought them. Here, the Ring was complete and magnificent, and the Xeelee, in their pomp, filled space. Already, she knew, the final defeat was inevitable, and the Xeelee were, in truth, huddling inside their final redoubt. But still, her heart beat harder inside her as she looked out over this, the supremacy of baryonic life.

The overlapping lengths of string slid down, smoothly, past the lifedome, as the *Northern* climbed. The nightfighters swooped like starlings through the string, and around the *Northern* – no, Spinner realized suddenly; the nightfighters were *flickering* across space.

'They're using their hyperdrive,' she breathed.

Yes. Poole stared up at the nightfighters, his lined face translucent. *And we're hyperdriving too. You're pushing it, Spinner; we've never tried jumps of this scale, even in test. Do you know how fast you're travelling? Ten thousand light-years with every jump . . . But even so, the Xeelee are easily keeping pace with us.*

Of course they are, Spinner thought. *They are Xeelee.*

These 'fighters could have stopped the *Northern* at any time – even destroyed it. But they hadn't.

Why not?

The ship was rising high above the plane of the Ring. The tangle of string fell away from the foreground, and she could see easily now the million-light-year curve of the structure's limb. And at the heart of the Ring, the singularity seemed to be unfolding towards her, almost welcoming.

The Xeelee 'fighters rose all around her, like leaves in a storm. *They can't believe we're a threat. I guess humans never were a threat, in truth. Now, it's almost as if the Xeelee are escorting us,* she thought.

'Lieserl,' she said.

'I hear you, Spinner-of-Rope.'

'Tell me what in *Lethe's* name we're doing.'

'You're taking us out of the plane of the Ring . . .'

'And then?'

'*Down* . . .' Lieserl hesitated. 'Look, Spinner, we've got to get away from the Xeelee, before they change their mind about us. And we've nowhere else to run, not in all of the Universe.'

'And this is your plan?' Spinner was aware of the hysteria in her own voice; she felt fear spread through her stomach and chest, like a cold fluid. '*To fly into a singularity?*'

Mark punched his thigh. 'I was right, damn it,' he said. 'I was right all along.'

The tension was a painful presence, clamped around Louise's throat. 'Damn it, Mark, be specific.'

He turned to her. 'About the significance of the radio energy flux. Don't you see? The photino birds have *manufactured* this immense cavity, of stars and smashed-up galaxies, to imprison the Ring.' He glanced around the skydome. 'Lethe. It must have taken them a billion years, but they've done it. They've built a huge mirror of star-stuff, all around the Ring. It's a feat of cosmic engineering almost on a par with the construction of the Ring itself.'

'A mirror?'

'The interstellar medium is opaque to the radio energy. So each radio photon gets reflected back into the cavity. The photon orbits the Ring – and on each pass it's superradiant-amplified, as Lieserl described, and so sucks out a little more energy from the inertial drag of the Ring's rotation. And then the photon heads out again ... *but it's still trapped by the galaxy mirror*. Back it goes again, to receive a little more amplification ... Do you see? It's a classic example of positive feedback. The trapped radio modes will grow endlessly, leaching energy from the Ring itself ...'

'But the modes can't grow indefinitely,' Morrow said.

'No,' Mark said. 'The process is an *inertial bomb*, Morrow. All that electromagnetic pressure will build up in the cavity, until it can no longer be contained. And in the end – probably only a few tens of millennia from now – it will blow the cavity apart.'

Louise glanced around the sky, seeing again the smooth distribution of galaxies she'd noted earlier. 'Right. And, in a hundred thousand years, the *Northern* will fly right into the middle of the debris from that huge explosion.'

Now the ship had sailed high above the plane of the Ring; Louise could see the whole structure, laid out before her like the rim of a glimmering mirror, with the sparkle of the singularity at its heart.

Lieserl said, 'Louise, the hostile photino bird activity we've noted before – the direct assault on the Ring itself with lumps of matter – is spectacular, but Mark's right: this radio bomb trick is what will truly bring down the Ring.' A subtle smile played on her lips. 'It's damn clever. The birds are draining the Ring itself, drawing energy out of the gravitational field using inertial drag. They're going to use the Ring's own mass-energy to wreck it.'

Subvocally, Louise checked her chronometer. Less than twenty minutes had elapsed since Mark and Lieserl had ordered Spinner to start moving the ship, but already they must have crossed eight million light-years – already they must be poised directly above the singularity.

'Mark. Where are we going?'

Poole, evidently trying to calm Spinner, told her what would happen to the nightfighter as it approached the disc singularity.

A timelike trajectory could reach the upper surface of the disc, Poole told her. A ship could reach the *plane* of the singularity. But – so said the equations of the Kerr metric – no timelike trajectory could pass *through* the singularity loop and emerge from the other side.

'So what happens? Will the ship be destroyed?'

No.

'But if the ship can't travel through the loop – where does it go?'

There can be no discontinuity in the metric, you see, Spinner-of-Rope. Poole hesitated. *Spinner-of-Rope, the singularity plane is a place where universes kiss.*

'Lethe,' Louise said. 'You're planning to take us *out of the Universe*?'

Mark swivelled his head towards her, unnaturally stiffly; the degradation of the image of his face – the crawling pixel-defects, the garish colour of his eyes – made him look utterly inhuman. 'We've nowhere else to run, Louise. Unless you have a better idea ...'

She stared up at the singularity. The AIs, working together at inhuman speed, had come up with a response to this scenario. *But are they right?* She felt the situation slipping away from her; she tried to *plan*, to come to terms with this.

Lieserl said drily, 'Of course, timing is going to be critical. Or we might end up in the wrong universe ...'

Morrow clung to his scooter, his eyes wide, his knuckles bloodless. 'What in Lethe's name are you talking about now?'

Mark hesitated. 'The configuration of the string is changing constantly. It's a dynamic system. And that's changing the topology of the Kerr metric – it's changing the basis of the analytical continuation of space through the singularity plane ...'

'Damn you,' Morrow said. 'I wish you'd stick to English.'

'The singularity plane is a point at which this Universe touches another smoothly. Okay? But because of the oscillations of the Ring, the contact point with the other universe isn't a constant. It's changing. Every few minutes – sometimes more frequently – the interface changes to another continuation region – to *another* universe.'

Morrow frowned. 'Is that significant for us?'

Mark ran a hand through his hair. 'Only because the changes aren't predictable, either in timing or scope. Maybe the changes cycle round, for all I know, so if we wait long enough we'll get a second chance.'

'But we don't have time to wait.'

'No. Well, we're not exactly planning this ... We won't be able to choose which universe we end up in. And not every universe is habitable, of course ...'

Louise pressed her knuckles to her temples. *Good point, Mark. We've decided to commit ourselves to crashing out of our Universe, and we have half the Xeelee nightfighters in creation on our tails already ... and now you bring me this. What am I supposed to do about it?*

'Tell me what you see through there right now,' she said. 'Tell me about the universe on the other side of the Kerr interface.'

'Now?' Mark looked doubtful. 'Louise, you're asking me to come up with an analysis of a whole cosmos – based on a few muddled glimpses – in a few seconds. It's taken all of human history even to begin a partial –'

'Just do it,' she snapped.

He studied her briefly, his expression even. 'Some of the twin universes feature a degree of variation to our physical laws. That's no great surprise; the constants of physics are just an arbitrary expression of the way the symmetries at the beginning of time were broken ... But even those universes with *identical* laws to ours can be very different, because of changed boundary conditions at the beginning of time – or even, simply, from being at a different stage of their evolutionary cycles to ours.'

413

'And in this particular case?' she asked heavily.

He closed his eyes. Louise could see that stray pixels, yellow and purple, were again migrating across the Virtual images of his cheeks. His eyes snapped open, startling her. 'High gravity,' he said.

'What?'

'Variation of the laws. In the neighbouring universe, the constant of gravity is high – enormously high – compared to, uh, *here*.'

Morrow looked nervous. 'What would that mean? Would we be crushed?'

More pixels, glitches in the image, trekked across Mark's cheeks. 'No. But human bodies would have discernible gravity fields. You could *feel* Louise's mass, Morrow, with a pull of about half a gee.'

Morrow looked even more alarmed.

'Stars could be no more than a mile wide, and they would burn for only a year,' Mark said. 'Planets the size of Earth would collapse under their own weight immediately ...'

Lieserl frowned. 'Could we survive there?'

Mark shrugged. 'I don't know. The lifedome would implode immediately under its own weight. We'd need to find a source of breathable air, and fast. And we'd have to live in free-fall; any sizeable mass would exert unbearably high gravitational forces. But maybe we could make some kind of raft of the wreckage of the *Northern* ...'

Lieserl looked up into the singularity plane, and her expression softened. 'We know there have been human assaults in the Ring – like the neutron star missile. So perhaps we are not the first human pilgrims to fall through the Ring. Mark, you said the bridge to the other universe goes through cycles. I wonder if there are humans on the other side of that interface even now, clinging to rafts made from wrecked warships, struggling to survive in their high-gravity world ...'

Mark smiled; he seemed to be relaxing. 'Well, if there are, we won't meet them. That continuation has closed off; a new one is opening ... Wherever we're going, it won't be *there*.'

Louise glanced up at the false-colour sky. '... I think it's time to find out,' she said.

The *Northern* reached the zenith of its arc, high over the plane of the Ring.

Spinner felt as if she were suspended at the top of some huge cosmic tree, a million light-years high. The ship was poised above the singularity's central, glittering pool of muddled starlight, and beyond that, at the edge of her field of view, was the titanic form of the Ring itself.

The flock of nightfighters hovered in a rough cap around her and above her, their wings spread. The 'fighters were sharp, elegant forms, filling space.

Spinner-of-Rope closed her hands over the hyperdrive waldo.

Now, it was like tumbling out of the tree.

The nightfighter *fell* through space, covering ten thousand light-years every second.

The singularity is a gateway to other universes, Michael Poole said. *Who knows? – perhaps to better ones than this.*

In fact, Poole told her, there had to exist *further* gateways, in the universe beyond, to still more cosmoses ... He painted a picture of a mosaic of universes, connected by the glowing doorways of positive and negative Kerr singularities. *It's wonderful, Spinner-of-Rope.*

Spinner stared down at the singularity. 'Is this what they intended? Did the Xeelee *mean* to construct the singularity as a gateway?'

Of course they did. Why do you think they made the singularity so damned big? ... So that ships could pass through it, without being destroyed by tidal forces from the singularity thread.

Spinner-of-Rope, this is the Xeelee's most magnificent achievement. I would have liked to tell you some day how this Ring was built ... how the Xeelee returned through time and even re-engineered their own evolution, to give themselves the capabilities to achieve this.

'You would have *liked* to tell me ... ?'

Yes. Poole sounded sad. *Spinner, I'm not going to get the chance ... I can't follow you.*

'What?'

It was as if she descended through an immense tunnel, walled by the distant, irrelevant forms of blue-shifted galaxies. The singularity was the starlit open base of that tunnel, out of which she would fall into –

Into what?

Still, the starling flocks of nightfighters swirled around the ship.

'You know,' she said, 'the Xeelee could have stopped us at almost any point. I'm sure they could destroy us even now.'

I'm sure they could.

'But they haven't.'

Perhaps they are helping us, Spinner-of-Rope. Maybe there is some residual loyalty among the baryonic species, after all.

'...Spinner-of-Rope.'

'Yes, Lieserl.'

'Listen to me. The trip through the singularity is going to be – complicated.'

'Oh, good,' Spinner said drily.

'Spinner, the spacetime manifold around here isn't simple. Far enough out the singularity will attract us – draw us in. But close to the plane of the singularity, there is a *barrier* of potential in the gravitational field.'

She sighed. 'What does that mean?'

'... *Antigravity*, Spinner-of-Rope. The plane will actually repel us. If we don't have enough kinetic energy as we approach the plane, we'll be pushed away: either back to the asymptotically flat regions – I mean, to infinity, far from the plane – or else back into the zone of attraction. We could oscillate, Spinner, alternately falling and being repelled.'

'What happens on the other side? Will we be drawn back into the plane?'

'No.' Lieserl hesitated. 'When we pass through the plane, there is a co-ordinate sign change in the metric ... The singularity will push us away. It will hurl us on, deep into the new universe.'

'So what do I have to do?'

'To get over the potential barrier, we need to build up our kinetic energy *before* we hit the plane of the singularity. Spinner, you're going to have to operate your discontinuity drive *in parallel* with the hyperdrive. The fractions of a second between jumps, when we're in normal space, will be enough to let us begin our normal-space acceleration.'

Spinner felt sweat trickle over her face, pooling under her eyes behind her spectacles. She was afraid, suddenly, she realized: but not of the singularity, or what might lie beyond, but of *failing*. 'That's ridiculous, Lieserl. How am I supposed to pull that off? What am I, a spider-monkey?'

Lieserl laughed. 'Well, I'm sorry, Spinner-of-Rope. We're making this up as we go along, you know ...'

'I can't do it.'

'I know you can,' Lieserl said calmly.

'*How* do you know?'

Lieserl was silent for a pregnant moment. Then she said, '*Because you have help*. Don't you, Spinner-of-Rope?'

And Spinner felt the warm hands of Michael Poole close over hers once more, strong, reassuring.

The discontinuity-drive wings unfurled behind the hulk of the lifedome, powerful and graceful.

'If it's any consolation, Spinner, we'll be a spectacular sight as we hit the plane,' Lieserl said. 'We'll shed our Kerr plunge radiation in a single burst of gravity waves ...'

The singularity plane was widening; it was a disc, filled with jumbled starlight, opening like a mouth.

'Michael, will there be photino birds, in the new universe?'

I don't know, Spinner.

'Will there be Xeelee?'

I don't know.

'I want you to come with me.'

I can't. I'm sorry. The quantum functions which sustain me don't traverse the plane of the singularity.

The Xeelee 'fighters swirled around her cage, graceful, their nightdark wings beating. They filled space to infinity, magnificent here at the heart of their final defeat. The plane of the singularity was a sea of silver light below her.

The construction material of her cage, of the wings, began to *glow*, as if white-hot.

Michael Poole turned to her, and nodded gently. The construction-material light shone out through his translucent face, making him look like a sculpture of light, she thought. He opened his mouth, as if to speak to her, but she couldn't hear him; and now the light was all around him, engulfing him.

'Come with me!' she screamed.

And now, suddenly, dramatically, the singularity was *here*. Its rim exploded outwards, all around her, and she fell, helplessly, into a pool of muddled starlight.

She cringed into herself and clutched her hands to her chest; her worn arrow-head dug into her chest, a tiny mote of human pain.

33

The lifedome was plunged into darkness.

The jungle sounds beneath Louise were subdued, as if night had fallen suddenly ... or as if an eclipse had covered the Sun.

The lifedome groaned, massively; it was like being trapped inside the chest of some huge, suffering beast. That was stress on the hull: the co-ordinate change, as the ship had crossed the singularity plane.

We have entered a new cosmos, then. Is it over? Louise felt like an animal, helpless and naked beneath a storm-laden sky.

Lieserl had spoken of how all of human history was funnelling through this single, ramshackle moment. If that was true, then perhaps, before she had time to draw more than a few breaths, her own life – and the long, bloody story of man – would be over.

... And yet the sky beyond the dome wasn't completely dark, Louise saw. There was a mottling of grey: elusive, almost invisible. When she stared up into that colourless gloom, it was like staring into the blood vessels she saw when she closed her own eyelids; she felt a disturbing sense of unreality, as if her body – and the *Northern*, and all its hapless crew – had been entombed, suddenly, within some gross extension of her own head.

There was a rasp, as of a match being struck. Louise cried out.

Mark's face, dramatically underlit by a flickering flame, appeared out of the gloom. Lieserl laughed.

'Lethe,' Louise said, disgusted. 'Even at a time like this, you can't resist showing off, can you, Mark?'

'Sorry,' he said, grinning boyishly. 'Well, the good news is we're all still alive. And,' more hesitantly, 'I can't detect any variation of the physical constants from our own Universe. It looks as if we may be able to survive here. For a time, at any rate ...'

Lieserl snorted. 'Well, if this universe is so dazzlingly similar to our own – *where are the stars?*'

Now the lifedome began to lighten, as Mark kicked in image enhancing routines. It was almost like a sunrise, Louise thought, except that in this case the spreading light did not emerge from any one of the lifedome's 'horizons'; it simply broke through the muddy darkness, right across the dome.

In a few heartbeats, the image stabilized.

There *were* stars here, Louise saw immediately. But these were *giants* – and not like the bloated near-corpse which Sol had become, but huge, vigorous, brilliant white bodies each of which looked as if it could have swallowed a hundred Sols side by side.

The giants filled the sky, almost as if they were jostling each other. Several of them were close enough to show discs, smooth white patches of light.

Nowhere in her own Universe, Louise realized, could one have seen a sight like this.

Beside her, Lieserl sighed. 'Uh-oh,' she said.

PART VI

EVENT: NEW SOL

34

The light of New Sol gleamed from the pod's clear hull, unremitting, blinding. Louise watched the faces of Mark, Spinner-of-Rope and Morrow as they peered out at the new cosmos. The pod turned slowly on its axis, and the brilliant young lamps of this new universe wheeled around them, bathing their profiles in intense white brilliance.

For their new sun, the crew of the *Northern* had selected a particular VMO: a *Very Massive Object*, a star of a thousand Solar masses – a typical member of this alternate cosmos. This star drifted through the halo of a galaxy, outside the galaxy's main disc. Huge shells of matter – emitted when the star was even younger – surrounded New Sol, expanding from it at close to the speed of light.

The *Great Northern* itself hovered, a few miles from the pod. By the harsh, colourless light of New Sol Louise could see the bulky outline of the lifedome, with the sleek, dark shape of the Xeelee nightfighter still attached to the dome's base – and there, still clearly visible, was the hull-scar left by the impact with the strand of cosmic string.

The battered ship orbited the new sun as timidly as ice comets had once circled Sol itself – so widely that each 'year' here would last more than a million Earth years. The ship was far enough away that the VMO's brilliance was diminished by distance to something like Sol's. But even so, Louise thought, there was no possibility that the VMO could ever be mistaken for a modest G-type star like Sol. The VMO was only ten times the diameter of old Sol, so that from this immense distance the star's bulk was reduced to a mere point of light – but its photosphere was a hundred times as hot as Sol. The VMO was a dazzling point, hanging in darkness; if she studied it too long the point of light left trails on her bruised retinae.

Externally, the *Northern*'s lifedome looked much as it had throughout its long and unlikely career: the ship's lights glowed defiantly against the glare of this new cosmos, and the forest was a splash of Earth-green, flourishing in the filtered light of New Sol. But inside, the *Northern* had become very different. In the year since its arrival through the Ring, the dome had been transformed into a workshop: a factory for the manufacture of exotic matter and drone scoop-ships.

Morrow, beside Louise, was blinking into the light of New Sol. His cupped hand shaded his eyes, the shadows of his fingers sharp on his face. He was frowning and looked pale. He caught Louise's glance. 'Things are certainly different here,' he said wryly.

She smiled. 'If we ever build a world here, it won't have a sun in the sky. Instead, by day there will be this single point source, gleaming like some unending supernova. The shadows will be long and deep ... and at night, the sky will shine. It's going to seem very strange.'

He glanced at her sharply. 'Well, it will be strange for those of you who remember Earth, I guess,' he said. 'But, frankly, there aren't so many of you around any more ...'

Now the pod's rotation carried the new sun out of visibility, below the pod's limited horizon. And – slowly, majestically – the lights of their new galaxy rose over their heads.

This galaxy was a flat elliptical, but would have seemed a dwarf compared to the great galaxies on the other side of the Ring: with a mass of a billion suns, the star system was a mere hundredth the bulk of the Milky Way, or Andromeda, and not much larger than the old Magellanic Clouds, the minor companion galaxies to the Milky Way. And – since the average size of stars here was a hundred times greater than in the Milky Way – there were only ten million stars in this galaxy, compared to the Milky Way's hundred billion ... But every one of those stars was a brilliant white VMO, making this galaxy into a tapestry of piercingly bright points of light. It was like, Louise thought, surveying a field of ten million gems fixed to a bed of velvet.

This universe was crowded with these bland, toy galaxies; they filled space in a random but uniform array, as far as could be seen in all directions. This cosmos was *young* – too young for

424

the immense, slow, processes of time to have formed the great structures of galactic clusters, superclusters, walls and voids which would one day dominate space.

Morrow stared up uneasily at the soaring form of the galaxy. Apparently unconsciously, he wrapped both hands across his stomach.

'Morrow, are you okay?'

'I'm fine,' he told Louise, unconvincingly. 'I guess I'm just a little susceptible to centrifugal force.'

Louise patted his hands. 'It's probably Coriolis, actually – the sideways force. But you shouldn't let the pod's rotation bother you,' she said. She thought it over. 'In fact, you should *welcome* your motion sickness.'

Morrow raised his shaven eyebrow ridges. 'Really?'

'It's a sensation that tells you you're *here*, Morrow. Embedded in this new universe . . .'

The laws of physics were expressions of basic *symmetries*, Louise told him. And symmetries between frames of reference were among the most powerful symmetries there were.

Morrow looked dubious. 'What has this to do with space-sickness?'

'Well, look: here's a particular type of symmetry. The pod's rotating, in the middle of a stationary universe. So you feel centrifugal and Coriolis forces – twisting forces. The forces are what is making you uncomfortable. But what about *symmetry*? Try a thought experiment. Imagine that the pod was stationary, in the middle of a rotating universe.' She raised her hands to the galaxy wheeling above them. 'How would you tell the difference? The stars would look the same, moving around the pod.'

'And we'd feel the same spin forces?'

'Yes, we would. You'd feel just as queasy, Morrow.'

'But where would the forces come from?'

She smiled. 'That's the point. They would come from the inertial drag of the rotating universe: a drag exerted by the huge river of stars and galaxies, flowing around you.

'So you shouldn't be worried by, or embarrassed by, your queasiness. That's the feeling of your new universe, plucking at you with fingers of inertial drag.'

He smiled weakly, and ran a palm over his bare, sweat-sprinkled scalp. 'Well, thanks for the thought,' he said. 'But somehow it doesn't make me feel a lot better.'

Spinner-of-Rope and Mark were sitting in the two seats behind Louise and Morrow. Now Mark leaned forward. 'Well, it should,' he said. 'The fact that general relativity is working here – as, in fact, are all our familiar laws as far as we can tell, to the limits of observation – is the reason we're still alive, probably.'

Spinner-of-Rope snorted; VMO light gleamed from the arrow-head pendant she still wore between her breasts. 'Maybe so. But if this universe is so damn *similar*, I don't see why it should be so *different*. If you see what I mean.'

Mark spread his hands, and tilted his head back to look at the dwarf galaxy. 'The only real difference, Spinner, is one of point of view. It's all a question of *when.*'

Spinner frowned. 'What do you mean, "when"?' Behind her spectacles Spinner's small, round face seemed set, intent on the conversation, but Louise noticed how her hands tugged at each other endlessly, like small animals wriggling in her lap. Spinner-of-Rope had been left too long in that nightfighter pilot cage, Louise thought. Spinner had seen too much, too fast . . .

Since she'd been retrieved from the cage Spinner had *seemed* healthy enough, and Mark assured Louise that she'd retained her basic sanity. Even her illusion of communicating with Michael Poole – an illusion she'd dropped as they came through the Ring – seemed to have had *some,* unfathomable, basis in reality, Mark said.

Fine. But, Louise sensed, Spinner-of-Rope still wasn't fully recovered from her ordeal. She still wasn't *whole*. It would take time – decades, perhaps – for the post-traumatic stress to work its way out of her system. Well, Spinner-of-Rope would *have* the time she needed, Louise was determined.

Mark said, 'Spinner, this universe is just like ours – except that it's around twenty billion years younger.

'This is a baby cosmos. It emerged from its own Big Bang less than a billion years ago. And it's *smaller* – spacetime hasn't had the time to unravel as far as in our old Universe, so this cosmos is something of the order of a hundredth the size. And the stars –'

'Yes?'

'Spinner, these are the first stars ever to shine here. Not one of the stars we see out there is more than a million years old.'

Out of the primordial nucleosynthesis of the singularity, here, had emerged clouds of hydrogen and helium, with little contamination by heavier elements. The new sky had been dark, illuminated only by the dying echo of the radiation which had emerged from the singularity. Then the gas clouds gathered into proto-galactic clumps, each with the mass of a billion Sols. Thermal instabilities had caused the proto-galaxies to collapse further, into knots with mass a hundred Suns or more.

Soon, the first of these smooth-burning stars had guttered to life: brilliant monsters, some with the mass of a million Suns.

Slowly, the sky had filled with light.

'The way these stars were born is unique,' Mark said, 'because they are the *first*. There were no previous stars. So the proto-galaxies were a lot smoother – the gas clouds weren't all churned up by the heat and gravity of earlier generations of stars. And the gas was free of heavy elements. Heavy elements act to keep young stars cooler, and to limit the size of the stars that form. That's why these babies are so immense.

'These are what we call Population III stars, Spinner. Or VMOs – "Very Massive Objects".'

'If they are so massive,' Spinner said slowly, 'then I guess they won't last so long as stars like Sol.'

Louise looked at her appreciatively. 'That's perceptive, Spinner. You're right. The VMOs burn their hydrogen fuel quickly. Each of these is going to stay on its Main Sequence for no more than a few million years – two or three, at best. The Sun, on the other hand, should have survived for tens of *billions* of years, without the interference of the photino birds.'

'What then?' Spinner asked. 'What do we do when New Sol goes out?'

Morrow smiled. 'Then, I guess, we move on: to another star, and another, and another … We have time here to work that out, I think, Spinner-of-Rope.'

Now New Sol was rising again, over the lip of the pod. The four of them turned instinctively to the light, its flat whiteness smoothing the lines of age and fatigue in their faces.

'In fact,' Mark said, 'the star we've chosen – New Sol – is already well past its middle age. It's probably got no more than three-quarters of a million years of its life left.'

Spinner frowned. 'That seems stupid. Why not choose a young star, and move there while we can? It may be that when New Sol dies we won't be *able* to move away.'

'No,' Mark said patiently. 'Spinner, we *need* an older star.'

The star called New Sol was nearing the end of the *second* phase of its existence. In the first, it had burned hydrogen into helium. Now, helium was fusing in turn, and a rain of more complex elements had formed a new, inner core: principally oxygen, but also neon, silicon, carbon, magnesium and others.

And later, in the third phase of its life, when the oxygen started to burn, the star would die . . . although *how* was far from certain.

'Terrific,' Spinner said. 'And we die with it.'

'No,' Mark said seriously. 'Spinner-of-Rope, we die *without* it. Don't you get it? New Sol is full of *oxygen* . . .'

Morrow was pointing, excitedly. 'Look. *Look.* There's the wormhole . . . I think it's almost time.'

Louise turned in her seat.

Now a new form emerged over the rotating pod's horizon: the familiar shape of a wormhole Interface. This Interface was only a hundred yards across – far smaller than the mile-wide monster the *Northern* had hauled across a different spacetime – but, like its grander cousins of the past, it shared the classic tetrahedral frame, the shining electric blue colour of its exotic matter struts, and the autumn-gold glimmering of its faces. A dozen drone scoop-ships prowled around the Interface, patient, waiting.

Louise felt a prickle of tears in her eyes; she brushed them away impatiently. *Already*, she thought, *we are building things here. Already, we are engineering this universe.*

Mark said to Spinner, 'If there were planets here we could land and try to terraform one. But there *are* no planets for us to land on. *Anywhere.* This is a very young universe. There are no more than traces of heavy elements here, anywhere, outside the interior of the protostars. There are no moons, no comets, no asteroids . . . We have no raw materials to build with, save the hulk of the *Northern* – save what we brought here ourselves. We can't even renew our atmosphere.'

Morrow nodded. 'So,' he said, 'we're mining the star.'

The second terminus of this wormhole had been dropped into the carcass of New Sol. Lieserl had accompanied the Interface – just as once she had travelled into the heart of Sol itself. Soon, enriched gases from the heart of the new star would pour into space – *here*, far from the heat of New Sol, accessible.

The scoop-ships had mouths constructed of electromagnetic fields which could gather in the star-dust across volumes of millions of cubic miles. When the wormhole started to operate, the scoops would sift out the few grains of precious heavy elements.

'The first priority is atmospheric gases,' Mark said. 'We lost a lot of our recyclable reserve during the string impact. Another blow-out like that and we'd be finished.'

'Are all the gases we need there, inside the star?'

'Well, there's plenty of oxygen, Spinner,' Louise said. 'But that's not enough. An all-oxygen atmosphere isn't particularly stable – it's too inflammable. We need a neutral buffer gas, to contribute to the hundreds of millibars of pressure we need to stay alive.'

'Like nitrogen,' Spinner said.

'Yes. But there isn't much nitrogen in New Sol. We should be able to use neon, though . . .'

'We can replace our other stores. Use the oxygen to make water and food.'

'We can do more than that, Spinner-of-Rope,' Mark said. 'In the longer term we can extract heavier elements: magnesium, silicon, carbon – maybe even iron. They are only present in traces in New Sol, but they're *there*. We can build a fleet of *Northerns*, if we're patient enough. Why, we can even make rocks.'

Spinner looked out at New Sol, and the point light glittered in her eyes, making her look very young, Louise thought. Spinner said, 'It's chilling to think that – except maybe for the Xeelee – we're *alone* here, in this universe. Stars like this once burned in our Universe – but they were all extinguished, destroyed, long before humans became conscious.

'We may survive for millions of years here. But, finally, we'll be gone. New Sol, and all these other stars, will destroy themselves. Eventually, a new generation of stars will form in the enriched galaxies – stars like Sol. And, I guess, intelligence will arise here ...

'But not for billions of years after we're gone.'

Spinner turned to Louise, her eyes large, her expression fragile, troubled. Her hands tugged at each other's fingers, and played with the arrow-head pendant at her chest. 'Louise, nothing we build could survive such a length of time. No conceivable monument, or record, could persist. We'll be forgotten. No one will ever know we were here.'

Louise reached over the back of her chair and took Spinner's hands in hers, stilling their nervous motions. Again she felt a surge of responsibility for Spinner's fragile state. 'That's not true, Spinner,' she said gently. 'We'll still be there. These VMOs will leave traces in the microwave background – peaks of energy against the smooth radiation curves. There were traces like that in the microwave spectrum of our own Universe – that's how we know of our own primordial VMOs. And there will be other traces, relics of this time. These giant proto-stars will enrich the substance of the young galaxies here, with heavy elements. Without the heavy elements stars like old Sol could never form ... and we'll be part that enrichment, Spinner-of-Rope, tiny traces, atoms which formed in a different universe.'

Spinner-of-Rope frowned. 'A blip in the microwave background? Is that to be our final monument?'

'It might be sufficient to let the people of the future work out that we were here, perhaps. And besides, we might have a billion years ahead of us, Spinner. Time enough to think of something.' She stroked Spinner's hands. 'It would take a long time, but we could *build* a planet for ourselves, out here on the lip of New Sol's gravity well.' She smiled. Maybe they could construct an ocean, wide enough for the *Great Britain* to sail again. What would old Isambard have made of that? And –

'No,' Morrow said mildly.

Louise turned to him, surprised. His face, gaunt, shaven of hair, was smooth and confident-looking in the light of New Sol.

'What did you say?' Louise asked.

He turned to her. 'Planets are *inefficient*, Louise. Oh, they're convenient platforms if they exist already. But – to *build* a planet? Why bury all that painfully extracted matter *inside* your habitable surface?'

430

Louise found herself frowning; she was aware of Mark grinning at her, irritatingly. 'But what's the alternative?'

Morrow said, 'We can build structures in space: rings, hollow spheres – the point is to *maximize* the habitable surface available for a given mass – to spread it out as much as possible. Louise, a spherical planet gives you a *minimum* surface for a given mass.'

Louise studied Morrow curiously. His motion sickness was still evident in the pallor of his thin face, but he spoke with a vigour, a clarity she wouldn't have believed possible when she'd first met him, soon after his emergence from the Decks. Was it possible that the centuries of oppression, of body and soul, which he had endured in there, were at last beginning to lift?

Mark smiled at her. 'You'd better face it, Louise. You and I grew up on worlds, and so we think in terms of rebuilding what we've lost. We'd better move aside, and leave the future to these bright young kids.'

She found herself grinning back. She whispered, 'Okay, I take your point. But – *Morrow*, as a bright young kid?'

'Maybe we'll just build ships,' Spinner said intently. 'Whole armadas of them. We can simply *fly*; who needs to land, anyway? We could spread out, here. Maybe the Xeelee are here already – we came through *their* gateway, after all. We could see if we can find them . . .'

Mark scratched his chin. 'That's a good agenda, Spinner-of-Rope. You know, I think Garry Uvarov would be proud of you.'

She glared at him. She pulled her hands away from Louise, and for a moment – with her streak of scarlet face paint, and spectacles glinting with New Sol light – Spinner reminded Louise of the savage little girl she'd once been.

'Maybe he would,' Spinner snapped. 'But so what? I'm not a *creation* of Garry Uvarov. Uvarov was an oppressor, insane.'

Louise shrugged. 'Perhaps he was, in the end – and capricious. But he was also insightful, iconoclastic. He never let us turn away from the truth, in any situation, no matter how uncomfortable that was . . .'

Uvarov hadn't deserved to die, blind and alone, in a remote, deserted future.

Maybe Uvarov had been right, too, in the motives behind his great eugenics experiment. Not in his methods, of course . . . But

431

perhaps a natural, technology-independent immortality was a valid goal for the species.

Louise was aware that she and her crew had gone to a great deal of trouble to preserve the *essence* of humanity, through the collapse of the baryonic Universe. They hadn't sent mere records of humankind through the Ring, or Virtual representations of what man had been: they'd brought *people*, with all their faults and ambiguities and weaknesses, and *plumbing*. And now that they'd succeeded, perhaps it was time for human stock to begin to develop: to face up to and exceed the limitations, of body and spirit, which had, at last, caused the extinction of humanity in the old, abandoned Universe.

She wondered if, in several generations' time, the descendants of Spinner-of-Rope would indeed sail through this new universe in their sparkling ships. Perhaps when they finally met the Xeelee, it would be on equal terms; perhaps the new humans would be strong, immortal – and *sane*.

'. . . It's starting!' Morrow said, his voice high and tense. He pointed, his sleeve riding up his arm. 'Look at *that*.'

In a sudden eruption of light, gas blossomed from the four faces of the Interface. Still fusion-burning as it emerged, the gas rapidly expanded into a growing, cooling cloud. Louise could see the tetrahedral form of the Interface itself at the blazing heart of this animated sculpture of gas.

Diffuse light flooded the pod. It was as if a new, tiny star had ignited, here on the fringe of New Sol's gravity well. The drones flickered open their electromagnetic scoops and moved into the glowing, dispersing clouds, browsing patiently.

'Lethe's waters,' Morrow breathed. 'It's beautiful. It's like a flower.'

'More than that,' Mark said with a grin. 'It's beautiful because it's bloody *worked*.' He turned to Louise, his blue eyes brilliant, and his face looked youthful and alive.

'Louise,' he said, 'I think we might live through this after all.'

Louise reached for the pod's controls. The first loads of atmospheric gases would be arriving soon. And there were homes to be built. It was time to return to the *Northern* and get back to work.

Life would go on, she thought: as complicated, and messy, and *precious*, as ever.

*　　*　　*

Once again Lieserl spread her arms and soared through the interior of a star. But now her playground was no mere G-type yellow dwarf like the Sun: this was *New Sol* – a supergiant, salvaged for her from the dawn of time, fully ten million miles across.

Lethe's waters. I'd forgotten how wonderful this feels – how restrictive a human body could be . . .

I was born for this, she thought.

She arced upwards towards the photosphere – the star's surface was a wall of gas which seared space at a temperature of a hundred thousand degrees – and then she dived, yelling, down into the core. In Sol, the fusing core had been confined to the innermost few per cent of the diameter. Here, the core *was* the star, extending out almost to the photosphere itself. There was fusion burning *everywhere*. All around her helium burned into oxygen, dumping prodigious quantities of heat energy into the star's opaque flesh. In response, immense convective cells – some of them large enough to have swallowed Sol itself – surged through the interior.

This star was no more than a couple of million years old. But already – to her intense regret – she'd missed one of the most interesting phases of its existence.

The star had formed as a ball of fusing hydrogen, two thousand times more massive than the Sun. There had been convection cells then, too, which had driven instabilities in the giant star; it had breathed, swelling and contracting through fully a tenth of its diameter in a day. The instabilities had grown, exponentially, resulting at last in the casting off of huge shells of material from the surface of the star, like a series of repeated nova explosions; the *Northern* had sailed in through those ancient shells, on its way to its orbit around the new sun.

Meanwhile, the helium core had grown, and steadily contracted, and heated up.

At last, the core reached half the mass of the original VMO – about a thousand Solar masses. And a shell of hydrogen around the core ignited.

The mass of *three* Suns was flashed to energy within mere hours – expending energy that could have fuelled Sol for ten billion years of steady burning. The wind from the explosion stripped off the still-fusing envelope, creating another expanding shell around a remnant helium star.

Now, as Lieserl flew through the star, the helium was in turn burning to oxygen, which was being deposited in the star's core. Eventually, the oxygen would ignite. And then –

And then, the outcome wasn't certain. Her processors were still working on predictions: gathering data, developing scenarios. It all depended on critical values of the star's mass. If the mass was low enough the star could survive, for many millions of years, its diameter oscillating slowly ... and rather dully, Lieserl thought. But a little larger and the star could destroy itself in a supernova explosion – or, if massive enough, collapse into a black hole.

Lieserl studied the data streams trickling into her awareness. She would know soon. She felt a shiver of excitement. If the star was unstable, the end would come well within a million years. And then –

... Lieserl?

The voice of Louise Ye Armonk broke into her thoughts. *Damn.* Lieserl lifted her arms over her head and plunged into a huge convection fountain; the fusing star-stuff played over her Virtual body, warming her to the core.

But she couldn't escape Louise's voice, any more than she'd been able to outrun Kevan Scholes.

Come on, Lieserl. I know you can hear me. I'm monitoring your data feeds, remember –

Lieserl sighed. 'All right, Louise. Yes, I can hear you.'

Lieserl – Louise hesitated, uncharacteristically.

'I think I know what you're going to say, Louise.'

Yes. I bet you do, Louise growled. *Lieserl, we're grateful to you for going into New Sol with the wormhole Interface. And you're sending us a lot of great data. But ...*

'Yes, Louise?'

Lieserl, you didn't leave a back-up.

'Ah.' Lieserl smiled and closed her eyes. The neutrino flux from the heart of New Sol brushed against her face, as delicate as a butterfly's wing. 'I wondered how long it would take you to notice that.'

Damn it, Lieserl, that's the only copy of you in there!

'I know. Isn't it wonderful?'

You don't understand. What if something happened to you? Louise went on heavily, *Lieserl, we've never dropped a wormhole into a VMO before. We're not sure what will happen.*

'No. Well, before my day no one had ever dropped a wormhole into Sol. Nothing much changes, does it?'

Damn it, Lieserl. I'm trying to tell you that you could die.

'Don't you think I know that? Don't you see – that's the whole point?'

Louise didn't reply.

'Louise, I'm very old. I've *watched* my birth star grow old and die. I'm grateful to you for retrieving me from Sol: I wouldn't have missed that ride through the Ring for . . . for half my memory store. But, Louise, I don't think I can be a human any more – not even a Virtual copy of one. And I don't want to build worlds . . . that is for Spinner-of-Rope, and Trapper, and Painter-of-Faces, and the other children from the forest and the Decks. Not for me.'

Lieserl, do you want to die?

'Oh, Louise. I've already died once – or so we think, on the neutron star planet with poor Uvarov – and I never even felt it. I don't want to go through that again.

'This is where I want to be, Louise. Here, inside this new star.' She smiled. 'It's what I was designed for, remember.'

Louise was silent for a while. Then: *Come home, Lieserl.*

'Louise – dear Louise – I *am* home.'

Lieserl –

Wistfully, she shut off the voice link to the *Northern*. She'd open it later, she told herself: when Louise had grown accustomed to the idea that Lieserl was *here* – here and nowhere else – and here she was going to stay.

And in the meantime, she realized with growing excitement, the processors lodged in the refrigerating wormhole had come to a conclusion about the destiny of her star, New Sol.

She called up a Virtual image of the star; it rotated before her, a crude onion shell.

Already, she knew, oxygen was burning in pockets throughout the star, depositing the more complex elements – carbon, silicon, neon, magnesium – for which the wormhole was designed to trawl. With time, the helium-burning core of the star would contract, leaving a mantle of cooling helium and ash around a centre growing ever hotter.

435

At length – perhaps in half a million years, the processors concurred – oxygen burning would start in earnest in the core . . .

With growing excitement Lieserl watched the Virtual diorama, ready to learn how she would die.

When oxygen burning started in the core, the star would become immediately unstable.

The mantle would explode. The rotating star would start to collapse, asymmetrically.

Then the core would implode, precipitously.

The giant star's gravitational binding energy would be converted into a flood of neutrinos, billowing through the collapsing core. Some of the neutrinos would be trapped by the implosion of the core. Others, in the last few milliseconds before the VMO's final collapse into a black hole, would escape as an immense neutrino pulse . . .

She remembered the first seconds of her life: her mother's hands beneath her back, a dazzling light in her eyes. *The Sun, Lieserl. The Sun!*

In the last moments of her long life, a neutrino fireball would play across the bones of her face.

Lieserl smiled. It would be *glorious.*

35

Time passed.

After a certain point, even the measurement of time became meaningless. For Michael Poole this moment arrived when there was no nuclear fuel left to burn anywhere, and the last star flickered and died.

Already the Universe was a hundred thousand times its age when the Xeelee left.

Sombrely Poole watched the stars evaporate, through collisions, from the subsiding husks of galaxies, or slide into the huge black holes forming at the galactic centres. Then, as the long night of the cosmos deepened, even protons collapsed, and the remaining star-corpses began to crumble.

Poole wearied of puzzling over the huge, slow projects of the photino birds.

He sought out what had once been a neutron star. The carbon-coated sphere, drifting in orbit around a gigantic black hole, was being warmed – at least, kept to a few degrees above absolute zero – by proton decay within its bulk. Poole, as if seeking comfort, clustered his attention foci close to this shadow of baryonic glory.

Maybe there were other baryonic sentients left in the Universe. Maybe there were even other humans, or human derivatives. Poole did not seek them out. With the closure of the Ring, the baryonic story was done.

Michael Poole, alone, huddled close to the chill surface of the neutron star. His awareness sparkled and subsided.

The river of time flowed, unmarked, towards the endless seas of timelike infinity.

Author's Note

Ring concludes the Xeelee Sequence.

The novel stands by itself, although events in three of my previous novels, as well as in related short stories, are referred to.

The high-gravitation alternate universe mentioned in Chapter 32 is explored in my novel *Raft*. The career of Michael Poole, first referred to in Chapter 2, is the heart of my novel *Timelike Infinity*. The neutron star colonization project discovered in Chapter 29 is described fully in my novel *Flux*.

The complete timeline of the Xeelee Sequence follows. Novels and stories in the Sequence are included, novels in capitals.

Be assured that, although *Ring* is the chronological end of the Xeelee story, there are tales left to be told ...

TIMELINE

Singularity: Big Bang

Era: Primeval

20 bya (billion years ago): First contact between Xeelee and photino birds. Xeelee timeships begin modification of Xeelee evolutionary history.

5 bya: Construction of Ring begins. Birth of Sol.

4 bya: Assault on Ring by photino birds begins. Life on Earth emerges.

1 bya: First infestation of Sol by photino birds.

Era: Expansion

AD 3000+: Opening up of Solar System with GUT and wormhole technology. First human extra-Solar expansion begins.

AD 3621: Birth of Michael Poole.
   'The Sun-Person'
   'The Logic Pool'
   TIMELIKE INFINITY

AD 3717: Launch of GUTship *Cauchy*.

AD 3829: Invasion of System by Occupation-Era Qax.

AD 3953: Launch of GUTship *Great Northern*.

'Cilia-of-Gold'
'Lieserl'

Era: Squeem Occupation

'Chiron'
'The Xeelee Flower'

AD 4874: Conquest of human planets by Squeem.

AD 4925: Overthrow of Squeem.

AD 5000+: Second expansion begins.
'More Than Time or Distance'

Era: Qax Occupation

AD 5088: Conquest of human planets by Qax.

AD 5274: Return to System of GUTship *Cauchy*.
'Blue Shift'

AD 5407: Overthrow of Qax. Humans acquire Spline and starbreaker technology.

AD 5500+: Third expansion begins.
'The Quagma Datum'
'Planck Zero'

Era: Assimilation

AD 10,000+: Humans become dominant sub-Xeelee species. Rapid expansion and absorption of species and technologies. Launch of Xeelee timeships into deep past.
'Vacuum Diagrams'
'The Godel Sunflowers'

Era: The War to End Wars

AD 100,000+: Human assaults on Xeelee concentrations begin.
'The Tyranny of Heaven'
'Hero'
FLUX
RAFT

AD 1,000,000: Final siege of Solar System by Xeelee. Defeat of Man.

Era: Flight

AD 4,000,000+: Migration of Xeelee through Ring. Sol leaves Main Sequence. Destruction of Ring by photino birds.
RING

AD 5,000,000+: Last humans return to Sol in GUTship *Great Northern*, and travel to Ring.

Era: Photino Victory

AD 10,000,000+: Virtual extinction of baryonic life. Michael Poole is last sentient human.

Singularity: Timelike Infinity